THE IVY CREEK COZY MYSTERY SERIES

RUTH BAKER

CLEANTALES PUBLISHING

THE IVY CREEK COZY MYSTERY SERIES

Books 1-5

WHICH PIE GOES WITH MURDER?

AN IVY CREEK COZY MYSTERY

ABOUT WHICH PIE GOES WITH MURDER

Released: September 2021
Series: Book 1 – Ivy Creek Cozy Mystery Series
Standalone: Yes
Cliff-hanger: No

Lucy Hale always wanted to make a name for herself. A name that people would associate with excellence, creativity, and fun. She thought she had found her calling in the big city and was on her way to becoming a world-renowned food blogger...

Until she got some tragic news that pulled her back to her small town.

Can she still make a name for herself in Ivy Creek and survive the suffocating attention of its citizens who think she's too big for her britches?

Discover how Lucy navigates her way through a rollercoaster of emotions as she tries to resolve a murder mystery that has her as the prime suspect.

She thought running a bakery would be a piece of cake, but she's in for a mighty shock as her fiercest competitor is found dead...

in her backyard!

Will she acquit herself in the court of public opinion and help to find the killer or become the killer's next victim?

1

T he town hadn't changed much since Lucy's last visit. She noticed this when she arrived at the cemetery earlier that day for her parent's funeral. It was a short ceremony, and she had made most of the plans together with her aunt while she was in Ivy Creek. When she arrived earlier that morning, she had gone straight to the cemetery.

Her aunt drove back to her house in the neighboring town as soon as the ceremony was over, and Lucy headed back home. The first thing Lucy noticed as she arrived at her parent's house was that the front lawn was still as beautifully kept as ever. Her mother had always paid special attention to it. She had loved the beautiful burst of flowers that bloomed, especially in the summer, and Lucy had grown to love that effect too.

She got out of her car and looked around the yard, unable to wrap her mind around the death of her parents. It was sudden, painful, and destabilizing. It'd been a few days, but she already missed them.

This town, Ivy Creek, was not a place for her, and she hoped she wouldn't have to stay in town for a day longer than necessary. She had moved to the city years ago, where she had carved out a life for herself, and she was thriving there. This tragedy was the only thing bringing her back to town.

As she walked towards the front door of the house, she turned around when she heard a dog bark. She saw the next-door neighbor, Maureen Jones, a woman Lucy remembered from when she was little, walk past holding her dog on a leash.

"Lucy, dear," the woman's edgy voice boomed, the corners of her lips lifted in a smile.

Lucy forced a smile onto her face and turned around to greet Maureen.

"It's a surprise to see you in town, and a tragedy what happened to your parents. They were such a lovely couple."

Lucy greeted her with a peck on both cheeks and stepped back.

"I hope you are handling everything fine?"

"Yes, I am," she replied with another smile. "Thank you, Mrs. Jones."

The woman nodded and pulled on the leash of her dog as she walked away. Lucy turned around and walked to the house. She went right to the flower pot at the corner of the front porch, took the keys from under it, and slipped it into the keyhole to open the door.

Once inside, she looked around, and a wave of nostalgia hit her. Tears instantly filled her eyes. The last time she was here, it was Christmas, three years ago. She had made it just in time for the traditional family dinner after her mother had nagged her about it for weeks.

She felt an instant wave of guilt overwhelm her for caring less about her parents these past years. *This is my home. I grew up here, but now it feels different... empty.*

I should have visited more often.

She sucked in a deep breath, headed for the stairs in the corner. Upstairs, Lucy looked around, taking in the perfect arrangements of the smaller living room. The pictures of her when she was younger hanging on the walls, and more of her dad holding her when she had won her first award in high school on the girl's sprinting team.

Lucy wiped at her eyes gently, then took a short tour around the rest of the house. Her old bedroom was still the same, her pictures hung on the wall, and her closet remained untouched. The wallpapers she had loved so much still hung on the walls.

She dropped on the bed, and gently stroked the sheets with her hands, then sniffed. "I'm so sorry mom, and dad. I should have been here more often," she muttered to herself.

In a few hours, she would be hosting guests in the bakery, and she didn't feel like she was up to it, but she dragged herself off the bed. She spent time staring at her reflection in the full-length mirror by the corner of her bed, then went into her closet to find a pair of jeans and a T-shirt that still fit. She grabbed the keys to the bakery from her parent's room and headed out.

The drive to the bakery on one of Ivy Creek's high streets was short. The outside remained the same, with its Norman Rockwell like painting. The inside was arranged in a pattern that drew the customers to the right side where the display glasses were, and a huge menu hung on the wall, listing everything they made. Minutes later, she was inside, cleaning up and gathering baking supplies from the shelves she could use to prepare snacks for her guests. She went into the storage room and came back with everything she needed in a large bowl, then went ahead to prepare

11

a mixture for blueberry streusel muffins and cookies.

Lucy used her mother's recipes she had learned when she was younger. She used to enjoy helping her out in the bakery a lot back then, and watching her parents work together had been fun. It was why she had successfully carved out a career in food blogging for herself and trying out new recipes was a favorite for her.

Lucy sat in the kitchen and waited after putting her dough into the oven. The bakery was still intact, and for a moment, she wondered what would happen now that they were gone. They had put so much effort and dedication into running the bakery for years, and Sweet Delights had thrived because of that.

The creamy and comforting scent of vanilla she had used in her dough filled the atmosphere, alerting her that her muffins were baked into a perfectly brown color, and as she took them out, and put in the next set, a soft knock on the front door told her the first guest had arrived.

*

In about an hour, the bakery was filled with citizens of Ivy Creek, some of whom Lucy recognized. They were all pleasant, chatting lightly amongst themselves as they enjoyed the confectionaries she had baked. She was proud she was able to pull it off in a few hours. Cleaning the bakery hadn't been hard at all as it was hardly ever dirty, and the majority of the work had been baking the pastries.

Lucy greeted an old friend of her father's briefly with a handshake, engaged in a light conversation with him for a few minutes before moving on to anyone else she recognized. Half an hour into the meeting, the door to the bakery opened again, and Lucy's heart did a slow dive in her chest as she noticed the man who walked in through the door. He was dressed in a black shirt tucked into navy blue jeans, and she didn't miss the gun belt on his waist. Lucy knew he had always wanted to go into law enforcement and could see he did it.

She swallowed as his eyes scanned the room, then settled on her. They stared at each other for a brief moment, and the only thing Lucy could think of at that moment was that in the five years since she last saw him, he hadn't changed one bit.

Of course, he had aged a little. His once boyish looks were gone and had been replaced with stubble that covered his face. Their gaze locked for a moment before he walked towards her. Lucy sipped from the glass she held and cleared her throat when he arrived and stood in front of her, slipping his hands into his pocket.

"Lucy Hale," he said in a low voice, his pale blue eyes not leaving hers. "It took a tragedy to bring you back home."

His statement was flat, with an underlying meaning they both understood, and Lucy plastered a smile on her face and extended a hand to him. He hesitated at first, but then slowly accepted the gesture.

"Taylor Baker—it's a pleasant surprise to have you here," she replied, and he cocked a brow. His gaze roamed her face again, and Lucy knew from the look in his eyes that he had not forgotten their history.

Taylor released her hand and slipped his back into his pocket. "Mr. and Mrs. Hale were friends of my parents too, and they are here, so it's only right that I pay my respects."

Lucy nodded, and just then Taylor's mother found them and greeted Lucy with a big hug. "Hello, Mrs. Baker."

"We are so sorry for your loss, dear," Taylor's mother whispered to her and took both her hands in hers. "It's a tragedy what happened to Morris and Kareen. They were such lovely people, the accident was a true loss for every one of us."

"Thank you," Lucy replied gently with a smile again, and Taylor whispered something to his mother before she walked away.

"So, you running again as soon as this is over?" he asked casually. "We both know Ivy Creek does not suit your exquisite needs," he added.

Her mind prepared a snappy reply to his question, but she suppressed it and nodded instead.

She didn't have the strength to get into an argument with Taylor, not at a gathering hosted in honor of her parents. All she wanted was for the night to be over, so she could slip into her bed and sleep for a long time. She was exhausted, partly because she had to stand here and accept condolences from almost everyone in town.

The gathering was her aunt's idea, and she wasn't even here to attend it because she had to get back to her daughter, who just had a baby back home.

"I don't think I'll stay," Lucy replied with a small smile, ignoring the contempt she saw in his eyes.

"I didn't think you would."

Three years ago, the Christmas she had visited, she ran into Taylor at the grocery store, and his attitude had been the same. Even though she had tried to apologize to him then, too. Lucy knew she didn't need to apologize every time they ran into each other. They had shared history, and she had chosen to move on for the sake of her career. If he couldn't forgive her for that, then there was little she could do about it.

"Thanks for paying your respects, Taylor. I appreciate it. I have to go now… to talk to other guests," she said, emptying the contents of her glass as she walked away from him, aware that his gaze was pinned on her the entire time.

She stole glances at him as he moved to join his parents in the corner of the bakery. She saw him join their conversation, and as he picked up one muffin and took a bite, she waited to see the reaction on his face.

He had enjoyed her baking once, when they were together, and he complimented it far too many times. She couldn't tell if he still thought it was good enough, and before she could look away, his gaze found hers across the room again, and lingered. He looked away first, and Lucy turned and focused on the conversation with her guests.

By the end of the gathering, Lucy cleaned up the place alone and finished late. She didn't want to go back to the main house tonight. The place held a lot of memories of her happy life there and it was painful to stay there alone.

She remembered there was a small apartment above the bakery, and as she closed the doors to the main entrance and locked the back exit, she hoped it would come in handy for her for the night. Lucy went up the stairs and flipped the light switch on, and the first thing she saw was her mother's cat, Gigi, huddled in a corner.

She bent over and touched its head as it came towards her. She let her gaze travel around the small living space, and she smiled. "This is better than I remember, and it'll be perfect."

She went in to check the bedrooms; there were two of them. It was more than enough for the night, or as long as she wished to stay. She made a trip downstairs to grab her luggage in her car, parked in the backyard. After closing her doors, she retired back to the living room upstairs to comfort herself with a cup of chamomile tea, hoping it would ease the stress of what had been quite an eventful day.

Seeing the number of locals who turned up in honor of her parents surprised her, and Taylor's presence too had shocked her, but his usual cold attitude hadn't. He was never going to forgive her. She had come to terms with that, and she could handle it.

As Lucy fell asleep, she hoped that time would heal the heaviness in her heart from her loss. When she opened her eyes the next morning, it was to the sound of something clattering downstairs. Lucy jumped out of her bed, and her heartbeat skyrocketed, leaving her with a rush of adrenaline that produced a tight knot in the pit of her stomach.

Who was out there?

2

As Lucy made her way towards the door, she grabbed a baseball bat she found in the corner of her room. And as she tiptoed down the stairs, different thoughts raced through her mind. Several things could have produced that sound, and she hoped it was not someone trying to burgle her.

Holding a baseball bat was a stupid idea. She could not defend herself from a burglar with a bat if they had a gun. She realized this and chastised herself as she climbed down the stairs, her heart pounding in her chest. When she pushed the adjoining door to the bakery and peered in, relief flooded her instantly.

Gigi, her mother's Persian cat, sat in front of the door, staring at an empty tin plate Lucy suspected made the sound that woke her up. She sighed and stared at the clean white cat and it meowed at her as she bent over to pick it up. Lucy had always loved her blue eyes the most, and she rubbed Gigi's belly as she purred.

"You scared me, Gigi," she whispered to her as she ruffled its fur and took it into the kitchen. "When did you slip out? And how did you stay down there alone all night?"

Lucy suspected Gigi must have followed her down the stairs when she went to grab her luggage, and when she returned, she had forgotten to check on her because she had fallen asleep on the couch after her cup of tea. "Let's fix your breakfast."

She took Gigi to the kitchen, placed her on the floor gently, and reached into the top of the refrigerator for a bottle of water. While Gigi drank the water, she fixed herself a bowl of cereal and made a mental note of the groceries she needed in the house.

Lucy wasn't certain how long she would be staying yet, but she still needed the supplies. After finishing her cereal, she took a shower, dressed in a pair of slacks and a red sweatshirt, then walked out to the nearest grocery store just around the corner.

The woman at the counter remembered Lucy the moment she walked into the store, and she waved at her with a huge smile.

"How have you been, Keisha?" she asked as she walked past her, and Keisha's response was as hearty as her smile.

Lucy went around the store, picking up toiletries and food items for the kitchen. She walked past the pet area and picked out a nail clipper for Gigi as she had noticed earlier that her claws were untrimmed. As she turned to walk to the counter, she bumped into someone.

"Oh... I'm so sorry," she blurted and raised her head to stare into the cold blue eyes of the man blocking her path. "Forgive me," she added, and stepped to the side to walk past him, but he blocked her again.

"You must be Lucy Hale," he said, and squinted his eyes. A slow smile spread on his lips, and the hairs on the back of her neck stood as she stared at his icy blue eyes.

WHICH PIE GOES WITH MURDER?

"I'm Dennis Fischer—I own Spring's Bakery on First Avenue."

Lucy smiled after he introduced himself, even though she couldn't recall the town having another bakery. As far as she knew, Sweet Delights was the only bakery in town. "I'm sorry… I haven't been in town for a long time, so I'm not used to the new places yet."

"I've run Springs for three years," he continued, ignoring her outstretched hand, and Lucy tucked it back to her side. "It's not new."

"Right."

"I heard about your parents' accident. I'm truly sorry about what happened," he said, and she got the slightest feeling that he was not sorry. She ignored it, and nodded, then politely excused herself so she could walk to the counter.

Dennis's words stopped her halfway. "You're not planning to stay in town, are you?"

She turned back to face him. "Is there a reason I shouldn't?"

He walked menacingly towards her. "There isn't," he replied. "But your parents and I were on our way to finalizing a deal that would make Sweet Delights a subsidiary of Springs."

Lucy had to laugh at that because she knew her parents would never sell Sweet Delights. It was their legacy; an embodiment of everything they had worked for. Why would they sell off when they weren't facing any issues?

"I sincerely doubt that," she replied. "I have to head out now," she added. "Have a nice day, Dennis."

"Watch your back, Lucy," he said.

She ignored him and walked to the counter. As Keisha entered her items into the system, Lucy bit her lower lip and pondered on Dennis's statement. *Could he be telling the truth?*

19

"I see you met Dennis Fischer," Keisha said, her wide eyes roaming the store.

"I did, and he is not a very nice man."

Keisha cleared her throat and handed over the bag of items to Lucy. "He is one of the town's richest and his reputation is formidable. I think he's rude," Keisha said as she punched keys on the cash register. "That will be fifty bucks."

Lucy paid her in cash. "Have you ever visited his bakery?"

"Yes… Although Dennis is a jerk, Springs is the finest bakery in town. I won't deny that the man has got good taste with all that interior décor and lighting, makes it look more like one of those fancy coffee spots in the city. Perhaps when you have the time, you could try out his tarts, they simply melt in your mouth."

Lucy smiled at her. "I will. Thank you, Keisha," she said and walked away from the counter. As she slipped out of the store, she caught Dennis's gaze on her through the glass door and noticed his jaw tighten as he watched her.

*

Lucy couldn't hide her curiosity, so later that evening, she located Springs Bakery and tried out the tarts Keisha had recommended. When she took the first bite, she moaned and had to admit it was awesome.

The place was lively; the interior was decorated with bright hues of green and flower wallpapers at the edges of the wall. Outside, there was a patio, with chairs and tables arranged in a rectangular form, and beautiful flowers on the decks.

She had to admit that the man had good taste. His workers were organized and polite in attending to their customers. She noticed the woman behind the counter always had a smile plastered on her face.

Lucy remembered her mother's words about hospitality as she watched the chef. *"It is easier to retain customers if they think you are hospitable, Lucy. Never forget that."*

Lucy ordered an apple pie when she was done with the tart and took it alongside a freshly made strawberry juice. When she finished eating, she left the place and strolled back home.

Dennis ran a fine business, but he lacked fine manners. Her mother would have been very clear with a man like him about that, so she was positive her parents never planned to sell Sweet Delights. Besides, if there was a reason to sell or a pending deal, the lawyers would have mentioned it when she finalized every detail of their life insurance and property with him.

They had willed her the bakery, and the house, and she was yet to decide what she wanted to do with them. Maybe one day, she might quit her job at the media house she worked for and come back here to plant roots? She couldn't tell because that would be a long time from now, but she was certain she wouldn't sell out. As she strolled, she recognized Taylor's house when she neared it, and just then he drove his truck slowly from the adjoining road leading to her street, past her, and swerved into his parking space.

She paused when he got out of his car and walked over to where she stood.

"You're still in town?" he asked, and Lucy nodded.

"I figured I could stay a few more days and see what I can do around here."

He laughed and crossed his arms over his chest. "There is nothing you can do around here. The town's too small for a girl like you, remember?"

His cynicism made her roll her eyes. "Come on, Taylor. Enough of your judgmental attitude. I could use a break from it."

"I am being honest, not judgmental. We both know you don't want to be around here and would rather go back to your big-shot media job in the city. That suits you more than flour-covered jeans and getting your hands dirty doing a real job."

"And what if I decide to stay?" she asked, and crossed her arms over her chest, raising her head defiantly. "I own the bakery now, and I grew up working there. Who says I wouldn't do a good job running it?"

"You wouldn't," he replied with a shrug, his brown eyes fixed on hers, so she could see how serious he was. "I don't think you can manage it, and when it gets tough, you'll probably run, anyway."

Lucy opened her mouth to say something, but snapped it shut again. Her eyes flared, and she bit her lower lip.

"Well, I have decided to stay," she replied, and the momentary drop in his jaw gave her satisfaction. *How dare he tell me what I can and can't do?*

"Sweet Delights is my family's legacy, and I will stay and see it through, no matter what you or anyone else thinks."

She expected him to say something else to kill her zeal, but he pressed his lips together, turned away from her, and walked into his house without another word. Lucy stood in front of his house for a few more seconds before turning and walking down the road, heading back home.

She grew up in this town and Sweet Delights was her inheritance, so she would take care of it in her parent's stead. *How hard could that be?*

It was a challenge, and she loved challenges... it was the reason she moved to the city in the first place. It had posed something new and thrilling, and she had gone for it. She believed she could become more than a small-town girl, living in her parent's nest her entire life.

She hadn't regretted her decision to live and work in Denver, not even for one day, and she didn't think she would regret this choice either. She could give running the bakery a try. *What's the harm in staying a few more weeks?*

Lucy sent in a letter to her manager at work before she went to bed, telling him she was needed to stay back in Ivy Creek for a few more weeks. As she hit the send button, she felt the first shiver of anticipation run down her spine. She walked to her window and stared out into the night filled with stars, admiring the beauty of the horizon, and the peak of the mountains teetering far into the sky, far from where her house stood.

"I hope I can do this, mom," she whispered to herself and closed her eyes. "I hope I can handle it without ruining everything you and dad worked hard for."

3

Running a bakery is not a piece of cake. Lucy knew this, so the next morning, the first thing she did was to put out a 'help wanted' sign. She cleaned out the inside of the bakery, wiped the windows clean and rearranged the chairs in a more suitable pattern.

When she had first started a food blog, it had been a crazy idea she didn't think would amount to much. The first few months proved she could do better if she was consistent, and that principle was what she applied to everything she did.

Lucy did a quick inspection of the bakery, satisfied that the walls were still good enough. She paid little attention to changing the wallpaper or stripping away the decorative mosaic she had made as a little girl hanging on the left side of the kitchen wall. Instead, she focused on making sure every inch of the store and kitchen was dusted out.

As she inspected the chimney inside the kitchen where the large industrial oven lay, she whistled to herself a familiar song she learned as a child. Gigi followed her around the bakery, making little purrs whenever she wanted to be noticed, and Lucy constantly flashed her a smile. She had always loved the idea of having a pet, but she never kept one because she was never in the house. Lucy's job required regular visits to different cities so she could keep her blog active and trending with the latest news and recipes on food.

In the last article she had published weeks before her parent's death, she had mentioned lots of native American dishes to try out, some of which she might include in the Sweet Delights menu.

She smiled to herself as she thought of all the amazing things she could do to generate more sales and publicity for the bakery. It felt like she could excel at this already, and she hadn't even begun yet.

By the end of the second day, she had completely cleaned the place and checked the equipment in the bakery for any that needed replacing. It was on the second day she got the first applicant for the position of a chef she had displayed out front. As Lucy sat in front of the red-haired teenager, she smiled, trying to appear warm and welcoming even though she could tell the girl knew nothing about baking.

"Hi, I'm Samantha, but most people just call me Sam," the girl said.

"I'm Lucy," she replied. "Do you enjoy baking?"

Samantha chuckled, then shrugged, and Lucy watched as she admired her nails individually.

"I don't have the slightest idea what baking is about," she replied, laughing. "Mom says I should get a job, and I have to admit, blueberry scones have always fascinated me. I love them. I love eating them."

Lucy had to laugh at the girl's facial expressions while she talked and crossed her out in her mind. They talked some more about her experimental baking, and Lucy had to end the interview early when another applicant strolled into the bakery.

The second applicant was a tall man, older than Lucy would have loved to hire, but witty and smart. He spent half the time cracking jokes about his experience in restaurants in town and then told her about his allergy to vanilla.

Another applicant walked in after she had finished her lunch.

"Do you have any prior knowledge of baking?" Lucy asked and listened as the woman explained baking cakes for dessert. She interchanged the steps, and if anyone was to bake using the steps she highlighted, they would end up with nothing close to a cake. She didn't even want to imagine what it would taste like.

Stifling a giggle, she dismissed the woman. "Thanks for applying, Tricia, but I would like to hire someone with good knowledge or interest in the field," she explained with a pleasant smile.

Lucy didn't want to make a mistake in the first stages of running the business by choosing the wrong candidate, not when she had strong competition like Dennis Fischer in town.

She spent the entire day interviewing just three applicants, and by the time she put the sign back out the next morning, she hoped she would have better luck. Lucy stood outside for a while, looking at the bakery.

Its exterior reminded her of a five-star restaurant she had blogged about in the city. She wondered if Sweet Delights would ever get to a point where it would garner international reviews, and if it did, could she still maintain this spot on the high street her parents had started the business on?

Lost in her thoughts, she didn't hear the footsteps of a person who came up behind her until she felt a gentle tap on her shoulder. She spun around and was met with a grin on the girl's face.

"Hi," the girl said in a pleasant voice and extended her hand.

"Hannah Curry," she said, her grin not fading.

Lucy stared at the girl, trying to place the face and the smile.

"You're Lucy, right? My God, the rumors are true, you look... different."

When Lucy kept staring at her in a confused state, Hannah pulled her hand away and chuckled. "You were in my senior class at Creek High. We played on the same basketball team for three years, remember?"

Lucy could finally place the face when Hannah mentioned the high school she attended, and she laughed. "Hannah... wow, you look... different yourself," she exclaimed, and spread her arms out for a hug.

Lucy led Hannah into the store, and as they entered, Gigi wiggled her short tail and rushed to Lucy's leg. She purred and lay flat on her back. Whenever she did that, Lucy remembered her mother always rubbed her stomach, so she bent over and did that, allowing her hands to fluff the fur on Gigi's body.

Satisfied, Gigi sashayed across the room, and Lucy offered Hannah a seat.

"Wow, this place hasn't changed," Hannah began as she looked around. "I used to get a lot of pastries from your mom."

"You haven't been in town much?"

Hannah nodded. "Just got back from Texas, and my dad mentioned what happened. When I walked by here a few days back, you weren't around, so I couldn't come in to say hello. It's a tragedy what happened," Hannah added.

"It's so nice of you to come around," Lucy replied. "I appreciate it."

"I see you have a sign out for hire. You plan on running the bakery?"

Lucy nodded, and Hannah sighed, and placed her hand on her chest. "I need a job to keep me busy so I can assist my dad, and baking happens to be something I'm good at."

"I didn't know that," Lucy said and reached for the file on the table in front of her. Inside it, she had made a list of the qualities she wanted in the worker she'd hire for the job.

"I do it as a hobby mostly, and I could learn more from you if you hire me."

"Will you be in town for a long time?"

"I'm back to stay," she replied. "Being in Texas didn't work out as well as I expected, so I came back."

Lucy scanned her notes. She wanted someone she could get along with, a fast learner, and someone pleasant. She had known Hannah for a long time. She also knew her parents, and they seemed like very nice people. "One last thing," Lucy said. "Any food allergies? You would try out a lot of samples while working here and I'd like to know."

"None," she replied. "I like it here, and I think this job will be good for me."

Lucy smiled at her. "You have the job," she said, after crossing out the list she made. She had spent the last two days interviewing applicants who wasted her time, and she was eager to move to the next phase in growing her business.

"You don't need me to do anything else?"

Lucy laughed. "Of course not," she closed the file. "You'll be learning most of my recipes anyway, so your knowledge in baking is enough to get you the job."

"When do I start?"

"Tomorrow… I'll make a trip to town to stock up, and then we are set to sail."

4

The local market was close to the bakery and Lucy went out with a comprehensive list to get supplies. Hannah had resumed at the bakery, and today she was ready to sell desserts and pastries to the citizens of Ivy Creek. She had gotten half the items on her list; baking soda, flavors, food colorings, cinnamon, and a smaller mixer she could use in teaching Hannah new cake recipes for their dessert menu.

When she returned to the bakery, Hannah helped in putting away the items. They discussed the menu she had drafted out for each day of the week.

"Do you have any ideas to add to the dessert menu?" Lucy asked.

"Scones, I've always loved them," Hannah replied with a smile.

Lucy loved scones, so she scribbled it down on her notepad and they walked out of the inner storage room together. "Today we should make bread for sale, and tomorrow we can start with other desserts."

"I'll get the items we need," Hannah replied as the door to the bakery opened.

Dennis walked in just as Hannah went into the kitchen, and Lucy walked to meet him as he looked around the place like he was inspecting it. There were some customers inside the bakery, enjoying their pastries, when Dennis walked in, and Lucy noticed the smug look on his face.

"I love what you've done with the place. Although you are lacking in loyal and passionate customers, just like your parents," he said to her, his eyes dancing around her arrangements.

"Thank you. Do you need something?"

He looked at her again and reached into the pocket of the blue suit he wore. Lucy noticed it was an expensive designer suit, and she noticed the platinum ring on his right finger. He handed over an envelope to her.

"I told you your parents were about to sell off this bakery to me. Here is a part payment cashier's check. You should take this and leave town."

Lucy scoffed, took the envelope from him, and looked at the writing on the front. "Ten thousand bucks is a lot of money to get me to leave town," she replied and handed it back to him.

"There is no room for you here, and besides, you don't strike me as the kind of woman who would want to sell pastries in a small town."

She rolled her eyes. "Are you scared of a little competition, Mr. Fischer?" she asked, raising her head in defiance. "This bakery existed before Springs' came to town. Why do you think a few measly dollars will get me to sell out?"

"Anyone can sell out with just the right amount of cash," he replied with a smile Lucy perceived as false. The man was obnoxious and annoying. How did anyone get along with him?

"Well, I'm not selling out, so you might have to get used to having me as your competition, Dennis, and trust me, I will be the last one standing," she replied, and crossed her arms over her chest. "If there is nothing else I can help you with, I suggest you leave my property now."

He nodded, then took a step back. "You'll regret this," he said, then turned around and walked out of the bakery.

Lucy remained in the same spot after he was gone, and when she turned around, her gaze fell on a woman staring at her. Three other customers in the bakery watched as the woman walked over to her and gently placed a hand on her shoulder.

"Maybe you should take the offer, dear," the woman said. "This place has lost its customers to Springs already."

"My parent's bakery existed before Springs," she insisted.

Hannah walked out of the kitchen with a bowl of everything needed to bake the bread, and Lucy proceeded to teach her a recipe for coconut bread.

Lucy had a positive feeling about the bakery. Together with her blogging skills, she could gather more customers this summer, and make more sales. She knew it would shock everyone, and that was what motivated her.

Dennis Fischer might think he ran the best bakery in town, but she was certain soon she would trump his services and make a name for herself.

*

By the end of the week, Sweet Delights was in full operation. Customers trooped in often during the day, and in the evenings, some stopped by to have order a late night dessert. She had to visit the local market sooner than she expected to get more supplies, and she ran into Dennis again.

He rolled his cart to where she stood, inspecting the crates of eggs on a stand, and he cleared his throat to gain her attention when she ignored his presence.

"Dennis," she said in an indifferent tone.

"I see you are still in town and making sales. Everyone is talking about you making it till the end of the month. They seem to mention that you left town because you felt the city had more need for talents like yours... What was it again? LFB... Lucy's food blog?"

"Yes, that's my blog," she replied.

"Don't you think blogging suits you better? You could write an article on Springs Bakery. I will pay you handsomely for it." He leaned closer to her and added. "Of course, before you completely ruin Sweet Delights."

Annoyed, Lucy stepped away from him. "Is that a threat? Any more threats Dennis and you'll confirm my impression that you're scared I'll do better than you," she said, suddenly realizing her loud tone had attracted a small crowd.

His smile dropped, and he looked around. People had stopped to watch, and she stepped closer to him.

"I should warn you I'm quite an ambitious woman, Dennis. And I'll not be intimidated by you or anyone else."

Lucy noticed that Dennis' mouth fell open for a moment. He regained his composure and made his way through the crowd. Satisfied that she had rendered him speechless, Lucy rolled her cart away and paid for her items at the counter.

When she returned to the bakery, Hannah was sitting alone on a chair in the small patio they had arranged, and she drove her car to the back of the building, and joined her.

"You won't believe the day I'm having," she said when Hannah pushed an unopened bottle of water to her. She grabbed it and drank half its content, then continued talking as she covered the bottle. "Dennis seems to be more of a jerk than I thought he was."

"Everyone in town knows he is," Hannah replied. "I think there are people who are naturally jerks. Dennis is one of them."

Hannah dropped her voice a notch. "Rumors have it that his wife went nuts putting up with his attitude, and sometimes when it gets bad, he checks her into a nursing home for weeks. She returned home to him and hasn't been in one for months since."

The revelation shocked Lucy. How much had she missed since she was away from town? "He keeps asking me to sell the bakery to him, and I think he's scared that I will be bad for his business."

Hannah laughed. "Anyone who's had your bread will admit that you are strong competition for Dennis."

Lucy smiled. It was nice to have someone encourage her for the first time since she opened up, and if Hannah felt this way, then there might be others who did, too.

They closed the bakery at eight pm, which had always been her parent's closing time, and Lucy retired to bed early after taking stock of the money she had already invested into the bakery. The next morning, she went for a run down the trail from her backyard. The path led to the town's field, and she remembered jogging through it countless times with Taylor in the past.

Standing at the back of the building where she parked her car, Lucy bent over to tie her laces before stepping down. She walked around the house, warming up her legs, and as she approached the small fence surrounding her mother's garden, a stench hit her nostrils.

It was a strong putrid smell similar to that of rotting cabbage. She followed it, wanting to see what it was. Lucy's eyes landed on shoes first, and she bent over to pick them up only to realize it wasn't just shoes, but a full body.

Her eyes landed on the man's pale face, and she fell on her butt. Terror tore through her as she landed on the ground and scrambled away from the body hurriedly. Her eyes widened, and she screamed in horror at the sight before her.

Dennis Fischer lay cold and lifeless in her backyard.

5

Lucy spent half the day in the police station, giving her statement. The officer who took her in had said it was just to give a statement, but what was going on was more of an interrogation.

"Where did you find the body?" the officer asked again, and Lucy groaned.

"I found him in my backyard," she said for the tenth time, and stared wide eyed at the bald officer focused on typing her words into his system. "Do you even believe anything I have said so far?" she asked.

The man shrugged and pushed back in his chair, rising to his feet. "It is my job to take your statement, miss, and not believe your statement," he replied, then walked away.

Lucy sighed and buried her face in her hands. Dennis' pale face flashed across her mind, and she raised her head immediately. *This could cause me a lot of sleepless nights.*

She had hoped she wouldn't have to call her Aunt Tricia for help soon, but it was obvious she couldn't handle this on her own. Lucy was grateful she had called her aunt the minute she got to the station, and she was expecting her any minute.

Footsteps approached the table where she sat, and Lucy raised her head when she heard Taylor's voice. He slammed the files he held on the table in front of her. "You're free to go."

Lucy sighed and jumped out of the chair. "Thank goodness, I was thinking that they were going to keep me here for longer than this," she said and flexed her neck muscles.

Taylor's jaw ticked, and he turned to walk away, but Lucy stopped him.

"Thank you… for helping," she said and slipped her hands into the pocket of the jeans she wore.

"Don't thank me… I filled out some paperwork, and that's it. Maybe what you should try doing is stop meddling and go back to the city."

"Taylor," she said and sighed. "You… you don't think I killed Dennis, do you? I mean, he was just lying there in my backyard and I…" her voice trailed off as she remembered the distant look in Dennis' eyes as she stumbled on his lifeless body.

"Many people heard you arguing the last time you two were seen together, and then he winds up dead in your backyard?"

Lucy scoffed and folded her arms over her chest. She looked around the room where other cops went about their job and fixed her gaze on his. "You're the Sheriff's deputy, so you tell me, if I murdered Dennis, would I call on the cops to come find him in my backyard?"

"I'm not the cop in charge of finding Dennis' killer," he replied. "But I suggest you quit meddling and do whatever it is you want to do before you leave again."

"Why do you keep suggesting that I would leave town?" Lucy said, and he shifted his weight from one foot to the other. "I'm not going anywhere, so when will you stop being mad that I did what was right for me back then?"

"That has nothing to do with this," Taylor replied, raising his voice a notch, and Lucy rolled her eyes. Taylor caught the movement, huffed, and added. "I mean it Lucy... don't do anything."

Her aunt walked towards them and spread her arms out wide when she saw Lucy. Relief flooded her as she hugged her aunt, and Taylor gave Tricia a stiff smile before he turned and walked away from them.

"I am so glad you came," Lucy said to her, and shoved her fingers through her hair. "It was so terrifying being here all by myself the entire day."

"It's a good thing you called, honey," Tricia replied, and gently patted Lucy's hair. "Are you alright? How long did they keep you here? I bet that felt like all day."

"A couple of hours," Lucy replied and glanced at her watch. She groaned inwardly and looked at Tricia. "I didn't get to open up the bakery today, and Hannah would be so worried," she said as Tricia took her hand and led her out of the station.

"You're running the bakery?"

Lucy nodded and looked at her. "I am trying to do my best, but I don't know if I'm out of my depth here."

"What do you mean?"

They got to Tricia's car, and Lucy got into the front passenger's seat. "The man who died was a competitor. Dennis Fischer... he asked me to sell out to him a few times, and I refused," she explained. "I might have said a few things in anger, and now these people think I killed him."

Tricia sighed and started her engine. "I knew Dennis Fischer, and I will tell you this, honey. Many would be glad that he was dead. He ran a fine business, but he wasn't a fine man," she said as she drove off and sped towards the highway leading to the bakery.

Tricia's words rang in Lucy's head, and she wondered who else stood to benefit a lot from Dennis' death. Whatever Taylor or anyone else thought mattered little, because the truth was she hadn't killed Dennis, but someone did, and the killer was still out there.

*

Dennis' funeral was the third day after Lucy found his body, and she attended the event with Hannah and her aunt. The entire time, she felt people's gaze on her. She tried not to think about it, but it made her self-conscious.

She knew the citizens of Ivy Creek could gossip. She had grown up here and experienced firsthand what it could be like to be the center of such gossip. When her best-friend in high school was involved in a scandal, Lucy had watched her withdraw into a shell. Every time they were in a public place, the murmurs would increase, and so would the stares. And Gina, her friend, had hated it.

Soon Gina had moved out of town with her parents, and Lucy had found it difficult to make a new friend. It was then she met Taylor Baker. He soon replaced the friend she lost, and they became very close.

Tricia drove her back to the bakery after the funeral, and they both walked in on Hannah, checking her phone. Lucy dropped on a chair after her aunt went upstairs, and she exhaled.

"This is exhausting," Hannah said as she emptied her second glass of strawberry milkshake. "Not even a single soul walked in here today, and this is the fifth day," she complained.

Lucy had tried to pretend like this wasn't getting to her, but she couldn't keep up the pretence. A business was like a living organism, and she had pumped a lot of money into getting the place running again.

"It's not evening yet, someone will come," she said, and continued typing her latest blog update on her laptop. Her aunt sang to herself as she joined them out on the patio and sat next to Hannah.

"Perhaps we should close up and go have fun for the rest of the evening? You both have been at this for the past five days."

"Someone will come," Lucy said again, and Hannah sighed.

She felt both of their gazes on her as she typed, and she raised her head briefly from her screen to look at them. "Fine, we can close up for today and go visit the park if it'll make you feel better," she said.

She was also exhausted from waiting the entire day and doing nothing. "That's better," Tricia said and got up from where she sat. "You're coming with us, right?" she asked Hannah, and Hannah nodded.

Lucy saved her blog post and closed the file. She would edit it later in the night and send it to her proofreader before uploading it. Minutes later, they were in her aunt's car and they drove down to the park on the outskirts of town.

It was a Sunday evening, and many people came to the park to watch their kids play while they enjoyed the cool evening breeze. Lucy remembered visiting the park often too, and every time she came here, she never missed out on the corn dogs, that

Big Joe's concession stand sold.

"Want some Big Joe's corn dogs?" she asked Hannah as they strolled, and Hannah shook her head.

"I prefer pretzels, or a jumbo dill pickle with some celery and peanut butter."

Lucy shook her head and giggled. "You sure eat a lot, don't you?" she asked as she walked over to the stand and stood in line.

She slipped her hands into the pockets of her leather jacket and pulled out a twenty-dollar bill, then rocked back on her heels as she waited for her turn. Lucy turned when she heard a whisper behind her.

"She runs the bakery… the one where the owner of Springs' was murdered," one whispered to the other. "It's all over the news."

Lucy cleared her throat and stepped forward when it was her turn, and Big Joe's huge smile made her smile. Lucy ignored the whispers behind her.

"Lucy, you're really back in town… thought the rumors were just rumors," Joe said and she laughed.

He had earned his name from his size. Joe Pennel was almost seven feet, with looks similar to that of a polar bear. It took a long time before Lucy could get used to his fierce looks, as she always struggled to reconcile how a man who was so tall, with hairy arms the size of an oak tree, could be so gentle and kind.

"Two corn dogs, Joe," she said and he saluted her.

"As always."

"Add a jumbo dill pickle, celery and peanut butter to that, please."

The girls behind her continued to murmur in hushed whispers, and she pretended not to hear.

"How are you?" Joe asked as he handed over her order. "I heard about…" he didn't finish his statement, and Lucy was grateful that at least someone was still sensitive about the recent demise of an Ivy Creek citizen.

"I'm doing alright, Joe. Thanks for asking, but I'm sure the cops will handle it, and clarify everything."

Joe nodded. "You take care then, and I'm sorry about your parents," he said as she took the pack. "They were nice people."

Lucy exhaled when she finally walked away from the stand, and she glanced back to see the girls' gaze still following her. When she got to Hannah and Tricia, she handed over a corn dog pack to her aunt, and jumbo dill pickle to Hannah.

They took a spot on a bench to watch the children playing with kites on the grass, and Hannah started a conversation with Tricia about the upcoming summer. As they discussed, Lucy couldn't stop her gaze from shifting over to where Big Joe's concession store stood. In the time they sat there, she counted over fifty customers standing in line, and she sighed.

When she first re-opened the bakery, she had at least gotten a few customers, but now no one even ventured around the bakery. *What can I do?*

Her mind was reeling with thoughts of how to turn things around, and she stared at the empty pack on her lap for a long time. An idea finally came to her, and she muttered, "That's it."

"What is that?" Hannah asked, and Lucy raised her gaze to find both her aunt and Hannah staring at her.

"I know a way we can make more sales," she replied and a grin spread out on her lips slowly as the idea lingered in her mind. "A concession store," she said to Hannah.

"Like Big Joe's?" Tricia asked, and Lucy nodded.

"Don't we need consent for that? Like from the council or something?" Hannah chirped in.

"We do, don't we?" Lucy asked Tricia and her aunt nodded.

"It's a crazy idea, but yes, we need a permit for that, and if you're going to get it, then you need a good recommendation. One that comes from a respected member of the town's committee board."

"Like the sheriff's deputy, or the local priest of the church," Hannah chirped in, and Lucy groaned as she realized to get started on this new idea, she might need help from Taylor Baker. He was the town's sheriff's deputy and was also the last person who would be inclined to help her.

6

"You think my idea is terrible?" Lucy asked her aunt as she sat in the living room above the bakery. She had called Taylor three times since she had her concession stand idea, and each time it went to his voice mail. He also returned none of her calls.

"I think it's brilliant, dear. It's an expansion and if you work hard on this, then you'd be able to pull a lot of positive attention to the bakery this summer when we'll have a lot of tourists coming to Ivy Creek. And one thing tourists love to try out is food."

Lucy chewed on her lower lip and toyed with the pen in her hand. "I sincerely doubt Taylor would want to help. He hates me... we don't get along very well."

Tricia chuckled and took off her reading glasses as she dropped the paper she was reading. "That young man always had the hots for you. Chances are he still does."

Lucy flushed at her aunt's comment and cleared her throat.

"It seems like you're still into him, too."

"I am not," she denied quickly. "We can never get along on anything," she added, and crossed her arms over her chest.

She picked up the remote and shrugged. "Fine, if that's what you say. You'd have to ask him to put in a good word, anyway."

Tricia lifted her legs and stretched it out on the table in front of her. At fifty-two, her aunt was still very agile, and Lucy admired her strength. She was grateful she agreed to stay with her until the entire death news blew over, and her presence brought some serenity to the chaos in Lucy's life.

Tricia started channel hopping. Most of the new channels reported the same story. Dennis Fischer's death was the top headline, even though two weeks had passed since his body was found. The cops had nothing new to say about his killer besides what they already knew and shared with the public.

He died from blunt force trauma to his head, and multiple stab wounds to his chest. The murder weapon was not found, and no DNA prints besides Dennis' were found at the scene. Lucy kept up with the investigation, mainly because she could do nothing else.

Her reputation was already linked to the man's death, and everything was a mess. She didn't expect that anyone would think she was innocent, but the least the police department could do was carry out a proper investigation.

"I should go to bed," Lucy said, as she got bored with watching the same news every night.

"Goodnight," Tricia said to her as she walked into her room and shut the door. Lucy had a restless night, and the next morning, to clear her head, she went for a run.

Hannah came to work early, and they opened up the bakery, baked little quantities of pastries, and set them out before she drove out again. They went to the store to pick out items. She needed to try out a new recipe for chocolate cake. As they strolled the grocery aisles, Lucy bumped into a man while rolling her cart, and she apologized immediately.

"I'm sorry," she said. He nodded and walked past her. Lucy's gaze followed him, until Hannah finished picking out food flavors, and joined her.

"That man looks so familiar," she said, and Hannah looked at the man.

"Who?" she asked and tossed the items she held into the cart. Her gaze followed Lucy's and landed on the man looking at the shelf where stacks of whipped cream were kept. "That's Michael Trent," she said.

Lucy rolled her cart away as Hannah continued. "He runs the largest poultry farm here in Ivy Creek and supplies most of the eggs used in town."

"I've seen him somewhere. I just can't place it," Lucy murmured as she paid for her items with her credit card and Hannah helped her take them out of the store. "I think it was at the funeral," she finally said. She remembered he stood behind the crowd on the far end, and she had seen him because she was standing right next to him, too scared to let anyone in the audience know she attended the funeral.

"He was at the funeral, but he left early. I think I also bumped into him then."

She was driving down the road, heading back to the bakery, when Hannah suddenly turned towards her.

"I've heard Michael and Dennis had a long-standing feud. No one really knows what it was about, but everyone knows they weren't exactly on speaking terms. And Dennis is the only businessman, with a food-related business, who buys nothing from Michael's farm."

Lucy thought Hannah's piece of information might suggest how the people of Ivy Creek viewed the murder case. If Dennis had a long-standing feud with Michael, then why wasn't he on the suspect list? Surely the cops had to know about this and also look into Michael Trent.

Lucy's intuition told her there was more to this case, but she tried to heed Taylor's words and take her mind off it. Dennis Fischer's murder was not her problem, and she had to focus on getting her bakery more sales. This was her parent's legacy, and she couldn't let it all come to nothing.

*

Taylor was standing in front of his truck when Lucy jogged past his house that morning, and she took the chance to talk to him. He was dressed in his cop uniform, and he turned when Lucy called his name.

"Taylor," Lucy jogged to meet him, panting as she wiped her forehead with the handkerchief tucked into the pocket of her sweatpants. "I have tried to reach out to you for days now, and it's common courtesy that you return missed calls when you see them."

"Do you need something?" he asked, and Lucy nodded. His expression was blank as he waited for her to reply, and Lucy cleared her throat and stepped closer to him. His intense, dark gaze remained on her as she spoke.

"It's about putting in a good word for me with the town's council committee. I intend to apply for a permit to run a concession store by the park and…"

"Wait," he said, cutting her short. "A concession store?"

"It's a means of expansion for the bakery. A way to attract more customers to the bakery."

"I don't care what it is. You plan to run it? Is there something that makes you think you'd be able to manage a concession store when you can't even get customers to the bakery?"

Lucy's breath hitched in her throat, and she flushed at his remark. How did he know the bakery was not getting any customers?

She bit her lower lip to hide her embarrassment, and she puffed out air from her mouth, hoping it would hide the color on her cheeks. "The concession store would solve that," she replied.

"I don't have time for this," Taylor said, and took out his keys from his pocket. "Business like a concession store requires commitment. What happens when you want to leave town again? All of it would be for nothing."

"Taylor… this has nothing to do with me leaving town or what you think about me. I need your help, and I am asking for it," she pointed out. "Now, I know you might not like me much, and yes, that's on me, but Sweet Delights is my parents' legacy, and ever since Dennis' death, everything has gone south. I am trying here to hold unto the little shred of hope I have, and this... this idea I got is that shred of hope for me. So please…"

Her voice trailed off, and she closed her eyes for a moment to gather her composure. "I need this, so please think about it, and put in a good word for me if you can. I will turn in a letter of request by the end of the week, and I know when the council meets to discuss it, as Sheriff's deputy, you'll have a say. So just please, think about it."

Without another word, she turned and jogged away from him.

She spent the rest of the day worrying about her conversation with Taylor and what his response would be. She hoped he would consider helping her out.

Another day passed in the bakery with no customer, and Lucy went out later that night after her aunt had retired to bring in the chairs on the patio. A woman walked up to the bakery just as Lucy took in the last set of chairs. She was exhausted from staying the entire day working on a blog post and waiting for at least one customer to walk into the store. A man dropped by earlier and ordered a scone, but Lucy was out of scones, so he had left.

"Hi," Lucy greeted her with a smile. "Do you need something?"

"Coconut bread," she replied, but her gaze left Lucy's and traveled around the bakery.

"Come on in," Lucy said, and she allowed the lady to step in before she closed the door behind them and went to get her order. The lady smiled as she took the bag from her, and Lucy took her payment in cash.

"Have a great night," she said, but the lady didn't turn to leave.

"You cleaned up nice," she said, and Lucy dropped the bagel she had picked up. The lady looked around the place again before bringing her gaze back to Lucy.

Her green eyes held a certain interest Lucy couldn't understand. She had never met the woman before, but it was obvious she had taken a keen interest in her bakery.

"I'm sorry, have we met?"

"No, but I know something that might interest you," she replied with a smile. "I think you are innocent in the Dennis Fischer murder, and I can help you find his killer."

7

L ucy closed the doors to the bakery and pulled a chair to sit beside the lady. "I'm Grace, by the way," she said, and gave Lucy a smile.

Lucy reminded herself that she had to be cautious and not believe everything the stranger before her was about to share. Still, she couldn't deny she was interested in whatever Grace had to say.

"What I'm about to tell you might be common knowledge to you, but I am quite certain about it, and I wonder why no one else has picked up interest in it."

Lucy linked her fingers in front of her and gave Grace her full attention.

"It's about Michael Trent," she said, then sipped from her glass. "I'm sure you might have heard about his feud with Dennis."

"I might have heard a thing or two," Lucy replied, not wanting to give away any more information because she still didn't trust Grace. "Dennis made a point of not patronizing Michael's local business even though he is the largest supplier of eggs in town."

"It was more than that," Grace replied. "I worked for Michael but quit recently because I wanted to make a move into the city. I can tell you they both had frequent arguments and Michael openly made a lot of claims and threats during those arguments."

"So, you think Michael killed Dennis?" Lucy asked, and Grace shrugged.

"I'm saying it is suspicious that Dennis wound up dead in your backyard. It's more like someone is setting you up to take the fall for it."

"Have you told anyone else about this?" Lucy asked.

Grace shook her head. "It's not my business. I'm leaving town tomorrow, but I was walking by and I couldn't help but feel sorry for you. Rumors spread in Ivy Creek, and they are talking about the girl who murdered her competition."

Lucy scoffed and clenched her fists. The people in this town were more brazen than she thought. They had no evidence that she killed Dennis, but it didn't stop them from spreading the gossip. It was maddening to think that even the ones who knew her when she lived in town did nothing to defend her, even Taylor.

She remembered the cold look in his eyes when he had arrived at her bakery the morning she found the body, and how he dismissed her when she tried to talk to him after spending half of her day at the police station.

"I have to go," Grace said and pushed back in her seat. "I hope this helps."

Lucy wasn't sure if the information Grace gave her could help.

She had only raised her suspicions about Michael and made it impossible for her to stay out of the situation because she was getting desperate. She needed a way out. A means to clear her name. Or else her business in Ivy Creek would be over before it even began.

"Can I contact you?" Lucy asked, and Grace nodded.

She took out a notepad, scribbled her number, then handed it over to her. "Everyone knows of Michael's feud with Dennis, but no one knows what really happened. They were once friends, and then Dennis betrayed Michael in a deal they both had. If anyone had enough reason to get back at Dennis, it's Michael. Trust me," she said with conviction.

Lucy's mind was spinning, and she tried to take her mind off the information Grace had just given her, but she couldn't. Restless, she spent the night preparing a pitch letter for the town's council board. This was her shot at turning things around for the bakery, and she had to get it right.

Lucy was exhausted the next morning, but she had promised to teach Hannah a new cake recipe, so she prepared a cup of coffee and headed down to the bakery. She put the chairs out on the patio, cleaned the tables, before getting out the ingredients needed for the day's lesson.

Lucy sat and scribbled down a list of things to do in her notepad, and she heard the door open. "Hannah, thank goodness you're here. We can get started early," she said without looking up from her notepad. "I have taken out the ingredients, so we can get started once you settle in."

Lucy expected a reply from Hannah and when she got none, she looked up to see Taylor standing by the entrance. "Hi," she said nervously, and jumped out of the chair she sat in.

"Hey," he replied, and slipped his hands into his pocket. "I thought about what you said," he began before Lucy could say anything else, and she swallowed, anticipating his reply. "It's a good idea, and I will put in a kind word for you with the board, but that is all I can do, and it guarantees nothing. It's up to you to make your pitch a persuasive one."

Lucy sighed, and a smile crept on her lips. "Thank you," she whispered.

Taylor nodded, turned around and walked out of the bakery. Tricia came down to the bakery minutes after Taylor left, but Lucy still stood in front of her counter, speechless, and unable to gather her thoughts.

This might actually happen. I might really get committee approval, and this… this could change everything.

"I thought I heard someone."

"Yes, Taylor was here," Lucy replied, and walked over to her aunt. "He's agreed to put in a good word at the committee meeting," she squealed, and Tricia laughed.

"Oh, honey. That's amazing. I knew he would come around."

"I know," she replied breathlessly, and laughed again. "Honestly, I thought he wouldn't. He made it very clear the last time that he didn't believe I could handle running a business in town."

"Well, you've got one chance to prove him wrong," Tricia replied and gave her a soft pat on her shoulder. Lucy ran her fingers through her hair and looked around the bakery. This was a huge encouragement, and now what she needed to do was impress the board members.

*

Her idea of impressing the council was to throw a dinner party. Lucy and Hannah worked to get wine and food available for the dinner, while Tricia did her magic with her parents' house. Lucy sent out invitations, taking advantage of the town's ability to spread gossip, and by evening of the fixed date, her parents' living room was swamped with guests, most of whom were members of the council board.

"I have to admit Lucy, you throw one hell of a party," Luke Sanders, the leader of the committee, complimented, and Lucy smiled. She had gotten as much information as she could on them. Hannah had helped as she had been in town longer than Lucy.

"Thank you, Mr. Sanders. I'm pleased to know you're enjoying yourself," she replied.

She walked away from him to talk with her other guests, then walked into the kitchen to meet Hannah, who was shoving huge portions of apple pie in her mouth. Her pale blue shirt had streaks of pie on it, and she picked up a napkin and wiped her lips.

"You alright?" Lucy asked, and Hannah grinned.

"I'm stress eating, I know," she replied with a mouth full of pie, and Lucy laughed.

"I should be the one stress eating; I don't know how much longer I can deal with the curious but yet polite glares from these people."

Tricia entered the kitchen, adjusting the black sequin dress she wore, and she smiled at both Lucy and Hannah. "What are we doing?" she asked.

"Stress eating," Lucy replied, and took a spoonful of Hannah's apple pie. "This is really good," she moaned while complimenting the pie Hannah made. "These pies will do murder to my hips. I wonder which pie goes with murder? You're getting the hang of the recipes."

"Tricia helped," Hannah replied.

"I have to get back," Lucy said, looking at her wristwatch. She was out of the kitchen in a daze and returned to mingling with the guests.

At some point, she stood with Hannah in a corner, sipping from her glass of wine as they looked around with a satisfied smile.

"You think this will butter them up?" Hannah asked, but Lucy's gaze had wandered to Michael. She watched him, and Grace's words flashed in her head. *If anyone has a reason to hurt Dennis, then it's Michael. Trust me.*

"Lucy?" Hannah said and followed her gaze. Lucy blinked and turned to her. "What's the deal with Michael?"

"Nothing," she replied and looked at him again. He turned, and his gaze met with hers from where he stood. Lucy's breath hitched in her throat, and she looked away immediately.

"It's not nothing. You keep staring at him," Hannah said and then frowned. "I also think it is strange that he's chatting with Mrs. Fischer, but you don't see me gawking at him."

"Don't you think it's weird?" Lucy asked, and the frown on Hannah's face deepened. "I mean Michael, and Dennis weren't exactly close, and now Dennis, her husband is dead. It's like she is fraternizing with the enemy."

"We don't know that he's the enemy," Hannah cut in, and Lucy sighed. She turned to Hannah, took her arm, and pulled her into the kitchen.

"I think Michael had something to do with it," she said in a hushed tone. "With Dennis' murder, I mean think about it. He has a long-standing feud with the man. Everyone in town knows this, and by all accounts, they've had several altercations, and Michael threw threats around. Does that not strike you as suspicious?"

"Yes, but… there's no proof that he did it."

"I know, that's why I have to find out what happened."

"You mean, you'll let the cops do their job, right?" Hannah interrupted, and Lucy straightened her posture. She had thought about what Grace said to her and the fact was she couldn't sit back and do nothing.

"The future of my bakery depends on clearing my reputation in this town, and I don't see any cops lining up to do that," she said.

Hannah sighed, then folded her arms over her chest. "What do you need me to do?" she asked.

Lucy smiled. "Entertain the guests and leave the rest to me."

She walked out of the kitchen with Hannah and noticed that Michael was gone. Lucy sucked in a deep breath and decided to speak with Dennis' wife. Sophie Fischer wasn't exactly the kind of woman she would expect to live with a man like Dennis. Unlike her husband, she seemed pleasant and gentle.

There was a warm smile on Sophie's face when Lucy walked up to her and extended a hand. "Lucy Hale," she introduced as they shook hands.

"You've thrown an amazing house party, Lucy," Sophie complimented, and Lucy fixed her gaze on her green eyes. "It's refreshing to have someone young around trying hard to keep the old ones happy."

"It's really nothing," Lucy replied. "My parents threw dinner parties like this all the time."

Sophie nodded and dropped the glass she held onto a tray that a server passing by held. Lucy watched her snuggle under the shawl wrapped around her shoulders.

"I'm really sorry about your husband, and I had nothing to do with it," she said apologetically, and saw Sophie's gaze turn cold. A chill spread through her arms, and she swallowed. "I just wanted you to know how sorry I am," she stammered.

"This must be inconvenient for you, the rumors about my husband, and..." Sophie's voice trailed off, but she continued, maintaining the smile on her face even though her gaze remained icy. "I am really sorry, that you have to take all the snide remarks and innuendo about his murder, dear."

Lucy didn't think a person could maintain a distinct proportion of two emotions at once, but Sophie's gaze sent shivers down her spine even though her smile remained warm. "Throwing a good party to butter up the committee members. Are you trying to expand? So, you want to get a permit?"

"Mrs. Fischer..."

"Sophie," she interrupted, and just then Lucy saw Michael walk towards them. "You bake a decent apple and pecan pie, so I'm sure you'll excel if you expand," she continued.

She expected the woman to curse her, considering the rumors around town, but Sophie's reaction was totally unexpected.

"I wish you well," she added when Michael reached where they stood and placed his hand on her shoulder.

"You ready?" Michael asked and flashed a smile in Lucy's direction. Sophie nodded and walked away with him.

Hannah walked over to Lucy minutes later and asked. "How did that go?"

"Unexpectedly, well," she replied, and her gaze remained on Michael and Sophie until they were out of sight.

Later that night, Lucy received a reply on her application to the committee.

8

"It wasn't really a no," Hannah said, trying to be encouraging after Lucy showed her the email she received from the board the previous night.

"It's a sugar-coated no," Tricia cut in from where she sat at the counter, nursing a cup of heavy-creamed coffee. Lucy buried her face in her hands and closed her eyes. "These people are so polite; they wouldn't tell you no in plain terms. They'd dance around it for as long as they want when in reality all they're really saying is no."

"They say your application is open to consideration. It means they could deliberate on it later on and change their minds," Hannah said.

"Are you sure Taylor put in a good word? Maybe we should..." Tricia said.

"I don't want to hear it, aunt," Lucy cut in gently. "I'm not asking Taylor for help again. This is already as humiliating as it can get," she added with a defeated sigh.

"Let's focus on running this bakery in the meantime," Hannah suggested. "We got two customers yesterday, and hopefully we'll get some more today," she said in a high-pitched tone.

Lucy smiled at her, grateful for her support, and glanced at her watch. "It's six pm. I don't think we'll get another customer, unless it's someone returning something they ordered," she said.

Tricia exhaled and walked over to where Hannah and Lucy sat. "I mean, dear, your pie is the best I've tasted in a long time. It's a refreshing blend of flavors and it has a rich, buttery taste. Only a person with no taste buds would say otherwise."

"Thanks, aunt," Lucy whispered as Tricia squeezed her shoulder.

Lucy loved how her aunt had a distinct way of encouraging her, and the humor she attached to everything always made being around her fun. Growing up, Tricia was her favorite relative, and whenever her parents needed time out from parenting, they dropped her for the weekend at Stone Creek, a town a few miles from Ivy Creek where Tricia lived. Those weekends were always spent in parks, swimming pools, and shopping malls, and Lucy had bonded with her aunt that way.

"Now, wipe that sullen look off your pretty face, dear, and go out and have some fun. Hannah and I will clean up here," she said, and Lucy looked at Hannah, who nodded at her.

She didn't feel like going out, but maybe a walk would clear her head. She passed the high road and entered an adjoining street leading to the town's library, when an art store caught her attention.

Lucy crossed the road and walked into the store to look. She went through the displayed paintings and then spotted a mural with bright, vibrant colors. Lucy stood, admiring the painting. It was a lovely, expressive piece, and as she stared at it, she tried to imagine it on a corner of her bakery's wall.

"It's a lovely piece of art," a female voice said behind her, and Lucy turned around to find a beautiful brunette smiling at her.

"Diane Keen," she said and extended her hand. Lucy smiled and accepted the gesture.

"Lucy Hale," she replied.

"Oh, I know you," Diane said. "The entire town's been buzzing with rumors about you for weeks."

Lucy felt heat rise to the back of her neck. *Did every person in this town know her as a murder suspect? Was Dennis' death the only thing they talked about in their spare time?*

"I'm sorry if I made you feel uncomfortable," Diane added immediately, and Lucy waved her hand dismissively. Diane was oddly familiar to her, but she couldn't place the face yet.

"It's not a big deal," Lucy replied. "It's a small town. People talk."

"They do," Diane agreed and then focused on the mural again. "I just hope the news blows over soon," she continued. "It's horrific what happened to Dennis," she paused. "And to you, of course. No one should be accused of such a terrible crime."

Lucy wished she would drop the subject, so she casually asked. "How much does this cost?"

"I have to check on that," Diane replied with a smile. "I'm new around here, and I'm not yet familiar with the price of these pieces," she added with a laugh. "It's not been an easy transition from being a chef to an art sales rep."

Lucy followed her as she walked over to the counter to check her system for the price of the mural, and she asked. "You were a chef?"

"Yes, I worked for Dennis," she replied without looking up from her screen. "Three years I slaved for him and helped expand his business. And the jerk pays me back by firing me for no just cause," she said when she looked up.

"Oh," Lucy exclaimed. *Just how many enemies did Dennis have?*

"Forty bucks," Diane said and Lucy blinked. "For the mural."

Lucy reached into her satchel purse hanging on her shoulder and handed over a fifty-dollar bill. It was a cheap artwork to add to the decorations in the bakery. "So, why did Dennis fire you?" she asked casually as Diane issued a receipt.

"I have no idea," she replied. "All I know is one morning I'm baking, and the next minute he's asking to speak with me privately. Turns out his crazy wife somehow convinced him to let some staff go because they were facing some financial hardship, and I was one of the workers to take the hit."

"Crazy wife?" Lucy asked and took the receipt handed over to her. Diane took a box and packaged the sixteen square feet mural painting.

"Yes, everyone in town knows she's got dementia. Dennis had her checked into a mental home out of town for some time, and later brought her back home when it seemed like she got better. But it turns out she wasn't better.

"I just want to put the entire ordeal behind me, and I needed a new job to get by, so I took the first thing I could get. Although it hurt me deeply that he could discard one of his workers without a second thought."

Lucy took the box from her and smiled. "Thanks," she said, then turned and walked out of the store. On her way back home, she decided to make a quick stop at Taylor's house and hoped he would listen to what she had to say.

She met his mother. Mrs. Baker was pleased to see Lucy had dropped by, and she offered her a glass of water while they talked about Lucy's bakery. Lucy was shocked to see his mother as she knew Taylor lived on his own, but she engaged in the conversation until Taylor walked in and his surprise to see her in his house was evident in the look he gave her.

"Do you have a minute?" Lucy asked when his mother excused them, and Taylor came to sit on the couch opposite her. "I got a reply from the committee," she began. "They refused my proposal."

"I'm sorry," he replied, his gaze not leaving hers, and she shrugged and forced a smile.

"That's not why I'm here though," she said and adjusted on her seat. "Is there any update on the investigation?"

"I'm not at liberty to tell you anything about the investigation, Lucy," he replied.

"I know that, but... I just need to know that you're one step closer to finding the culprit and this entire ordeal will be behind me soon."

"I'm not at liberty to say," he replied and stood up. "It's best you find something else to keep you busy," he said and moved to walk past her, but her next words stopped him.

"Did you know about Michael's feud with Dennis? And that he was going bankrupt?"

Taylor sighed as he turned to her, and she rose from where she sat. Lucy raised her chin when he fixed his gaze on hers, and she added. "I found out from a chef he recently fired before he died, and she had a lot to say about his wife."

"Did you go around asking questions about Dennis' murder?"

"No, but..."

"Good, you shouldn't do that," he warned. "If you're not his killer, then that means his killer is still out there. So, what do you think happens when you dig into matters that do not concern you?"

"I'm trying to clear my name here. I don't see you or any other cop in line to help me do that."

"Just let us do our job please, and focus on running your bakery," he replied. "Murder cases are not the same as stories you upload on your blog, and it takes a lot of work to catch a killer. If you go about digging, you'll either get the killer on your tail or you'll wind up dead."

His gaze softened on hers a little, and he added. "It's not safe." Lucy retreated and walked out of his house.

Lucy spent most of the night staring at the mural and replaying the chef's words in her head. Something told her there was more to the story, and she could find out more if she followed the chef around a little. Something about Diane's story piqued her curiosity, and she couldn't push down the thoughts racing through her mind. She dozed off late and awoke to the sound of a loud crash from her bakery downstairs.

9

Tricia had her arms around Lucy, and they watched as the cops hauled a teenage boy away the next morning. Lucy cleared her throat when Taylor walked over to where she stood with her aunt and tried to act like she wasn't freaked out. The cops had asked around, and the eyewitness descriptions of some passersby matched the boy's physical description.

"That's him?" she asked, and Taylor nodded. "A teenage boy threw some stones at my window for no reason?"

"He will give his statement to the cops. For now, what we know is that someone paid him to do so. All he said was they wanted to send you a message."

"A message?"

"Have you been digging around Dennis' murder when I asked you to sit back?"

Lucy shrugged. "I spoke with you last night. How much digging do you think I would have done in a few hours?"

Taylor sighed, then placed his hands on his hips, and turned to watch the cop's car drive away. Lucy kept her gaze focused on the road. "This is not what I expected when I decided to stay in town," she murmured beneath her breath, and Tricia, who was beside her, gently patted her shoulder.

"I will keep you posted," Taylor said, then walked away, leaving Lucy and her aunt to clean up the mess.

When she had heard the first crash, she had jumped out of her bed and rushed to her window to check out what was happening. By the time she got downstairs, there was no one outside, and three of her windows were broken.

"I don't understand any of this," Lucy lamented as Tricia helped her take out the broken shards of glass. The repairs would cost her a lot of money and she wasn't even making any profit from the bakery to justify the capital she had put into running it.

"Do you think there is a reason for anyone to target you?" Tricia asked.

"I have no idea," she replied and wrapped her arms around her chest. "They all think I killed Dennis anyway, so I don't know what's going on."

Tricia scrunched her nose. "I'll tell you what, we'll get to the bottom of this together," she said and stepped outside to throw most of the pieces of glass in the waste bin. When she returned, she handed over an envelope to Lucy.

"I think someone dropped this," she said. "Found it lying around on the patio."

Lucy took the envelope and opened it, and color drained from her face. "No, they didn't just leave it lying around," Lucy replied as her eyes scanned the two words written boldly in red on the piece of paper inside the envelope.

It read, *STOP DIGGING.*

Tricia took the paper out of her hands and read it out loud. Her aunt's face paled, and Lucy dropped to a chair so she wouldn't lose her balance. "This has to do with Dennis' murder," she whispered and her thoughts whirled around everything she had uncovered just by asking questions.

Dennis had fired his chef unjustly, and he also had a long-standing feud with Michael Trent. To Lucy, those were two suspects in the murder, and she still couldn't figure out what Taylor was doing about it.

"I met someone," Lucy said to her aunt. "She used to work with Dennis, but he fired her before he was killed. She had some interesting things to say about Dennis Fischer."

"What did she tell you?" Tricia asked and took a seat in front of Lucy.

"Dennis was bankrupt."

Tricia's eyes widened, and Lucy nodded. "That was my exact reaction because this man flaunted cash at me to get me to sell Sweet Delights."

"Who else have you talked to about this?"

"Taylor... he is the sheriff's deputy, and he said he would look into it," Lucy replied, and shook her head. "But I'm done being the obedient girl while this town sucks the life out of everything I'm working so hard for. I have to look into this myself, and I need your help."

"Where do we start?" Tricia asked, her eyes gleaming with mischief, and Lucy's brilliant idea was to pay the chef another visit.

*

Lucy drove out with her aunt to the high street and parked at a corner of the street where they could look into the art shop. Her eyes widened in surprise when she saw Diane talking with Michael.

Seeing Diane and Michael together put her on edge, and she suspected she was the center of their discussion. Everyone in town seemed to be talking about her. Every inch of her wanted to know what their discussion was about, and she could see from her aunt's focused look that she shared the same view.

"When I spoke to Diane, she mentioned nothing about being close with Michael," Lucy murmured as she watched them hug before Michael walked away from the store, and Diane went back inside.

"Should we go in?" Tricia asked, and Lucy shook her head.

"Let's watch from a distance," she suggested, and popped a stick of gum in her mouth. Tricia's keen gaze remained fixed on the entrance to the art store, and Lucy took out her phone and checked the time.

She yawned, closed her eyes for a minute. She startled when she felt a double pat on her arm.

"She's leaving," Tricia announced in an excited voice, and Lucy looked.

They watched Diane close the door to the art store, then flag down a cab. Lucy started the engine of her car and drove down the road behind the cab.

They drove a while and stopped at the town's clinic.

"Is she ill?" Tricia asked and Lucy shrugged.

"I think you should wait here," she told her aunt, then took off her seatbelt and got out of the car before Tricia could suggest anything else. She walked into the clinic while adjusting the black cap on her head and took the seat at the corner of the reception area.

Diane stood at the counter, and Lucy watched the woman standing on the other end give her directions. She waited, watching closely as Diane smiled and thanked the lady before following the directions.

Lucy sprang into action. She followed her down the corridor, careful not to gain her attention, and stopped when Diane knocked on a door, and walked into a room with the sign, OB-GYN.

Lucy did a double take. *Was Diane pregnant?*

Was Michael the father? Both of them had seemed quite close. Maybe they had such a relationship?

She didn't know what to think, but this was a positive step towards finding out more about what was going on in Ivy Creek. She had a strong feeling of Michael's involvement, and now all she had to do was find some evidence to back it up.

Lucy returned to the car.

"What did you see?" Tricia asked the moment she got in.

"She went in to see an Obstetrician, I think she's pregnant."

Tricia gasped. "You think it's Michael's?"

"I don't know what to think," Lucy replied as they drove back to the bakery to meet Hannah. "I think we have to find out what Michael is up to ourselves, and it will involve following him around."

"I have a better idea," Tricia said later that evening when they had closed up for the day. Lucy was in the middle of fixing dinner, and she listened to her aunt.

"We get into his house and search."

"That's a crime," Lucy pointed out, and Tricia shrugged.

"Not if we don't get caught," she replied, a wide grin on her face that made Lucy laugh and shake her head.

"This is fun for you?"

"Come on, you have to admit it's thrilling… We're like private detectives, and watching that chef today made me realize we might actually be good at this."

Lucy smiled and shook her head. She needed little convincing. They watched Michael for a few days and monitored his every move. He lived alone in a house close to the entrance of his farm and drove a white truck.

It was the biggest farm in town, but what caught Lucy's attention was the fact that he had no workers living on the farm with him. The perfect opportunity presented itself when Michael drove out one Sunday evening to take supplies to the local market.

Lucy watched him drive out in his truck with the back fully loaded, and once he was out of sight, she got out of her car parked close by, then approached the farm house with her aunt. She hoped they would find at least one clue that would help with the puzzle.

After crawling through an unopened window, they found nothing linking Michael to Dennis. The man had a simple house, and most of his belongings were personal. Lucy found pictures on the wall of him and a little girl. He had no wife, no children, and she thought it was a sad life. They ended the search early because of the fear of getting caught.

"I still think if we keep digging, we could find something," Tricia said one evening as they watched the local news.

It was the middle of summer, and many tourists were in town. It made visiting the parks or hike grounds tedious because there were many people in line.

Lucy preferred to stay indoors at times like this. When her parents were alive, the bakery would have had a lot of customers strolling in, wanting to taste her mother's famous lemon meringue pie.

Feeling nostalgic, she had baked the pie herself, copying the entire recipe she had learned as a girl, and it tasted perfect. Lucy gave Hannah the day off because she had been working diligently, opening the bakery early, setting up only a quarter portion of all the snacks they had on the menu. They hardly had any customers and staying the entire day doing nothing wasn't fair to Hannah.

"I was very positive when I started this out," Lucy said in a low voice, and took the last bit of pie. "I said to myself... you can do this, Lucy," she added, groaned and dropped her plate. "Mom would be so disappointed."

"Don't say that," Tricia cut in. "There is nothing to be disappointed about. Every failure is a stepping stone to success."

"Well, I don't even have time to fail," she replied with a huff, and waved her hand. "Look around... this place is deserted. No one drops by, and even when one person does, they seem more interested in wanting to know where or how I found the body. It's all they want to know."

"It's a rumor that will fade, Lucy. When I was eighteen, I went for a frat party and got arrested and no one in town would shut up about it for months. Eventually they got over it and found some more juicy story to talk about. The same will happen with Dennis… they'll catch the killer, and soon no one will remember any of it."

Lucy ran her fingers through her hair and stared at the painting she had gotten hanging on the wall. *How long was soon going to take?*

"I don't know how much longer I can hang onto a tiny shred of hope," she murmured. "Maybe Taylor was right... This town is not for me," she added, then stood up and headed to her apartment upstairs.

10

L ucy was showing Hannah some icing techniques when someone walked into the bakery. She wiped the icing sugar off her hands, then went out to check on the customer, but gasped when she saw Sophie standing by the counter.

Lucy forced a smile as Sophie smiled at her.

"I love what you've done with this place," Sophie said. "And that mural hanging over there is lovely. Did you make it?"

"No, got it at a iocal store," Lucy replied casually, and Sophie smiled. "Do you need something?"

"I'm leaving town," she announced, and smiled. "I know… I just walk in here and tell you I'm leaving town for no reason," she continued, and Lucy could only blink. "But it's been a thought process for now, and it's best I leave."

"What? Why?" Lucy asked, not understanding what angle Sophie was coming from, or why she was even here telling her this. "What about Springs' bakery? I mean, you own the place now, right?"

"I completed a deal and sold out. It was something Dennis and I wanted to do for a long time, but we both didn't see any of this coming," she continued, and her eyes watered. Lucy watched as Sophie tried to control her confused expression. She exhaled and closed her eyes for a moment. When she opened them again, she looked calmer, more in control as she added. "I hear the rumors in town, and I know how difficult it must be for you, trying to fit in here when everyone thinks the worse of you."

Yeah, you have no idea.

"I'm trying my best," she replied instead of the words that flashed through her head, and Sophie nodded.

"I know. That is why I completed the deal to sell the place. My husband wanted all of this, but I didn't. Now that it's done, you're the only bakery available to the locals, and they will have no choice but to patronize you."

Lucy didn't know if to feel grateful for the thoughtful gesture or angry that Sophie would think she desperately needed to make sales. "Either way, I just wanted to stop by here and let you know that."

"Is there any specific reason you've decided to sell?" Lucy asked, but Sophie shook her head. "I met with Diane Keen, a friend of your husband's," she continued, and saw the vein in Sophie's temple pulse and her eyes bulge.

"Employee," she replied. "Diane Keen was his employee, not a friend."

"Right… she told me she was unjustly fired, and I just thought that maybe your selling out was a result of internal staff issues you couldn't manage?"

Sophie shook her head. "It was the right call to sell out," she replied, and adjusted her purse beneath her arm. "Diane Keen was fired because she wasn't useful to the bakery anymore."

"Alright," Lucy said and raised her hand. She had mentioned Diane specifically because Diane stated Sophie was behind her losing her job.

Sophie nodded. "I should get going," she said and as she turned away, Lucy noticed she was reluctant to leave. She waited until Sophie walked out of the bakery, and then she returned to the kitchen to join Hannah.

"That took a long time," Hannah said, and she nodded.

"That was Sophie Fischer," she announced.

"What did she want? Pie? Tacos?"

"She's closing up Springs' bakery, said it was the right call."

Hannah stopped piping designs unto the cake and looked at Lucy. "That's strange."

"I think so, too," she replied, then continued with her work, but she couldn't get her mind to stop spinning with thoughts of how Diane and Michael were possibly linked to Dennis' death. Lucy made time that evening to visit the art store with Tricia.

They watched from a distance as Diane closed up the art store, and they tailed her down the street. Her house was a few blocks from the art store, and Lucy parked her car by the corner of the street, then followed Diane towards the entrance of the building.

She planned to follow her and find out where she lived, so she could come back with Tricia some other time to search the house. While she loitered around in reception as Diane talked to a man by the security post, she didn't notice when Diane slipped away.

Lucy groaned and rushed towards the elevator, hoping she could meet up with her, but it was too late. She couldn't find Diane anywhere.

The next evening as Lucy sipped a cup of coffee, she wondered how she could have let Diane slip out of her gaze. She was determined to be more vigilant, as she couldn't afford any more blunders.

She left Tricia and Hannah at the bakery and followed the woman everywhere. Diane met with Michael every evening. He walked her to her apartment down the street, but Lucy never followed her inside when Michael was around. She didn't know how dangerous he was, and it was best she avoided running into him for now.

She got another chance to find out her apartment number one evening after Diane closed the art store, and she took it.

Lucy followed her into the elevator, but she kept the black hoodie she wore over her head, and dark shades over her eyes so Diane wouldn't recognize her. They had met only once, but she suspected the woman would find her familiar.

The elevator door opened, and Lucy hesitated, giving Diane room to get out first before she followed. They walked down the corridor, and when Diane turned around, she turned to a door by her left, and pretended to unlock it until Diane stopped in front of her apartment door, then slipped into it.

Lucy sighed, and rushed to the door she saw Diane enter, and made a mental note of the apartment number. "207," she muttered, then turned to walk away, but the door opened suddenly, and someone grabbed her arm.

Lucy yelped as Diane dragged her into the apartment, shut the door, then pushed the hoodie off her head. "Are you following me?" Diane shrieked and stepped away from her. She saw recognition flash in Diane's eyes, and she sighed.

"Yes," she admitted.

"All week? What are you… a stalker?"

"No, not all week, but a few days," she replied quickly, but Diane shook her head and reached into her pocket.

"I'm calling the cops."

Lucy raised a brow. "Really? You want to call the cops when you are hiding something yourself?"

"What are you talking about?"

Lucy rolled her eyes. "Dennis Fischer's murder? And your secret pregnancy, and meetings with Michael Trent?"

Diane shrieked again, and her eyes widened. "You think I killed Dennis?"

Lucy crossed her arms over her chest as Diane scoffed. "Well, you have good reason to," she replied.

"I'm not a psychopath. I wouldn't kill someone who fired me unjustly. Suing them would work much better."

"Then why didn't you?"

Diane rolled her eyes at Lucy, then pushed her hair away from her face. "You had every right to sue him, but you didn't. Looks to me like you took matters into your hands, or asked Michael for help. You two seem really close."

"I didn't kill Dennis, that's the truth. His death was as shocking to me as it was to you," she said, and her voice trailed off. "I would never do that to the father of my child."

Shocked, Lucy stammered. "Dennis is the father?"

"We had an affair," Diane admitted. "For years he told me he loved me and he made me believe he would leave his wife for me, but he never did that. Whenever I brought it up, he always got out of the argument by saying his wife was sick and it wasn't the right time. I found out I was pregnant a few weeks before he fired me," she continued and crossed her arms over her chest. "The bakery was running at a loss. Had been for months because Dennis was deceived into purchasing a fake property and he was laying off workers, so he saw it as a perfect opportunity to get rid of me. He offered me cash to get rid of the baby, and then he turned up dead the next day. I have no idea what happened to him… that's the truth."

Lucy blinked and looked away from her. *Could she believe what Diane was saying? She had figured the part about the pregnancy, but she would never have guessed that the child was for Dennis. Did Sophie know about this too? Was that why she was so tense when Diane's name came up?*

"I didn't kill Dennis, but I can't say the same for Michael," Diane suddenly said, and Lucy lifted her gaze to hers again. She saw the scared look in the woman's eyes as she added. "Michael and I have been close friends a long time, and the night I told him about the pregnancy, I had never seen him more enraged."

*

Lucy told Tricia everything Diane said to her. "Dennis is more of a jerk than we all thought he was," Tricia said when she finished her story, and she nodded. "I think Michael did it."

"Me, too," Lucy admitted. "He has more than one reason to want him dead, and he's never hidden his dislike for Dennis because everyone in town knows."

"We have to find proof."

WHICH PIE GOES WITH MURDER?

Lucy was chopping vegetables and tossing them into a bowl of water. She prepared a kale salad for lunch and spent the time with her aunt plotting another visit to Michael's farm.

It was a cool Sunday evening, and he would be driving out to make supplies any minute, so all they needed to do was get ready. They snuck into Michael's house through the kitchen window. Lucy knew this wasn't the best approach to solving Dennis murder. Breaking into Michael's house was a criminal offense, and if she got caught then she'd be in so much trouble, but she couldn't think of any other means.

The end has to justify the means, she thought to herself when they got into the house.

Tricia searched his living room, and Lucy found a door in the corridor that led to the basement. She called her aunt, and together they went into the basement. It was dark and dusty down there.

"I don't think there will be much to find here," Tricia said as Lucy mistakenly knocked over a flower vase on the table and it crashed to the ground. They both froze, and looked around, trying to make out objects with the flashlight Lucy held tightly in one hand.

Tricia sneezed and took out a handkerchief from her pocket. They walked over to the shelf hanging on the wall, and Lucy looked at the stack of papers, then pulled out one.

She opened it and flipped through the pages.

"What did you find?" Tricia asked.

"A ledger," she replied as her gaze narrowed down on the notes scribbled on different pages. She used her phone to take pictures of the pages so she could go through them later, then she dropped the paper and took out another.

"This is a cute picture," Tricia said and Lucy walked over to look at it. "Isn't that…"

"It's Sophie," Lucy interrupted as she stared at the picture of Michael and Sophie, with his arms around her neck and his lips on her cheeks. They both looked happy in the picture, and Lucy cleared her throat. "I don't think anyone is supposed to see this."

Tricia took out her phone and took a picture. "I will send it to you, it might come in handy."

Lucy nodded. "This might mean Sophie had a relationship with Michael, and this is one more reason why he would want Dennis out of the picture."

"There's more," Tricia announced, and took out a small album. She flipped through the pictures, most of Michael alone, and others with Sophie. Lucy looked around some more and saw a baseball bat on the floor beside a soccer cleats.

"Let's get out of here," she said when she found nothing else of importance, and Tricia dropped the album. As they made it out of the basement, they both heard the loud sound of cop sirens close by and knew that this time there was no way out.

11

"I told you to stay out of it," Taylor chided, pacing around his office while Lucy sat with her head bowed. "You don't listen... you never listen," he continued. "You broke into a man's house. That is a chargeable crime, and you could get a year for that."

Lucy closed her eyes as he continued to rant. *This is so embarrassing,* she thought. Michael had returned early from his trip into town and realized someone had broken into his house when he found the door to the basement ajar. They had been lost in their search and lost track of time, and Michael had used that opportunity to call the cops.

"Taylor..."

"You don't seem to get it, do you? You go about causing a scene, not caring about what it would take others to get you out of the mess you put yourself in. You're no different from the spoiled brat you were five years ago when you left town."

"Is this about me leaving town? Or about Michael's house?" she retorted and raised her head. "I don't see you or anyone else doing anything to get this murder solved," she said.

"Do not accuse me of not doing my job, Lucy."

"Why? I found out Dennis had a secret affair with his chef. I got the chef to point me in the right direction, and I got to find out Michael has a thing for Sophie."

"If you stayed out of it, then I wouldn't have to be here, saving you, again," he threw back at her. "Can you not cause any more trouble?" he asked and shoved his hands through his hair. He squeezed his eyes shut, and she noticed the fine lines around the corners of his eyes.

"I had to do something," she muttered. Lucy had mixed emotions about the situations she found herself in. She was one step closer to finding out the truth, and that was what mattered to her, not what Taylor thought of her.

"I'm not backing down now," she said in a quiet tone, and stood up. "You either have to charge me for this crime or let me get back to work."

Taylor turned to face her again. His cheeks reddened, and Lucy raised her chin defiantly, preparing herself for whatever he was about to say next. *I can handle whatever he throws at me.*

He gritted his teeth. "Just do as you're told and stay out of this because I won't let you go free the next time you break the law."

Taylor left his office, and Lucy walked out after him minutes later. "God, I can't stand him," she told her aunt as they walked out of the station, and Tricia laughed.

"Did they charge you?"

She shook her head. "I will have to pay a fine, but I think that's it."

As they got outside, Lucy saw Sophie and Michael get out of a car and walk towards the station. "I overheard the cops talking," Tricia said. "They are here for questioning."

"Why would they come in together?" Lucy asked.

"They are each other's alibi," Tricia replied. "I heard they were together the night Dennis was murdered, so their whereabouts sync. And it takes them off the suspect list."

Lucy shook her head as they flagged down a cab to take them back home. "They are no longer hiding their affair. Maybe this means they murdered him together... I mean, what better way to have Sophie all to himself, than get rid of her husband who was sleeping around himself?"

*

Lucy went for a run early the next morning. It was a good way to start her day. When she stepped out of the building, she saw Michael's truck parked in a corner of the road. He started the engine the minute she spotted him, and sped down the road, leaving a trail of dust behind him, and Lucy turned white with fear.

She focused on her path and completed her jog in thirty minutes, and by the time she returned to the bakery, Hannah was already setting up the patio. Her schedule for the day got less vigorous with each passing day, and recently they barely baked anything for sale because no one came by.

Lucy focused on running her blog and making more posts. A few emails came in from her publishing house, and she had been tempted to reply and tell them she was coming back to town, but what stopped her was the thought of leaving the bakery and everything she grew up with.

Since her parents died, she had been feeling nostalgic, and the urge to fit back into life here was growing. Lucy wanted to focus on something bigger than herself. She had her blog, and even though it was running smoothly, it didn't seem enough.

Running the bakery was an achievement she would have loved to add to the list, and proof to herself that she could handle anything. But so far, all she could prove was that the town she felt so attached to, had changed so much in her absence. And there was nothing she could do about it.

Lucy drove to the park and dropped by Big Joe's stand. She spent time walking in the park and finally sat down to watch the children playing. From where she sat, she spotted a cop playing with his child on the field, and the mother standing by a corner watching, and the image made her laugh.

She remembered taking walks with Taylor some years back. They joked about everything they saw and admired watching families having fun. Back then, she had imagined a life in Ivy Creek; setting up a family, running a business, and being content. But a big opportunity had come, and she changed her plans.

For the first time, Lucy wondered how things would have been different if she had stayed. She would have earned the respect of Ivy Creek and they wouldn't all see her as the spoiled brat who ran and abandoned everyone.

Maybe Taylor was right, and she shouldn't have tried to run the bakery at all. Things wouldn't have been so messy if she had just taken Dennis' offer.

It was late when Lucy finally got back in her car to drive back home. As she made it down the high road, a van came out of the adjoining road and sped in her direction. Lucy stepped on her brakes, but the car didn't slow down. She swerved, trying to dodge the oncoming van, but couldn't control her speed.

She crashed into a fire hydrant at the corner of the road. Her head lolled forward and collided with the air bag that popped out of the steering wheel.

*

The next time she opened her eyes, the pain that shot through her head was unbearable, and all she could hear were murmurs. Lucy swallowed, and blinked. Then slowly the murmurs made sense as she saw Hannah and Tricia peering down at her with worry written all over their faces.

"Are you alright? You were hurt," her aunt said as she swallowed again and tried to speak.

"What happened?" She asked as she touched her head and felt the bandage wrapped around it.

"You were in an accident," Hannah replied. "The cops are here to ask what happened."

Lucy cleared her throat when a cop walked into the room alongside Taylor, and her aunt walked out with Hannah.

"How are you feeling?" The officer asked and she nodded gently. "Can you tell us what happened?"

"A truck…" she stammered, then cleared her throat again. Her gaze landed on Taylor's and for a moment, there seemed to be a flicker of concern in his eyes. It disappeared as quickly as it came, and he focused on his partner. "It came out of nowhere, and I tried to slow down, but I couldn't... The brakes..."

"The brakes didn't work?" Taylor asked, and she nodded.

"Have you had issue with your brakes in the past few weeks or months?"

"No," she replied. "Its been fine."

"Do you think someone tampered with them?" The other cop asked Taylor, and just then she remembered seeing Michael by her bakery that same day. *What if he had tried to hurt her, and tampered with her brakes?*

She swallowed again. "Michael," she said. "I saw him loitering around my bakery earlier before the accident happened. You think it's related?"

The cop was about to reply, but Taylor cut in. "Don't assume anything... we'll look into it carefully," he said, then walked out of the room. Tricia and Hannah entered again, and Lucy sighed.

"You would think Taylor would show a little compassion or pretend to like me when I'm hurt, but he's plain cold."

"The man has never been a pretender," Tricia replied, and that was true. In the years Lucy had known him, he was pretty easy to read, and she could instantly tell when he was offended or happy.

How had the years changed him? They used to be such good friends who enjoyed each other's company so much, but leaving town had changed that. It had changed him just as much as it changed her.

Lucy was discharged the next morning after the doctors ran a routine scan to make sure she had no internal injuries, and she spent the rest of the day resting in her room. When she finally got down to the bakery, Hannah offered her a piece of cake. Lucy sat back and enjoyed the thick cinnamon filling that gave it a rich taste.

"Did you hear?" Tricia asked as she entered the bakery holding shopping bags. Both Lucy and Hannah chorused.

"Hear what?"

"They arrested Michael Trent this morning after the cops searched his house and found brake parts of a car in his basement."

Lucy was not shocked by the news. Her intuition had told her Michael had something to do with it. It was payback for breaking into his house, or a way to scare her off from digging into Dennis' death. Either way, he was wrong, and all of this only made her more desperate to know what really happened the night Dennis died.

12

Her intuition turned out to be wrong. Lucy was lost in reading through the ledger pictures on her phone when someone barged into the bakery. She looked up from her laptop and saw Michael storming towards her, his face red and the veins on his temple pulsing.

"You should be in jail," she said and rushed out of her chair, backing away from him as he came closer. "Come any closer and I'm calling the cops," she threatened and raised her cell phone so he could see she wasn't joking.

"Turns out they have no reason to charge me," Michael snapped, and she shook her head.

"Why?" *do I need to give the cops evidence myself?* "You tampered with my brakes; they found the brakes in your house... The basement."

"Those belonged to my car," he pointed out. "I came to warn you to get off my back. I have nothing to do with whatever mess you're in, and I don't care what you are doing. Just stop dragging me into this mess."

"Oh, come on. Cut the crap," Lucy replied and pushed back a stray strand of hair from her face. "We both know you're not innocent. Not while you're sneaking around with Dennis's wife everywhere in town. Does she know? Does she know you killed him? Or did you both plan it together?"

"I didn't kill Dennis," he said, and Lucy raised her eyebrow. "Look, I don't have to defend myself to you, or anyone else. I told the cops everything I know, and I don't have to defend your baseless accusations. I'm sorry you got hurt, but that wasn't me."

"I read your ledgers… Dennis tricked you on a business deal and walked away with all the profit. You hated him, and all the while you were having an affair with his wife."

"I'm not in a relationship with Sophie," he interrupted, then burst into laughter. "You think I'm having an affair with her? She's a friend, a close friend and she came to me when she found out her husband was having an affair. All I've done is to support a friend and make sure she's getting by because even after Dennis did that to her, she still loved him. I always told her he was a jerk, but she wouldn't listen. Diane is also a friend and I have to admit, it annoyed me that Dennis toyed with and hurt two women close to my heart, but I sure as hell didn't kill him."

Lucy flushed in embarrassment when Michael revealed he was just friends with Sophie. "If you think I'm lying, then ask the cops. We've given our statements together from the very start of this, and everything you think you know; they know too."

Lucy turned away from him for a moment. When she turned back, Michael added. "If you hadn't assumed I killed him from the start, then you could have followed up on the investigation instead of gossip."

"I didn't…" she replied and sighed. "Taylor… the sheriff's deputy wouldn't fill me in. They all seem to think I did it."

Michael was quiet for a minute, and Lucy chided herself mentally. "I'm sorry," she apologized. "About breaking in… that was stupid, and…"

"Just stay out of my way henceforth," he said and walked out of the bakery. Alone, Lucy dropped into a chair and buried her face in her hands. The door opened again, and Michael walked in. Lucy raised her head when he said. "Sophie knew about Dennis' affair, but she did nothing about it. I was with her the night Dennis was killed, but that was only from ten pm. Before then I have no idea what she was up to, and I told the cops this."

"Why are you telling me this?"

Michael sighed and closed his eyes for a moment. Lucy watched as he sucked in a deep breath. "Because she's my friend, and…" his voice trailed off, and Lucy could tell it was difficult for him to get the words out. "Because she's my friend, and yet a part of me… A part of me doesn't know what she's capable of. When she found out about Dennis' affair, and that he had shipped her off to a nursing home out of town so he could have time to indulge in sleeping with his chef, she was enraged."

"Did you tell the cops this?" Lucy asked, her heart in her throat, and Michael nodded.

"It doesn't matter. Any woman who finds out her husband is cheating, has a right to be enraged. I just don't know how much she was willing to express her outrage."

Lucy spent the next day thinking about her conversation with Michael. His side of the story confused her, because she couldn't tell if he was saying the truth or trying to cover his tracks by throwing the blame and attention to Sophie.

WHICH PIE GOES WITH MURDER?

*

Lucy convinced Tricia to stay a week longer before she left town after she announced she had to get back to Stone Creek.

One evening, Lucy decided to check in on Sophie, so she drove to her house with Tricia. She had pondered on what Michael told her the last she saw him, and her curiosity made her make this trip to Sophie's house. Perhaps, if she struck up a conversation with Sophie, she might find out more.

Lucy knocked first and waited for a response. "Sophie?" she called and shifted her worried gaze to Tricia.

"I don't think anyone is home," Tricia whispered as Lucy touched the doorknob.

The door gave way and creaked as it opened, and Lucy jumped back. "Sophie?" she called again as she walked into the living room.

Inside the house was neatly arranged, the kitchen was spotless, and Lucy didn't think anyone made use of anything in there. "Sophie isn't here," she said as she swirled around the living room before her gaze landed on a door by the corner of the staircase leading upstairs. Lucy considered leaving the house with Tricia for a moment, but Michael's words suddenly flashed in her head.

I just don't know how far Sophie was willing to take hers.

What if Michael was telling the truth? She was in Sophie's house, and this was a chance to find anything that could help clear her name. She exhaled and shook her head, trying to dispel the idea, but when she opened her eyes again, her gaze landed on the door and she groaned.

"Tricia…" she started, but her aunt cut her words short.

"We should leave. Sophie isn't home," she said, and picked up a photo album on the center table. Tricia flipped the first page and an envelope fell out.

"What is it?" Lucy asked and rushed to her side.

"I think it's a letter," Tricia replied, and opened the envelope. She gasped after reading through it, and Lucy grabbed it from her and did the same.

"These are emails printed off from a computer… these seem to be from Diane," Lucy said. "She was blackmailing Dennis," she said as she read through the lines of texts and flipped over to the back page.

She read through the words quickly, then tossed them aside. "I think Sophie found out about his affair through these black-mails."

"Dennis was a jerk," Tricia commented and bent over to replace the envelope into the album on the table. They heard footsteps approach, and Lucy tensed.

"Not again," Tricia groaned.

"You think the cops caught us?" Lucy asked, and her questions were answered when the door swung open and Sophie stood in the doorway pointing a gun at them.

The smile on her face was cynical, and her eyes were bulging out of their sockets. It chilled Lucy to her bones.

"Surprised?" Sophie asked, and walked in.

Tricia backed away with Lucy, but Sophie stopped in front of them, then cocked and aimed the gun at Lucy. "I told you to stop digging."

WHICH PIE GOES WITH MURDER?

It was Sophie all along? The break into her bakery, the car crash... she killed Dennis.

Lucy was standing face to face with a killer and she never expected that it would ever get to this. *Michael was right, she had taken it too far.*

"The cops have been following me for a while and I was expecting to leave town before anyone caught on to this mess," she continued.

"The mess you created when you killed your husband?"

She shook her head, and her eyes teared up. "I suffered and built everything we had with him, and he wanted to pay me back by running off with some whore? He wasted everything we had on some stupid deal and when there was no way out, he planned to shove some divorce papers down my throat and hang me out to dry."

"So, you killed him, and left him in my backyard."

"He seemed to be obsessed with you the moment you came to town. Forgive me if I thought he was repeating the same cycle as he did with Diane. My husband never really cared about anyone but himself, and you... you were just collateral damage.

"I followed him the night he came to your place to speak with you. But you had already locked up, so he went around the property. That was my only chance, and I couldn't waste it."

Lucy's heart was pounding so fast in her chest and when she stole a glance at her aunt, she saw Tricia was sweating with her arms raised above her head. Lucy turned back to Sophie, who had taken off the bag hanging on her shoulder.

"I have to admit, you're brave, but not so smart. You should have taken what Dennis offered and fled town, then you wouldn't be in the center of all of this," she said and laughed.

"You're a sick woman," Lucy retorted and her laughter died.

"Really?" She asked, then fired the gun at Tricia. Lucy screamed as the shot went off, and her aunt dropped to the ground with a thud. Tears rushed out of her eyes as she dropped beside her and screamed again.

"You killed her?" She yelled and reached for her aunt. *What do I do? Please, don't die. This is all my fault? I shouldn't have dragged you into this.*

"Aunt Tricia," she called, shaking her aunt as blood seeped through her hands.

"She's probably not dead, but you will be in a few minutes," Sophie boasted. "How sick is that?" she asked and cocked the gun again.

Lucy closed her eyes and waited to feel the pain as another shot went off again. *Was this the end?*

13

Lucy was still alive. She could feel her heart beating. Was it a dream? Had Sophie actually shot her aunt? She couldn't tell because it was like she was floating.

It felt like she was in a trance, but the screaming ambulance, the faint voices of the cops talking to each other, proved it wasn't.

"Miss Hale?" a voice called, dragging her from her thoughts, and she rubbed her eyes. "Are you alright?" the cop asked, and she nodded, her throat too dry to speak.

Two cops wheeled her aunt on a gurney out of the house, and Tricia winked at her. For a moment, she thought she lost the only family member she had left. But Tricia was alive, and the ambulance rushed her to the hospital while Taylor drove Lucy to the station in his car.

As she sat in front of him after giving her statement, she waited for his usual scolding, but none came. His lips pressed into a tight line. He handed over a bottle of water, which Lucy accepted..

"We were handling it," he said to her. "I placed cops to watch Sophie's every move, and I was carrying out a full investigation. What you did was reckless and stupid, and you could have gotten yourself killed."

She blinked and said nothing. Her mind was still reeling from everything that had happened.

Taylor sighed and ordered a cop to take her to the hospital. When Lucy walked into the room where her aunt was, she broke down crying when she saw her lying on the hospital bed, awake.

"I thought you were dead," she shrieked out and Tricia forced a smile.

"She got my shoulder, but I recorded her on my phone. There's no way she's escaping her crimes."

Lucy exhaled and sat beside her on the bed, then took her hands. "Thank you so much," she sobbed. She couldn't have gotten through this without her aunt's support, and she couldn't be more grateful than she already was.

"I love you, Lucy, and you're my little girl," Tricia said as they hugged. "You will always be my little girl."

Tricia got discharged four days later, and Lucy prepared a celebratory dinner. Hannah made the meal; chicken soup and pasta, and they dined in the bakery that evening together. It felt like a huge weight had been lifted off her shoulder, and with Sophie in police custody, Lucy felt safe in Ivy Creek for the first time since she returned.

"I think I'm out of my depth here," she said to Tricia later that evening as they cleaned up the dishes. "Running the bakery, trying to expand. Maybe it was too much to handle too soon."

WHICH PIE GOES WITH MURDER?

"You're quitting?" Tricia asked, and she shrugged.

"I had a job in Denver, a life I left to be here. Maybe I need to get back to that instead of trying so hard to start something here."

"That's sad," Tricia replied. "You make such a delicious double crust fruit pie, and if I think that, then I'm sure others do as well. Give it time, now that the killer has been found, they'll come around," she advised, and her words gave Lucy a fresh jolt of hope. "You could start something new here, and make it something solid, something to hold onto. Besides… I can always eat all the pie you bake," she joked, and they both laughed as Lucy locked the doors and they headed up to the apartment above the bakery.

Tricia had a point. She could start a new life here in Ivy Creek. She had found a way to stand on her feet and persist against the odds, and Lucy had never been as optimistic about anything as she was about the bakery.

She wanted this. It was why she opted to stay back at first, and life in the city might never be enough for her again. Not when she knew she could start something new here.

14

Three weeks later, it was as if Lucy had never been at the center of a murder investigation. There was a long line in front of the Sweet Delights' concession store, and Lucy had to trade places with her newly hired chef, Diane Keen. Lucy had hired Diane because she had skills best suited for a bakery and not an art store. She had a full schedule today at the bakery with Hannah as they prepared to deliver a wedding cake contract.

When she arrived at the bakery, the lemon summer berry cake they baked together stood tall on the counter. It was ready to be delivered, and Lucy smiled as she took out her phone and took shots of it for her blog. She still uploaded posts every week, and she had started a new trend that involved different recipes for every Tuesday. She called it *The Tues-delight.*

"It's amazing, right?" Hannah asked, and she nodded. "I've

asked the delivery van to be here, so we can both take this to the venue."

"I think I'll add this lemon berry cake to the new menu. It's really nice, and would gain a lot of attention," Lucy suggested and Hannah agreed with her.

"Personally, I think I might come to prefer it over the regular cakes we sell."

"What time is the wedding?" Lucy asked, and Hannah glanced at her watch.

"Ten am, that's exactly one hour from now," she replied with a sigh. "I better get changed," she added, then turned around and dashed up the stairs leading to Lucy's apartment.

Whistling to herself, Lucy grabbed a napkin from the stand and wiped out the counter, then went into the kitchen. She heard the front door open, so she walked back out to greet the customer with a happy smile.

Taylor stood on the other end of her counter, and beside him was a face she hadn't seen in a long time. "Dylan?" she called, and Taylor's younger brother laughed. "Oh, my God," she exclaimed, then walked around the table to wrap her arms around his neck. "When did you get back?"

"Few days ago, and I've already heard the gossip about this place," he commented and looked around. "Had to come see for myself."

"I'm glad you came," she said and her gaze moved to Taylor, who stood quietly and watched the happy reunion. After Dennis' case was resolved, and Sophie was found out to be his killer, Lucy had left town for a few days to wrap up her life in the city and tender her resignation to the publishing house officially. When she returned, she had rushed back into business.

She now ran the only bakery in town as Sophie had sold out

Spring's bakery before she was arrested, and Diane Keen had decided to stay in town and keep her pregnancy after Sophie was caught.

"Hey," she said to Taylor when his brother wandered away to look around the bakery. Lucy had added more artwork to the walls and changed the wallpaper to give the place a fresh look. And so far, everything seemed perfect.

"Hi," Taylor replied, his gaze fixed on hers.

For a moment, Lucy forgot all about their feud and was about to thank him for helping her out with the case.

"I see you stuck around," he said and looked around the bakery.

She shrugged. "I did. Turns out running a bakery is fun and I don't get to do that in the big city," she replied with a smile, and their gaze met for a moment. She looked away first, and when he said nothing else, she added. "Thank you, for helping with Dennis' case."

Lucy turned towards Dylan. "Now that you're back, we're going to have so much fun," she said and wrapped her arm around his shoulder, grateful she had an old friend around again.

"Just like old times," Dylan added, and the duo laughed.

Hannah came down a few minutes later, fully dressed for the wedding, and it was Lucy's turn to dash up the stairs and get ready for the long day ahead.

When she got back down, Dylan and Taylor had left, and Lucy joined Hannah in attending to the fresh stream of customers in the bakery.

"I would like a tart, please," a lady said when she walked over to the counter, and Lucy gave her brightest smile as she reached into the display glass for a lemon tart. Sales had improved drastically in the last three weeks and Lucy hoped it was the beginning of better days.

The End

TWINKLE, TWINKLE, DEADLY SPRINKLES

AN IVY CREEK COZY MYSTERY

ABOUT TWINKLE, TWINKLE, DEADLY SPRINKLES

Released: October 2021
Series: Book 2 – Ivy Creek Cozy Mystery Series
Standalone: Yes
Cliff-hanger: No

When Lucy is invited to serve her pastries at a charity gala, she's excited at the opportunity to rub shoulders with the movers and shakers in town

Things turn better than expected when she's approached by a wealthy couple who want her to cater for a landmark event in their lives.

Lucy's life is thrown into a tailspin when she hears that this warm couple have been found dead.

Things go from bad to worse when the rumor mill in Ivy Creek goes into overdrive with insinuations that Lucy's pastries might have been what killed the couple.

Lucy knows it couldn't have been her pastries as many people ate them but didn't die.

So, if her pastries didn't kill them, who and what did?

Lucy has to set aside her frustrations and fears and find a killer who's happy to let her take the rap for a heinous crime.

1

It was a sunny afternoon, and the birds chirping in the sky above reminded Lucy of a time when she played on the patio while her parents worked in the bakery. She had grown up happy, her hours spent learning recipes from her mother's cookbook, and holidays full of entertaining events like the summer kid's camp and marathon races. Those fond memories she held on to filled her leisure time.

She sighed when the door behind her opened, and Hannah, her employee and friend, walked out, holding two glasses.

"Freshly made orange juice," Hannah said, smiling as Lucy took a glass.

"Thanks," Lucy replied, and took a sip. Hannah settled into a chair close to Lucy's and took out a notepad from her apron's pocket. "Have you made a list of the needed items?"

Hannah pushed the notepad to Lucy. "We have a week to the delivery date, so we should get them tomorrow, and then we begin preparations."

She had made great sales since the bakery reopened, and there were more to come. She was certain of it. Lucy took out a pen from her shirt pocket and scribbled down additional flavors.

She was trying out a new recipe and if she perfected it in time, it would be a new addition for their menu. "Thank you, Hannah," she said, after making the notes.

Hannah placed both her hands on the table, and Lucy sipped her juice as she turned to her friend.

"Have you heard?" Hannah asked, clearing her throat.

Hannah was Lucy's source for town gossip. She lived down-town, and since Lucy remained in the apartment upstairs, she barely had contact with the citizens of Ivy Creek unless they came to Sweet Delights.

"Heard?"

"About the merger." Hannah's eyes widened as she continued. "It's the talk of the town. *James Anderson* took over a small ac-counting firm. This is the third time in two years they've taken over some small firm."

Lucy was aware of *James Anderson*, the town's biggest account-ing firm owned by Roland Anderson, who belonged to one of the town's founding families. His father had started the company, and they had expanded a lot in the last few years. She had never done business with him, but he had a lot of clout in town.

"Some say his wife got him the deal," Hannah continued. "I think they worked hand in hand on every acquisition, but the glory goes to the husband every time."

As Hannah talked, Lucy spotted a red Mustang approaching. The driver stopped and parked by the corner of the street, and when the door opened, a lady stepped out.

Hannah looked at it, and her jaw dropped. "That's Mrs. Anderson," she announced in a shaky voice, and Lucy saw Hannah's cheeks turn red.

Blushing, Hannah excused herself and scurried into the bakery. Lucy watched as Mrs. Anderson walked towards the patio with short, calculated steps.

She wore an immaculate white Chanel pantsuit that gave her an exquisite business look and a pair of designer sunglasses that made her look like a Hollywood celebrity. Lucy also did not miss the hot red color of her lipstick. Her black stilettos clicked on the floor with each step she took and made a distinct sound that was hard to ignore.

The rumors are probably right about her; everything about her exudes wealth, Lucy thought.

What were the odds that they were just talking about her and she came here? What did she want?

Lucy shook the thoughts away and rose to her feet when Mrs. Anderson got to the patio. The subtle scent of magnolia and jasmine reached Lucy's nostrils as Mrs. Anderson slowly took off the shades she wore.

"Hi," she greeted in a silky tone, and extended a hand. "Becky Anderson."

Lucy accepted the extended hand and smiled.

"Lucy, right?" Becky asked, skipping formalities, and Lucy nodded.

"Yes," she replied. She noticed her well-manicured red painted nails and the elaborate stitching on the pantsuit she wore. "Have a seat," she offered, and Becky sat. "Is there something you need?"

Becky smiled. The corners of her lips curved, and the sides of her eyes wrinkled. "Of course, dear," she replied. "I wouldn't drive all the way out here if I didn't." She glanced at the gold watch on her slender wrist for a second and when she raised her gaze, Lucy met her deep velvety brown eyes.

"My husband and I are hosting a charity event next weekend, and I need services for baked treats," she continued. "I always hire the very best, and I've…" She took a slight pause, and she looked around the patio. "I've heard you're good at what you do," she added.

Becky smiled again. "Are you?"

Lucy chose not to answer the last question. With a deep sigh, she linked her fingers on her lap and replied. "I would like to know what you have in mind for the treats, your budget, and of course, guest list."

Becky reached into her designer purse, took out a piece of paper, and handed it over to Lucy. "I've made a list of everything required of you. It's all written there."

Lucy scanned the notes on the paper and frowned. "There's no budget. A budget plays a role, as it helps us work smoothly," she explained, and dropped the paper. "You should state a budget which, of course, includes my pay for the event."

Lucy raised her chin, determined not to let Becky's intimidating presence bait her. She could handle business deals and she was every bit as professional as Becky Anderson.

Becky chuckled softly. "Like I mentioned earlier, it's a charity event. Surely you know what charity events are?"

"I do…"

"That's great," Becky interrupted. "You offer your services for free, just as I am hosting the event to gather proceedings for charity. My husband and I do this every year, and this year we're trying to raise more… for a good cause."

Lucy pressed her lips together, but Becky remained persistent.

"If you agree to do this, of course you will gain the right amount of publicity for your bakery. As director of the local chamber of commerce, I will have many guests in attendance who are all potential clients of yours with the right recommendation."

Lucy analyzed her offer quietly as she stared at the list of treats needed and the number of guests. *Over two hundred guests meant some were non-locals. It was definitely going to be a major event.*

"I take it you're thinking about my offer," Becky said after a minute of silence. She waved her hand as she continued. "There are a few potential clients on my list I can hand over to you right now once you agree to this deal."

"What's in it for you?" Lucy asked. "Seems like you're offering more than you'll be receiving."

Becky shrugged. "Let's just say I have a knack for helping people," she replied.

Lucy sighed, and the smug grin on Becky's face widened when she said. "Fine, I'll do it."

Becky clapped her hands together. "This will be fun," she murmured, took out a pen and scribbled her contact details on the paper. "I will expect a call from you."

Lucy watched her walk away after that and rubbed her forehead. "Did you just agree to work an event for free?" Hannah asked, stepping out of the bakery. "I heard the entire conversation," she added when Lucy raised her brows. Hannah pulled out a chair and sat. "You let her bait you."

"She offered excellent prospects," Lucy replied. "More clients… corporate and wealthy clients if I work on this, and the best part is I get to meet them in person. Isn't that great?" she asked, as if in doubt of her decision. She had heard rumors about the Andersons and their need for perfection. There was constant gossip surrounding them, revolving around Becky Anderson's short temper, and the need to stay in control. She wondered if working for the woman was the right choice.

If their alliance didn't turn out as planned, she would offer compensation, right? She rubbed her jaw again and looked at Hannah. "You think it's a good deal? Considering you know all about Becky Anderson through the gossips."

"It's a great deal. Working for Mrs. Anderson shouldn't be that hard," Hannah replied. "But you don't sound so sure… do you think you made a wrong decision?"

"I don't know." They both fell silent, and Lucy added. "I have a weird gut feeling about it though, and I have to admit, she's quite intimidating," she said as an image of Becky's cool smile flashed in her head.

"I think it will be huge," Hannah exclaimed, and the excitement in her eyes brought a smile to Lucy's face. She pushed down the tingle that had formed in the pit of her stomach and blamed it on over-analysis.

Lucy grinned and handed over the paper she held to Hannah. "Here's a list of the treats needed," she said. "We will start work immediately."

Hannah walked back into the bakery after their brief conversation, and Lucy relaxed in her chair and sighed. This was a new prospect for her, and it could lead to another expansion in her business. "You've come a long way, Lucy," she murmured and exhaled again as she raised her head and shut her eyes, mentally congratulating herself on her accomplishments.

But why did it feel like there was another wave of unrest coming and something was about to go wrong?

2

Lucy hummed to the soft music in the background and sipped from her glass of cranberry juice. She looked around the hall, satisfied at the brilliant smiles on the faces of the guests as they enjoyed her treats. She turned to Becky as she walked across the room to where Lucy stood, and she smiled.

"Lucy," Becky began after she placed a soft peck on Lucy's cheeks. "Every guest in attendance loves your treats. It's all they've talked about since the evening began."

"Thanks," Lucy replied.

"I guess people open their pockets when they have wonderful treats to feast on." Becky laughed and sipped from her glass, her eyes twinkling. An old couple walked towards them, and Becky leaned in and whispered. "Here comes Mr. and Mrs. Wilson."

The couple reached where they stood, and Becky lifted her chin. Lucy watched in amusement as she greeted them. Becky had a stylish way with words. Her rich southern accent made her sound different from the locals, and she played it to her advantage when she spoke in her low, silky tone.

"I'd like to introduce you to the mind behind the wonderful treats," Becky said, and touched Lucy on her shoulder. Lucy smiled.

"Nice to meet you, Lucy," Mrs. Wilson said as she shook her hand.

"Likewise."

"I'll leave you all to get acquainted," Becky chirped in with a laugh before walking away. Lucy fixed her attention on the couple, and Mr. Wilson smiled at her.

"Wonderful evening," he said. "I enjoyed the cupcakes best," he added, and his wife slapped his arm playfully.

"You've had way too many of those tonight, Lucas," she chided. "You're not having any from the next serving."

"Fine," he laughed. "I'll take the kale chips next or maybe I'll try some of those truffles."

Lucy joined in the rumble of light laughter, and Mr. Wilson continued. "I love the cupcakes because of the sprinkles, dear. They twinkle, just like the stars in the sky."

"Thank you," Lucy replied, and turned to Mrs. Wilson. "Did you enjoy the treats, too?"

"Of course, I did."

"Sarah will turn seventy-five soon, and we would like something with sprinkles for the party," Lucas cut in. He turned to Sarah and gave her a warm smile. He grinned at Sarah, and Lucy saw his eyes gleam, and she could tell they loved each other.

"It's also our fiftieth anniversary. Would you like to cater for the event?"

Lucy was giddy with excitement at what she had just heard and couldn't hide the grin on her face that seemed to stretch from one ear to the other. "I would love to!"

They walked away after Lucy accepted the business card Mr. Wilson handed over, and as she stared at it, she smiled.

Guess this wasn't such a bad idea after all, she thought, grinning.

Still staring at the business card in her hand, she picked up a glass of cranberry juice from a waiter's tray. Lucy hadn't expected working with Becky to turn out easy, but everything, so far, had worked out just fine. They had agreed on the treats and Becky had no problem with Lucy adding a few items like kale chips, truffles, and caramel-apple tarts.

"It's amazing what you did with the cupcakes," a voice said, pulling her out of her thoughts, and Lucy turned to see Taylor, the town's deputy sheriff. His dark eyes flickered from her face to the cupcake he held.

Lucy had been romantically involved with Taylor before she left Ivy Creek for the big city. Everyone thought they would be together forever. Lucy thought so too, and she knew Taylor felt the same. But she chose to pursue her dreams to have a career in the big city and that had spelt the end of their relationship. Ever since she had gotten back in town, Taylor had made it known implicitly and explicitly that she wasn't welcome.

"You're turning into a celebrity," he said when they both turned to see Becky smile and wave at her from a distance.

"I wasn't expecting to see you here," she replied, licking her suddenly dry lips. She didn't always know what reaction to expect whenever she saw him, considering their shared history. Her relationship with Taylor lasted a while, so she was used to reading his facial expressions.

"I got an invitation as a member of the town council committee," he replied and looked around the hall. "The party is well organized."

Lucy accepted the compliment and assessed him briefly. He wore a jet-black suit, and clean black shoes. The look made him fit into the business world perfectly. *He cleans up nicely for a guy who loves jeans and plain baggy t-shirts,* she thought.

"Well, I hope you enjoy the rest of your evening," she said and he smiled.

"I will."

Lucy excused herself and joined Becky, who stood beside her husband, sharing a conversation. She saw their lips move as they talked, and when she got to them, she greeted Mr. Anderson with a smile and made eye contact with Becky.

"You've put together a lovely event," Becky complimented. "It's been a wonderful evening."

"We owe you our gratitude, Lucy," he replied. "Without the treats, we wouldn't get half the response we've gotten from the guests. You've impressed them, and also opened their wallets."

Lucy laughed at his remark and withdrew her hand from his. "I will definitely recommend you to my clients who are glad to pay for quality services like yours. *James Anderson* represents most of the wealthy members of the town, and I will always recommend you."

"Thank you, sir," she replied, and he shook his head.

"Please, call me Roland," he corrected. "I'd love to be on a first name basis."

He gave Becky a brief kiss on the lips before he walked away, and Becky turned to her. "So, was working with me a success?"

"It was," she admitted, wondering why everyone in town thought Becky was a socially distant, rude woman. Lucy found her intimidating at first, but when they conversed more, she realized there was nothing to Becky's personality besides outstanding self-esteem.

"You've only just begun," she added and walked away.

Lucy spent the rest of the evening socializing amongst the guests, and by the end of the event, all she could think of was getting home and taking off the black stilettos she had to wear all evening to complement her red, backless evening dress.

Hannah joined her in the parking lot when it was time to go, and she helped her lift the bag she held into the back seat of the car.

"Have fun?" Hannah asked as she took off the cap she wore over her short blonde hair. Hannah had worked with the catering team Becky had hired to make sure they served the treats and presented drinks to the guests properly.

"I met a few prestigious guests and guess what?" Lucy replied. She took out the business card Mr. Wilson gave her. "I got a new job offer."

Hannah squealed, and laughing, they both got into Lucy's car. She explained the details of the birthday deal to Hannah as they drove down the road and headed for Hannah's house downtown.

Still overwhelmed with joy, Lucy hummed a nursery rhyme to herself as she drove back to her apartment after dropping Hannah off. When she walked up the stairs and entered her room, Gigi, her white Persian cat, greeted her with a loud purr.

"Hey, Gigi," she greeted. Lucy squatted and ruffled Gigi's fur, smiling as Gigi rubbed her body around her legs. "Miss me?" she asked as she sat on the floor, unbuckled her shoes, and kicked them off.

Lucy sighed and massaged the heels of each foot gently, and

relaxed against the wall. "I had a great night," she continued as Gigi watched her with wide eyes, her tail straight and upright. Lucy stroked Gigi again and closed her eyes.

I shouldn't have worried so much, she thought as she settled in bed thirty minutes later.

The evening had turned out great. She had prospective new clients and a growing reputation in town. Everything was perfect, and she had a lot of work to look forward to this summer. *What could possibly go wrong at this point?*

3

The next day, Lucy kept herself busy with preparing a new batch of pastries for sale.

Humming to the music playing from her ear pods, Lucy spun around in the kitchen and stepped to the beat. She didn't hear Hannah come into the kitchen, but when Hannah reached the table where Lucy stood, watching the dough in the industrial mixer, she took off the ear pods.

"I set everything else for the pecan pie in the refrigerator," Hannah announced, wiping her flour covered hands on a napkin she picked from the table. "Do you need anything else before I go home for the evening?"

Lucy paused and thought about the question for a second before replying. "No, I've got everything else covered."

Hannah pulled out a chair and sat while Lucy tasted the already mixed dough. She had to deliver bread to the grocery store tomorrow, and also cupcakes to a parent who ordered treats for her child's school bake sale.

"Is the bake sale order set?" Hannah asked. "I could help you deliver them tonight before heading home," she offered.

Hannah was always of great help at the main bakery, and without her, Lucy was certain she would overwork herself. She definitely couldn't handle the bakery and her concession store on her own. "You deserve a raise," she replied, and Hannah chuckled.

"Does that mean I will get one soon?"

"Of course." Lucy smiled as she wrapped the dough in a cling film and placed it in her refrigerator. She had to wait forty-five minutes before placing it in the oven, and she could use those minutes to sort out the cupcake order for the bake sale.

"I should call the Wilsons this weekend to follow up and get more details about the birthday," Lucy said as they wrapped each cupcake in a fancy material.

"That's a brilliant idea," Hannah replied. "The Wilsons own more than half the grocery stores in Ivy Creek, and if this deal goes well, you might become a major supplier of their pastries."

Lucy looked forward to the possibility of being their major supplier. She could work towards opening another bakery soon if things continued running smoothly, and her blog - Lucy's Food Blog - still brought more publicity to her business.

"Working that event with Becky has turned out to be a blessing," she commented. When they finished wrapping the cakes, Lucy's phone rang, and she stepped out of the kitchen to take the call.

"Aunt Tricia," she said when she heard her aunt's smooth laugh on the other end. "It's been a while."

"I've been great, dear... how are you?" she replied, and Lucy smiled.

The last time she spoke with her aunt, Tricia had mentioned her decision to move back to Ivy Creek, and Lucy had helped her check out some houses her real estate agent had suggested. Two of them were a stone's throw from her parents' house on Third Avenue, and the last one was close to the town's high school.

Whichever choice Tricia made, she would be a thirty minutes' drive away from the bakery, and Lucy preferred that. "I've been great, Aunty. A lot has happened here, and guess what... I got to work for the rich and famous owner of *James Anderson*," she said, unable to hold the news from her aunt. Her voice oozed with conviction as she added. "I think that's just the beginning of my expansion, and soon Sweet Delights will be all over the country."

Tricia laughed. "You have big dreams, dear," she replied, and cleared her throat.

"How's the relocation plans coming along? I should have called sooner, but the past week has been hectic on my end," Lucy explained, and turned around when Hannah stepped into the dining area.

"I turned down the heat of the oven," Hannah whispered, and walked back into the kitchen.

The warm, slightly sweet aroma of the bread, filled the air and it reminded Lucy of her childhood before the bakery started running. Her mother's passion was always baking, and Sweet Delights was her parents' dream. They started it, but never got to see it expand beyond that single shop before they passed away. Lucy was fulfilling those dreams with each sale and deal she made.

Lucy shifted her attention back to her aunt on the other end, who was explaining the bits of her relocation plans.

"So, you'll make the last move by the end of the week?" Lucy asked when Tricia finished her explanations.

"Yes… I never thought I would move back to Ivy Creek, but here I am," she replied, and laughed again. "I will talk to you later, Lucy. Have to take another call."

"Bye," Lucy said, and the phone beeped as the call ended. With a sigh, she joined Hannah in the kitchen. "That was Tricia," she said, and Hannah pulled open the top shelf and took out a bowl. She placed it on the table, took out a pack of whipped cream from the refrigerator, and measured out the amount needed.

They had to prepare coconut flavored whipped toppings for the cupcakes they'd be selling the next day. Lucy loved to prepare everything beforehand to make the day less stressful.

As Hannah whipped the cream, she asked. "When is she making the final move?"

"By the weekend. I'm glad she's moving back to town… having her around is helpful."

Lucy enjoyed having Tricia around because she was the only extended family she had left. Tricia was her mother's elder sister, and her father had no siblings. Later that evening, Lucy was happy to send Hannah off with the packed cupcakes which she'd be delivering to their customer. She stayed a few more hours in the bakery before turning in for the day.

*

The next day was unlike any Lucy had experienced in her bakery's short existence. It was super busy. Customers strolled in and out of the bakery, and orders kept coming in for delivery. John, the driver Lucy hired for home deliveries, came into the store while Lucy was closing a client's birthday cake order, and she beamed at him.

"Here's a tip," she said and handed over a ten-dollar bill to him. John smiled and tucked the note into his wallet before taking the paper bag of orders. "Thanks, John."

"Anytime," he replied, and strolled out of the bakery. Lucy walked around the counter and smiled when another customer walked in.

"Welcome to Sweet Delights. What would you like?"

"Three cupcakes with sprinkles to go please," the girl replied, and stuck out a ten-dollar bill.

"That will be seven dollars, and thirty-five cents," Lucy said.

Lucy attended to a few more customers until Hannah returned from the restroom and took over. Lucy went into the kitchen to prepare the bread delivery she had for the day.

She supplied three grocery stores in town with pastries twice a week, as well as two families who ordered special pastries like gluten-free and vegan bread. When she finished arranging the bread inside her delivery basket, she glanced at her watch.

"Keisha will be here any minute," she murmured and took off the apron she wore. Lucy stepped out of the kitchen and as she got into the sitting area, the door opened and Keisha, the sales assistant from the grocery store down the high street, walked in.

"Hey, Keisha," Hannah greeted. Keisha placed her hands on the counter and exhaled. Lucy noticed she looked flushed, and her eyes were wide as she panted.

"Are you alright?" she asked, and Keisha struggled to catch her breath. "You look flushed."

Keisha placed her hands on her cheeks and swallowed. "I'm also hot," she replied and shuddered.

Lucy watched Keisha shut her eyes tight for a moment, and then she reopened them as she wiped some beads of sweat that her were forming on her forehead.

Hannah asked, "Did something happen?"

"You both didn't hear?" Keisha replied, her wide hollow eyes darting across Lucy's and Hannah's. "The entire town has heard about it."

Lucy stiffened, and color drained from her cheeks as Keisha added. "Mr. Wilson died last night, and his wife is still unconscious."

4

K eisha's announcement left Lucy speechless. She blinked multiple times as she tried to process what she had just heard.

"I heard they got ill from food poisoning. Mr. Wilson is dead, but his wife is still unconscious," Keisha said.

"When... when did they get hospitalized?" Lucy stammered. She exhaled, trying to keep calm, but her insides tightened and the horror of Keisha's news made her heart ache.

"After the Andersons' party," Keisha replied, and Lucy took two steps backward. She collided with the counter behind her, and Hannah reached a hand out to steady her. *The night of the party?*

Shivering, Lucy wrapped her arms around her sides and turned away, hurrying into the kitchen. Minutes later, Hannah joined her. "Keisha just left with the bread supplies," Hannah said, and Lucy turned to her.

Lucy murmured, "I can't believe I might be linked to another murder in town."

"Why would you say that, Lucy?" Hannah replied. "A lot of guests had your treats that night. You don't see them dying in hospitals, do you?"

"I know that, but…"

"Let's relax, Lucy," Hannah advised. "The cops will sort this out."

Lucy hoped that was the case, and she swallowed, trying to fight the gut-wrenching feeling of doom closing in on her. Keisha's words replayed in her head, *Speculations are they got ill from food poisoning.* An image of Mr. and Mrs. Wilson's smiles flashed in her head, and she clenched her fists as a wave of nausea hit her.

Lucy rushed to the sink, turned on the faucet, and splashed the cold water on her face, hoping it could jar her out of this bad dream. She could feel tears forming in her eyes, so she splashed the water again, and placed her hands on the edge of the sink, leaning in towards it.

"We have a customer," Hannah said, but Lucy didn't turn back.

What do I do? Why is this happening again? Who could have done this?

Her mind reeled with questions, and she reached for her phone and dialed Tricia's number. Her aunt picked up on the second ring, and her smooth voice helped Lucy's nerves relax. The first time she was involved in a murder investigation, her aunt's support helped get her through it.

"Aunt Tricia," she began in a shaky voice.

"Are you alright, dear?" Tricia replied in a hushed tone.

"I'm in trouble again," she replied and shut her eyes tight. The dull throb in her head spread, and when she opened her eyes again, tears slipped down her cheeks. "There's another murder investigation in Ivy Creek."

Lucy spent the next ten minutes on the phone with her aunt, explaining the events of the night and the news of Mr. Wilson's death. She ended the call when Tricia promised to come into town sooner than planned, and Hannah rushed into the kitchen.

"Lucy, Taylor's here," she whispered. Lucy wiped her cheeks, tucked her phone into the back pocket of her jeans, and exhaled to steady herself. She headed out to the dining area, and when Taylor turned to her, she saw the question in his eyes, and she spoke before he said anything.

"I don't know how this happened."

"I can't believe there's another murder, and somehow it involves you," he replied, shaking his head and tapping his fingers on the counter.

A few months ago, Lucy had been involved in a murder investigation when the owner of a rival bakery had died. His corpse was found in Lucy's backyard and she had been identified as a prime suspect. Taylor had been in charge of the investigation and because of the history between them, he had done nothing to allay her fears that she would be found guilty. Thankfully, the real killer was eventually found but it seemed she was still in Taylor's bad books.

"Is it a murder investigation?" she stammered.

Taylor hesitated before replying. "Nothing is certain for now. We're trying to rule out foul play, and that's why I am here," he paused, and looked around the dining area. "I'm here to collect samples of the treats served that night."

"My treats can't possibly be the cause," Lucy defended. "You know that. You had them too and you're not dead."

"Lucy…" he called, his voice trailing off. "Please, just go along with this investigation. Let's make this easier on both of us this time, and I suggest you don't leave town while the investigation is ongoing as that puts you in a difficult position."

She lowered her head for a second. "I think I have some cupcakes and kale chips left," she replied, and led him into the kitchen. Taylor collected the treat samples in an evidence bag, and Lucy walked him to the front of the bakery before asking.

"Any news about Mrs. Wilson's condition?" Taylor rubbed the back of his neck. "Will she be alright?"

"Mrs. Wilson died a few hours ago."

She staggered backwards, her mouth suddenly going dry. Lucy clutched her chest and watched as he walked to his truck parked on the other side of the road. The knots in her stomach tightened, and she lifted her shaky hands to her cheeks.

Her chest was so tight, she couldn't breathe properly, and the urge to scream built up with each second. *Would screaming help?* She wondered. *Would it take away some of this tightness in my chest?*

Hours ago, she was certain her fate had changed, and her business was on the verge of expanding, and now… everything was spiraling downhill so fast, it gave her no time to prepare for the impact of a crash.

Shoulders dropping low, Lucy walked back into the bakery, and turned the door sign to *Closed*. She stared at the *closed* sign and wondered if it was a sign. A sign that it was time to pack in and return to the big city where she previously had a life.

5

Lucy flipped over to her left side on her bed and dragged the sheets over her body. She willed her mind to stop spinning, so she could get a decent amount of sleep, but nothing she did brought relief to her racing heart.

It was barely dawn, and this made it the fourth day since news about the Wilsons' death broke. Over the past few days, Lucy had listened as rumors about their death, spread throughout the entire town.

The previous night, a client of hers had called to cancel her order for a birthday party. She gave the excuse of not hosting a large party anymore, so homemade desserts would suffice. But Lucy could tell it was a lie because the woman stuttered a lot as she framed her sentences.

Her aunt promised to come in before the weekend, and she desperately needed the support of family if she was going to get through this stage.

With a sigh, she threw the covers off her body and slipped out of bed, heading to the bathroom for a quick, cold shower to calm her nerves. Lucy spread her rose-scented wash over her skin, and inhaled the blends of floral scents, hoping it would help ease her insides.

When she finished in the shower, she strolled to the kitchen downstairs to fix a quick cup of hot cocoa. Lucy weighed her options. She could stay in town, and allow the investigation to run its course, or she could drop everything now and leave town. The last time a murder investigation involved her, business had flopped, and she had struggled together with Hannah and her aunt Tricia to keep the bakery afloat.

She had been so optimistic about the future of her business a few days back, but now she couldn't think of one reason to keep the business running. Lucy finished her cocoa, stood up from her seat, and opened the bakery. Hannah was due to arrive at 8 a.m., but Lucy always opened before she arrived. She cleaned the front glass, turned the outside sign to 'Now Open', and walked into the kitchen to note the pastries they had in stock.

"I have made no sales in the past two days," she muttered, chewing on her lower lip as she opened the refrigerator and took out a bowl of sliced fruits. At this rate, she would run at a loss soon. "What's the point of all of this, anyway?"

With her stomach rumbling, Lucy took out her phone to call her aunt. She needed some reassurance as nothing she did seemed to stop her heart from thudding louder with each passing second.

She heard a soft knock, and the slow creak of the front door caught her attention. She dropped her phone on the table and rushed to the dining area.

"Aunt Tricia," she exclaimed as Tricia stepped into the bakery. A black duffel bag hung loosely on one shoulder, and she held her car keys in the other. Lucy was in her arms in a split second. She exhaled and stepped back after a second.

"You look like you've lost some weight," Tricia commented as Lucy took her bag. "Have you been overthinking?"

The rumbles in the pit of her stomach slowly subsided, and she rubbed the back of her neck as she dropped the bag in a corner of the kitchen. "I can't help it, Aunt Tricia. It's like I'm deep in quicksand, and things might keep going downhill from this point."

"Don't be quick to assume things, honey. I know life isn't fair but giving up so easily isn't your style."

"I hate this," Lucy whispered. "Hate that I'm in this position again... helpless again. Taylor dropped by here a few days back. He took some cupcakes as samples for testing."

"They think your treats caused their death?" Tricia asked. "You have no motive to want the Wilsons dead," she pointed out.

Lucy nodded, bit her lower lip, and dropped into a chair. She crossed her hands on the table. "They died after the party hosted by the Andersons. I was with them for a while during the party, and they both looked healthy and so in love. The doctors suspect food poisoning, and the last place they were seen alive and well was at the party."

Tricia tapped a finger on the table continuously, and she tilted her head. "I lived in Ivy Creek the first thirty-five years of my life, and I know what it's like around here when there's something newsworthy, but the gossip mongers can't feast on one piece of news for too long and soon latch on to something else."

Lucy remembered Aunt Tricia moved out when her husband got a job in Denver. They had rented a condo by the lake in a nearby town called Castle Pines. Lucy had visited one summer with her parents and Tricia had shown them the mountainous path of the Colorado leading to the Denver River. The memory was special to her as Tricia had tucked her in that night and told her a story about a one-eyed monster who lived in the mountains.

"What happens to my business while I wait for this to blow over? Just like the last time, no one comes by here anymore, and it's only just the first week."

Tricia placed her hand over Lucy's and squeezed. "Don't beat yourself up. I believe the truth will eventually come out. In the meantime, how about we distract ourselves with a trip to the convenience store? I need some personal items."

"Hannah should be here any minute," Lucy replied, and rose from her chair. She glanced at her watch and added. "We can leave for the store once she shows up."

Lucy carried her aunt's bag to the extra bedroom upstairs and Gigi followed her into the room, flicking her tail. Tricia came into the bedroom and took off the shawl wrapped around her neck.

"Hi, Gigi," Tricia greeted, and squatted to stroke Gigi's fur. Gigi gave a high-pitched meow. "I will take a brief nap, and join you downstairs soon," she said and smiled at Lucy. "Try to worry less dear."

"I will."

Lucy walked out of the bedroom with Gigi, shutting the door gently behind her. "Come on, let's fix you breakfast," she whispered and scooped Gigi into her arms.

Hannah arrived while she was waiting for the homemade salmon recipe to cool off, and she greeted Lucy with an enthusiastic voice. She stroked Gigi's fur and walked over to the sink to wash her hands. "I see Tricia's sedan parked behind yours in the corner. When did she get here?"

"Not so long ago. She's resting upstairs right now."

"It's good to have her around," Hannah replied. "You need to stop worrying so much about everything. I'm sure it will blow over soon, and now that Tricia is here, you can distract yourself a little."

Lucy remained quiet, and Hannah checked the stock. "Did we get any orders this morning?"

"No," Lucy replied, and stopped stirring the kibble. "Mrs. De Luca called to cancel the order for her son's birthday next weekend. She claims they won't be having a large scale party anymore."

Hannah wiped her hands on a dry napkin. "Mrs. De Luca never entertains guests on a small scale. That's obviously a lie."

Lucy squeezed her eyes shut for a second. "I know it is," she replied, and swallowed as she reopened them. Hannah pulled out their inventory notepad from the mini drawer on the left of the kitchen and pulled out a chair at the rectangular table to seat. "There's nothing we can do besides wait for the cops to clear this up and find the killer."

"Did you hear from Taylor?" Hannah asked.

"No," she replied in a tiny voice. "But I hope to hear something soon."

Gigi finished her meal, and Lucy cleaned the plate before heading back to her room. When she returned to the bakery minutes later, Tricia was sitting with Hannah on the patio, enjoying a glass of lemonade.

Lucy stepped onto the patio and shut the door behind her. She took a seat at the table and picked a crepe from Hannah's plate. "Ready for a drive to the store?" Lucy asked.

Tricia nodded her reply and emptied her glass. "I was just telling Hannah of my theory after thinking about the details you told me."

Lucy arched a questioning brow in Hannah's direction. "What theory?"

"The Wilsons are a close-knit family, and many people in Ivy Creek envied the relationship they had," Hannah replied. "It seems preposterous that anyone would hate or want them dead… They had no enemies anyone was aware of."

"Which brings my theory to life," Tricia said. "What if the killer is a close relative? Someone whom no one would suspect?"

"What are you thinking?" Lucy asked, her face scrunched up. Whatever Tricia's theory was, it could prove useful. Everyone was a suspect until proven innocent, and if Lucy didn't kill them, then their killer was out there. A chill coiled up Lucy's spine from the thought of someone ending two innocent lives, and her stomach rumbled.

"The Wilsons had two sons. I met them once while I lived here, and again last year," Tricia replied. "If we want to dig into close relatives, then their sons come first."

"They each run a subsidiary of their parents' grocery store business," Hannah said. "You think one of them is the killer? Isn't that a wild assumption?"

"She's not saying one of them is the killer," Lucy replied before Tricia could speak. "She's saying we have a premise to dig up what we can."

Tricia's smile turned upward. "It's a good thing we planned a trip to the convenience store," she mumbled, and rose from her seat. "Let's see what we can find out."

6

A sheen of sweat broke out on Lucy's forehead as they walked into the Wilsons' convenience store downtown twenty minutes later.

She walked over to the counter behind her aunt, and Lucy's gaze wandered around, sizing up the store's symmetrical arrangements. She picked up the fruity smell, and the clean atmosphere made the place relaxing.

Although the store was empty, the man at the counter kept busy. He kept his focus on the screen before him, his fingers punching his keyboard as if he had a personal vendetta against it. Tricia leaned towards Lucy as they neared the counter. "That's Bruce… he's their first son. I recognize him because we passed by each other a few times last year when I was in town. He was with his father one of those times."

Lucy assessed his slight frame, noting the crease lines on his forehead as he focused on what he was doing. He stopped typing, rubbed the stubble on his jaw, and continued.

"Mr. Wilson," Tricia called, gaining his attention, and his jaw dropped when he looked in their direction.

His gaze landed on hers, and Lucy nearly cowered behind her aunt when his brown eyes bulged out.

"I'm Tricia King," her aunt added.

"Lucy Hale," she said after Tricia.

"I know who you are," Bruce replied, and took his hands off the keyboard. He slipped them into his pockets and leaned away from the counter. "The town keeps talking about you."

"I'm here to relay my condolences about your parents," Lucy replied. She placed her hand over her chest gently. "You should know I had nothing to do with it like the rumors say and accept my sincerest condolences."

"I don't pay attention to the rumors," he replied in an edgy tone. "People lose sight of what's important when they focus on what everyone thinks. Whatever information I need about my parents' death, I will get from the cops."

Lucy nodded and shifted her weight from one foot to the other. Bruce Wilson turned away from her, and she released an exasperated sigh. His reaction was far different from what she had imagined. She had expected him to meet her with anger.

"Still, it must be hard for you," Tricia added. "Losing your parents in such a way… it's not something I would wish on anyone. We are truly sorry for your loss."

He nodded, his tight expression easing a little. "Thank you," he replied. "I've had many condolences come in since they passed away, and yours seems more genuine than curious. I appreciate that…" His words trailed off as the door swung open, and a man walked in, holding three large boxes.

Lucy and Tricia exchanged curious looks as Bruce ordered the man to place the boxes in the back and handed over the receipts.

"They are new stock. I'm doing a general restock of this store and our branch on sixth avenue," he said when he turned back to them. "It's Thanksgiving soon, and a lot of families have guests for Thanksgiving. It's a good business time for the store, and it would help with our expansion next year."

"Expansion?" Lucy asked. Would anyone who just lost their loved ones a few days ago be thinking of expanding a business? Lucy tried to hide her suspicion with a follow-up question.

"Wouldn't those plans take a back burner considering the ongoing investigations and funeral preparations?"

Bruce shrugged. "My parents weren't religious. They would have wanted to be cremated without a funeral, and we've pushed back plans of expansion for long enough. It's now or never," he replied with a wave of his hand.

"It's good to see you making steady plans," Tricia chirped in. She took Lucy's hand in hers and squeezed. "Take care," she added, and led Lucy out of the store.

Outside, Tricia released Lucy, and Lucy combed her fingers through her hair. "Seems to me like Bruce Wilson has everything figured out," she commented, and glanced back at the store as they walked to Tricia's car in the parking space.

Tricia turned on the engine when they got in and sped down the road. She tapped her finger on the steering wheel as she drove. "Don't you think he's suspicious?"

"It just seemed to me like he wasn't grieving at all. Either that, or he is excellent at masking it or shoving it away."

"He was quick to dismiss the rumors surrounding his parents' death and his talk of expansion made him seem like he didn't care about his parents' death."

"Let's drop by his brother's store and see what we can find."

*

The location of Wayne's store was a mile away from Bruce's, and Lucy had a hunch that they didn't see eye to eye on the expansion because when they arrived at the store Wayne was closing up.

Lucy glanced at her watch, wondering why he would close the store so early in the day. "Wayne Wilson," she called, and he turned around.

Wayne was a foot taller than his brother, and his height, coupled with the broad expanse of his shoulders, made him look older than Bruce.

He adjusted the bag on his shoulder and waited till they reached him. "Lucy Hale?" he called in a shaky voice, and a dull ache formed in the pit of her stomach. *Maybe Wayne Wilson would treat her with anger and not indifference like his brother*, she thought.

"Yes," she replied.

He frowned, and Lucy began in carefully spaced words. "I'm here to relay my sincerest condolences for your parents' deaths. I met them once, and they were really friendly people."

Wayne's head bobbed nervously, and he licked his lips. "They were," he replied, his voice cracking.

"I'm truly sorry about the news," Tricia added. "It must be so hard on you, having to work on funeral arrangements, and the store expansion."

Wayne stared at the ground, and when he raised them, his eyes were watery. "I admit I've had it rough, but I'm holding it together. When it gets too hard, I take time out to cool off. I've never imagined a world without my parents in it."

His words reminded Lucy of the ache in her heart when she received the news of her parents' death some months ago. She remembered being confused at first, before her aunt's words sank in fully, and the tears that came after did nothing to reduce the gut-wrenching pain.

"It gets easier with time," she assured him, and looked around the surroundings of the store to the black model T Ford parked in the tall grass beside the store.

Wayne jiggled the keys in his hands as Tricia asked, "Were you heading out?"

"Yes," he replied. "I have an appointment, and I really didn't feel like opening until the funeral passed, but Bruce insisted. He has always had more zeal for the business, and my parents thought he made a better successor because I ran things differently. But even though I don't share his focus and zeal, I have compassion and I think the key to running a successful business is making your customers comfortable, and happy. I'd rather close up than allow my poor state of mind to affect the business."

"You do what you have to do to feel better," Tricia sympathized, and a sigh escaped his lips.

"Thanks for your visit, Miss Hale. It means a lot that you both dropped by."

"Please, it's Lucy," she replied and gave him a warm smile.

Wayne walked away from them, and they watched as he entered the Ford, kick started the engine, and disappeared down the rutted road.

"Well, that sure looked like grieving," Tricia said as they walked back to her car. "He seems more affected by his parents' death than Bruce."

Lucy shook her head. "He showed compassion… it's human to show your pain," she replied and stared at the road as Tricia swerved the sedan down the single lane. "I think Bruce is ambitious."

"That makes him dangerous," Tricia replied. "A person with ambition always craves more, and you never know the lengths they'd take to achieve their ambition. But then again, Wayne wasn't as good at business as his brother, and his parents made it clear Bruce was a better successor. He could have just the same ambition as his brother."

Lucy agreed with her. Wayne was just as suspicious as his brother because he also had a motive. If his parents undermined him, then at some point he would seek to disprove this, and that made him as dangerous as Bruce.

"We might be on to something here," Tricia said, and stole a glance at her. "I have a feeling there's more to Bruce Wilson."

"Likewise, Wayne," Lucy replied, replaying the emotional scene with him earlier. She couldn't trust either of them because the chances that they both put on an act were high.

7

L ucy noticed Hannah was sitting outside the bakery with a glum look on her face as they got out of the car. She walked over to her and dropped into a chair. "Any customers?" she asked, hoping some news would brighten her mood.

"None," Hannah replied, and rubbed the back of her neck. "I've been sitting out here all day, and not even one person dropped by."

Lucy lowered her head into her hands. She rubbed her temples slowly, hoping it would dull the slow ache she had there all day, and ease some of her tension.

A minute of silence passed between the three women before she spoke. "I had a bad feeling about working with Becky Anderson," she murmured. "Guess I should have listened to my gut!"

"You can't blame yourself for any of this," Hannah said. "Becky presented a good business offer, and you took it."

"I'm in this mess because I agreed to make treats for her party."

"Were you compensated for the work done?" Tricia asked. "You put in a lot of effort and now have more troubles because of the murder."

"I did the work for free," Lucy replied, and Tricia's jaw dropped. Lucy shook her head and unwrapped the shawl around her neck.

"You knew better, Lucy," Tricia chided. "You're a talented businesswoman. I've watched you grow this place over the past few months. How did you let some uppity woman talk you into working for free? You should have gotten something for your troubles."

Lucy groaned and closed her eyes for a second. *I shouldn't have worked at this party.... I'm in this mess because of Becky Anderson's proposal.*

"Have you heard from her since the beginning of all of this? Has she contacted you to say anything? Maybe offer to defend you?" Tricia asked.

"She hasn't," Hannah replied for Lucy, and a heavy sigh escaped Lucy's lips. An engine roared from across the road, and Lucy straightened her spine. The car slowed by the side of the bakery and stopped.

"That's Becky," Hannah announced once the driver stepped out of the car.

Tricia and Hannah walked into the bakery, leaving Lucy to confront Becky alone. Lucy remained in her seat as Becky marched towards her patio. She wore a neatly pressed white chiffon blouse tucked into green pants, and her hair tied into a sleek ponytail.

"I should tread carefully when hiring for an event next time," Becky began, with no niceties. "What exactly did you do? How did you make such a mess of the opportunity I handed over to you by causing a ruckus and a murder investigation?"

"I don't know what you mean, but if it's about the Wilsons, then you've come to the wrong place. I am just as confused as you are or anyone else in this town."

"This entire episode has damaged my brand, and it's all your fault, Lucy Hale. You served those treats at the party. You should be responsible."

"Are you accusing me of killing the Wilsons?" Lucy asked, raising her voice a notch. Her eyes widened in disbelief, and she blinked rapidly. "What reason would I have to kill them? I never met them before your party."

"You did this… you should be responsible… perhaps you made a mistake with the recipe or something? Maybe they were allergic to something in your cupcakes. I don't know, but it was something they ate from your treats. That's on you!"

"No, it's not," Lucy defended. Her cheeks burned with the ferocity of her growing anger, and she could barely contain the tremble in her voice as she jabbed a finger at Becky. "You don't get to drive here in your expensive suit and car and accuse me of killing people. It was your party… your association, and if someone poisoned the Wilsons, then it would be someone on your list of guest. Other guests had my treats. How many of them did you see dropping dead from poisoning?"

The door opened, and Tricia stepped out of the bakery. Lucy shoved her fingers through her hair when her aunt placed a hand on her arm to calm her.

"I won't let you blame me for any of this," Lucy added, and turned away from Becky.

She struggled to regain composure. Her nerves were spiraling from her recent outburst, and from the ashen look on Becky's face, she could tell she had surprised her, too. Lucy prided herself on having a tight control over her emotions. She never let them get the best of her, but everything about this situation was testing her resilience.

Becky dropped into a chair. Her purse landed by her feet, and she rubbed her forehead.

"I understand how difficult it is trying to run a business right now because of the ongoing investigation, but throwing accusations around won't change that," Tricia pointed out.

Lucy turned to see the pout on Becky's lips. "I'm sorry," Becky muttered. "Since all of this started, I've had a massive decline in profits and my husband and I are trying hard to get to the root of this. When I heard the Wilsons died, and they suspected it was food poisoning that killed them, I dropped by here. I don't think your treats caused their death… I had some of your cupcakes and they were amazing. I guess I let my emotions get the best of me."

"I'm sorry, too," Lucy replied.

A relieved look washed over Becky's face, and she continued. "I know the cops will sort this out. We just have to give them time to do their job. All my customers withdrew their orders, and the bakery makes no daily sales."

"It's hard," Becky murmured and crossed her legs. "I have Roland's support, and it makes things easier to know I have that one person in my corner rooting for me."

Lucy leaned forward and tapped her finger on the table. *I wish I had that;* she thought. *A person in my corner, rooting for me, backing me up all the way.*

"How are you holding up?" Becky asked.

"I'm hanging in… holding on to a shred of hope it will work out." Lucy replied.

"If you need anything, or any help, please reach out to me. I would be more than glad to help in any way I can," Becky replied with a soft smile. She sprung out of her chair then and turned to Tricia. "I'm sorry I barged in here and caused a scene."

"It's not a problem," Tricia replied with a nod. They watched Becky walk to her car and drive away before Tricia added. "That could have quickly escalated if you didn't control yourself. You should keep Becky Anderson in your corner for the time being. She might be of help someday."

"I'm just so tense... I need to cool off," Lucy replied, and cast Tricia a slight glance.

The creamy scent of buttery cinnamon rolls reached her nose, and her stomach grumbled. She ran a hand over her face, rubbed her nose and inhaled the scent. "Becky's lucky," she whispered, turning to Tricia. "She has someone backing her and helping her through this rough patch. I have no one to lean on besides myself."

"You have me, Lucy," Tricia reminded her, and reached out to touch her hand on the table. "You will always have me."

8

B usiness worsened over the next three days, and by the weekend, Lucy's clients were not picking up her calls or were canceling their orders. She checked her watch for the tenth time since Hannah arrived an hour ago and let out a heavy sigh when she realized it was almost noon.

Hannah, sitting at a corner of the bakery's dining area, repeatedly tapped her finger on the table, and the noise made Lucy nervous. She shifted in her chair and cast a glance in Hannah's direction.

"Can you stop doing that? It's making me nervous," she said.

Hannah withdrew her hands from the round wooden table and lifted her left shoulder. "I can't help it, I'm sorry."

Lucy stood up and crossed over to where Hannah sat. "I'm just as worried as you are, maybe even worse than you are. I don't know what to do at this point… It feels like I've lost everything over the past two weeks."

"We need to hang in longer. This will pass, and everything will be back to normal as soon as the cops clear it up," Hannah reassured her, but Lucy's unsettled insides continued to roll. She couldn't bring herself to stop worrying.

She threw herself into an intense round of cleaning, finding new places to clean in the kitchen and dining area when she had finished the first round of cleaning. Hannah had worked on making a new batch of bread and cupcakes for sale, but in small quantities to minimize loss, and her aunt had worked in the backyard.

Lucy was exhausted by the time she finished. She was still unsettled. *If I could just get an update, anything to give me a shred of hope to hang unto.*

"One customer would encourage me to keep at this," Hannah muttered, but Lucy heard her. "Would you like some salad?"

"Sure," Lucy agreed, and Aunt Tricia walked into the bakery holding a round basket of garden tools Lucy's parents had kept on standby.

"I'm exhausted!"

Lucy re-focused on the task at hand, and Tricia returned from the kitchen with a bottle of cold water. She sat beside Lucy, took a long gulp before asking. "Any customers?"

Lucy shook her head and turned around to see Hannah walking towards her.

"Your cell phone," she said. "Found it buzzing on the table in the kitchen."

Lucy took the phone, and did a double take when she saw the caller ID. Every muscle in her body went rigid, and her breath quickened. "It's Taylor," she murmured. The hand holding the phone trembled slightly, and she broke eye contact with Tricia and focused on the phone.

She watched as the phone vibrated in her hand, contemplating if she was ready to receive the ominous news she was sure he was calling to deliver.

Seconds later, her phone stopped ringing and she closed her eyes. A rush of fear flowed through every vein in her body as she contemplated how bad her situation had become. *What is the worst that can happen? I'm innocent in all this, so I have nothing to worry about.*

"Will you call him back?" Tricia asked, and she nodded twice.

She licked her chapped lips and picked her phone up from the table.

"What's up?" she asked when he picked up on the third ring and stilled herself mentally for his next words. "I have heard no updates from you. Did you call because you have news?"

"Yes," he replied.

"Is the sample testing done? Do we know what killed them yet?" she tried to hide the tremor in her voice but she knew it was obvious.

"We have yet to get the results, but the investigation is officially a murder investigation."

Heart sinking in disappointment, Lucy lowered her gaze to her feet. *What else can go wrong?* She thought in despair, and her eyes turned red from the pool of tears welling up in them.

"Regardless of what happens, please remain in town. We will call you in for questioning, and we will leave no stone unturned," he continued in the same straight tone. "I will be in touch."

Her hand slid to her side when the call ended. She couldn't find it in herself to look at the ladies who she knew were expecting some feedback.

"What did he say?" Tricia and Hannah asked at the same time.

Lucy masked her watery eyes with a grin. "They haven't received a report from the testing yet," she replied. "He promised to be in touch."

"Then why do you look so pale?" Tricia asked, a concerned look on her face.

"I'm fine," she replied. "Excuse me," she added, and hurried out of the bakery. Once outside, she rushed to the side of the building, and dropped both hands on her knees as she fell to the ground.

Lucy's breath came out in haggard puffs, and she struggled to keep breathing against the knot in her throat that promised to suffocate her. *There is no getting out of this... What if this is the end, and they can't prove my innocence? What if the Wilsons truly died because of my treats?*

A torrent of questions bombarded her mind and a hot tear slipped out of her eye. There was a possibility someone had sabotaged her treats to hurt the Wilsons. She couldn't rule out anything yet and it wouldn't be the first time someone in this town was setting her up for a fall.

I have to contact Becky Anderson...

Becky organized that party. She had the list of guests who were also possible suspects in Lucy's opinion.

Chest still burning, Lucy regained a bit of composure when she wrapped her hands around her shoulder, and gently patted herself, counting the seconds until her breaths slowed. She heard footsteps followed by her aunt calling, and she staggered to her feet.

"Are you alright, dear? You don't look good." Tricia placed a hand on her arm and led her back to the patio.

"I'm fine," Lucy murmured, stopping Tricia with her hand. "I just need a minute to catch my breath… I'm fine." She had to clear all of this and wrap it up before it got any worse.

Later that evening, Lucy contacted Becky via text. They chose a time and place to meet, and she hoped meeting with Becky would answer her questions.

9

The sky was clear the next afternoon, and the air carried a light musky scent of pine and sappy cottonwood. Lucy and Becky met at a local cafeteria downtown, not far off from Ivy Creek High, the school Lucy had attended.

She walked into the cafeteria and chose a spot by the left corner where anyone walking into the shop could easily spot her. It would make it easier for Becky to find her once she got there.

The interior of the shop was cute, with well-polished wooden floors and walls covered in thick, silvery-patterned wallpaper. The choice of colors made the place come alive, and she was impressed with the design as she looked around the half-empty shop.

She imagined that supplying cafeterias like this with her pastries could be a great income earner. It would bring both her bakery and the cafeteria more customers, she thought and turned to the man on the other side of the counter.

He wore an apron over his shirt, and he smiled as he handed over a to-go coffee cup to the girl at the counter, took the dollar bills she handed over and waved her goodbye.

Lucy flushed when he looked in her direction, and she glanced away. She ran a hand over her sleek ponytail and linked her fingers.

"Hi there," a voice said by her side.

Lucy saw the charming smile on the man's face out of the corner of her eye before turning to meet him.

"I'm Richard Lester," he said, and sat on the chair in front of hers.

She blinked and took in his features. He had a left dimple, she noticed, and the auburn brown shade of his hair matched his golden skin.

"Lucy Hale," she said as she cleared her throat that had suddenly gone dry.

"New to town?" he asked. "I noticed you keep looking over the walls and counter."

"Oh, no, no… I'm here to meet someone," she replied.

Lucy immediately noticed his deep brown eyes as his grin widened. She looked away first when they lingered.

"May I offer something to calm you? You seem rattled, and chamomile tea never goes wrong for soothing nerves," he offered.

"Thank you, but I'm fine. My friend should be here any minute."

"Come on… I insist. It's on the house, I would appreciate if you accepted the gesture."

Lucy looked at him again, and he clasped his hands in a plea gesture. "Alright," she said.

Richard disappeared into the kitchen behind the counter and returned minutes later with a mug on a saucer. Lucy accepted the mug with a warm smile and lifted it to her lips. The underlying refreshing scent of daisies hit her nostrils as she took a sip.

She tasted honey and licked her lip as she lowered the mug to the table. She noticed him watching her, his hooded lids trailing over her face, and Lucy's cheeks turned red.

He leaned forward and laced his fingers on the table. "Soothing, right?" he asked.

Lucy's head bobbed twice, and she sipped from the mug again, wondering if she should suggest a partnership between them. "It's lovely."

"Mind sharing what's bothering you?" he asked.

"It's just business problems," she replied, carefully pacing her words.

"We all have a few of those," Richard replied. "I've had many of those... from renovation problems to lack of customers."

"Really?" Lucy asked and scanned the shop. It seemed like the one thing he didn't lack here was customers. Although the shop was half empty, she had counted eight walk-in customers since she arrived.

"I opened up two years ago, and it was difficult to keep the business afloat at first, especially because I started off with a loan to cover the furnishing and renovations. The former owners of the shop did very poor maintenance, and I had to change a lot to make it presentable."

"Did you get the cafeteria on lease?" she asked, genuinely interested in talking about his business progress. It helped get her mind off waiting for Becky's arrival.

"No, it belonged to my grandmother. She rented it out when she closed down her diner, and I made use of it when I moved back to town. I got a loan and started the business, oblivious to how difficult it would get at some point.

"Was it a cooperate loan?"

Richard shook his head. "I got it from a relative."

"Oh…"

He looked at her half-empty mug, and he smiled. "I guess you enjoyed the tea."

"I did." A smile crossed her face. "Thanks."

"You're welcome," he replied, and rose to his feet.

The door opened, and Becky made her way into the cafeteria. She beamed and waved at Lucy, then cat-walked towards her.

"My friend is here," Lucy said as Richard gathered the mug and saucer.

"I'll see you around, Lucy."

He left as Becky arrived and took over his seat. "I see you've met Richard Lester… he's one of Ivy Creek's eligible bachelors," she said and eyed Richard at the counter. "If I was single, I might have snatched him up for myself."

Lucy eyed her, and Becky broke into a short laugh. "That was a joke, relax. Why did you want to meet?"

Lucy raked her fingers through her hair. "I need a list of the guests at the charity event you hosted last time. Every person in attendance that night, and also the team of ushers you hired for the job."

Becky's brows furrowed, and she lowered her purse to the table. "Why? Did something happen?"

"No, no," Lucy replied with a dismissive wave of her hand. "I would like to network with other businesses, and I know you have a lot of connections with the wealthy people of Ivy Creek," she stammered. "I just need a new client list."

"I can help with that," Becky replied in an enthusiastic tone. "Connecting people is what I do." Her eyes lit up, and she took out a notepad from her purse. She handed it over to Lucy with a pen. "Write down your email address, and I will send it to you once I get to my laptop tonight."

"Thanks, Becky."

Lucy scribbled down her email address and slid the note back to Becky. Once she got the list, she would go through it, and try to find out each guest's relationship with the Wilsons. Becky snatched her purse from the table and glanced at the golden wristwatch on her left wrist.

"I have to go now," she said, and gave Lucy a sly smile. "You should give the young man your number. Seems like he can't take his eyes off you."

Lucy stole a glance in Richard's direction and their eyes met briefly. He smiled at her, winked, and then focused on the customer by the counter. She gathered her things and exited the cafeteria with Becky.

Lucy flagged down a cab after Becky drove away and rode back home thinking about her brief encounter with Richard Lester. She wondered if he was truly interested in her, as Becky speculated, or if he was simply a playboy.

10

Tricia's car was missing from the corner of the building when Lucy arrived at the bakery.

Inside the kitchen, Hannah hummed to the music playing through her AirPods as Lucy entered the bakery and took off her coat. She unwrapped her shawl next and rolled the sleeves of her sweater up before walking over to the counter.

Hannah flashed a grin. "We had two customers today," she announced in a cheery tone. "I feel relaxed now."

Lucy saw the corners of Hannah's eyes lift as she smiled, and she shrugged off the heaviness weighing down on her and reached for a napkin.

"It's a good thing," Lucy replied as she folded the napkin. "Everything will get better," she added. "Where is Aunt Tricia?"

"She went off to get some items from the grocery store."

Lucy checked the display glass and counted the pastries they had left. They would make a new batch of bread tomorrow, and hopefully, more customers would come by. Lucy hoped she could put the entire ordeal of the Wilsons' death behind her and move forward.

A lady walked into the bakery holding her daughter as Lucy finished counting the remaining cupcakes and Hannah greeted her.

"Welcome to Sweet Delights. What would you like?"

"Do you have an apple pie?" the lady asked and turned to her daughter.

The little girl stared at the cupcakes on display and Lucy saw her eyes widen.

"What would you like, sweetie?" her mother asked, running a hand over the girl's blonde pigtail braids.

"Uhhhm…" she licked her lips and lifted her saucer round eyes to Lucy's. Her cheek colored, and she glanced at the display glass again. "I want… I don't know what I want," she exclaimed in a tiny, unsure voice.

"You should try our cupcakes," Lucy chirped in, and signaled to Hannah to get the lady's pie packed while she helped the little girl make a choice. "The sprinkles are amazing, and we have different flavors and blends too."

The girl jumped and tugged at her mother's hand. "I want the cupcakes then," she sang out, giggling. "Mom, I'll have two cupcakes please, the ones with the sprinkles."

"Alright, Zoey." The lady giggled, and Lucy shot her an amused look. "She learned how to pedal her bike on her own today, so she's really excited."

"That's amazing, Zoey. Learning to pedal on your own is an achievement."

Zoey flashed Lucy a wide smile, showcasing her set of white teeth. "I know," she replied, swinging her arms. "My dad taught me, and he promised to let me ride at the park once winter is over. It will be so much fun."

"I'm sure it will be," Lucy replied, and Hannah returned with a package. Lucy wrapped Zoey's cupcakes and added an extra piece. "I've added an extra for you to try out with your dad," she said and handed over the pack to Zoey's mother.

"Thanks," Zoey said, and spun around. She jogged towards the door singing a popular children's rhyme, *Twinkle, Twinkle, Little Star.* Her mother chuckled, and paid for the items in cash, waving at Hannah and Lucy before walking out of the store.

Zoey reminded Lucy of when she learned to ride her bicycle and she shook her head, smiling to herself as a memory of her riding in the park with her father flashed through her mind. "She's cute," she whispered, and turned to Hannah.

Hannah dusted her hands together. "We've run out of cupcakes and chips."

Lucy walked around the counter and took a seat. She spread her legs out in front of her and sat upright when Richard Lester crossed her mind. She hadn't seen him around town before, and when Becky had mentioned *Lou's Café,* a mental image of some old barista crossed her mind.

"I dropped by *Lou's Café* today. It's a lovely place with beautiful scenery, and I met Richard Lester for the first time. He's a charming young man."

"Richard Lester?" Hannah rasped. She scoffed and shook her head. "He's charming sure, and he's got honeyed words."

Lucy caught the cynicism in Hannah's venom laced words.

"You know him well?"

"He used to date my sister," she replied. Lucy's ears perked up as she listened to Hannah.

"They got along as friends at first when he moved into town two years ago. We all thought he was perfect for her, but he strung her along and then acted like she didn't exist when he moved on to his next girl. He never commits to anything long term, that I can assure you."

Richard's genuine smile as he offered her a cup of tea flashed in her mind and also when he winked at her as she left his shop. She shook it away, amazed at the interesting twist of Hannah knowing him so well.

"How did you two meet, by the way?" Hannah asked, pulling Lucy out of her thoughts.

"I met with Becky at his café earlier today to get the list of guests at her party the night the Wilsons died."

"You suspect one of the guests might have had something to do with their poisoning?"

"Yes. Whoever poisoned them had to have access to the treats beforehand. Once Becky sends over the list, I will go through it and try to see how many of the guests have a personal relationship with them."

"That's a brilliant plan."

Hannah and Lucy continued their conversation, shifting from talking about Becky's guest list to updates on the concession she had set up close to the park four months ago. After her hired assistant, Diane, who ran the store, tendered her resignation last month, she had closed down the store.

Lucy hoped to reopen it once the Wilsons investigation was complete. Having a few customers at the bakery had renewed her passion for her business and ignited some hope that there was some light at the end of a very dark tunnel.

I hope I keep getting customers like Zoey and her mother, who happen to care little for town gossip.

She made plans with Hannah to reduce their daily stock, but include newer recipes, and as they mulled over new ideas, the door burst open. Her head whipped up and she spotted Bruce Wilson.

Lucy braced herself immediately as he marched towards her menacingly.

11

B ruce reached where Lucy stood, and color drained from her face as he stared at her.

What do I do?

Hannah scurried into the kitchen, leaving Lucy to face Bruce on her own, and Lucy's mind reeled with different thoughts. *Why was Bruce Wilson here? Did he hear the rumors? Or about the cops' investigation of her treats? And why had Hannah left her to confront him all by herself?*

"Bruce…" she began.

"I heard about what you did," he interrupted before she could finish her sentence. "It's commendable, and it's why I'm here."

He wasn't here to fight her? Lucy bit her lower lip and closed her eyes for a second, slowly exhaling to ease the pressure building in her chest. So he wasn't here because of his parents' murder? She blinked, and a shaky laugh escaped her lips. Her racing pulse slowed, and she clapped her hands. "Thank you, Bruce," she replied, and offered him a seat, even though she wasn't sure what he was talking about.

"I met with a close friend who works on the local business committee, and he recommended your treats for my expansion plans. He says you supplied the treats at the Andersons' charity event weeks ago."

"I did."

A satisfied smile crossed Bruce's lips, and he looked around the bakery. "You have a nice setup here, but I'm certain walk-in customers aren't enough to generate huge profits," he paused, and took out an envelope from the breast pocket of his blue shirt. "How about we work together?"

She took the envelope and ripped it open, reading through the brief words. "That's a grant I just got from the local bank, and it will cover all my expansion expenses. Working with me means you will have a sublet in my grocery stores where we can put your pastries on display for sale. Of course I'll be offering upfront payment for whatever supplies you bring, and I would need a lot to cover all my stores."

Her lips curved into a wide smile until the sides of her mouth hurt, then she muffled a squeal of excitement. "I... I would love to work with you, Bruce."

"Great! My assistant will contact you by next week to draw up a plan and please add whatever new ideas you have to the list."

"I sure will."

Bruce got up, gave her one last smile before walking out, and Lucy released a pent-up breath. He had seemed upset when he walked into the bakery, and for a minute, she feared he would accuse her of his parents' murder.

Hannah returned to the dining area and sat with Lucy. "What was that about?"

"Bruce offered a business deal," Lucy replied, still giddy with excitement at Bruce's news. "He wants me to supply his chain of grocery stores with pastries… we would have a sublet for our goods."

Hannah breathed out an easy laugh, and her eyes danced. "That's amazing!"

"I know, right," Lucy tittered, unable to control her joy. Ideas already bounced inside her head like tiny rubber balls, and she couldn't wait to get started on the new project.

"We should try perfecting the recipes for at least three new pastries to add to our current menu."

"First off, we should celebrate," Lucy replied. She went into the kitchen and returned seconds later with a bottle of sparkling grape wine and two glasses.

"To more good news," Hannah toasted as their glasses clinked. They drank and continued discussing the recipes when Tricia returned. She drifted through the doors and joined them, slipping into the conversation easily about Bruce.

Bruce's determination to expand the store regardless of the murder investigation of his parents was a powerful move, and she couldn't settle the tiny sprout of envy in her heart. *I wish I could focus more, and not allow any circumstance to derail me.*

"Bruce Wilson wants to work with us on his expansion," Hannah said.

"It's true," Lucy said when her aunt turned to her. "We would supply his grocery stores pastries."

Tricia sipped her wine and cocked her head to one side. She

grinned and reached for the bottle again. "This definitely calls for a celebration."

They toasted again, and minutes later, Hannah said her good-byes as her shift had ended. Lucy and Tricia stayed in the bakery longer before retiring to the apartment upstairs. As Lucy prepared for bed, she thought about Bruce's proposal again.

Gigi strolled over to where she sat and she picked her up. "We are doing better, Gigi," she whispered, and Gigi purred. "We got a new business deal, and things are looking good." She stroked Gigi's fur repeatedly, enjoying the fluffiness.

Gigi was fast asleep in a minute, and Lucy gently placed her in the snug bed by the corner of the room and switched off the light. She dropped on her bed and pulled the sheets over her body and snuggled into her pillows.

She couldn't wait to start on Bruce Wilson's order, and she hoped the outcome of this job would differ from the disappointment of the lost orders in the past few weeks. *This is all I've got now.* Lucy planned to impress Bruce Wilson with her skills.

Her phone pinged on the dresser, and she reached for it. Becky's email flashed on the screen, and she sprang up. She positioned a pillow to support her back as she sat.

She hoped the email would lead her to something useful as she clicked it open and read the brief note attached to it.

This is a list of the guests and the business or companies they run. I hope you find it useful... xoxo Becky.

The first name on the list was Richard Lester.

12

The next morning, Lucy did not hear her phone's alarm buzzing. She snored lightly, dragging the sheets over her face to shield her eyes from the rays of dawn entering her room.

She finally stirred awake when something warm lapped at her feet, and she opened her eyes to see Gigi purring and licking her feet. Lucy groaned and sat up, ruffling her hair with both hands. She pushed stray strands away from her face and focused on Gigi.

"I need more sleep," she complained and searched the bed for her phone. It was past 7 a.m. She had overslept, missing the time for her early morning run. Lucy slipped out of the bed and stretched her arms out.

She spent half the night reading Becky's email, and interesting facts had popped up. The Wilsons not only owned two grocery stores in town, they also had buildings out on sublets, and one of them was 6 Dune Street. That was the exact location of Lou's Café where she met Becky.

Lucy couldn't remember seeing Richard at Becky's party that night, but he had gotten an invitation, so why didn't he attend? Besides, Richard told her the building had belonged to his grandmother. *Was that a lie? What else did he lie about?*

Lucy began dressing up after a hot shower. She stepped into her navy-blue pants and slipped into a floral-patterned cream-colored shirt. She planned to drop by Becky's office that morning, and confirm for herself all she could about Richard Lester.

When she reached the kitchen, Aunt Tricia sat with a mug of hot cocoa, and she waved a newspaper in Lucy's direction. "Come join me, dear. Are you heading out?"

"Yes," Lucy replied, and sat down. "Can I borrow your car?" She picked a pancake from the plate on the table, and after taking a bite, she added. "I want to meet with Becky."

"Did something happen?"

Lucy shook her head. "I just need to confirm a few things with her," she replied.

"Sure, you can drive my car. The key is upstairs."

Lucy finished her pancake, helped herself to a cup of hot cocoa before stepping out of the bakery. She drove to Becky's office address and walked into the building, stopping by the reception to ask for directions.

"Walk down that corridor, and stop by the fourth door," the short, plump woman at the front desk pointed at Becky's office down the hall.

"Thanks," Lucy breathed, then followed the directions.

She knocked before twisting the knob. Lucy entered the office, and Mr. Anderson's smile greeted her.

"Lucy," he said, and stood up from his chair. "What a surprise visit."

She crossed over to the table and accepted his extended hand, smiling as she eased into the chair he offered. "I came in to check on Becky," she replied, and looked around the office.

The office had seamless windows and a breath-taking view of the lawn outside. A dark walnut colored bookcase lined the right-side wall, and on the left was an exquisite black rug that matched the two-seater couch in the corner.

"Unfortunately, Becky had to leave town this morning for a business meeting, but she should be back in a few hours," Roland replied. "Did you need something? I'll be glad to assist if I can."

Lucy contemplated asking him about Richard Lester. He represented most of the town's rich members, so he could provide answers to some of her questions. Roland raised a brow when she didn't reply immediately, and she flashed him a smile.

"Actually, you can be of help. I was contemplating working with some other businesses in town, and I would like your input on some of them. I have interest in Lou's Café, and I want to know if he owns the café or…"

"Richard Lester owns the café," Roland replied before she finished. "However, he doesn't run it on his own, the Wilsons do."

"I don't understand."

"Richard is a nephew of Mr. Wilson, and he took a loan years back to start up the business. Rumors say he didn't pay back in time, and that led them to have some issues, but I represented Mr. Wilson, and I know for a fact that he cared little about a few thousand dollars his nephew borrowed to run a cafeteria."

So, Richard didn't lie about owning the building.

"Was he at the party that night? I don't remember seeing him."

Roland nodded his reply and picked a wrapped candy from the tray on the table. Lucy watched him pop it into his mouth and chew.

Lucy studied him, and she noticed how he toyed with a fancy colored candy he picked from the side of the table, and a grin broke out on his face, but his lower lip quivered as he looked at his hands.

"I have a sweet tooth," he explained. "Becky always complains about it, but it doesn't stop my cravings. I will definitely be popping into Sweet Delights one of these days."

"I appreciate that," Lucy replied. "It's nice to have someone compliment my work considering people fear my cupcakes had something to do with the Wilsons' death."

Roland's brows creased, and he wrinkled his nose in a worried expression. "That must be so difficult," he sympathized. "I believe you're innocent, and anyone with an ounce of sense would think so too."

"Thank you, Roland. It means a lot that you think so."

He nodded his agreement. "Keep working hard, and Sweet Delights could grow to be the premier bakery in the state of Colorado."

Lucy hoped that would happen one day, too. She thanked Roland for his time and left the building. She sped down the road, taking the first right turn that would lead to a connecting road taking her to the highway.

She slowed when her phone beeped, and she accepted the call from her smart watch.

"Hey, Lucy, where are you?" Hannah's tense voice floated through the speaker, and Lucy stopped when she spotted the red traffic light.

"I had something to take care of, but I'm driving to the bakery right now. Is there a problem? Do you need something?"

"Mr. Wilson's here," Hannah replied. Her voice trembled as she added. "Please get back fast."

The call ended, and Lucy felt an ominous feeling wash over her. *Why was Bruce Wilson at her bakery again? What did he want this time?*

She pressed down the accelerator and zoomed onto the highway, heading to the bakery. *What if Bruce found out about the presumptions surrounding my treats and he is there to cancel our contract? What do I do next?*

13

Lucy was surprised at what greeted her when she walked into the bakery. It wasn't a snarling, angry man who wanted to rip apart the contract they had agreed to. It was a more tentative man who was pacing the dining area. And it wasn't Bruce Wilson. It was his brother, Wayne. She took off her coat, handed it over to Hannah, and walked over to him. *Thank God, it isn't Bruce;* she thought.

"Mr. Wilson," she called. He turned around to face her. His sharp, irritated gaze swept up her face, and Lucy held her breath in anticipation. "Did you need something?"

Wayne brushed back his hair and straightened his spine. "Lucy," he replied, eyeing her. "I got news about my parents' investigation from the detectives. They died from poisoning..." he paused and glared at her. "Food poisoning."

Lucy remained quiet, counting the seconds until the accusation came. "I saw them eat your cupcakes at the Andersons' charity party the night they were hospitalized."

His words crashed on her, and Lucy sucked in a deep breath, trying to stop her panic. "Wayne..." she whispered, but he raised a hand, silencing her.

"You killed them? You poisoned those cupcakes... and I will make sure you pay for that," he yelled. "I will make sure you pay," he repeated.

"Wayne, please listen to me," Lucy tried again. Her temples pulsed, and out of the corner of her eye, she saw a woman and her daughter leave their seats. "I had nothing to do with it... The cops are..."

"Liar," he accused again. "I can't believe a word you say," he added in a quivering voice. Lucy saw tears pool in his eyes before he looked away from her, and she swallowed against the tightness in her throat.

Did Wayne really believe she poisoned his parents? Why would he think she did? Did everyone in town also doubt her innocence?

A woman walked into the bakery and rushed to Wayne's side. "Come on, honey," she said.

Lucy pressed her lips together, and the woman shot her an apologetic stare.

"Please, Wayne, let's go outside," she cooed.

Wayne hesitated at first, before walking out of the bakery with the woman. Lucy staggered backwards, unable to hold her weight with her wobbly feet.

Hannah rushed to steady her, and Lucy leaned against her. She couldn't take any more of these accusations and attacks on her business. The detectives still had no news, and she remained patient because she trusted they could get to the real culprit.

"What do I do?" she asked Hannah as they walked over to a chair. Lucy slouched into it and buried her head in her palms. "I need to do something. Today it's just Wayne Wilson. It might be someone else accusing me of murder tomorrow."

"You should reach out to Taylor," Hannah replied, and patted her shoulder. "He should have news about the sample testing by now. It's taken long enough."

The lady who led Wayne out walked back into the bakery. Hannah and Lucy turned to her, and she offered an apologetic smile.

"I'm so sorry," she muttered, crossing her fingers in front of her. "I'm Jane Wilson, and my husband was so out of line earlier."

"It's okay," Lucy replied. "I understand how he feels… it's a lot to lose both parents out of the blue."

"It's been so hard on him since they died, and he's…" she croaked, sniffed, and raised a finger to rub the corner of her eyes. "He's developed an anxiety issue… lots of anger outbursts like what happened earlier. I'm sorry for any inconvenience," she added, gave Lucy one last smile before walking away.

The bakery had emptied during the scene with Wayne, and Hannah walked around to gather the dishes on the tables. Lucy's chest was tight enough to explode, and she knew the one way she could get relief was to get answers.

"I have to see Taylor," she whispered, adjusted her purse on her shoulder, and hurried out of the bakery.

*

Taylor stood outside the station with another cop when Lucy arrived. She got out of her car and crossed over to him with determined steps. "Taylor," she called, and he turned to her. "We need to talk."

He whispered something to the cop, then walked over to her, slipping his hands into the pocket of his pants. "Lucy... Do you need something?" he asked in a cool tone.

Lucy swallowed and extended her clenched fists. "If you think I'm responsible for the Wilsons' death, then arrest me," she replied.

She saw him look at her outstretched fists, and Lucy raised her chin, determined not to back down. He could either give her answers that would clear her name or arrest her as a suspect. Whichever way, she was not leaving without answers.

"I have no reason to arrest you," he said. "Investigations are still ongoing and more evidence came to light recently."

"More evidence?" she asked, her heart hammering in her chest. "What... What evidence?"

Please let this be something positive.

"Your treats did not contain any poisonous substance, so you didn't do it," he said, and Lucy exhaled. Her lower lip quivered, and she wiped her sweaty forehead with her forearm.

"We are still testing other samples of what the Wilsons had that night, their drink, and food samples we collected from their house. The forensic team will determine which of those items contained the poison."

Lucy placed a hand over her chest. "So this means I'm free?" she asked, her tone light. Taylor shook his head, and she frowned. "What else?"

"You should be careful henceforth," he replied. "The killer is still out there, and whoever it is, they are trying to pin it on you."

Lucy's blood chilled, and she blinked. *Why would anyone want to frame me? I have no connections to the Wilsons or any rich resident of Ivy Creek.*

"Why would anyone do that?" she breathed out.

Taylor shrugged. "Beats me... just make sure you are careful," he added.

14

"Let's get some gas," Tricia said, and swerved her car into the gas station by the highway. Lucy got out of the passenger's seat and walked over to the stand while Tricia wandered into the fuel station's store.

Lucy filled the tank and sat in the driver's seat to wait for Tricia. It was the first Sunday in the month, and Tricia's house renovation was complete. They drove downtown to inspect the work done, and the changes satisfied Tricia.

Lucy especially liked the landscape of the front lawn. The daisies gave the air a sweet scent, and Lucy already imagined having Thanksgiving dinner at her house. They could host a small get-together in the front yard just like her parents did and invite friends over.

A white truck pulled into the station and parked by the empty pump. Lucy saw Bruce Wilson get out from the driver's seat, and he waved when he spotted her.

"Hey," he said when he got to where she sat. "It's good I found you here. I planned to visit your bakery this evening to apologize about my brother's behavior the last time… I heard about what happened."

Lucy groaned. She couldn't believe her brief altercation with Wayne had gotten on to the Ivy Creek rumor mill.

"No apologies necessary," she replied. "I understand what your family is going through, and I hope the cops get to the truth soon."

"Yeah, me too."

"How are you coping with your grief?" she asked. Bruce quirked a brow up, and she quickly added. "I mean… you seem alright, and more business focused than your brother. I just thought that it should be hard on you too."

"It is," he replied, and his countenance changed. "I've known my parents all my life and being without them is difficult. I distract myself with work. It's why it might come off like I'm not grieving. I know it gets easier with time, but I still dread going back home to an empty house, and knowing they aren't coming back. I wonder what it will be like this Christmas without them," he added ruefully.

"You will get through it," she said, hoping her words offered a bit of comfort. "When my parents passed, everything reminded me of them, and it hurt, but it got easier."

Bruce blinked his puffy eyes and looked around, then back at her. "Did you get a call from my assistant?" he asked, changing the subject.

"No, not yet."

"I will make sure she gets back to you this week. I've made a list of the pastries I would like to have. You can list a few and run it by me before you begin production."

"That's perfect… looking forward to it," Lucy replied. He waved at her, then retreated to fill up his tank. Lucy watched him drive away when he finished, and she sighed.

What's keeping you, Aunt Tricia, she wondered.

Another car drove in, and Lucy admired the neat jet-black sedan. The door opened, and Richard Lester stepped down. He spotted her immediately, and the corner of his lips moved.

"I haven't seen you around," Richard said when he strolled over to her. "I hoped you would drop by because you could not stay away from my chamomile tea," he teased, and Lucy laughed.

His light laugh came easily, and Lucy noticed the dimple on his left cheek.

"How have you been?" he asked.

"I've been good, just getting around my usual activities. How are you holding up since your uncle, Mr. Wilson, just passed?"

His eyebrows flew towards his hairline and he raised a hand to stroke his clean-shaven chin. "How did you know he was my uncle?"

Lucy lifted a shoulder. "It's a small town, people talk. Besides, there's a striking resemblance between both of you."

Richard chortled. "I get that a lot," he replied and dropped his hand. "When my father died many years ago, my uncle took me in and treated me like a son. I loved being around him and my aunt so much, and he planned to let me run one of his grocery stores in town."

Lucy's ears perked up. She tapped her fingers on the steering wheel and asked. "So why didn't you?"

"Well, it seemed like there were some issues between his sons. They believed my uncle was being partial, and I didn't want to create any issues in the family, so I opted to start my own business. He gave me a loan, and I put the plans for Lou's Café in motion. But things didn't turn out well. He kept changing the terms of the loan to suit him, and I got fed up."

"What do you mean terms of the loan?"

"He increased the interest on the loan and made changes to the partnership contract I signed without notifying me. I wanted it to be over, so I promised to pay him back all I owed, and close the café, but unfortunately, he passed away before I could.

His face sagged, and his voice turned hoarse as he continued. "It's been a mess since he died, I must confess. I'm getting pulled in every corner by extended family members, and the cops trying to investigate. I had to close my shop on Friday because the sheriff summoned me to the station for interrogation."

Lucy held back the urge to batter him with more questions. She pressed her lips together, and Richard gulped in air, releasing it intermittently before looking at her again. "I think maybe it's time to close up and move on to something else," he whispered.

"You shouldn't give up," she replied, and reached out to touch his arm. Lucy spotted her aunt walking over to them, and she withdrew.

"I'll see you around, Lucy," Richard said, and walked away.

Tricia reached for Lucy and handed over the shopping bags she held.

"Why did you take so long?" Lucy asked as she entered her side of the car.

Tricia grinned while Lucy started the engine. "The salesman was fun to chat with," she replied, and turned to Lucy. "Who was the young man I saw you flirting with?" she asked in an amused tone.

"I wasn't flirting," Lucy said. Her cheeks gained color as Tricia chuckled and teased her with her look. "He's Richard Lester, Mr. Wilson's nephew, and I was trying to get any information I could about his relationship with the Wilsons."

"Did you find anything?" Tricia asked and took the turn leading to the bakery. "He is a fine young man. What reason would he have to kill his uncle?"

She replayed her conversation with Richard in her head, and Taylor's warning flashed through her mind. *I think someone is trying to pin this murder on you.*

"I don't know," she replied, and stared outside the window. Richard had seemed distraught as he talked about his uncle's death, and she didn't know if she could trust his reaction.

Is he the broken man she talked to? Or is he just desperate enough to do something extreme to get his way?

She didn't know what to believe about either Richard or Bruce or Wayne.

"He has a reason to want his uncle dead," Lucy whispered, and Tricia looked in her direction. "He took a loan, and he told me Mr. Wilson kept changing the terms without his consent.

"There was tension between them before he died, and on the night of the party Richard Lester was there," she continued. "I don't remember seeing him but Mr. Anderson confirmed his presence that night. Bruce is overly ambitious, that's probable cause. Wayne feels over-looked, and Richard thinks they extort-ed him. It could be any of them."

Tricia said nothing, and the unanswered question of the killer's identity hung in the air.

She spent the rest of the night replaying her conversations with

Bruce, Wayne, and Richard.

There was no evidence to back her suspicions about any of the men. She thought for a moment and took her phone to go through the list Becky sent her again.

Halfway through it, a thought occurred to Lucy for the first time. *What if it was some other business partner?*

15

T he next morning, Lucy's phone beeped twice on the table in her bakery. She snatched it, took the call and lifted it to her ear, hoping to hear good news.

She and Hannah had emailed most of the business owners on Becky's list the previous day and anyone interested could reach her through her contact address, but so far, they had gotten no response yet.

"Hello," Lucy spoke into the receiver, and held her breath, waiting for the person on the other end to speak up.

The voice on the other end mumbled something in Spanish, and Lucy frowned. "Hello?"

She sighed and dropped the call when the caller continued to speak Spanish. "Probably a wrong number," she whispered when she met Hannah's expectant gaze.

"Try calling Becky," Hannah suggested. "She could speak to the business owners directly, and I think they will respond better to her."

"That's a brilliant idea."

Lucy dialed Becky's number, toying with the hem of her blouse as she waited for the call to connect. It rang through to voicemail thrice, and she dropped the phone. "It keeps ringing to voicemail," she said.

"Maybe drop by her office? She might be too busy to take your calls."

Lucy picked up her notepad and stared at the list of contacts she had scribbled down. Becky could help her connect to these people effortlessly. "I will drop by her office."

Minutes later, she was driving past Lou's Café and heading towards Becky Anderson's office downtown. Three cops stood outside the building, and Lucy wondered what they talked about as she walked in.

Becky welcomed Lucy with a huge grin when she walked into the office. "How are you doing?"

"I'm great," Lucy replied, and took a seat. "I called earlier, but it rang straight to voice mail, so I dropped by."

Becky glanced at her phone on the table. She picked it up and flashed her an apologetic smile. "I'm so sorry. I'm swamped with organizing deals and I didn't hear it ring."

"It's fine," Lucy said with a smile. "I sent out business proposals to the people on the list you gave me, and I was hoping you could introduce me to them in person or put in a good word, so they read my proposal."

She opened her purse and handed over the list she had emailed. "Here is a list of those I contacted."

"Alright," Becky replied, accepting the notepad. She glanced at it and dropped it on the table. "I will place a call to each of them during the weekend when I have some time, and I will make sure they consider your proposal.

"Thanks Becky, I really appreciate this." Lucy looked around the office, and noticed the pile of books on the couch by the corner. A black suit jacket draped over the couch, and a pair of black shoes lay neatly by the corner of the rug.

"You had a guest?" Lucy asked, pointing at the couch.

"They're Roland's," she replied. "He works here often and sometimes receives guests."

"Oh..." Lucy rose to her feet.

"Let's meet on Monday so I can update you on my progress," Becky suggested and picked up her glasses from the table.

*

Lucy arrived at Sweet Delights before she realized she left her notepad in Becky's office.

She had some recipes she was perfecting written in the notebook, and she needed it for the weekend.

Lucy flagged down a cab and instructed the driver to take her back to Becky's office. When the cab arrived, she jumped out and darted towards the building.

She was almost out of breath as she rushed in through the door. "I left my notepad."

181

"Right." Becky gathered her items from the table as she spoke. "I got a call from one of the business owners on your list minutes after you left, and he's agreed to meet and hear me out. I need to meet with him right now. Your notepad is somewhere on my table… I'll be back in a few minutes."

"Oh, that's fine. I'll wait," Lucy replied as Becky slipped into her green stilettos and patted her cheeks.

"How do I look?"

Lucy raised her right thumb. "Perfect."

Becky sashayed out of the office with a smile, shutting the door with a loud thud, and Lucy sighed. She looked around the place, and the huge mahogany bookshelf on the left wall caught her attention.

The bookshelf had three sections. They displayed awards in the lowest section, and the other two contained books. She picked up an award for a promising firm in the state, admired it before replacing it gently on the shelf.

She looked in the books section and landed on a misaligned book jutting out. She reached for it, opened the first page, and read the notes.

Lou's Café figures.

Lucy scanned the pages of the book, her fingers tracing out the debit and credit balance on each page. Richard mentioned the skyrocketing interest on the loan he took from Mr. Wilson, and she wondered if Roland kept records of everything concerning the businesses he handled like this.

She noticed every month had the same closing balance, and that didn't seem right. The same closing balance could only mean there was no profit at the end of the month. If Lou's Café didn't make any profits, then how did Richard survive after paying off his loan?

182

Lucy froze, and she nearly screamed out in shock when the door burst open and a voice boomed.

"What do you think you're doing?"

16

L ucy's hands turned cold and clammy. As Roland stepped forward, Lucy saw something flash in his icy blue eyes.

Was it anger? Or fear? She couldn't tell the difference because he masked it with a grin that resembled a sneer.

"You shouldn't go through people's stuff. What do you have behind you?" he asked.

Lucy shifted until she collided with the shelf. Pain radiated through her back at the point of contact, and she bit her lower lip to keep from yelping. There was something different about the way Roland looked at her. The grin on his face disappeared and was replaced with a thick glare that made her shiver.

"I was reading a book," she replied in a tiny voice, her heartbeat racing. Lucy swallowed. "I wasn't snooping around. Becky asked me to wait, and I didn't know you were here. I should leave," she added hurriedly. Roland took three long strides and grabbed the hand at her back.

"You're a terrible liar," he snarled and snatched the book from her. "I could see this book behind you the entire time," he added, his grip still tight on her arm.

"You're hurting me," Lucy whimpered. She rubbed her arm when he released her and glared at him. "Fine, you caught me... I found the book on the shelf, and I was going through the numbers. Turns out they don't add up... the interest Richard pays don't reflect in the books," she accused. "What did you do?"

Roland burst into a cackle. He flung his head back as his laugh rocked his entire body. "You still don't get it, do you?" he asked when he stopped.

"You drove a wedge between Mr. Wilson and his nephew," she repeated, wondering what else he did.

Roland sneered. "Oh, come on Lucy... I didn't do anything that hasn't been done before. We live in a world where the rich get richer, and the poor get poorer. It's a known principle, and as a businesswoman, you should know that."

She watched him, her insides recoiling in fear as he paced the room. He rolled up his sleeves, unknotted his tie, and turned back to her.

"A sales offer for Lou's Café came in a while back. The investors wanted to pay a huge sum to get the building, and still allow Mr. Wilson to have shares in whatever business they used the place for. It was good business, the best deal anyone could get, but he turned down the offer because his nephew had built a business there."

He paused and pointed a finger at her. "A business he couldn't keep afloat."

"You increased the rates of the interest and the terms of payment. How did you expect him to keep up?" Lucy asked. "He thought his uncle did that. He had a hard time because of it, and you think you did nothing wrong?"

Lucy saw him assess her. She shook her head. *How could he lack such human decency? Lying to his client and falsifying ledgers was a crime.*

"I told Wilson about the deal long before Richard came to town, but he didn't listen. I gave him a lot of reasons to make that deal and he promised to think about it, but the minute his nephew came to town, he jumped at that offer. Don't you see what he did wrong?"

"No, I don't," Lucy replied defiantly.

His nostrils flared, and he scoffed. "You're just like them, aren't you? You think you're better than everyone else with your self-righteous attitude." Roland lunged for her, and she couldn't escape because he backed her into a corner.

He gripped her shoulders and shook her hard. "I worked hard for Wilson and when I needed him to do just one thing for me, he refused. All he had to do was take the offer, and they would compensate us handsomely, but he was stubborn."

"So, you killed him?" Lucy yelled.

Roland struck her cheek hard. It stung, and tears welled in her eyes as she staggered away from him. He followed quickly, yanking her by her hair when she tried to get away from him.

"You're right, I did," he growled. His large hands circled her neck, clamping down on her throat so she couldn't speak. Lucy whimpered. She struggled against him, her hands pinching his skin.

I want to live; she thought as she struggled to breathe. His crazed gaze remained steady on hers, his lips curved, exposing his teeth. *Please,* she tried to speak as she slowly slipped out of consciousness.

"I'm sorry, Lucy," she heard him say as she blacked out. "But some things have to stay as secrets."

17

A loud beep cut through her unconscious mind, jarring her out of the darkness, and Lucy opened her eyes wide.

She choked, her chest tightened as she struggled to breathe, and it was like Roland's hands were around her neck again. *Help me... someone please.*

Lucy tried to move her hands, but she couldn't. She floated in her surroundings, trying to find a balance amongst the beeps and noises in the background.

What happened? How did I get here?

Images of her struggle with Roland Anderson flashed in her mind, and her heart rate sped up. A nurse rushed into the room, and Lucy realized the continuous beeping monitor was connected to her arm.

The door opened again and Tricia and Hannah rushed in, each taking a side of the bed.

"Oh, God, Lucy. What happened?" Hannah said.

"Can you hear me? It's alright, you're in a hospital, and you'll be fine," Tricia cried, and Hannah latched on to her hand.

Lucy's chest tightened, her throat burned, and she tried to speak. Tears slid down her cheeks at the failed attempt, and Hannah reached out to wipe them.

"You'll be fine."

She nodded frantically and took in her surroundings. The nurse adjusted the IV fluids connected to her arm and walked out of the room. Lucy looked out of the window blinds and saw Becky.

Becky was sobbing with her face in her hands, her shoulders heaving up and down. She saw Becky briefly raised her head, mumble some words to the man by her side, and break down in tears again. Aunt Tricia reached for the blinds, pulling them closed.

Lucy's head suddenly spun as another wave of dizziness hit her. Her eyelids fluttered closed as the darkness called, and she slipped out again.

*

When she opened her eyes, Taylor was looking down at her.

"Hey," he whispered, and Lucy blinked.

189

"Hi," she croaked. She swallowed, hoping to ease some of the dryness in her throat, and she raised a hand to her neck.

"You sustained bruises and swollen airways. You speaking is a good sign."

She managed a faint laugh and dropped her hand to her side. "My aunt?" she asked when she noticed they were alone in the room. "Hannah?"

"They went to the station for questioning. You've been out for a day, and you're lucky to be alive."

"How did I get here? Who found me?" she asked in a wobbly voice.

"Becky returned to her office just in time," he replied. "Roland Anderson had no way out of it because she called the cops immediately."

Lucy remembered seeing Becky crying outside, and her heart sank a little. She had admired Roland, and she knew Becky had loved him.

"We're still investigating, and we'll know the entire truth soon. You just need to hang in there and get better."

"I will," Lucy whispered with a smile. "Thank you, Taylor."

A moment of silence passed between them, and he returned the smile, the side of his mouth quirking up a little. "It's nothing… I was just doing my job."

Taylor got up and walked to the door. He glanced back and added. "You were brave, Lucy, and I never doubted your innocence."

Lucy chuckled when he left and sighed. The burden of the Wilsons' death no longer pressed on her conscience, and she was certain everything could only get better from here.

She fell asleep again after a nurse came in to check on her, and

190

by evening she was feeling strong enough to sit up in her bed. Hannah dropped by with her aunt again, and they were laughing at a joke when Richard Lester walked into the room.

Tricia and Hannah excused themselves, grinning, and he took a seat by her bedside.

"I heard you almost died," he said. "You should be more careful, Lucy."

He reached over, patting her hand on the bed and Lucy's insides warmed.

"Are you alright?" she asked him, studying his face. He must have heard about Roland's deceit by now, she thought. *I wonder how he feels.*

Richard sucked in a deep breath. "I'm hanging in there," he replied. "I've been to the station twice today, and they told me everything. Roland added the numbers to the loan because he wanted to scare me off the property. It makes sense now… my uncle wouldn't have changed the terms without consulting me.

"When I confronted him, he denied it at first, but I didn't believe him. Turns out it was all part of Roland's manipulative scheme to run me out of town so he could sell off to some rich investor."

"I'm sorry you had to go through that," she whispered.

"Yeah… me too," he paused, and lifted a finger to touch her cheek. "I'm glad you didn't die, Lucy."

Lucy nodded.

He shifted in his chair. "I'll see you around."

"Yeah."

Her aunt returned to the room seconds after Richard left, and she had a teasing smile on. "He's into you, I can tell," she said.

Lucy shook her head. "He's not my type," she replied, laughing, and Tricia patted her shoulder playfully.

"Time will tell."

Lucy didn't agree with her aunt on that note. No matter how charming Richard Lester was, Hannah had told her of his past, and she was not looking to get hurt by any man. "I'll find the right man one day. Don't you worry," she replied and hugged her aunt.

For now, she was just relieved that the pandemonium of the last few weeks was over.

18

wo weeks later

"Cheers," Lucy said and clicked her glass to Hannah's, then Tricia's. "To many more orders and paychecks."

They laughed, and she sipped from her glass. "I'll bring the cake."

Lucy wandered into the kitchen and returned with the cream frosted cake. She cut into it, and served everyone a piece, then settled on her seat to eat her slice.

"We got three new orders from the proposal emails you sent out, and Bruce called to commend our work. He says he'll need a new batch of orders by next week," Lucy said.

Lucy was glad things were returning to normal. It had been discovered that Roland had poisoned the drinks of the Wilsons on the night of the charity gala. He knew they both loved sweet things and whoever served nibbles on the day would be a key suspect. He had slipped some poison pills into drinks he had offered them. His intention was to kill Mr. Wilson but since he wasn't sure if he would take the poisoned glass, he had spiked both drinks. Taylor had assured her that there was enough evidence to get him sent to jail for a very long time.

"I'm happy," Hannah beamed. "I knew business would bloom again, and now you can reopen the concession," she suggested.

"I will interview new candidates for the position," Lucy replied.

Halfway into their celebration, Becky walked into the bakery.

"Excuse me," Lucy said to Hannah and Tricia.

She led Becky out to the patio and sat with her. It snowed heavily earlier in the day and melting snow covered her front lawn. She noticed that the car Becky had driven to the bakery was an unfamiliar one.

"Lucy..." Becky said as her voice trailed off, and she reached into her purse for a handkerchief. She wiped her nose and shut her eyes for a second. "I came here to apologize for everything," she added in a croaky voice. "I planned to visit earlier, but I couldn't find the right time... the investigation is over, and I couldn't put it off much longer."

"I'm alright, Becky," Lucy replied, hating to see Becky so distraught. When they first met, she thought Becky was a snob, but now, she was more empathetic. "You shouldn't apologize."

Tears filled Becky's eyes, and she shuddered. Lucy reached for her hand on the table and squeezed it.

"It's water under the bridge," she added.

"I can't believe Roland did such a thing," she said, dabbing at her eyes. "We've been in debt for a while because of his gambling habit, and he told me he had it under control. He told me he had settled everything, and I shouldn't worry, and I didn't.... I should have known he was up to something," she continued.

"You didn't know, Becky. Don't beat yourself up... it was Roland's crime, not yours. He poisoned them... that's not on you."

"I'm lost and alone. I didn't know who I married. They are charging him with murder, and I might never see him again."

Lucy understood Becky's pain, and she wished she could help her. Becky always offered help when she needed it, and she wanted to do the same. She moved her chair closer to Becky's and wrapped her arms around her shoulders.

"You'll be fine, Becky. Trust me, you'll get through this."

Becky sobbed in her arms for a while. Minutes later, she pulled away and wiped her face. "I'm sorry," she apologized with a nervous laugh.

Lucy shook her head. "It's fine."

Becky rose to her feet and picked her bag from the table. "I should go."

"You could join us inside for a celebration," Lucy invited, hoping company would help lift her mood. "I want to help you feel better before you go, so please, come in," she offered.

She pleaded again when she noticed Becky's reluctance. "Please?"

"I don't want to intrude."

"You're not intruding," Lucy corrected and took her hand. "Come in and have a drink and some cake. I promise you'll feel better afterwards."

Becky entered the bakery with her. Hannah brought her a glass and a plate for the cake and she joined in the celebration.

As they talked and laughed, Lucy was glad she had made a new friend, despite all the pandemonium that had engulfed her world and taken her on a whirlwind ride of disappointment, rejection and redemption. Things were returning to normal and with the holiday season on the horizon, she was looking forward to the rest of the year. She had some great recipe ideas she couldn't wait to share with Ivy Creek.

The End

EAT ONCE, DIE TWICE

AN IVY CREEK COZY MYSTERY

ABOUT EAT ONCE, DIE TWICE

Released: December 2021
Series: Book 3 – Ivy Creek Cozy Mystery Series
Standalone: Yes
Cliff-hanger: No

It seems Lucy has finally gotten the hang of running a bakery and serving the good citizens of Ivy Creek. She knows she has a lot to learn but she's up for the challenge. She just never bargained for competition from a new couple in town.

When one half of this dubious couple is found dead, Lucy is torn between minding her own business or helping the grieving person find justice for their loss.

Matters aren't helped when it appears all circumstantial and testimonial evidence points to this person as the killer.

But Lucy knows what it's like to be falsely accused in the court of public opinion.

Will she unearth the secrets that surround a building in town that seems linked to the murder?

Will she find out why the accused has so much to hide even though they've professed their innocence?

Will she help to find a killer that doesn't want to be found and restore normalcy to her life and small town?

1

Lucy loved new things. And as she looked through her window at the golden, orange, green and brown leaves that were gently swaying on the tree outside, it was clear a new season had rolled by. This new season deserved a new look, and she was feeling brave to try something different. Staring at herself in the mirror, she wondered if she had made the right decision.

Her shoulder length normally brunette hair had grown a few inches over the past months, and she kept the length as part of her current style.

She angled her head and got a clearer view of her face in the mirror. The new platinum color suited her pale skin, but she wasn't sure it made her brown eyes pop.

"How do I look, Gigi?" she asked her white Persian cat.

Gigi purred and rubbed her fur on Lucy's feet. Lucy chuckled and ran her fingers through her hair.

"Is it too light?"

She sighed and turned away from the mirror, walking out of her room to the bakery downstairs, leaving Gigi behind.

Her employee, Hannah, sat in the kitchen alone, holding a mug of hot chocolate in one hand, and a magazine in the other. She lifted her eyes from the magazine when Lucy entered the kitchen.

"Oh my God, Lucy, what did you do to your hair?" she asked with an amused laugh. "You weren't kidding when you mentioned changing your hair color. I didn't think you'd go through with it though."

Lucy shrugged. "I wanted a change. Experimenting with a new color seemed like a good idea," she replied, and poured herself a glass of lemonade.

"Do I look good? Or is it too light? I applied the color and dozed off."

Hannah was a natural blonde, and another pair of eyes would confirm if Lucy needed to find the nearest hair salon to undo her decision.

"It's lovely," Hannah replied, assessing her. "It really does suit you."

Lucy tucked strands of her hair behind her ear, and Hannah slid the magazine she held towards Lucy. "The annual Creek's

Christmas fair," she said out loud. "Registration starts soon. This is a chance for Sweet Delights to share our pastries with a new clientele. There will be lots of foreign tourists at the fair," Hannah explained.

Lucy had never attended the Annual Christmas Fair because it was an event introduced after she moved out of town three years ago, but it was a brilliant idea. She imagined it would be an excellent opportunity for various businesses to display their products and make massive sales.

"We should try registering once the fair begins," Hannah said.

Lucy closed the magazine. "Yes, it's a good idea," she agreed. "We have lots of customers, and this fair will help raise more revenue to open one more outlet next year."

A banging noise from across the street caught Lucy's attention, and she walked over to the window to peek outside. The ongoing reconstruction had spanned a few weeks, and Lucy wondered what business would occupy the space once it was completed.

Hannah came over to where she stood. "It used to be a restaurant, but the owners sold out weeks before you moved back into town. I think a new designer boutique will take its place," she said.

Lucy noticed the brick patterns on the new walls and the humongous sized windows. She imagined that only a designer boutique would require such enormous windows.

The door swung open and Lucy walked over to the counter where a customer stood.

"Hi, welcome to Sweet Delights. What would you like?" she said.

The lady adjusted her tote bag on her shoulder. She scanned the counter for a second and finally made a choice. "I'll have the banana nut bread."

"That will be four dollars, and seventy-five cents, please."

The customer paid in cash, and as she walked out, two more customers walked in. Hannah attended to one, and Lucy took an order from the other person for six cupcakes. She added an extra cupcake to the order since the woman was a regular and wrapped them up in a fancy bag.

"Here you go," Lucy said. "Eighteen dollars for everything."

"Your pastries are always so pricey," the woman complained as she reached for her wallet. "I spend a lot on your cupcakes every week because it's the only thing I can use to bribe my twins to do their chores."

Lucy grinned. "Sweet Delights serves only the best because we know only the best come to Sweet Delights," she said as she winked at the lady. The lady chuckled and left the bakery with a smile on her face.

Lucy exhaled and cleaned some fingerprints off the counter.

"It's the first day of the week and we're out of banana bread and chocolate chip cookies," Hannah said. "We still have orders to fulfill by the end of the week, and we're almost out of flour."

Lucy hopped with excitement and counted the rest of the cupcakes in the display glass. This meant they had to produce more for the rest of the week. "We could make them tomorrow," she replied, after noting twenty cupcakes left.

She scratched her ears as loud scrapes and creaks echoed from the construction site across the road. Lucy stepped outside the bakery to get a better view of the work in progress.

She sat down on a chair, enjoying the cool afternoon breeze. It ruffled against her hair and she caught a whiff of her jasmine-scented shampoo.

A young boy stood by the corner of her mailbox dispensing fliers to anyone walking past. He stopped two women heading to her bakery and handed over fliers to them.

"Hey," Lucy called out in a loud voice to get the boy's attention.

His eyes popped wide as he spun around, and he fled down the street before she could say anything else. Her brows creased as she watched him disappear down an alley.

Lucy welcomed both women, who entered the bakery with warm smiles.

"Hi, Lucy," the lady with a red beret greeted.

Lucy recognized her as a regular customer of Sweet Delights. She dropped by every afternoon and always ordered cheesecakes.

"How are you, Kasey? And the twins? Hope they're doing okay."

"They are," Kasey replied. "Have you heard about the new bakery coming to town? Sounds exciting, doesn't it?"

"New bakery?" Lucy repeated.

"Right across the street from you. They're advertising all around town," she replied, and pointed toward the construction site across the road.

Lucy's jaw dropped for a second as the ladies proceeded into the bakery. One of them tossed the flier away, and it landed at her feet. She picked it up and read the words out loud.

"Opening soon: Sweet Bites Free treats on opening day."

She slowly shook her head as she gazed at the flier in her hand. Her head whipped up as the sound of a roaring car engine drew closer.

A man stepped out of a black Bentley that pulled to a halt in front of the new bakery and her gaze traveled up the building to see a sign with bold letters going up.

'SWEET BITES,'

Lucy crumpled the flier in her hand and tossed it into the bin with one perfect throw. She looked back at the black-haired stranger who had gotten out of the car and was now staring at her. She noticed he had a smirk on his face that triggered a sickening feeling in the pit of her stomach.

It seems I have new competition; she thought as the dull ache spread through the rest of her body.

2

The man didn't move from where he stood as Lucy crossed over to the other side of the road where he stood by his parked car. As she drew closer, she got a better view of his features. The smirk on his face disappeared, and his lips formed a thin line, making her wonder what caused the change in his expression.

The color of his hair matched his dark suit, and she saw him slip his hands into his pockets. Lucy extended a hand when she got to him, and the car door slid open. A brunette woman sat inside, staring straight ahead with thick, dark shades covering her eyes.

"Lucy Hale," she said, shifting her attention back to the man. She met his brown eyes, and her stomach tightened and twisted as questions about this new business owner in town bounced around in her mind. Why is he starting a bakery here, right beside mine, out of all the places in Ivy Creek?

He accepted her gesture, squeezing her hand. "Solomon Mumford," he muttered in a smooth southern accent no one could miss.

Lucy allowed her gaze to travel to the building behind them as he released her hand. The workers seemed to round up for the day because the pounding noises had stopped, and the men who pulled up the sign minutes ago were making their way down.

She got a glimpse of the inside from where she stood and noticed the well-polished marble floors and light green wall papers spanning the entire inner wall. Her curiosity got the best of her, and she blurted out the first question that came to mind. "You opening a new bakery?"

A ghost of a smile crossed his lips, and he replied with a simple nod. "The first of many Sweet Bites shops opens here," he announced. Her eyes traveled to the building again, and she noticed the signboard light up. The outlook of the new place already looked expensive, and Lucy's palms became sweaty.

There's no way Sweet Delights can compare to this, she thought.

The woman in the car stepped out, and Lucy greeted her with a smile, extending a hand as Solomon turned to her. "Nessa, this is Lucy. She runs the bakery across the street," he began.

A pout formed on his wife's lips. "I have better things to do than speak with Susie, or any of the locals," she snapped.

"The name's Lucy," she said and her jaw dropped as his wife walked away without turning to acknowledge her.

"That's my wife Vanessa," Solomon said with a short, nervous laugh when she disappeared inside. "She's Sweet Bites' manager, so you'll be seeing more of her and less of me once the bakery opens up."

"Why choose to set up in a small town instead of a big city like Denver? Or Aspen, where you'd have a larger pool of customers?"

"You run a bakery yourself, Lucy," he replied and rocked back on his heels. "The return-on-investment matters, and there's less competition here. Setting up branches in relatively small towns like Ivy Creek will generate more profits than the city because of the lack of competition."

His eyes twinkled as he spoke, and Lucy fought the urge to scoff. He didn't think of her as competition? His brazen conclusion that he could come into town and garner customers so easily left her with a sour taste in her mouth.

"I've run Sweet Delights for quite some time myself, Solomon, and I don't think gathering customers is as easy as you make it out to be. Customers prefer quality, and if you can't offer that, then I don't think you'd grow a business successfully," she countered, raising her chin in defiance.

"I have started and run other businesses successfully. I can pass the quality test if it comes to that," he replied, and shot her an amused look. "Don't worry, Lucy, if you ever run out of business, I'd be more than happy to employ your skills here at Sweet Bites."

Lucy crossed her arms over her chest.

"That wouldn't be necessary," she replied, her eyes burning into his unrelenting stare. "I can keep my business running as I've done over the past months."

"The offer still stands regardless," Solomon replied.

Lucy turned and stormed away. Back in her bakery, Lucy burst in through the doors, and rushed to the counter where Hannah stood, attending to a few customers.

Lucy couldn't keep down the urge to rant as she entered the kitchen and filled a glass with icy water. She downed it in one gulp and dropped the cup on the table. "How could he insinuate

I am not good enough to keep my business running?" she asked, pacing around the kitchen with a hand on her right hip.

Lucy rubbed the back of her neck since she felt beads of sweat trickling down her back as she continued mumbling to herself. She stopped when Hannah walked into the kitchen a few seconds later.

"Did something happen? We still have customers eating in the bakery, and it's unsettling to see you storm through the bakery."

Lucy met her gaze. She ran her fingers through her hair and replied. "A new bakery's opening up in the new building right across the street, and the owner is a smug jerk."

"What?" Hannah asked, her eyes wide like saucers. "A new bakery?"

"Sweet Bites," Lucy said, chewing on her lower lip. "He offered me a job in case we run out of customers."

"That's rude."

"I know, right," Lucy said with a wave of her hand. She paced around the kitchen some more, and Hannah stood quietly by the doorway. "I don't know how to handle this."

"Having a new competitor who's promising everything I can't will harm Sweet Delights. We just got back on our feet after our involvement in two murder investigations that drove customers away from the bakery. How do we handle the demands of being compared to another promising business right across the street?"

"We can handle anything," Hannah reassured. "Try to relax."

They heard someone call out for attention from the front, and Hannah hurried out of the kitchen. Lucy dropped into a chair and stared at her empty glass, and Solomon's words rang in her head like an alarm bell.

If you ever run out of business, I'd be more than happy to employ your skills here at SWEET BITES.

Lucy was never one to doubt her skills. She prided herself on her vast baking knowledge and incorporated popular recipes her mother taught her while adding new ones frequently.

Sweet Delights was thriving, and she didn't need to bother about her new rival. She knew this, but still her stomach growled like a bear at the thought of the new bakery.

What do I do?

Half an hour later, Lucy was still antsy when the bakery emptied. She stood by the high-arc windows and watched Solomon and his wife in front of their building. Their conversation seemed heated. Vanessa flung her hand in the building's direction continuously, and it seemed to Lucy like they were arguing about the renovation.

Lucy saw Vanessa scowl as she marched away, got in the car and drove off, leaving Solomon standing there with his hands buried deep in his pockets. He suddenly lifted his head, and Lucy's breath hitched in her throat when his eyes landed on her. She saw the corners of his lips lift in an odd smile before he turned around and went into the building.

A shiver ran up her spine and she retreated from the window and exhaled deeply. This is all I've got, and I'll do anything to keep it running, regardless of what Solomon offers.

3

Later that week, Lucy saw a furniture van park in front of the new bakery as she opened for the day. She admired the mahogany wooden chairs the workers carried into the building. The huge art work and display counter they offloaded all looked exquisite. The sight brought back her fear of losing her customers and it piqued her curiosity, too.

She wanted to see what Sweet Bites looked like on the inside once they opened, and she also wanted to try out their pastries. That way, she could satisfy her curiosity about how their desserts and pastries compared to hers.

An hour later, Lucy made her way to the local grocery store to pick up some food stuff. She rolled her shopping basket past the canned food stand and stopped by the fresh vegetables counter to select some items to make a salad. She spotted Taylor Baker at the other end, examining a cabbage in one hand, and a smile crossed her lips.

Her past romance with Taylor before she left the city was no longer a topic for gossip in town. That brought relief because she had moved on completely from that chapter in her life, and she wanted others to forget it as well.

He hadn't noticed her yet, so that gave Lucy time to observe him for a bit. His blond hair had grown longer, and she wondered if he would get a haircut soon. The new hair-length gave him a more relaxed look, and she allowed herself to inspect him further. He wore a baseball shirt over black shorts.

When he turned, Lucy thought he would walk over to her, or say something. She braced herself, but his gaze trailed over her head.

He rolled his basket away, and it took a second for Lucy's heart to stop thumping. She hurried to catch up with him as he stopped by another counter, then she matched his pace.

"Hey," she greeted, and picked up a carton of milk. "I haven't seen you around in a while."

Taylor didn't spare her a glance as he replied. "I've been busy."

"Right. If I didn't know any better, I would have thought you were avoiding me," she continued with a light chuckle. He glanced at her, and their eyes met.

"When did I avoid you?" he asked.

"Back there at the vegetable stand," she replied, pointing where he stood earlier. "It was like you saw me but chose not to act like it. Looks to me like our shared history still makes you edgy."

He cleared his throat, and she remembered it was an old habit to do that whenever he was uncomfortable with a situation.

"I wasn't avoiding you, and I don't reminisce about us. Trust me," he replied.

He lifted a hand to rub the back of his neck, then added a carton of milk to his cart. Lucy stared at the full basket and raised a brow.

"You sure you need that much milk?" she asked, enjoying watching him squirm.

"Did you need something?" he asked.

"Is there a way to get the new bakery across from mine to move somewhere else? I mean, isn't there a law restricting that much proximity to similar businesses? The council should be able to do something on my behalf."

"There's no law stopping two bakeries from operating side-by-side, Lucy," he replied and continued. "If you feel threatened by new competition, maybe you should work harder to make sure your pastries are the best."

"My pastries are top-notch. Trust me," she replied. "I don't worry... there's no reason to."

"Good," he replied, and she saw a smile on the corner of his lips as he added. "You make wonderful treats."

Lucy grinned widely as he walked away from her, appreciating his compliment even though he didn't stay long enough for her to thank him.

Lucy shoved away her assumptions, but even though she still disliked the idea of having a new competing bakery so close to hers, it seemed like her heart was lighter as she went to the counter to pay for her items.

"You're in a good mood," Hannah commented when she returned to the bakery, humming to herself. Lucy sat in the kitchen after arranging the groceries.

"Have we had many customers today?" she asked.

Hannah replied with a nod. "We've sold out our cupcakes and

scones. We'll bake a new batch for the rest of the week."

Lucy bolted to her feet with renewed energy. "I'll get right to the preparations."

Hours later, a new batch of cupcakes was ready. Lucy could see that Hannah had completed her tasks for the day, so she told her she could leave before her official closing time. Once she left, Lucy stayed behind to clean up.

Later that evening, she sat alone on her front porch. She saw Vanessa address a group of people all dressed in multi-colored uniforms outside Sweet Bites. Lucy suspected they were the new Sweet Bites employees, and a dull ache formed in the pit of her stomach. She rolled her neck, trying to find relief from her building panic, and called her Aunt Tricia, who recently moved back into town.

Lucy was glad she could count on her aunt's support. After her mom passed, Aunt Tricia had become that mother-figure she could confide in and lean on for counsel. Aunt Tricia being close by was a source of comfort. Lucy visited her house on Sundays when the bakery wasn't open, but since Aunt Tricia got a day job at the town's nursing home, they only got to see each other during her free days.

"Aunt Tricia," she said when she picked up on the first beep. The raspy sound of her aunt's voice eased some of her developing tension.

"Lucy, honey, how are you?"

"I'm all right," she replied and relaxed in her chair. "Have you heard of the new bakery across the street from Sweet Delights?"

"There's a new bakery?" Aunt Tricia asked. "Wow, I should try out some of their treats then," she added with a light, mischievous chuckle.

"Not funny, aunty," Lucy muttered. "I'm sure they'll have a lot of customers already."

"You find that unsettling?" Tricia asked. "You're good at what you do, Lucy. Having a little competition is good sometimes, you just have to make sure you keep doing your best."

Lucy remembered Solomon Mumford's smug statement about giving her a job, and she couldn't see the good part of having Sweet Bites so close to her, especially when she remembered the small army of staff she saw earlier who'd be working there.

"I don't know if this is good competition, Aunty. I've met the owner and he's not a small-town kind of guy. It's odd he'd started a bakery here when he had a chain of them in the city."

"You're probably overthinking it, Hun," Tricia dismissed lightly. "New things attract people, but they eventually go back to what they are used to. I don't think you have anything to worry about."

The call went on for a few more minutes and Tricia promised to come over at the weekend before ending the call.

Lucy went to bed that night thinking over her aunt's words, and as much as she appreciated the comfort it offered, she couldn't tell if her customers would come back after trying Sweet Bites, or if they would simply prefer what the new bakery offered.

4

A week passed, and the day for the grand opening of Sweet Bites had finally arrived. As Lucy went over some paperwork, she hoped and prayed that she'd be able to manage her emotions and the flood of thoughts that would make her a nervous wreck. Hannah walked into the kitchen with a notepad in one hand and the other buried inside the pocket of her apron.

"We still have one delivery to the grocery store for the day," she announced.

"What's in the order?" Lucy asked and turned off the oven. She took off the gloves she wore and the cap covering her hair.

"Ten dozen cupcakes and two gluten-free loaves of bread."

"Have you tried calling the pickup van?"

"Yes," Hannah replied, and they walked out of the kitchen together. The dining area had emptied minutes ago, so Lucy used the chance to clean the floors for the second time that day.

As she swept towards the door, Hannah peered out of the window. "We should check out the new bakery tonight," she suggested.

Lucy shook her head. "What would we do there?"

"Try out their pastries? See what the interior looks like. Come on, Lucy, aren't you at least curious about what this new bakery is like on the inside?"

"I am curious," Lucy muttered. She exhaled, finished sweeping, and joined Hannah by the window. "I just don't want to compare Sweet Delights to what they have over there."

They stared at the bustling activity in front of the bakery for some time in silence, and Lucy pulled her thoughts together when a familiar car parked in front of her bakery.

"Someone's coming in," she said, straightening her blouse. "We have to be extra nice to all our customers from now on."

"We're always nice," Hannah said with a smile.

Lucy cleared her throat. "Right, then we should show extra, extra care."

The door swung open, and Kasey walked in. "Hey, Lucy," she greeted as Lucy walked around the counter to attend to her. "The usual, please."

She packed six cupcakes, and included an extra, wrapped them up in a customized bag, and handed them over to the lady. "Eighteen dollars, please."

The woman's smile dropped a little as she paid in cash. "I look forward to trying out the new bakery opposite yours. I hear they sell cupcakes for as low as one dollar, and if I'm lucky, my twins might like their pastries."

Lucy paled at her statement. She said nothing while staring at her blankly, and the woman burst into a short laugh.

"That was a joke," the woman added, laughing as she picked her customized bag from the counter. She winked at Lucy before making her way towards the door. "I think nothing will ever compare to your cupcakes. See you around, Lucy."

Lucy's color slowly returned, and she joined in the laugh to lighten the moment. When the woman left the bakery, she exhaled, and she gripped the counter until her knuckles turned white.

Her chest tightened further with each passing second. Hannah was by her side immediately, helping her remain on her feet. The surrounding walls suddenly constricted as her panic rose. She could barely catch a breath without the pain in her chest jabbing at her.

Hannah helped her to a chair, disappeared into the kitchen, and returned with a paper bag.

"Try to breathe into this," she suggested.

Lucy grabbed the paper bag, opened it, and blew air in. She mentally counted to three and repeated the act until she slowly regained control of her breathing.

Her eyes reddened when she looked at Hannah again, and Hannah placed a hand on her shoulder.

"Do you feel better?" she asked.

Lucy could barely speak, so she closed her eyes and bobbed her head twice.

"You really have nothing to worry about, Lucy," Hannah said, and pulled a seat closer to Lucy's. "Sweet Delights is successful, and we have our loyal customers. It's best you take your mind off wondering if you'll lose customers and focus on making them happy instead."

A moment of silence passed as Hannah's words sank in. "You're right," Lucy replied, and she wiped her palms on her jeans. "I know I can be neurotic sometimes, and I worry a lot, but I'm too good at what I do to fear being run out of business."

"That's the spirit," Hannah encouraged with a lopsided grin and extended a hand.

Lucy placed hers in Hannah's and rose from the chair. "Let's check out the bakery tonight," she said as the door opened and another customer walked in.

She wanted to see what Sweet Bites bakery looked like for herself. That was the only way to know if there was anything to worry about.

*

Sweet Bites had a cozy interior. Eccentric lighting illuminated the inside, and the warm yellow tone of the walls brought the place alive. Soft music played in the background as customers swarmed the area, each of them in line to order some treats.

"A cupcake and scone, please," Lucy said when it was her turn. The dark-haired attendant took her order quickly and moved on to Hannah in line behind her. They settled in a corner of the bakery to enjoy their order, and out of the corner of her eye, Lucy spotted Vanessa trudge out of an inner office.

She wore a gloomy expression and signaled for a worker. Lucy watched the interaction between Vanessa and the boy, and she could pick up some of her words from where she sat because she spoke in a raised tone.

"What do you think that's about?" Hannah asked in a hushed tone.

Lucy shrugged. "I don't know, but everyone's definitely watching this go down."

Curious gazes skimmed towards Vanessa, and the door behind her opened again. This time, Solomon stepped out and placed his hand on her arm to calm her down.

"Let me go," Vanessa yelled, and entered the office, swinging the door closed with a loud thud. The music playing in the background stopped, and Solomon, still facing the door, made a strangulating sign with his hands before walking away.

Lucy turned back to Hannah and took the first bite of her scone. She savored the blend of coconut and butterscotch flavor in the scone and took another bite.

"How is it?" Hannah asked, her wide eyes giving away her curiosity.

"Not bad," Lucy replied, even though she tasted something off. *Was that cinnamon?*

"The cookies are too stiff and flat," Hannah commented as she shoved the last piece in her mouth. "A bit too sugary, but there's the right crowd who might like it. Anyone with a sweet tooth will."

Around them, some other customers shook their heads in dismay at what they were eating.

Lucy was about to say something when a scream cut her short. A male staff rushed out of the office Vanessa had entered minutes earlier. He had a wild, horrified look, which made Lucy and some other customers in the bakery jump to their feet.

The man screamed again, and this time, he pointed to the office. "She's…. I think she's dead."

Lucy slapped a hand over her mouth to muffle her gasp and hushed murmurs around the bakery followed the announcement. In a split second, the once peaceful bakery became chaotic.

5

Lucy spread more flour over her work tray and continued kneading the bread dough as Hannah prepared the coffee for the day.

"Last night was crazy, I mean," Hannah was saying as she turned on the coffeemaker. "I wonder what caused her death. I mean the uproar and the scene last night was horrific, and everyone wanted to stay till the cops came."

Lucy hadn't stayed. She was one of the few customers to leave the bakery before anything else happened. Besides, she had satisfied her curiosity, and she didn't want to get caught up in another murder investigation in Ivy Creek.

I think I've had enough of that to last me a lifetime.

She, however, still imagined scenarios of what caused Vanessa's death. *Was she terminally ill? Or did she eat something bad? Perhaps poison? It could also be the stress of working so hard to open a bakery in a new location.*

"You're awfully quiet," Hannah said, dragging her out of her thoughts.

Lucy shook her head. "I was just thinking of what could have happened. When I saw her the first time, she didn't look sick."

"You've met Mrs. Mumford?"

Lucy vividly remembered the brief introduction and Vanessa's snobbish attitude. "Yes, and she called me Susie." She didn't think Vanessa had a likeable personality, and a woman like that could easily make enemies.

"Well, I hope the cops sort this out. Sweet Bites just opened up, but it seems like no one will go back there for treats soon."

Hannah had barely finished her sentence when the front door swung open. "I'll take it," she said and left for the dining area.

Lucy wiped her hands clean after setting the bread dough on a baking sheet. She waited a few more seconds for the oven's timer to go off before putting the dough in to bake and setting the timer again.

Briefly, she looked around the place to make sure everything was in place before joining Hannah in the dining area. Lucy smiled when she saw her regular customer. Kasey walked in with her twins.

"Hi there," Lucy greeted the kids with a wave. "What would you like?"

Both boys looked a lot like Kasey. They had the same blonde hair, and a dimple on their left cheek. The resemblance amazed Lucy as she watched them look over her display counter before whispering to themselves.

"They'll have cupcakes," Kasey decided for them.

Lucy packed the usual number of cupcakes and handed it over to Kasey. "I saw you at Sweet Bites last night," she said, accepting the cash payment.

"I wasn't at Sweet Bites last night," Kasey denied. Her cheeks flushed beet red as she took her change.

"That's strange. It was definitely you with a pink dress, and cute black shawl wrapped around your neck. You were with some woman wearing a similar dress... I think a black one," Lucy said, re-counting the details she remembered from the previous night. "I am certain it was you."

Kasey pretended to cough, and Lucy chuckled at her discomfort. "Or am I wrong?"

Another woman came into the bakery then, and the second she spotted Kasey, she headed over to the counter. "Oh my God, Kasey, it's so good I ran into you here," she began, flashing Lucy a brief smile before adding. "Look what you left at Sweet Bites last night."

The lady took out Kasey's shawl and handed it over. Lucy met Kasey's wavering gaze, and she didn't miss the color on her cheeks before she grabbed the shawl and hurried out of the bakery with her kids.

"What treats would you like?" Lucy asked the second customer.

"Kale chips please."

"Coming right up."

Hannah was no longer in the dining area, so Lucy packaged the kale chips with extra cupcakes. "Here you go."

"Thanks ... you know I still think your baking is the best in Ivy Creek," she commented and handed over her debit card.

"That's really nice of you to say," Lucy replied while processing the lady's payment. The compliment made her happy, and it seemed like she was going to have a wonderful day ahead.

"You're welcome, and it's the truth. I was at Sweet Bites, and nothing they made was enticing enough. I tasted cinnamon in their cake, and it completely ruined the experience for me."

The lady leaned closer over the counter and continued in a hushed tone. "I also think his wife didn't just slump and die. I think she was poisoned, and rumor around town suggests it might be her husband. The two didn't seem to get along well before the incident."

Lucy's eyes widened at the bit of information she had just heard and she tried to hide her disbelief. "I know the cops will figure out what really happened," she replied. "They'll get to the bottom of it."

The lady shrugged. "I hope so, too. I mean, look what happened the last time there was a murder in town. The Wilson's investigation took over a month and look how it affected you...."

Lucy's eyes tightened around the corners. *Was this lady being chatty or insensitive?*

"Anyway… you're right, the cops will handle it."

"They will," Lucy answered. When the lady walked out of the bakery, Lucy crossed over to the window and peeped out through the blinds. Solomon stood in front of his bakery, his hands propped on his waist and his head lowered.

Police tape surrounded the shop, and it was obvious he wasn't open for business. *How could he open? He just lost his wife.*

I think she was poisoned, and rumor says it might be her husband. The two didn't seem to get along well before the incident. Her customer's words played in her head again, and she shivered.

It's best I don't get involved in this, she thought, and gave Solomon one last sad look. To her, he seemed broken in more ways than one.

6

As Lucy stared out of the window, she saw someone cross the road and head for the door. Without thinking, she sprinted over to the counter to wait. Seconds later, the door opened and Richard Lester walked in.

The first time she met Richard two months ago, he helped her relax in his cafeteria for a few minutes, and she had run into him in town a few times after that.

He got to the counter and placed both hands on it. "Hi, Lucy," he said with a grin. "How is it going?"

"Going great," she replied. "How have you been?"

"I'm all right," he replied. His gaze flickered over her face for a moment before he continued. "I heard about what happened last night at the new bakery and thought I should come over to check on you... Just to make sure you're fine."

Lucy examined him, and the upward slant of his lips as he stared at her. "That's very nice of you," she replied.

A minute of silence passed between them, and Richard made a slight hand gesture when he spoke again. "I love what you did with your hair. The color really suits you."

"Thanks." His compliment made her insides warm a little, and a blush crept over her cheeks.

Hannah walked into the dining area then, interrupting their conversation, and Lucy asked if he needed any of her pastries, just to make sure Hannah didn't notice the sheepish smiles exchanged between Richard and herself.

"Would you like some cupcakes? Or bread?"

"Actually, I came for some macaroons," he replied, and dipped his hand into his pocket to produce some cash. "How much for three?"

"Oh, don't worry, it's on the house."

Lucy brought him three macaroons with an extra sandwich and passed it over the counter. "Thanks for stopping by to check on me, Richard."

"It's nothing," he answered, then winked at her. "See you around, Lucy."

Lucy stared at the door for five seconds after Richard left, and Hannah's gentle nudge on her side pulled her back to reality.

"Oh, my God! You're fawning over him."

"I'm not... fawning," Lucy replied, and rubbed her hands over her apron to get rid of the sweat on her palms. She only got sweaty palms when she was nervous, and Richard's smile caused a spike in her heart rate.

"You are," Hannah countered, and rolled her eyes. "You were

practically drooling over him. I noticed you didn't notice that I had come in."

"Come on, don't give me that face," Lucy said. She took in the disapproving arch of Hannah's brows and the crease on her forehead. "Richard's nice... he came by to check on me because he heard about the incident in Sweet Bites last night, and that was it."

Hannah sighed. "I care about you, Lucy, and I'm telling you, he's trouble. He dumped my sister and made her look stupid... he's nothing but trouble."

"I know... Richard Lester is trouble, and that is the last thing I want right now, okay?"

Hannah gave her a soft nod, and Lucy exhaled. "I'll go check on the bread... the timer will go off any minute."

She went into the kitchen to check on the bread, and after making sure it was properly baked, she switched off the oven and set out the bread loaf to cool. Whistling to herself, Lucy measured out more flour to prepare more cupcakes.

"I should try out a strawberry flavored one this time," she muttered to herself as she put all the dry ingredients into a bowl, set them aside, then moved on to measure some butter for creaming. Lucy enjoyed different flavors of cupcakes because they were her favorite pastry, and also the first item she had learned to bake.

Her mother's recipe always made the cake come out moist and sweet without too many crumbs. It was always perfect.

As the mixer worked on the cake, Lucy put the baking sheet of cookies Hannah had mixed into her small electric oven and set the timer to fifteen minutes.

Thinking about her mother's recipe reminded her of fun times with her family, and she felt a familiar dull ache in her chest. It wasn't even a year since they passed away in a car crash, and she had come so far.

She had pulled off her parents' dream of holding the bakery together. To congratulate herself, she planned a renovation of the dining area. That way, Sweet Delights could have a new look.

Lucy was busy with her thoughts when Hannah came into the kitchen again. She turned around when she heard Hannah call her name, but the noise of the mixer prevented her from hearing the rest of Hannah's words.

Lucy turned off the cake mixer so she could hear her.

Hannah repeated. "Someone's here to see you."

"Who? Richard?" she asked, taking off her apron and cap. "Did he come back?"

"No, not Richard. It's Taylor that's here to see you," Hannah corrected, and left the kitchen again.

Lucy's fists bunched up the apron in her hand. *Why is Taylor here?*

Knots formed in the pit of her stomach as she approached the dining area, fully aware that whenever he came by her bakery after an incident like last night's, it was always to deliver bad news about the ongoing investigation.

What could he possibly want? Lucy dreaded whatever he was about to say, but she knew she had to hear it, anyway.

She stilled her shaky insides and stepped into the dining area. Holding her chin high, she kept a straight face so her composure would give nothing away.

7

Taylor wore a grim look on his face, and he followed Lucy to a corner of the bakery. They sat near the window, and from where she sat, she could get a perfect view of Sweet Bites. A police car was parked in front of her bakery, and she suspected Taylor had come with some colleagues to conduct interviews.

But why do I need to be interviewed, too? I really don't want to be dragged into this.

Taylor spoke first, cutting the silence. "I'm speaking to everyone who was at Sweet Bites last night, so you have nothing to worry about." His voice was steady, and he crossed his fingers in front of him on the table.

"I'm not worried. What gives you the impression that I am?"

He lifted one shoulder casually and looked around her bakery.

"You've had it tough with two murder investigations already. Everyone in town knows that."

Lucy swallowed and relaxed a bit in her chair. "So, what did you want to ask?"

"Did you see anything unusual at Sweet Bites last night before the incident? Or before last night? You live right across the street from their bakery, so have you noticed anything off?"

Lucy thought of her reply for a second. "No, actually… besides the fact that Vanessa had a snobbish attitude when I first met her, I didn't think anything was unusual or out of the ordinary."

"Rude?" Taylor questioned. He uncrossed his fingers and rubbed his chin with his right hand. The thoughtful look on his face egged Lucy on to continue.

"Yes. She completely ignored me when we first met days ago in front of their bakery, and it seemed like they were at each other's throats. Last night, it also seemed like she made Solomon angry, judging from his expression before they found her dead. She seemed condescending towards Solomon."

Lucy looked out of the window again, and when she turned back to Taylor, she caught him staring at her. "What is going on with the investigation? Do you need anything else? I'd like to help in any way I can."

Lucy wanted to know what the cause of death was. *Could it really be poison?*

"No, there's no way you could help, so that will be all," he replied and rose to his feet.

The finality of his tone told her he wouldn't say anything else on the subject, and Lucy dropped it. Taylor had always been that way about his job.

"I'd like some bread, though. My mother can't get enough of

232

your banana nut bread, and the grocery store close to us ran out."

Lucy let out a short laugh, and she swatted the strands of hair on her forehead away, tucking them behind her ear. "Is it just bread? Would you like some cupcakes too?" she asked, remembering Taylor liked her cupcakes as well.

His replying nod was all the answer she needed.

"I'll get it for you."

Lucy left him chatting with some other customers who walked into the store, and she went into the store to get a loaf from the freshly baked bread. Taylor paid for the bread and left the bakery after waving at Hannah briefly.

He didn't spare her another glance, and seconds later, she saw the police car drive away. Lucy joined Hannah to serve the rest of the customers, taking their orders efficiently, making sure no one had any complaints.

The bakery emptied again in a few minutes, and Lucy was wiping the counter clean when Hannah came to stand beside her. "You know, I think Taylor still likes you. It's obvious to me," she said.

Lucy chuckled. It was impossible for Taylor to still have feelings for her. He made it clear when she first moved back to town. "He doesn't... that ship sailed and sunk a long time ago. We're both over it, and we're in a good place."

"Sounds to me like you're trying to convince yourself of that. From what I see when he looks at you? He's into you, trust me... I know that look."

Lucy tossed the napkin on the counter at Hannah and giggled. "How can you even tell how he looks at me?"

Hannah dodged the napkin while laughing and she adjusted the cap on her head after. "I just know. It's hard to miss, and if you ask Tricia, I'm sure she will tell you the same thing."

"Well, I don't see it." Lucy maintained her stance because listening to talk like this could put ideas in her head. She didn't need any of those thoughts... not now, when she was focused on making sure her bakery stood out in Ivy Creek.

Her bakery was successful, and a bit of her worry that she would lose customers because of the new competition had faded. She tried out Sweet Bites offerings to compare to her treats, and Lucy was sure hers tasted way better. It made her relax because she realized she didn't need to worry so much.

The thick, rich scent of vanilla reached her nostrils, and she remembered she had put a batch of cookies in her electric oven minutes before Taylor dropped by. She dashed for the kitchen to check on the cookies, and relief washed over her when she found they were fine.

She turned on the mixer again and went about the kitchen, gathering the ingredients she needed for a whipped cream frosting on the strawberry cupcakes. Lucy buried her attention in her work and wasn't aware Hannah came into the kitchen to call for her again until the mixer went off.

"Someone out front is here to see you," Hannah said, and took the hand mixer Lucy used on the whipped cream.

"Is it Taylor again? I answered all his questions."

"No, not Taylor, it's Solomon Mumford this time."

8

Solomon looked different from the man she met a week ago. His shoulders were slumped and gloominess radiated around him. Her initial conclusion that he was an arrogant man melted away, and all she could see in that moment was a broken man.

He looks so pitiable; it must be so tough on him going through these pat few days without his wife.

Solomon rocked back on his heels and took a hand out of his pocket. "Hello, Lucy," he said.

"How are you doing, Solomon?" she responded, leading him to a corner to sit. Lucy slipped into the chair opposite him and pinned her eyes on him.

"I'm all right... I think. Just dropping by to speak with you. I've stayed at my bakery all day, and there's nothing to do, and no one to talk to. You know, I just thought some company would be nice."

Lucy raised an eyebrow in surprise but masked it away when Solomon lowered his gaze from hers and exhaled deeply. "Is there something you want?" she asked.

"I would like some coffee with cream, and a sandwich to-go, please."

"I'll bring it over." Lucy went to the counter and returned with a plastic cup of creamed coffee and a sandwich.

He offered her some cash when she set the meal in front of him, and she refused it with a wave of her hand. "You don't need to pay," she said, and settled in the chair opposite him.

His stress and worry are written all over his face.

"How are things with you? I'm sorry about what happened last night ... It was really horrible." Lucy hoped her words would offer some comfort.

"I spent the entire night trying to convince myself it was a dream. After returning from the hospital, I couldn't stay in our house alone, so I booked a hotel." His jaw quivered as he spoke, and he lowered his head again. "What has happened seems surreal. Vanessa and I had such big plans for the bakery, and she believed in me through it all."

Lucy saw him blink back the tears, and she reached out to touch his hands on the table. His palms were large, and two gold bands sat on his ring finger. "I'm sure she was a good woman," she consoled.

Even though Vanessa was dismissive at their first meeting, Lucy knew she didn't know the woman that well. *To some people, she might have been a saint.*

"Do you know what happened?" she queried. There was no news

on what the cause of death was yet, and Lucy wanted to confirm if what the lady in her bakery had said earlier was true. *Was she really poisoned?* "Did the doctors, or cops, say anything?"

"No, not yet," he replied. He looked around her bakery and added. "I hope they do soon. Not knowing what happened to her is killing me."

Although she couldn't imagine Solomon being involved in his wife's death at this moment because he seemed shaken by the news, she had also learned to not rule out anything in instances like this.

He looked at her, sniffled, and wiped the corners of his eyes. "No... all I know is someone took my queen, and I will get whoever it is by any means possible." He gritted his teeth as he spoke, then pressed his lips together after. "I can't wait to re-open the bakery and honor her memory. I will work hard to make sure every dream she had for Sweet Bites comes true."

Lucy withdrew her hand and crossed her fingers on her lap. "If you need anything, I'd be more than happy to help."

Solomon offered her a brittle smile. "Actually, I want to apologize for how I spoke to you when we first met. I know I came off as a condescending jerk, and I'm really sorry about that. I came here to say I'm sorry, and I hope we can start off again, but on an amicable note this time."

"It's fine... water under the bridge," Lucy agreed, and rose from her chair as he did. "I hope to see you around soon and take care of yourself."

"Thanks for your time, Lucy. I hope we can work together when the bakery re-opens so you can give me some useful tips. We had some teething issues on our first night, and I'd like to correct them."

Her heart went out to him. "I'll be glad to help," she answered and waved as he turned to walk away.

He was barely out of the door when Hannah came over to her immediately to sit on the chair Solomon just occupied. "What did he want? The conversation seemed long and touching."

"He apologized to me," Lucy announced. "I never imagined a man so arrogant could become so humble. It's like he changed overnight. He seemed really devastated over his wife's death."

"Do you think maybe you misjudged him?" Hannah interrupted. "Sometimes people are humbled by tragic events in their lives. Losing his wife must have been such a hard blow."

"I hope he gets through this," Lucy said. Her head whipped up when the door opened again, and she saw Solomon re-enter the bakery. He backed towards the counter as Lucy jumped to her feet, wondering what was going on.

Two cops walked in after him, flashing a badge, and hushed murmurs filled the dining area as heads turned towards Solomon.

"Solomon Mumford, you're under arrest for the murder of your wife," one officer announced, and took out his cuffs.

9

The next day, Lucy drove down to the closest grocery store to pick out some personal items. She walked through the aisles of the grocery store, trying to find cat food. As she entered the third row, she saw a man straighten from his crouching position. He turned to roll his basket away, and Lucy immediately recognized him as the worker who found Vanessa's body that night in Sweet Bites.

She rolled her cart towards him. "Hi, I'm Lucy," she introduced with a smile. "I own the bakery across from Sweet Bites, and I remember you. You work there, right?"

"Daniel Evans," he said. "Yes, I work... worked there."

"What happened was a tragedy, and it must have been horrific to find the body that way... I hope you're all right?"

"I am," he replied. "I've known the Mumfords for a while, and it's so sad to lose Vanessa that way. She was problematic but overall, she had a good heart."

"You've known them for a long time?"

His head bobbed twice. "I worked with them at a designer store out of town and it came as a shock when Solomon informed me they would open a bakery. I joined them because I had some restaurant experience, and I needed the cash. But frankly, I didn't think they could make it work... Those two never agreed on anything."

Daniel's words piqued Lucy's interest. She angled her cart out of the way to allow other customers to pass. "Do you know if the cops released Solomon yet? They arrested him in my bakery yesterday."

"That doesn't surprise me," Daniel muttered, and looked at her again. "Vanessa undermined Solomon a lot. She never respected him, not even when the workers were around. I just didn't think that was enough reason to kill her."

Lucy recalled an image of Solomon trying to ward off tears as he spoke to her the day before, and she just couldn't imagine that same man murdering his wife. "Do you remember anything else?" she asked, not wanting to jump to any conclusions.

Daniel hesitated, his eyes darted around the store, and his lips pursed like he was about to say something. A second passed, and Lucy held her breath, waiting for him to speak.

He cleared his throat. "No, nothing else comes to mind," he answered. "I should head out now, bye."

Lucy followed behind him to the counter and waited till he hurried out of the store with his bags after paying. She then proceeded to ask the lady behind the counter where she could find cat food.

"The last row by your left," the lady directed.

"Thanks."

"I saw you talking to Daniel Evans over there," the lady said before she could walk away. "Did he share anything about why Solomon killed his wife?"

"No, he didn't. No one seems to know even the cause of her death. The cops are being tight-lipped about everything."

"It's probably for the best. I'm Keisha," she chipped in, and slumped her shoulders. "Although people are guessing it was poison. That building they rented has a cursed history. The town's founding fathers used to host their council meetings there, and the last two occupants lost their loved ones shortly after they moved in. They moved back out after that."

"Still, don't you think that's a little preposterous? I mean, it could simply be coincidence?'

Keisha wagged a finger at Lucy. "No, I don't think it is. It's barely a week since the Mumfords moved in there, and the wife was murdered. The rumor around town is that the husband killed her with poison. "We never can tell who is innocent," she added with a shrug.

Her words filled Lucy's mind with doubt about Solomon's innocence, but she shook them away.

"I guess I've said too much. About your cat food... check the last row. I'm sure you'll find what you want."

"Yeah... thanks."

Still pondering on the Keisha's words, Lucy strolled over to the last row with her cart and took the tiny curve leading down the aisle. She stopped in her tracks when the customer with his back to her turned around.

"Hey, Richard."

10

Lucy walked over to where Richard stood. "How are you?" she asked, then turned to scout the shelf for cat food.

"I've been great," he replied. "What about you? How are things holding up?"

Lucy saw him pick a pack of cat food, toss it into his basket, then prop a hand on his waist to listen to her.

"I drove down here to pick up a few baking supplies, and some cat food," Lucy answered and took two more cans so she wouldn't run out quickly. "I didn't know you had a cat."

"Yes. A Siamese cat. She's a real beauty, and she's in the back seat of my car right now. We're just headed back from the vet downtown."

"Is she sick?"

"I think she ate something bad," he replied, stroking his hair with his right hand.

Lucy rolled her cart forward, and he followed her past that row into the other, where she could pick some fresh food items.

They reached the section of canned foods, and she stretched a hand to reach for a can of green peas on the top shelf. Richard swooped to help her get it. Their hands brushed a bit, and she offered a light thank you as she took the can from him.

She regarded him closely when he rubbed a hand on his chin as if contemplating something before he picked some cans.

"You know, there's this jazz bar on Fifth Avenue—if you're free this evening, we could check it out together. I hear there'll be a live jazz band there this week, and I think it'll be fun if you come along."

"Are you talking about Roddy's Bar? On Fifth Avenue?" Lucy asked, tapping her fingers on her cart gently. Roddy's Bar was the town's only jazz bar she knew, and she didn't think any others had opened up recently.

"Yes, that's the one," Richard replied enthusiastically. "Ever been there?"

"Twice. My father listened to a lot of Jelly Roll Morton when I was young, so that's my type of music amongst others."

"That's cool, so you'll make it?"

Lucy lifted one shoulder in a light shrug as she replied. "I would have to get back to you on that one."

"That's okay."

She parted ways with Richard after they paid for their items, and when Lucy got back home, she called her aunt while Hannah arranged the new items on the shelf.

Lucy sat on the patio to enjoy a glass of cold lemonade as she talked to Aunt Tricia.

"Still coming around this weekend?" Aunt Tricia asked.

"Yes, I am. It's been a while since we hung out," Lucy replied with a short laugh. "With everything going on here, I think I deserve a break." She paused for a second. "Do you know they arrested Solomon for his wife's murder in my bakery yesterday? I can't understand it though, but something in my gut tells me he is innocent."

"I'm sure the cops had a justifiable reason to arrest him. I mean, they'd do a thorough investigation before identifying someone as a suspect. Or maybe there is incriminating evidence against him."

Lucy rubbed her eyebrow. What kind of incriminating evidence? After speaking with Solomon the other day, she had developed some pity for him.

"Let's just see how it all unfolds," Tricia was saying, but Lucy's mind had drifted.

Now, her thoughts centered on Richard and the decision to join him at the jazz bar. She remembered Hannah's warning about him when he had asked her out at the grocery store, and that was why she hesitated.

If the rumors about his love life are true, then I would rather not get hurt.

"Are you there?" Tricia asked.

Lucy pretended to cough as she replied. "Yes, of course I am. My mind just wandered to Richard Lester for a second."

"Richard Lester?"

"He asked me out on a date to the jazz bar dad used to spend time at."

"Oh, crazy… you should go, Lucy," Aunt Tricia replied in an excited tone. "This is good. You say you deserve some time to cool off… well, a hot date with Richard Lester is the perfect chance to do that."

"It's not a hot date," Lucy said as her cheeks turned a bright shade of red.

"Come on, why are you hesitating? It will be fun; you love jazz and it's just one evening out."

Lucy fell silent. She chewed on her bottom lip, then closed her eyes. "It's best I don't go," she said, hoping her aunt would drop the topic.

"All right… if that's what you want. I'll see you this weekend then."

"Take care."

She sighed and relaxed further in her chair after the call ended. It's just one evening of fun and jazz music, so why am I so hesitant to go?

11

S oft music played in the bakery's background, and Lucy hummed the lyrics to herself as she served her customers.

"Add an extra cupcake, please," the lady in front of her said, while eyeing the muffins Lucy displayed in the glass. "And two muffins."

Lucy dusted her palms together when she served the last girl on the queue. Customers swamped the dining area, ordering take-outs that morning. Maybe an expansion of the building would be great, she thought as she surveyed the crowd for a second, loving the feel of having so many customers.

"This is good," Hannah said behind her.

Lucy turned to find her peering into the display glass.

Hannah raised a hand and said, "We're making three times the number of sales we were making at the beginning of this month."

"I know, right?" Lucy replied, her grin wide.

A customer came back to the counter to order more sandwiches, and she quickly prepared the order. The lady thanked Lucy and dropped a tip before leaving the bakery.

Minutes later, the bakery had emptied, and she put out the closed sign while they cleaned because they had exhausted most of their items for the day and she wanted a breather. Hannah worked on cleaning the tables and picking up leftovers while Lucy swept the floor.

When they finished, they sat by the window to rest. "Do you think we would have this many customers if Sweet Bites was still open?"

"I didn't see them as competition," Hannah replied. "I mean, look at how much change you've brought to this place. You have a unique skill in creating recipes and you underestimate what you bring to the table." Hannah stuck out a hand and placed it over Lucy's. "Relax, you've got something great going on here."

Lucy appreciated the vote of confidence. "Thanks, Hannah," she replied solemnly. Their eyes met, and they exchanged a brief smile before she rose to her feet to check some muffins that were in the oven.

Most times, when they sold out early in the day, they rested a while before baking more items for the next day. That way, they reduced the work for the coming day and they could have more time on their hands.

Lucy was grateful she had hired Hannah. There's no way I could have handled all of this on my own, she thought. They had a concession store running near Ivy Creek's park, and they supplied a chain of grocery stores, bread with other pastries every weekend.

She still had external orders coming in, and Sweet Delights' successes kept growing. Lucy hoped none of that would end, and the fear of a setback was why she had feared having competition so close by.

"I think we should try out something new," Hannah suggested. "Let's add eclairs to the menu, and maybe brownies and some tarts."

"All brilliant ideas," Lucy replied. "I just have to draw up a plan for the items we might need to purchase to make these yummy bites you talk about."

They continued munching on their chips, and she remembered she still hadn't given Richard a response to his invitation, and she wondered if he was expecting her reply. The more she thought about it, the more she had doubts about the date. She just wasn't sure getting involved with him was a good idea.

Although Hannah had her reservations, Richard didn't strike her like the man who would take advantage of a woman. He seemed genuinely nice each time she saw him, and it was difficult imagining him as a bad guy.

Maybe I am just a poor judge of character?

"There's this jazz club down at Fifth Avenue," she began. "Its old and has been there a while, but I think it has new management now and they're hosting a jazz night."

"Roddy's bar," Hannah answered, lifting another chip to her mouth. "The place is the talk of town right now. Why? Do you want to go? We could go together if you're interested."

"Richard Lester invited me," Lucy said, gauging Hannah's expression to see how she would respond. The change in Hannah's mood was clear, and Lucy saw the smile on her lips wither before she pressed them together, releasing a resigned sigh.

"You're going?" Hannah asked. "You said yes to this date?"

"It's not a date, it's just one fun evening," Lucy said, raising her hand. "I'm telling you it's not," she added when Hannah shot her a look of disbelief.

Hannah lifted a brow. "Remember, I told you about who he really is, and how much he hurt my sister. Don't fall for his charm, Lucy, it won't end well."

Lucy opened her mouth to respond, but snapped it back shut when Hannah stood up and went into the kitchen. She took out her phone from the side pocket of her jeans and scrolled to Richard's number.

It's just one evening, and it will be nice to do something fun. What could go wrong?

Lucy didn't see a problem with going to the jazz club. She could enjoy the music with a friend, have a few drinks and then call it a night. She contemplated her choice for a few more seconds before deciding.

Hey, Richard... turns out I'll be free tonight, so we can hang out at the jazz bar.

She clicked send, heard it tick and held her breath when the screen showed delivered.

She noticed Richard began typing almost immediately, and his response made the corners of her lips lift a little when she saw the excited emoji he used.

Great! Lucy... we can meet up at the bar if that's alright with you.

Chuckling under her breath, Lucy affirmed his last text, then dropped her phone on the table. She ran a hand through her hair, and her head whipped around to see a car pull to a halt by the side of the street.

Lucy's pulse skipped a bit this time as the man got out of the car and strode towards the bakery.

What does he want this time?

12

L ucy saw Taylor walk into the bakery and look around till he spotted her. She crossed over to him. "Hey," she greeted. "Come to arrest me?"

The corners of his eyes crinkled, and a smile played out on his lips as he looked at her. "I'm not. How are you doing, Lucy?"

"Fine, fine," she answered, matching his light tone. Lucy slipped her hands into the back of her pockets and observed him for a while. "Did you need something?"

"Yes," he replied, then paused. He made a hand gesture towards the display counter behind her and continued. "The boys at the station keep talking about and praising your treats. And since I was driving down this way… anyway, they asked me to place an order."

"Oh, what would you like?" Lucy responded. She reached for

her small notepad in the pocket of her apron and also grabbed a pen to note down his order. After writing down the number of cupcakes, chips, and bread needed, she raised her head and met Taylor's gaze on her face. "Anything else?" she asked after a second passed.

"Uh, no," he said, rocking back on his heels. "You can deliver them before the end of the day, right? Or do you need me to wait for them?"

"You don't have to wait. I'll drop them off before the day ends."

"Cool."

Lucy maintained eye contact with him when he didn't make a move to say goodbye or walk away. He looked at her as if there was something on his mind, and Lucy remembered there was a time they used to enjoy each other's company in silence.

"I should get back to work," she said and turned to walk away.

His next words stopped her. "You remember Roddy's bar? We used to hang out there before you moved out of town. I hear they're having a concert tonight. Almost everyone in town is planning to be there."

"I heard," Lucy replied. "Something about a live jazz band."

"Yes, that's the one. If you're free, I can take you."

His request made her blink in surprise, and her jaw dropped slightly.

"I hear it'll be fun," he added. The genuine interest she saw in his eyes made her heart sink a little because she already had plans with Richard, but attending the concert with Taylor wouldn't have been a bad idea. They both used to enjoy jazz a lot.

"I have plans to attend with Richard Lester," she replied. "I'm sorry, but maybe we could hang out some other time? You know I'd love that too," she quickly added, when the smile on his lips vanished.

"It's all right," he said. He gave her an indifferent shrug and added. "I'll see you around."

She watched him wave to Hannah as he walked out of the bakery. Lucy was still staring after him. Hannah poked her in the side gently, so she turned to her.

"I definitely heard Taylor trying to ask you out," she said, her eyes shining with excitement. "What did you tell him?"

Lucy shook her head. "I said some other time," she replied, and turned to Hannah. "I already have to go with Richard, too bad."

She returned to the kitchen to bring out the muffins from the oven. When she returned to set them in the display glass, Hannah had turned the sign outside to open again, and they resumed the day's activities. She hoped her date with Richard would be worth the hassle she was getting.

13

Lucy sang along to the music from the radio as she drove towards the police station. She had closed the bakery early, and Hannah joined her to deliver the order at the police station, before dropping her off at home and then going on to her date at the jazz bar.

She had been feeling bubbles in her stomach all day and the only thing she could attribute to the giddy excitement she felt was the date she had later that night. She didn't know if feeling this way was good for her, but she enjoyed it. Hannah joined her in singing as they waited for the traffic light to turn green.

"You know the last time I went on a date?" Lucy asked, turning to Hannah. "I haven't been on one in months. The last time was in the city, and that was three months before I moved back to Ivy Creek. Do you think that's why I'm so excited? It could be, right?" she rambled.

Hannah chuckled. "Yeah, right, or it could be you like Richard Lester that much. I mean, look, you even put on red lipstick, and styled your hair. That's a bit too much."

Lucy gently shoved Hannah's shoulder away and moved the car when the light turned green. The song playing changed into a slow tune, one she recognized, and she sobered up immediately. This song reminded her of Taylor. It used to be his favorite.

As Lucy parked in front of the station, she wondered how much of Taylor was still the same. They had known each other for a long time, but did they still know each other?

"I'll drop off the order," she said to Hannah and got out of the car.

Inside the station, the first person she saw was Sheriff Johnson, and he greeted her with a wide smile. Sheriff Johnson had held the position for some time before Lucy moved back to town. She knew his family well, and he had kids scattered across the country. None of them returned home during the holidays, and she didn't think it mattered to him.

"Lucy Hale," he said, and stopped in front of her. "What a pleasant surprise to see you come over here. How have you been?"

"Great, Sheriff. I trust you're fine, and Angela?" she asked, checking up on his wife.

"She's wonderful."

"My regards to her."

Taylor and three other cops Lucy recognized stepped out of an inner room then, and Lucy raised the basket she held to notify him she had brought their orders.

All four cops came to her as the Sheriff excused himself, and Lucy greeted each of them with a handshake.

"Good to see you, Lucy," one officer said as Lucy handed him the basket.

"Good to see you too, Dan."

"Taylor talks about your baking a lot, and we have a team night out today, so we thought your treats would be the perfect compliment," he said with an enormous smile.

Lucy didn't miss the alarmed look on Taylor's face as he elbowed his teammate, and Dan let out a loud laugh. He waved at Lucy and walked away with the other officers, leaving her with Taylor.

"Thanks for delivering," he said and took out his wallet from his back pocket. "How much will that be?"

"Twenty-seven dollars and ninety-cents."

He counted the cash, handed it to her, and their fingers brushed slightly as she took them from him.

"Thanks," he murmured this time.

Lucy gave him a soft nod. She left the station, aware that he was watching her as she walked away. When she got to her car, Hannah was standing outside, resting on the door.

"You good?" Hannah asked.

"Yeah." Lucy took out her phone when she heard a soft ping. She looked at the text from Richard and smiled.

Hey, can't wait to see you tonight.

"Ready to go?" she asked Hannah. Her insides tingled with excitement, and she couldn't wait to see Richard as well. She saw a cop car drive towards the station, and two officers stepped out. The officers walked into the station talking and she got into the car with Hannah.

"You're heading to Roddy's bar now?" Hannah enquired.

"Yes, the concert starts in thirty minutes, and I think Richard's waiting for me there. I'll drop you off at home first?"

"Yes, please."

Lucy started the engine and reversed onto the road. She was about to press down the gas pedal when she remembered her basket.

"Shoot! I forgot the basket. We need it for tomorrow's deliveries." She parked the car again, took off her seat belt, and opened the door. "I'll go get it."

Lucy hurried back into the station and asked around for Taylor. A lady directed her to a room at her right where they kept people brought in for interrogation, and she dashed into the room. She saw Taylor sitting with his friends from the doorway and sighed in relief before heading his way.

"Hey, I forgot my basket," she said when she got to him.

"I was going to deliver it to you tonight," he said and reached for the basket by his side. "These cupcakes are amazing, by the way. Good work, champ!"

His compliment made her blush, and she took a step back, waving her right hand once. "Later."

Lucy made her way out of the station again, but as she got to the door, someone yelled her name.

"Lucy!"

Her steps faltered, and Lucy turned slowly to look see Solomon Mumford staring at her from inside a cell. He stood up from the bench where he sat and gripped the bars.

"Help me, Lucy. I'm innocent... I didn't kill my wife—I would never!"

14

Lucy sipped her drink and turned to look at Richard. The past thirty minutes since she arrived here, their attention had been on the performance. He seemed to be enjoying himself, nodding along to the music as he drank his Mojito.

Richard glanced at her. "Enjoying the show?" he asked.

"It's a brilliant performance." She looked around the bar, noticing how many people were in attendance. The turn-out was impressive, and Lucy was certain if they held a special event every night, the place would be packed.

She saw two cops standing at each exit of the bar, and it reminded of her brief rendezvous with Solomon at the station hours ago.

I didn't kill my wife, I would never.

Was he telling the truth? Although Solomon didn't look like a killer to her, she could never be sure. She had been wrong in the past, when she was linked to two murder investigations. The last people she had thought were capable of the murders turned out to be the guilty, and she never knew who to be cautious of. Richard was someone she had previously thought was guilty of a murder that had occurred in Ivy Creek a few months ago.

She stole a glance at him as the last thought crossed her mind. How could she even suspect he was a murderer?

Richard looked so at ease with his Mojito in one hand. She couldn't tell if he really enjoyed jazz, or this was an excuse to take her out because he barely knew a thing about the band. She dragged in a deep breath, gaining his attention.

"What do you think about the recent murder in town? Vanessa Mumford's sudden death? I mean, do you also suspect the husband?"

Richard lifted one shoulder casually. "In times like this, there is never a concrete reason to suspect someone from the grieving family, except there's concrete evidence."

"You're saying you think he murdered his wife?"

"I'm saying the cops definitely must have solid evidence to suspect him." A moment of silence passed between them, and he extended a hand over the table to touch hers. "We should enjoy the night and not worry about the town's latest events. Tonight is about fun, remember?"

Lucy matched his smile. She chased thoughts of Solomon's case out of her mind and re-focused on the music. When the musician on the saxophone played a few notes, the crowd cheered, and Richard joined, pumping a fist into the air as he sang along to the next song that came up.

She stood up to join, singing at the top of her voice and giggling as she mimicked Richard's dance steps, rolling her shoulders and hips alternatively to each side. He took her hand when it was over, and they sat back down.

"That was exciting," he remarked.

Lucy pushed the strands of hair clinging to her forehead. She struggled to catch her breath, her eyes locked on Richard's for a second before she puffed out air from her lips, and broke contact.

"I'm definitely getting a ticket next time this band is in town," Richard commented.

"I've watched them before—one summer when I came for a visit. My dad never missed a show when they came around. Do you remember the fifth guy? The one who left for a singing position out of state? I hear he's returning too, isn't that exciting? A re-union after almost eight years?"

Richard blinked. It was noticeable he did not know what she was talking about. She searched her mind for what to say next since the singers had taken a break and she didn't want this interlude to feel awkward.

"Do you remember 'Roll with the dice', the very first single they released fresh after their thirty-song album?"

Richard emptied his glass. "No… I wasn't much of a jazz fan till after the release of their Christmas album in 2007, titled '07'. I loved that album because it stood out."

It was Lucy's turn to finish her drink. She knew the album he was referring to, and as much as she loved jazz and this band… that was their worst album in her opinion.

So, we both love jazz, but have different tastes… splendid.

"I should get more drinks," she said, grabbing his empty glass, and made her way past the crowd of bodies to the bar on the other end of the room. Lucy sighed after placing an order. Lucy propped her hands on the counter and lowered her head.

"Not having as much fun as expected?" someone asked beside her.

She turned her head to see Taylor sitting there. "That's weird, you enjoy jazz a lot."

"I still do," she replied and faced him squarely, noticing he sat alone at the counter. He tipped his glass in her direction, and she released a light chuckle before teasing. "Drinking on the job?"

Taylor shook his head and released a short laugh that breezed past her ears. "I'm not on duty tonight, and you know I would never miss Jeanie's performance."

"I think the next song coming up is *Roll with the dice*. You remember it has this slow interlude, and it just feels like that's what's coming next." Lucy's statement barely ended before the exact prelude she was referring to came up.

The crowd celebrated the next song, and Taylor's grin matched hers.

"I was right."

"Yes, you were." His smile slowly faded when she grabbed her glasses, and his gaze trailed over her face before he said. "If you feel the urge to talk more about jazz, I'm right by the bar."

Lucy looked at him for a second, taking in the wistful look she saw in his blue eyes as he looked at her.

"Right," she replied, then turned away from him. As she approached her chair, she wondered why recently every time she saw him, he always had that expression on.

15

"So overall you had fun?" Hannah asked her the next morning as they arranged the freshly baked muffins and cupcakes in the display glass. "You seemed really excited about the night."

"I had a little fun in the end," Lucy replied, remembering her conversation with Richard about wildlife after she got them a refill. The event ended shortly after her favorite song 'Roll with the dice', and as people filed out of the bar, the noise quieted down enough for them to have a conversation.

Richard had vast knowledge of zoology, which was a topic that interested her, too. "It felt nice to be out with someone after such a long time."

Hannah went into the kitchen, and Lucy followed behind her to check on the last batch of cakes in the oven. This one was a special order from a family downtown who had a birthday cele-bration that weekend, and she already mapped out frosting dec-oration tips in her head.

"I've been craving some baklava," Lucy said, and placed both palms on her waist.

"Baklava?"

"It's Turkish. My mom used to make it when I was little, but I just can't seem to remember the recipe, and how to make them."

"Tried googling it?" Hannah asked. She was wiping the kitchen surfaces clean as they had finished with the first set of baking for the day, and it was past nine, the regular time to open up.

"I can't find any definitive recipe. It's all basic, and I doubt it'll taste like my mom's. I just need to remember how she used to make it." Lucy sat down and combed her fingers through her hair.

"You can try the cooking books section in the local library," Hannah suggested. "I've used the library a lot, and I know they have lots of useful books there on those dusty shelves. No one appreciates the beauty of good-old book reading anymore."

"Some do," Lucy answered, chuckling as she left the kitchen to the dining area to turn the door sign to open.

Two hours later, when the morning rush of customers had sub-sided, she drove to the library to check some cooking books like Hannah suggested. Lucy gathered three Turkish recipe books, found a quiet spot, and settled in a corner to go through them.

Minutes into browsing the second book, she stumbled on the information she needed. "Super," she murmured, then reached into her purse for her cell phone to take a quick snapshot of the page with the different recipes of baklava.

She felt a light tap on her shoulder and jerked around to see Daniel Evans smiling at her.

"Hey… you're still in town," she greeted as she rose to her feet. "How are you doing?"

"I'm fine, and you?" Daniel replied. "I think I'll stay in town and get a job while waiting for things to settle with Solomon," he continued. "Solomon and Vanessa gave me a second chance after mistakes I made as a young man, and although I am still loyal to them, it might be time to try out new things for myself."

"Trying out new things is always good," Lucy encouraged. "In the end it helps you discover yourself, and learn things you didn't know about yourself."

Daniel nodded softly, then his eyes dropped to the books she held. "Are those Turkish books?"

"Yeah, translated versions. I dropped by because I needed to confirm some recipes."

"Cool. The entire town praises how much effort you put into making your pastries, and I also think it's commendable that you run Sweet Delights how you do. Keep it up, Lucy!"

His compliment made her spirits soar, and Lucy beamed. "Thanks. You should also stop by for a treat sometime," she offered.

"Actually…" he began, then paused.

Lucy maintained her smile when she saw him falter. "Do you need help with something?"

"No, it's just… I wouldn't mind helping at Sweet Delights while I try to get on my feet here in Ivy Creek. I'll be taking on lots of side jobs, and if you ever need any more help."

"You should drop by for an interview later today," she replied. "I'll see what skill you're strongest at and I'm sure we'll find something for you to do."

"That's very nice of you," Daniel said. "Thank you so much, Lucy."

It was then she noticed he also held a book. The cover page caught her attention, and Lucy peered down to stare at it. Daniel angled the book towards her to give her a better view, and she read the name in red ink out loud. "Ivy Creek: The Unwinding Landmarks of Nature."

"You're into geography?" she asked.

"Yeah," he replied with a dismissive shrug, and gave her a smile again. "Thanks, Lucy. I should get back to my reading."

"Right… have a nice day."

"Yeah, you too."

Lucy watched him walk away, wondering what piqued his interest in geography. She returned the cooking books to the counter and made her way to the front desk to sign out. She was driving home and replaying the scene with Daniel in her head when she realized she might have offered him a job at her bakery.

She panicked, and images of a tense atmosphere in the bakery while working with Hannah and Daniel entered her head. Daniel seemed peaceful, but how would Hannah feel about having him as a counterpart?

"Why didn't you think of this before inviting him over?" she questioned with a groan.

What! What were you thinking, Lucy? She chided herself and took the turn leading onto the highroad. Lucy exhaled to relieve her worrisome thoughts and chewed on her lower lip. She remembered she had offered him an interview, so now she hoped he would give her a good reason not to hire him.

16

By evening, Lucy was pacing around her kitchen. What do I do? It's best he doesn't show up for the interview. Won't working with him be awkward since he was on Solomon's team?

Hannah came into the kitchen for the second time, dropped the serving plates she held into the sink, and faced Lucy. "Okay, I've pretended to not notice you pacing for the past…" she glanced at her watch before adding. "One hour. What is it? Did something happen? Did you run into Taylor?"

Her last question made Lucy frown. "Why would you think I ran into Taylor?"

Hannah raised both hands. "Well, whenever you both meet there's tension or sparks."

Lucy rolled her eyes. She stopped pacing and shot Hannah a

mortified look, her eyes widening, and forehead creased into a frown. "I did something stupid. I kind of asked Daniel Evans to drop by for an interview."

Hannah looked oblivious to what Lucy was saying. "Daniel Evans?" she asked.

"Yeah, he worked at Sweet Bites, and I might have offered him a job when he asked."

Hannah's eyes brows furrowed when the meaning of Lucy's words finally settled in, and Lucy grimaced. "I know, I know. It was a terrible idea. I hope he doesn't show up."

"You offered him a job, Lucy. Of course, he'll show," Hannah replied, and joined Lucy in pacing. "Wait, don't you think it'll be like… weird?"

"I know, right?" Lucy groaned and smacked her forehead gently. "Why didn't I think of that? I just wanted to give him a chance, and I asked him to come over without thinking about it properly."

"Yeah, well, you're a sucker for being nice," Hannah remarked, and crossed her arms over her chest. The next minute, they heard the front door swing open.

Lucy and Hannah rushed out of the kitchen to see who it was, and Lucy's panicked gaze flew to Hannah when they saw Daniel walk into the bakery, and assess the place briefly before turning to them.

He flashed a smile and waved in their direction.

"I'll be in the kitchen," Hannah said, huffed, and walked away while Lucy joined Daniel.

She offered him a seat, and sat opposite him, linking her fingers in front of her on the table.

"You have a nice place," Daniel complimented. "I love the wallpaper designs and the setting, it's lively."

"Thanks."

Lucy cleared her throat and searched her mind for the right question to start with. She needed to know Daniel's experience with baking and customer service. Also, if he was a fast learner, then that would be helpful because she loved adding tweaks to her recipes.

"So, you're knowledgeable about baking? What's your experience when baking cupcakes? How do you make sure your recipe is fluffy and well-aerated?"

Daniel smiled and launched into his reply. He spent the next three minutes explaining details on baking cakes, the dos and don'ts and the tips to getting a yummy result.

He's better than I hoped, Lucy thought and feigned a smile when he gave her tips on making bread, avoiding crusts and burnt bits.

"You have impeccable knowledge, and you've got the job too," she announced, blown away by his replies.

"Really?"

"Yes."

Daniel pumped his fist in the air, and both of them burst out laughing. She hoped working with him would be easy, and he would get along with Hannah.

"I'm so grateful, Lucy. This will help me plan for the future since I won't have to worry about giving up the room I occupy in Solomon's house. It's really discomforting staying there in his absence, and I'm glad I wouldn't have to stay longer than a few weeks now."

"The Mumfords own a house here in Ivy Creek?" she asked.

"Yes, they planned on going into real estate as a long-term investment. Ivy Creek seemed like a good place to start. It's small, cozy and has the potential for development. Vanessa's brother is into real estate, and it was her idea to try it out. I also think her brother was funding the business… the bakery, I mean. Before we moved here, he visited a lot, and they discussed big plans," he explained. "Little wonder why she was always so rude to Solomon. He never had a say of his own," Daniel added in a low tone before looking at her again.

Lucy masked her shock with a grin and pretended not to ponder on the bit of information he just revealed. He really knows a lot about the Mumfords, she thought.

"Well, you're free to start tomorrow, and I look forward to working with you," Lucy said, standing to her feet. He got up as well, with a fat grin on his face.

"Me too, Lucy. Thanks again. I'll see you first thing tomorrow morning," he agreed.

Daniel left after that, and Lucy went back to the kitchen to join Hannah.

"So, he got hired?" Hannah asked, taking out whipped cream from the refrigerator.

"He knows a lot about baking, and I think he'll learn quick, and gives us an edge. We get an extra set of hands around here, so it's a good thing."

Hannah said nothing, so Lucy went to her and put a hand on her shoulder. "Think about it this way. We have someone who knows a lot about the Mumfords in our corner now. This is a good thing."

"I just worry that there might be some tension around here, especially when Solomon gets released. Do you think it will please him we poached off his worker? And what if Daniel is here to steal recipe ideas? I know it's preposterous, but what if?"

"You both will get along fine," Lucy replied. "We shouldn't worry about any of that, okay?"

Hannah sighed and returned to work. Lucy was confident about her decision. She just hoped it wouldn't spoil the beautiful working relationship she had with Hannah.

17

T he next morning, Lucy showed Daniel how to set up the electric oven for baking and how she made sure her pastries never burn. He was a fast learner and good listener, like she expected, taking his time to watch her do a thing before mimicking the same steps to perfect it himself.

By mid-day, he had mastered her frosting recipe, while Hannah served the customers out front. They switched places when Lucy finished decorating the cake. Hannah came into the kitchen to mix another batch of macaroons, and Daniel attended to the customers out front.

"He's good, isn't he?" Lucy commented. She peeped out of the kitchen to check on Daniel's rapport with the customers and caught two teenage girls giggling at a joke he made while he served them. "He charms the ladies and is polite to the men."

"I don't trust him," Hannah replied, and dropped the palette knife she was holding. "The charmers are the ones worthy of our suspicions. He has a bad vibe that I don't like."

Lucy could understand Hannah was apprehensive over someone else stepping in to disrupt the beautiful dynamic they had together. Still, what was to dislike about Daniel?

"I saw him rummaging through some files in here this morning when you were on the patio," Hannah continued, pointing toward the small locker room Lucy used as a store to keep dry baking items. "I don't know what he was looking for, but it definitely threw him off when I walked in."

"Try to relax, Hannah," Lucy replied, and returned to her work. "Daniel doesn't seem like a bad guy at all. I have good instincts with stuff like this."

"Do you?" Hannah asked with her questioning eyes fixed on Lucy.

Lucy gave up after re-thinking her last statement. "Okay, fine, I might not be the best judge of character, but come on, look at him," she urged, and pulled Hannah to the door so they could watch Daniel. "He looks okay."

"I just need you to be careful," Hannah added, not backing down either.

Lucy sensed she was coming from a place of jealousy when she noticed Hannah's glare, but she didn't voice that. If she was going to make sure they got along, she had to maintain neutral ground here, and take Hannah's point into consideration, too. She had been with Hannah a long time, and she trusted her.

"All right—I'll be watchful and careful, but you have to promise to keep an open mind with Daniel too."

"I promise," she replied grudgingly.

Lucy went out to join Daniel in the dining area. They formed a good partnership as they attended to the customers. Lucy took the orders, Daniel prepared them, and brought the packages to her, before she got cash from the customers.

The work was efficient that way, and customers didn't have to wait long before it got to their turn. When the dining area emptied, she continued her lessons with Daniel, teaching him how she packaged her bread loafs after baking.

He did most of the packaging, helped her set them into the large delivery baskets, then she offered him a cool glass of lemonade to help him relax since they didn't have any customers in the bakery.

Lucy was aware of the tension in the kitchen as the three of them worked. Hannah wore a grim expression and Lucy wished she would open up a little. She thought Daniel was worth giving a chance.

Daniel rinsed out his glass and moved to join Hannah, where she was rolling out dough and setting them in baking sheets.

"Can I try that?" he asked her.

"I got it," Hannah replied in a gruff voice.

Hannah glanced in Lucy's direction and Lucy returned her stare by slowly shaking her head. Lucy gave her a hand signal to let him try the rolling, and Hannah reluctantly stepped away from the table.

"You're doing it all wrong," Lucy heard Hannah say.

She closed her eyes, pretending to relax while watching them, and she saw Hannah snatch the rolling pin, then flex her wrist in demonstration, showing Daniel the proper way to roll dough.

Daniel got it on the next try, and he beamed afterwards. "Thanks, Hannah," he said and stepped away from her.

He left the kitchen, and Lucy rose to her feet. "See, that wasn't so hard," she said, propping both hands on Hannah's shoulders from behind. "Just try to be nicer."

Hannah's frown made her giggle, and she went up to her apartment to freshen up and prepare to drive out to make deliveries for the day since she couldn't get ahold of her drivers. Usually, they came around in the morning to check if she needed to make any deliveries. She only drove out to drop urgent orders or Sunday orders.

She returned to the kitchen minutes later, dressed in black jeans and a white chiffon shirt. She tied her hair in a bun, and she let some strands fall loose in front because she thought the look flattered her.

"I should go deliver these items," she told Hannah. "There's still no word on the delivery driver."

"Cool, I've got everything here covered," Hannah replied.

"Okay."

Lucy assisted her in putting the baking sheets in the oven, then she went into the storeroom to pick up her shoulder bag. She reached for the handle of the basket to lift it, but a loud crash from the dining area halted her movement.

Lucy froze for a second. She went limp, as if all her bones had dissolved away, leaving only her skin standing. Angry voices followed, and she pushed the shot of adrenaline that zapped through her away, found her feet again and dashed towards the dining area to see what the problem was.

18

Lucy and Hannah rushed into the dining area, and Lucy stopped in her tracks when her gaze landed on the gigantic figure standing beside another man she soon recognized as Solomon when he turned around to face her. Daniel was cowered in a corner.

Some customers rushed out of the bakery, while the others watched the scene unfolding before them. A hushed silence fell on the room, and Lucy could hear her own heart beating. When was Solomon released?

"Solomon? What's happening?" Lucy said.

The huge man stepped between Lucy and Solomon when Solomon took a step towards her. Solomon's cheeks flushed with anger; his ears reddened as he wiped a sleeved hand over his lips.

"Talk to me, Solomon. I can explain this. Lucy did not poach me or try to steal me from you." Daniel said as he slowly got up.

"Is that how you explain working for the enemy? You went right behind me, and took a job from her," Solomon retorted, jabbing a finger in his direction. "She pretended to be my friend, then went behind me to steal my employees," he announced so everyone in the bakery could hear.

What? Why am I the enemy? And why is he even here?

Lucy's stomach sank as eyes turned in her direction, and she felt a tight knot in the pit of her stomach. She was too shaken to do anything, and Solomon's accomplice seemed intent on handling the situation, as he wouldn't move away from standing in front of her.

"Solomon, you're not even open for business and I need a job," Daniel explained. "Lucy runs the best bakery in town. There's nothing wrong with me taking a job here."

"You are my friend," Solomon replied. "I never expected that you'd betray me like this."

"I did not betray you, Solomon," Daniel pointed out in a high-pitched voice. "I am still your friend, and Lucy… she's not the enemy."

Solomon's jaw tightened, and he lurched forward again, attempting to grab Daniel, but the huge man was faster. He held onto Solomon and stopped his attack. Solomon gritted his teeth and fought to free himself.

"Let's not cause a scene here, Solomon," the huge man advised, as Solomon struggled to free himself from his hold. "This is a business place, and we can do this some other time. Let's go home."

"No, I want to do this now. Why would she do this? I'm trying to get back on my feet, and then she steals my best man, and friend, and offers him a job."

"She stole nothing," the huge man said. "I think you should go home, and I will come sort this out with you."

"He's right, Solomon," Lucy said, finding her voice again. "It's best you leave now."

Solomon gave her an unflinching glare, and the huge man pulled his arm, leading him out of the bakery.

Lucy sighed as the bakery door swung shut behind them. A hand moved to her chest, and she wiped the beads of sweat that had formed on her forehead. Seconds later, the door re-opened, and huge man returned into the bakery.

"I'm sorry about this," he said, and handed Lucy his business card. "John Stanley," he said. "Don't worry about Solomon, I'll make sure something like this never repeats itself."

"Thank you." Lucy took the card and slipped it into the pocket of her apron without checking it. "No problem."

"I'm so sorry about this," Daniel said when he turned to her. He looked pretty shaken himself, his face sweaty, and eyes wide. His lower lip quivered as he added. "Let me clean up this mess."

It was then, Lucy realized; Solomon had shattered a saucer when he entered the bakery. That was the loud shattering sound that caused the ruckus she heard. Grateful that the scene did not scare away all the customers inside the bakery, she gave Daniel a soft nod.

"I'll clean it." Hannah swooped in with a brush, while Lucy led Daniel into the kitchen.

"I didn't know Solomon would have a problem with you working here," Lucy said inside the kitchen.

"It's not a problem, and he will get over it. He couldn't have expected me to sit and wait around for him while doing nothing for myself. All the other employees already got other jobs. He is just angry because I'm his friend, and he's probably stressed out, too. He will get over it."

"I didn't think it would be a problem, or even imagine he would come here to cause a scene," she lamented.

"I hope he gets over it soon."

Lucy hoped so, too. She had no intention of making any enemies in Ivy Creek because she was enjoying the simple life she now led.

She ran a hand through her hair and sighed. "You should take the rest of the day off. Hannah and I will take care of the bakery."

"Sure?" he asked, taking out a towel to wipe his face. "I'm all right, and since you have to deliver items, I can still work."

"No, I want you to take the rest of the day off," she insisted.

She also needed some fresh air at that moment. Solomon's boldness in calling her the enemy really threw her off, and she just needed a minute to breathe. Daniel could use one, too.

"All right. Thank you, Lucy."

He left her in the kitchen, took off his apron, and walked out. She grabbed a bottle of cold water and emptied its content in one continuous gulp before going into the storeroom to fetch clean napkins to cover the baskets.

Inside the storeroom, Lucy stumbled on a rucksack lying near the shelf where she stacked papers and bakery inventory. She remembered Hannah claimed she had seen Daniel going through the files in the storeroom and she wondered if Hannah had been right.

A book fell out when Lucy picked up the bag - *Ivy Creek: The Unwinding Landmarks of Nature*. She remembered this was the same book he was reading at the library the other day, and kept it for him.

When next he came to work, she would give it to him.

19

An early morning jog was a good way to start the day. Lucy enjoyed the cool morning breeze on her skin each time she went for a run. It made her feel alive and energetic.

She stopped running for a second to stretch her legs and arms out behind her. "Oh, that feels so good," she murmured, and turned when she heard footsteps behind her.

Taylor headed towards her, jogging at a steady pace, and she bounced on her feet while waiting for him to catch up.

"Hey!" she said when he was almost close to her, and he stopped.

"Lucy… good morning. How are you?" he said, taking out his headphones from his ears.

"Great. Do you mind?" she asked and joined him to jog at his pace when he replied with a gentle shake of his head.

They moved in silence for a while before she asked. "So, why was Solomon released?"

"We released him on bail. His wealthy brother-in-law bailed him out."

"Guess that's what happens when you've got connections, right?" she asked rhetorically. When Taylor didn't give her a direct reply, she continued. "What happens next? Do you have any other suspects in custody?"

"You ask a lot of questions; do you know that?" Taylor replied, glancing in her direction as they approached the end of the road where there was a bend linking into another road.

Lucy laughed. "I like to be informed, you know the saying— knowledge is power," she said, remembering a famous scene from the TV series, *Game of Thrones*.

"Power is power," Taylor replied.

They both giggled and stopped jogging when they reached a fork in the road. Taylor could get home by continuing straight ahead, but Lucy had to go back the same way she came to join the high street.

"We arrested him because there were some financial transactions that seemed off, so we took him in for questioning to get to the root of the situation."

"And did you? Get to the root of the situation," she probed, wanting Taylor to give her a definitive answer. "I mean, when will we know for certain who the killer is?"

She placed her hands on her waist, panting to catch her breath from the recent physical exertion. Taylor trailed his gaze over her for a second, then rubbed his palms on his sides.

"This is a sensitive case, Lucy. You know I won't be able to reveal any information about it. I've already said enough."

"I know," she agreed and sucked in a deep breath.

They fell into silence for a moment, and he spoke again. "I should go now. I must get to work. See you around, Lucy."

"Yeah, see you around."

She turned to head back down the road and stopped abruptly when a car came out of nowhere and nearly sent her flying across the road.

20

Taylor rushed back to her side and held her arms. "Are you all right? Did the car hit you?"

"Are you okay?" the man, who stepped out of the car, asked as he rushed to her side. Lucy was staring at her feet, and when she raised her head to look at him, she realized it was someone she had seen before.

"Yeah, I'm all right."

"I'm so sorry, I didn't see you coming, and I was trying to get somewhere in a hurry."

"It's fine," Lucy replied, and Taylor released her. "I think we've met," she continued when the initial shock of what just happened eased her a bit.

"Yeah, I was in your bakery yesterday," he said. "With Solomon," he added when she still didn't remember. "I'm John Stanley, Vanessa's brother."

"I'm so sorry for your loss, John," Lucy offered after his introduction. "How are you holding up?"

Before she could answer, Taylor helped her up.

"Are you sure you're okay?"

"Yes, I am. Stop worrying about me."

Taylor nodded at John and Lucy and started jogging in the opposite direction.

"I'm doing okay," John said, returning his gaze to Lucy. "It's been a lot to try to take in, but I am getting over it. I just hope Solomon will, too. It's been difficult for him."

"I can only imagine," Lucy said. "He must be going through a lot. Have the cops been able to find out anything? How's the investigation going?"

"There's no concrete evidence yet. I know Vanessa and Solomon had their differences and problems, but they were good together, and I know they loved each other deeply."

"So, you also don't think he's guilty?"

"I could never think that," John replied. He paused and skimmed his fingers through his thick, black hair. "Our parents left us a small fortune when they passed, and I grew it by investing in real estate. Moving to Ivy Creek was my idea. I think this place has the potential to be a property hot spot," he said as he looked around and smiled. "Vanessa always wanted to run a bakery. Even though she barely got along with people, I don't think she ever did anything so awful that someone would want her dead."

"I met her once," Lucy said, remembering her run-in with Vanessa the day she first met Solomon. "I just hope the cops find the killer soon. Where were you on the night she died?"

Stanley's expression went dark, and she saw anger flash in his eyes.

"What are you insinuating by asking me that sort of question?"

"I... just... I don't think there's anything wrong with me asking," Lucy quickly added. She blinked when John's jaw hardened.

"You think I killed my sister?"

"No... that was not what I thought or said. I just simply wanted to know your version of what happened that night. I mean, if you saw her before the incident."

"Well, you're not a cop, Lucy, and I won't stand here and let you insult me while acting like one."

"Wait," Lucy said, and followed him as he headed for his car. "I didn't mean to insult you."

"Stay away from me, and watch your back," he warned, wagging a finger at her.

She stared at him, speechless, as he drove away.

When Lucy finally got back to the bakery, she saw Aunt Tricia sitting in the kitchen with Hannah.

Lucy hugged her before she went to the fridge to get some water. "I ran into John today," she said, launching into a conversation with Tricia and Hannah.

"Who is John?" Tricia asked.

"Vanessa Mumford's brother. Hannah, do you remember the man who came here with Solomon yesterday."

Hannah nodded. "Yeah."

"Well, I bumped into him earlier today and he explained to me they wanted to go into real-estate and purchase properties in Ivy

Creek."

"So, does he know what happened to his sister?"

Lucy shook her head. "When I tried to ask him about his where-abouts that night, he took offense and said I insinuated he killed her. I didn't have that in mind."

"You think he got angry because he's guilty," Hannah said, and everyone in the room fell silent. "Sometimes our guilt gets the best of us, and we react without thinking."

For the rest of the day, Lucy couldn't get her encounter with John out of her head. She wondered if his actions were that of a bereaved brother or that of a ruthless killer.

21

The next morning, Lucy was cleaning the tables on the patio while Hannah worked on displaying the baked goods for the day. She checked her watch and sighed. Daniel still hadn't turned up for work, and she was getting worried.

Did something happen to him?

Lucy finished wiping the tables and dropped on a chair to rest for a while. She closed her eyes, enjoying the rays of the rising sun on her face.

Hannah came out to join her, and she wore a worried look on her face. "Daniel still hasn't shown up?" she asked.

"No," Lucy replied.

She didn't want to think that Daniel bailed on his job after the scene with Solomon, but the more time passed without a word from him, the more her thoughts went in that direction.

"What do you do now?" Hannah asked.

Lucy was about to reply when she saw Daniel's motorbike grind to a halt on the other side of the road.

"He's here finally," Lucy said.

He came towards her, taking off his helmet as he approached in quick strides, and Lucy rose to her feet while Hannah went into the bakery.

"Daniel, I was worried about you. How are you? You didn't show up yesterday, and you're late today."

"I know. I'm so sorry about that, Lucy. I just dropped by to tell you I won't be able to keep working here."

"What?"

"I met with John, and he convinced me to come back to work in Sweet Bites. John Stanley has connections in political circles, and Solomon is my friend. I want to help him re-open Sweet Bites."

"Oh…" Lucy masked her surprise with a wavering smile. "That's fine. I understand you want to stick with Solomon. It's commendable."

"Thank you so much, Lucy," he said. "I'm really grateful."

She watched him walk away, and when he drove away on his bike, Hannah came out of the bakery again. Hannah put a hand on her shoulder and squeezed. "I heard everything," she said.

"Yeah, it's fine."

By afternoon, Lucy had finished baking and cleaning for the day. She sat alone on the patio, and Hannah came to join her. "Hey, have you read this book?" Hannah said and took out a small novel she had been reading. "I picked it up from the library."

Lucy took the history book from Hannah and looked at the title. It reminded her of the book Daniel left in her storeroom. "You know, Daniel left something like this here the last time he was around."

"A history book?" Hannah asked.

"Yeah, I forgot. I wanted to give it back to him. The book talks about Ivy Creek's history. Did you know this bakery used to be the Sheriff's office? And then after that it was a bank."

"No, I didn't know that." They ended up talking about the town's history, and Lucy was glad Hannah brought up the topic to distract her. Talking to her about other matters helped take her mind off the disappointment she was feeling at Daniel's decision to go back to Solomon.

She had enjoyed working with him the day he had been at Sweet Delights. Lucy's mind continued wandering while Hannah left her to get a glass of orange juice for both of them.

When Hannah returned, Lucy accepted her glass absent-mindedly. Her gaze focused on Solomon's bakery building across the street from hers. Although Sweet Bites was still closed, she imagined Solomon re-opening the bakery when everything settled down, and John Stanley using his political connections to run her business out of town.

The thought, no matter how far-fetched, scared her. Hannah must have noticed the pale look on Lucy's face because she pulled her chair closer, and she reached out to touch Lucy's hand on the table.

"You sure you're all right?" she asked. "Look, I know how much you enjoyed working with Daniel for the day he was here, and I can tell you thought he was good. But he made a choice, and it shouldn't bother you."

"That's not what bothers me," Lucy said. "I might have angered Vanessa's brother with my question the other day, and now that I know he's got big connections in town, I'm scared he'll try to get back at me."

"How do you think he'll do that?"

"He might try to run me out of town?"

"That can't happen," she laughed, shaking her head. "Come on, Lucy, stop worrying about the impossible, okay?"

Lucy hesitated for a while before she responded. "I hope so."

Later that night, she fell asleep after tossing and turning in bed for a long time.

She couldn't get rid of the feeling that something was about to go wrong. A noise from downstairs jerked her out of sleep, and Lucy's stomach took a slow sinking dive when the sound persisted.

Her first instinct was to call the cops, but when she reached for her phone on the nightstand, and realized her battery was dead, she knew she had to confront whoever this intruder was on her own.

Lucy gathered her wits, sucked in a deep breath to calm her jittery nerves, and tip-toed towards the door leading to the bakery downstairs.

22

When Lucy got downstairs, there was no one in the bakery. Gigi leaped towards her from a corner of the kitchen, and she bent down to scoop her up. "How did you get down here?" she muttered to herself and looked around the kitchen.

There was no one there, but Lucy could see that something had been moved.

She noticed the door connecting the kitchen to the dining area was slightly ajar, and when she went out to check, Lucy realized one window was open. A chill ran down her spine, and she immediately went back to her apartment to get a charger.

Her phone came up back to life minutes after she plugged it in, and she quickly dialed 911. After Lucy reported the incident to the cops, she went around to make sure she locked every door and window before she went back to bed.

She was up early because she couldn't fall asleep. The cops dropped by that morning to question her, and Hannah's call came in while she talked to them.

"Hey, Hannah, how are you?"

"I don't feel too well, Lucy. I might not come around today," she said.

"What's the matter?" Lucy asked.

"I don't know. I woke up feeling feverish. It seems like I might be coming down with something."

"Oh… okay. I guess it's best if you stay at home."

"I hope you make a lot of sales today."

Lucy didn't want to bother Hannah with what occurred that morning, so she cleared her throat and made sure her voice was cheery as she replied. "I hope you get better soon. Everything is going well here. I can handle things today, just take time to get better."

"All right, thanks, Lucy. I'll drop by later in the evening."

Lucy ended the call with Hannah and returned her attention to the cops. They left after getting her statement and promised to keep someone on the watch in case the burglar returned.

She spent the rest of the day serving customers, and her worry subsided when Daniel came into the bakery that evening.

"Hey," she said, wiping her hands on a napkin.

Daniel smiled as he walked to the counter to greet her.

"How are you doing?" she asked

"Great, Lucy. I remembered I left a bag here, and I came to pick it up."

"Oh, it's in the office."

Daniel went into the room that served as an office to get the bag, and when he returned, he waved at her and made his way to the door when she remembered she had kept his history book somewhere else.

"Daniel, wait," she called. "You forgot your book."

She went into the office to bring the book, and he thanked her again as he took it from her. "I found this and kept it for you. Your history book... about Ivy Creek."

Daniel gave her another smile, stuck the book in his bag, and turned to walk away when she stopped him again.

"I read through it. The town has a lot of history and it's all noted in the book. I understand why you like the book so much. I mean, who knew this place used to be a Sheriff's office, and then a bank? Meaning there could be a vault somewhere around this building. It's crazy... I plan on telling the cops, anyway."

"There's no need for that. They might think you're nutty," he said as he put his hands in his pockets and rocked back and forth on his feet.

"Imagine if there really was a vault? With a lot of money or treasures?" she said, clasping her hands together.

"I never knew you had such a wild imagination," he said, and they both started laughing.

"You're right. Sometimes my imagination runs wild."

"Maybe that's why you thought someone tried to break in earlier."

"How do you know someone tried to break in?"

"Um... I didn't say someone tried to break in... I said someone might try to break in."

"No, Daniel. You said that's why someone tried to break in earlier."

Daniel looked as if he wanted to say something, then slowly shook his head. Lucy crossed her arms over her chest.

"Daniel... Do you know who tried to break in here?"

He moved, and turned the door sign to closed, then dropped his bag to the ground. Lucy's gaze dropped to the bag on the floor, and when she looked at him again, she saw a dangerous look in his eyes.

"Dan...."

His hands gripped her throat before she could say anything else.

"I'm sorry, Lucy," he said as he tightened his grip on her neck and squeezed hard. "I didn't think it would end this way, but this has to be it. I'm tired of serving people, and I won't let you ruin what I am working so hard to get. I didn't let Vanessa, and I definitely won't let you."

She freed herself from his grip when Daniel got distracted by the loud voices of people walking past the bakery and ran to the corner of the room. She rubbed her hands on her throat where he had gripped her. In an instant, she saw him moving towards her.

"Daniel, you don't have to do anything stupid."

"Are you calling me stupid? You're just like all of them. Well, it ends today. I'll end your life like I ended Vanessa's and find me that treasure."

Lucy fought him as he lunged towards her. She struggled to free herself from his hands, which had found their way around her neck again. Her nails dug into his hands around her neck and she felt her chest tighten as she felt her legs turning to jelly. Lucy's eyelids fluttered close, and the last thing she thought as she slipped away was what a sad fate it would be if she ended up like his first victim, Vanessa.

23

S uddenly, Lucy heard the best word she had heard in a long time.

"Freeze!"

The door had burst open, and cops surrounded them.

The minute Daniel's hands left her neck, Lucy gasped for air. She scrambled away from him, terrified, as she struggled to fill her lungs with air.

"Are you all right, miss?" the cop who came after her asked and put a hand on her shoulder to console her. "It's fine, you're safe. Just take in a deep breath slow and easy," he encouraged.

Lucy obeyed his instructions, and after a second, she could breathe properly even though her throat burned. She broke into a sob, and tears fell freely as she sank to the ground, her shoulders heaving as she buried her face in her hands.

Taylor walked into the bakery and was at her side in a split second. She saw him whisper something to the female cop talking to her, and the others dragged Daniel out of the bakery as he struggled.

"Don't worry, you're safe now," Taylor said to Lucy. "The paramedics are on their way, and they'll check on you soon."

Lucy's hand remained on her neck, and Taylor reached out to pry her hands away from her neck. "I'll make sure Daniel pays for this," he said in a gruff voice and she met his gaze briefly before a cop came to call him out.

The paramedics arrived a while after, and Lucy watched the cops loiter around as they attended to her. She swallowed some pills they gave her and closed her eyes, exhaling with relief. Taylor was still talking to his colleagues, but he glanced in her direction a few times, and his gaze trailed over her each time.

Hannah came into the bakery then, and she hurried towards Lucy. "Oh God, Lucy what happened?"

"It was Daniel," Lucy murmured. "It was him all along, and he tried to…" she stopped when Hannah enveloped her in a hug, and Lucy realized she desperately needed that form of consolation.

She released a shaky breath, and Hannah pulled back again. "I'm so sorry, Lucy. I should have been here when it happened. If I came around this morning, then maybe…"

"No, no, Hannah, none of this is your fault," Lucy whispered. "I'm all right, so you have nothing to be sorry for. You warned me, but I trusted Daniel and gave him the benefit of the doubt."

"Turns out he approached me and asked for a job because he thought he could find some kind of vault buried down here in my building. I told you about the history book I found in his bag.

He's been reading that in hopes of one day accessing the vault."

"That's crazy," she said, and Taylor walked into the bakery.

"Ladies," he said when he reached where they sat. "Lucy, I hope you feel better now?"

Lucy nodded, and she rubbed her neck again. "So, is it true? This place used to have a vault, and Daniel thought he could access that vault?"

Taylor sighed and a small smile crept over his face. "He was wrong. When the bank moved out of the building years ago, they cleared out all the vaults. My father told me about that operation. Even if he got there, he would have been very disappointed."

"He probably was spending too much time listening to Solomon and his brother-in-law and thought he'd find a piece of real estate with the best return on investment," Lucy said

"So, he was on a fool's errand?" Hannah asked.

Taylor nodded his next reply. "He was wrong. I should get back to the station now. I have tons of paperwork. Take care of yourself, Lucy, and make sure you apply something to that bruise."

"Thank you."

Lucy exchanged a quick glance with Hannah and relaxed further in her chair when they were alone again.

"It's finally over," she said with a deep sigh.

Hannah dropped her bag on the table. "I'll get you an ice compress for your neck."

Lucy reached into the pocket of her jeans to get her phone. She called her Aunt Tricia to break the latest news to her.

"Hello, aunt… guess what, they found the killer," she announced, and told her aunt the details of her near-death experience.

24

News of Daniel's crimes spread in town like wild-fire over the next week. Everywhere Lucy went, someone was talking about the concluded murder investigation. Daniel's antics made it to the local news station, and the cause of Vanessa Mumford's death was finally announced as ingestion of a poisonous substance.

Lucy still couldn't believe she had misjudged Daniel. She went around town in the days following the attack with a scarf around her neck to hide the hideous bruise. She hoped no one in town would directly ask her about the incident.

Hannah came into the bakery that morning with her sister, and Lucy greeted them both with a wide smile as she walked around the counter.

"Hey, Lucy," Hannah said. "This is my older sister, Stacey," she said, and Lucy smiled at her.

"You have a lovely place, Lucy," Stacey said when Hannah let go of her hand and went into the kitchen. "And I've tasted your treats. I love them."

"Thank you," Lucy replied with a blush.

She offered Stacey a seat and brought her a cool glass of lemonade. They were chatting about the news of the next jazz event in town when the door opened, and Richard Lester walked in.

"Hey, ladies," he greeted, and made his way towards the counter.

Lucy excused herself to attend to him after Stacey waved back at him and returned her attention to her glass of lemonade.

Lucy served him the cupcakes and cookies he ordered. "I'm sorry about what happened with Daniel. How do you feel now?"

"I'm much better, thank you," Lucy replied. "I'm just glad everything is back to normal now."

"Yeah, me too. I heard Solomon Mumford moved out of town with John Stanley, and John is suing Solomon for embezzling money from their business account. It's such a pity what happened to Vanessa."

"It's really sad," Lucy added.

What do you say to joining me for another night in Roddy's bar tomorrow?" Richard asked. "I had fun the last time we were together, and I'd like to go with you again."

"Oh, just say yes already," Lucy heard Hannah call from inside the kitchen and she broke into a short laugh.

"Sure, I'd love to join you," she agreed.

She returned to Stacey when Richard left, and Stacey asked. "You and Richard are together? As in a couple?"

"Not really a couple," Lucy replied with a light giggle.

She pushed a stray lock of hair behind her ear and shrugged. "We just both enjoy jazz."

"He might not be the most knowledgeable about jazz, but he definitely enjoys the music," she replied, and they both laughed.

Lucy had noticed that bit about him on her own, and even though she kind of wished she could attend the concert with a die-hard fan, she still enjoyed her time with Richard the last time they went to Roddy's.

"Hannah told me about you and Richard. I'm sorry about that."

"It's water under the bridge. Hannah just held a little grudge because Richard was always really nice to her."

"I get it."

They continued talking about how much Lucy enjoyed staying in Ivy Creek, and she learned a few things about Stacey and her love for the town, too. She was glad she met a new friend, and Hannah joined them after mixing bread dough in the kitchen.

Someone else came into the store a while later, and Lucy stood up to attend to the slender blonde lady who had walked in.

"Hi, you must be Lucy," she said, and extended a hand to her.

Lucy took the flier she was handing out and read through it.

"Jessi's designs?" she asked.

"Yeah, and I'm Jessi," the lady replied. "I just moved in across the street, and I run a fashion store. I look forward to living and working here—I've heard so much about this town."

"I look forward to seeing you around, too," Lucy replied, and she meant it.

Lucy was glad some sense of order had been restored to her

town. She realized she had something unique that would always attract the citizens of Ivy Creek, regardless of any competition that appeared on the scene. She made a mental note to focus on her strengths and serve her customers with more yummy treats. As a ray of sunshine suddenly shone through the window, she let out a sigh and looked forward to better days ahead.

The End

SILENT NIGHT, UNHOLY BITES

AN IVY CREEK COZY MYSTERY

ABOUT SILENT NIGHT, UNHOLY BITES

Released: January 2022
Series: Book 4 – Ivy Creek Cozy Mystery Series
Standalone: Yes
Cliff-hanger: No

Lucy is looking forward to a holiday season that's filled with Christmas carols, remembering and making new holiday memories and yummy food. She's also excited about all the new festive recipes she'll be introducing into the menu at Sweet Delights bakery.

When she finds out that an obnoxious woman at an event for the homeless has stolen some of her treats for her business, Lucy gives this lady a piece of her mind in no uncertain terms.

She's left bewildered and sad when this lady is found dead. Did Lucy's harsh words, spoken in the heat of the moment, have an effect on the lady's life or is something more sinister at play?

It seems almost everyone wants to sweep this murder investigation under carpet but Lucy knows there's something seriously off.

With Christmas just around the corner, Lucy knows she has to find a killer on the loose or her small town will be having a blue, blue Christmas.

1

"This is definitely my best time of the year," Lucy commented and glanced at her assistant, Hannah, who was sitting next to her, enjoying a cup of caramel flavored ice cream. "Does that taste good?"

"Hmm, this is so good. I can't tell you how stress-relieving this is," Hannah replied, taking another scoop of her ice cream.

Lucy had finished her cup of mint mixed with strawberry ice cream earlier, and watching Hannah indulge in hers made her crave more.

"You'll make me order some more," she said with a groan and stood up to retrieve some cupcakes from the kitchen for them to share. "You know, my mother used to make extra treats for the house during Christmas. On Christmas Eve, we spent it here at the bakery with my aunt, and anyone from the town who wanted to join us," she said, flashing Hannah a wistful smile. "I don't think that will happen this year."

Lucy gasped when Hannah finished the last scoop of her ice cream and punched her playfully on the arm. "Well, Christmas is all about making fresh memories, so I am sure this year we'll find something fun to do."

"Yeah," Lucy agreed and lowered her gaze for a bit. She raised her head when an idea slipped into her mind, and her lips widened into a grin. "I have an idea," she blurted out and jumped out of her chair.

Lucy paced around the open part of the dining area and propped her hands on her hips. "Decorating," she said.

"Decorating is your idea?" Hannah asked, scratching her head. "Doesn't everyone decorate at Christmas?"

"They do, but I meant decorating Sweet Delights. Putting up some lights and a Christmas tree. Then hosting a small party here for the local kids." Lucy could already imagine what it would look like on Christmas Eve, having kids over for some treats and then selling everything in the bakery at a discount. Maybe she could also take part in the seasonal bake fair.

Her mind was already buzzing with different ideas she could use to create a new tradition for Christmas this year. Her parents were no longer here, but she could never forget them, or the fun she had each year.

"Well, your plan sounds fun," Hannah agreed. "It will be nice to do some sort of bake sale too, you know. Ivy Creek's seasonal bake sale is a sure way to make money and then there's the publicity too because many families will reunite with their loved ones this season and you could get customers from out of town."

Lucy loved Hannah, and her brilliant ideas, but this time around she was really thinking about doing something purely fun. She shook her head, walked over to Hannah, and patted her shoulder.

"Do you even know how to have fun?" she teased.

"I'm more fun than you are, Lucy. Trust me," she replied, and they both burst into a fit of laughter. "Last year, I got my entire family presents for Christmas, and we went to the cinema to see a Christmas-themed movie before the carols on Christmas eve. What fun did you have on your end?"

Lucy remembered she still lived in the city back then, and she had done little. "I had a hot date," she replied, then stuck her tongue out at Hannah.

"What hot date? You're lying," Hannah replied, shaking her head as she turned away from Lucy.

The bakery door opened, and Hannah gathered the empty ice cream cups while Lucy welcomed the customer she recognized as the town's local pastor.

"Hello, Lucy," he greeted with a warm smile, his brown eyes settling on hers. "How are you?"

"I'm doing fine, Pastor Evans," she replied. "How are you doing? And your wife, Sarah?"

"Please, Noah is fine."

Noah Evans ran the town's local Baptist church Lucy and her parents attended when she was younger. The man had blessed her parents' marriage; he was also present when Lucy was born in the town's local clinic, and then again at her parent's funeral earlier that year.

In the years since she last saw him, he had aged. Most of his brown hair had streaks of white in it, and he had even gained a little weight.

"It's good to see you're doing well here, Lucy," he said.

"Is there something I can get you?" Lucy asked as she walked around the counter. Noah followed and placed both hands on the counter, leaning closer to it.

"Some cinnamon cake," he replied. "A church member dropped by my place and gave my wife and me some of your cinnamon cake and it tasted amazing. Reminded me so much of your mother's baking. She used to bring my wife and me pastries on Sundays when she had the chance, and I loved them."

The recipe also reminded Lucy of her parents. It was the first flavored cake she learned to bake when she turned sixteen, and she could never forget the look of pure joy on her parent's face when they tasted her baking for the first time.

"It reminds me of her, too," Lucy replied, and sealed up his paper bag. She handed it over to him, and he nodded as he took the bag from her. "I'm glad you enjoy them."

"Your mother would have been so proud to see how much you've accomplished here," he complimented, and looked around the bakery. "You're a tough one, Lucy Hale, just like your parents."

Lucy rubbed her palms together. "Thanks, Noah. I've added an extra chocolate cupcake for your wife. I remember how much she loves those."

"That's so sweet of you. You know the church made a tradition of giving out to the homeless and singing carols every Christmas. We'll be doing the same this year and it will be nice if you could bring us some treats and join in the entire event. It would feel nice to have you around, Lucy."

"What day is the event?"

"Sometime before Christmas," he replied, taking out some cash to pay for his order. "We stroll the streets singing carols and end up in the church or anywhere someone has volunteered to host us for the night. I think we would have the name of a host soon for this year's carol."

Lucy thought about contributing to the event for a second. She had just suggested creating a new Christmas tradition for Hannah, and this sounded like the perfect opportunity to do that. It would be more interesting because a lot of the citizens of Ivy Creek would take part in it and they could even meet new people—potential customers.

All she had to do was bake some treats and join in the fun.

"I'd love to bring some treats to the carol, Noah. If you inform me of a time and venue, I'll definitely work towards it."

"That's so nice of you, Lucy," he replied. "I'll sure let you know the venue. Happy holidays," he said and waved at her before making his way out of the bakery.

"Say hello to Sarah for me, and happy holidays," she called after him. Lucy's smile remained after he left the bakery.

Hannah returned to the dining area just then, and Lucy asked. "We're baking treats for the town's Christmas Carol night," she announced in a cheery tone.

Hannah dropped the pan of cookies she had already wrapped. "I heard Lucy. I just don't think it's such a great idea," she replied with less enthusiasm than Lucy expected.

"Why not? Sounds like fun and it's a good way to give back to the community. It will just be like Halloween when the kids go trick-or-treating. We will sing carols while walking from house to house, and afterwards, the participants would have a lot to feast on. Also, the homeless in town will enjoy some of our treats," she explained, already open to the idea. Lucy wanted Hannah to warm up to it too, as she joined her in arranging the packed cookies on the counter.

"I know it sounds like fun, but we could make sales here if we sell at the store instead of wasting our time on some road trip carol," she shrugged as she spoke. "I just don't think it's a good idea. Think about how many sales we might miss."

"Oh, come on! Loosen up a little. It's Christmas. We'd meet new people and advertise our products by sharing our treats. I am so positive about this, Hannah. It's something new to do over the holidays, a new tradition."

Hannah was quiet for a while before she released a defeated sigh that made Lucy reach out for a high five. "If you say so, then let's do it," Hannah said as she forced herself to smile.

"Trust me, it's Christmas, and we'll have fun doing this." She had known Pastor Evans for years, and this was the town's Christmas Carols.

What was the worst thing that could happen?

2

A few days later, Lucy woke up bright and early and had a spring in her step. She sang along to the lyrics of a pop song, and she moved her hips in rhythm to the song. She applied more frosting on the top of the cupcakes and perfected each one with care, while enjoying the tune playing in her head.

She took a step back when she finished with the frosting and clapped her hands together to admire her work. "Perfect," she muttered to herself, grinning as she admired the red and green Christmas-themed design on the cupcakes.

The kitchen door swung open, and she looked up to see Hannah walk into the kitchen carrying three shopping bags. Hannah paused when her gaze landed on the cupcakes arranged on the table in delivery paper boxes, and she lifted her eyes to Lucy's.

"Don't you think this is too much?" she asked, walking to meet Lucy where she stood at the table. "Oh, Lucy, how many cupcakes did you bake?"

"Maybe over a hundred," Lucy replied with a sheepish grin. She groaned when Hannah arched a brow.

"A hundred and fifty?" Hannah said as her eyes widened.

Lucy continued with a wave of her hand. "Come on, it's for charity, and besides, this is Christmas. You need to get in the holiday spirit and loosen up, Hannah."

"Oh, I'm loose," Hannah replied with a gentle shake of her head. "I went to a nearby clothing store today, and I got everyone at home a pair of pajamas."

"Pajamas? Really?" Lucy teased. "You got your parents, sister, and yourself... pajamas?"

"Yes," Hannah replied proudly as she strolled over to the counter. "In my family, we wear pajamas on Christmas morning, and sit in front of the decorated tree to open our presents—It's tradition."

"And you have to wear pajamas for that?" Lucy burst into laughter and shot Hannah an apologetic smile. "I don't mean to tease but, I think sharing cupcakes sounds better."

Hannah rolled her eyes and emptied the cup of water she held in the sink. "I'm happy to bake cupcakes for charity. I just think you might have gone overboard on this one."

Lucy sighed when Hannah came over to her and placed both hands on her shoulder. "Maybe you're too excited about this. Wait, let me guess... Richard Lester will be there, right? It's a town occasion, and his late relatives were huge donors to these kinds of events. Is that why you're so excited? Oh, my... are you trying to impress him?"

It was Hannah's turn to laugh, and Lucy punched her playfully in the arm before turning back to clean up the kitchen.

"Impressing Richard is the last thing on my mind. I'm doing this because Christmas is the time to share, and this is an opportunity to do that. Besides, we'd be giving out free treats. That means many happy bellies in Ivy Creek."

"Hmm, I believe you," Hannah replied, her eyes dancing.

Richard Lester popped up in her conversation with Hannah once in a while since Lucy went on her first date with him weeks ago. He ran a cafe in town, and Lucy enjoyed popping in there for some chamomile tea whenever she was in that part of town.

Lucy knew the tone of her voice suggested she didn't believe a word she just said, and she chuckled.

She finished cleaning the kitchen and hurried up to her apartment to get ready for the occasion. When she returned, Hannah had packaged the cupcakes and put them in the back seat of Lucy's car.

"Ready to go?" Lucy asked as Hannah locked the kitchen doors.

Hannah turned to her and replied in a sing-song voice. "You're wearing make-up, and you claim you're not trying to impress the man. Dream on, Lucy."

Hannah's statement ended with a laugh, and Lucy joined in as they headed out to her car so they could make it to the venue in time to watch the choir sing the Christmas carols.

*

Lucy sang along as the carolers belted out popular songs. She had set up a stand at the back of the tents set in the churchyard, and the attendance was more than Lucy expected.

She saw some people she hadn't seen in a while. Aunt Tricia, her mother's sister who recently moved back to town, sat close to her stand, humming along to 'Silent Night' as the pianist performed a solo. She also saw Becky Anderson, a businesswoman she worked with months back in the front row with some women, Lucy didn't know.

Lucy sucked in a deep breath. It was good she had attended the event. At least this way, she could blend in more than she already had. She angled her head towards the entrance again and saw Taylor, her ex-boyfriend, and the town's deputy sheriff walk in with his mother.

Lucy's heart warmed from watching the crowd. When she was younger, the town had celebrated like this during Christmas, but her parents hosted most of such gatherings, and it was usually a typical dinner hosted in the town's hall on the evening of Christmas Eve where they would sing songs, eat, and enjoy long discussions.

She believed things like this brought people together, and she was glad she had contributed to it.

"Having fun?" a voice asked behind her, and she turned to see Richard.

Lucy gave him a brief hug, and he pecked her on both cheeks, bringing heat to the back of her neck before he pulled away.

"Wow, you made a lot," he said, commenting on her full stand.

"What can I say? I love Christmas."

The carol ended minutes after Richard arrived, and people flocked towards her stand in pairs to get their fill of her treats. Lucy happily served them, alongside Richard and Hannah.

When most of them had received a cupcake, Pastor Noah Evans

came to her stand with his wife, Sarah. Lucy greeted them both with a warm smile, hugging Sarah briefly.

"Thank you so much for doing this, Lucy," Sarah said. "You've made many people here happy."

"I'm glad I could be of help, and I'd do more anytime," Lucy replied.

Lucy's discussion with the pastor and his wife was interrupted when a lady walked up to them and asked Lucy in a curt tone. "Do you have any more treats other than what I see on this table?"

Lucy turned to the lady. "Hello," she said and handed her a cupcake.

The woman took it. "I mean, I need more," she continued briskly as she took a bite of the cupcake and chewed. "I run a shelter for homeless people, and a lot of them could not make it here today because, well, they couldn't afford to. Don't you think we should give them some treats, too?"

"Tabitha, take yours and let others have a taste of the treats," Sarah said before Lucy could reply.

"I wasn't talking to you," Tabitha replied. She hissed and looked at Lucy, her gaze flickering over her body. "I was talking to Miss Nice Pants over here."

Lucy blinked, taken aback by the woman's rudeness. Tabitha wore a sneer, and she didn't mind that people had stopped and were staring at Lucy's counter.

"I want more cupcakes for the hungry souls back at my shelter. This is charity, right? Then you don't mind showing the poor folks some kindness."

"Well, you can have some cupcakes for them," Lucy replied and masked her annoyance with a grin. She wanted nothing to spoil the cheery mood she was in.

Hannah was about to protest beside her, but she gave her a cautious look that made her stay put.

Lucy packed some cupcakes into a free box, added three extras, and handed it over to Tabitha. "Here you go."

"Is that it?" Tabitha asked as she snatched the box away. "Do you know what it means to be homeless? Surely you can't assume that this will be enough," she continued, eyeing Lucy.

Quietly, Lucy packed a dozen more cupcakes for her. She noticed a few people from the crowd had turned around to watch the scene, and she didn't want all the attention on her.

Tabitha collected the second pack. "You seem like a caring one, Miss Nice Pants," she remarked and her gaze dropped on the jeans Lucy wore. "Not everyone is as lucky as you folks," she hissed and pushed past Pastor Noah and his wife as she walked away.

"Well, that was some character," Lucy murmured when she was gone.

Noah and Sarah nodded in agreement. "I apologize on her behalf," Noah said.

"Oh, it's nothing. I just hope those cupcakes make some homeless person's day brighter," she replied and looked in the direction where Tabitha had departed moments ago.

Noah and Sarah said their goodbyes and moved on to talk to other people at the event while Lucy turned to Hannah and Richard. "This was fun, wasn't it?" she asked, her eyes mainly on Hannah because she wanted to see her expression.

"Oh, yes, it was," Hannah replied with a laugh. "I'm glad I came, but it doesn't trump my pajamas morning with the family."

They started packing up the stand. Aunt Tricia joined them as they rounded up, and she joined in their small talk about the event and how angelic the carolers sounded as they sang.

As they drove back to the bakery, a song about Christmas was playing on the radio, and they all sang along to the lyrics. Lucy was glad she found a new tradition for Christmas, and as she rounded the corner leading to the main street, she wondered about Tabitha and the homeless souls she had referred to.

Lucy wondered if the homeless would overlook Tabitha's brutish behavior and enjoy the cupcakes with gladness in their hearts.

3

The good vibes from the caroling event stayed with Lucy the rest of that evening. The next morning when she got down to the bakery, she met Hannah at the front counter taking notes from a man standing with his identical triplet daughters.

"You have really lovely little girls," Hannah complimented as she packaged his order of kale chips, bread, and a double latte espresso.

"Thank you, Hannah," he said and took the hand of the nearest girl. "My girls are a lot to handle on my own, but they're still a joy."

"I can see," Hannah replied with a chuckle, and Lucy joined her to wave as the man took his order and left the bakery.

Lucy walked over to Hannah and joined her in serving the other customers in line. Hannah took the orders while Lucy packaged them and handed them over before Hannah took the cash.

They worked like that in sync for a few minutes before the store emptied again. "We have a lot of customers trooping in today. I think word has spread about Sweet Delights and people are driving down from the far end of town to try out our pastries," Hannah said. "Turns out the charity work at the church paid off, even though we were giving away free cupcakes."

"I know, right," Lucy replied, and tucked her shirt into her jeans. "I'm glad it's working for us."

They went into the kitchen, and Hannah took out the notepad in the pocket of her apron. "We've got two deliveries this morning. One downtown, and the other at the police station. We don't have any available drivers to make the delivery. Do you think you could handle these two?"

"Of course," Lucy replied.

Hannah was saying something about deliveries, and she had lost track for a moment because her mind wandered, but she quickly re-directed her attention back to Hannah.

"Right, I will drive down to drop them off. When I come back, we can start working on the last order you just took from the man with the triplets."

"Mr. Johannesen?" Hannah said. "He's well known in town as the ever-dotting father. When his wife gave birth to the triplets, he stepped back from a 9-5 routine job, started a local business, and hired an operations manager to handle the day to day running of the business, while he spent time with his family."

"I admire him," Hannah said wistfully.

"You'll find your Mr. Right. Don't worry," Lucy told her.

She turned around to pick up the order Hannah had prepared on the table, and bent down to stroke her white Persian cat, Gigi, who had just sauntered in.

Lucy's heart melted when it purred, then flipped over to lie on its back. "I'll see you later, Gigi," she said and straightened again. She took the orders out with the note Hannah handed her and drove down to the station first to drop off the chips and cupcakes the officers ordered.

Lucy met a few of them standing outside the station when she arrived, and she handed over the package to Dan, an officer she knew.

"How are you, Lucy?" he asked as he paid for the order.

"I'm doing great, Dan. How are things around here? Is there a lot of trouble during the holidays?"

"Well, there's always trouble in Ivy Creek. We just try to do our best and hope no one spoils the fun for others."

"That's great work you do," she replied.

Lucy craned her neck and looked around a little, trying to see if she could spot Taylor. He hadn't come over to the stand yesterday to say hello, and she saw him leave after the carolers stopped singing.

Maybe he was in a hurry to get to work, she thought, and looked at Dan again. "I should go. I have deliveries to make."

"Bye, Lucy," he said, waving as she headed back to her car.

She drove to the second address, which was an office near the church building, and delivered the bread and macaroons. At the front desk, she noticed the receptionist opening a paper bag of cupcakes. He took one out after he handed her cash for the order, and the wrapper design caught Lucy's attention.

Lucy paused instead of walking away and edged closer to the table again.

"Hey," she said, gaining his attention. "You know, that cupcake looks delicious, and I'm wondering where I can get one for myself?"

"Oh, you can get one at a hotel right around the corner from here. I sometimes go there for breakfast and it was on the dessert menu today. The place is called Blue River, and it's not far off from here."

"That's very kind of you, thanks," Lucy replied before walking off.

Lucy drove down the road, rounded the corner, and saw the building with a big maroon sign in front. She went to the hotel and made her way inside.

The ground floor had a restaurant, dining room, and several conference rooms. She imagined the upper floors housed the rooms for guests. The hotel staff she walked past were dressed neatly in well-pressed shirts and matching pants, and she admired the city landscape paintings on the surrounding walls.

Lucy noticed they were running a buffet service when she saw the setting and display of dishes on a table by the far end of the dining room.

"Hello, what would you like? Our menu for the day is on the other side," the waiter said to her.

Lucy forced a smile. Her curiosity peaked when she saw more customers stroll towards the buffet stand and return with cupcakes.

Is this pure coincidence? Or is someone intentionally serving my cupcakes at this restaurant without my knowledge.

She headed for the buffet stand to see what else they had on the menu for herself, and she heard some customers whisper about how good the cupcakes tasted as they walked past her.

"I hope they serve them every day," one lady said to the other as they picked another cupcake from the display table.

"Hello, excuse me," Lucy called, tapping on the shoulder of the man in front of her in the buffet queue. "Do they serve these regularly?"

"No, it's the first time the owners brought them in," he replied. "They're really worth it. Try one… this is my third cupcake."

"I'd like to meet the owner. Do you know where I can find—"

The man pointed at the entrance before Lucy ended her question. She spun around to see the woman she met at the church the previous day, and her eyes narrowed to tiny silts.

"There she is. I guess she just came in."

"Thanks," Lucy murmured as the man walked away with his plate, and Lucy walked over to where she stood.

She took in her round frame, noticing she was quite bigger than she remembered from seeing her yesterday. She wore a red dress that did nothing to hide her rounded mid-section and full limbs. The look on her face was displeasing, and in Lucy's opinion, Tabitha would look a lot better if she tried to not frown or glare often.

"What you did was wrong. You know there were other people who could have benefited from my cupcakes, and what you did deprived them of it," Lucy said.

She jabbed a finger in Tabitha's direction and added with an unflinching stare, her anger bubbling higher. "I can't let you get away with this."

Tabitha flung her head back and cackled softly. "What will you do?" she asked, taking a step towards Lucy. "You can't do anything, Miss Nice Pants. You really thought I was going to give all those cupcakes to homeless people? You're gullible…. It's best you get out of my building, or I'll have you thrown out."

Lucy stood her ground, unwilling to let Tabitha have the final say. "This is deceitful," she accused again.

"Well, what are you going to do about it?" Tabitha tossed back, gently lifting one shoulder. "John, please see the young lady out of my building," she said, turning to the security man standing by the curve near the receptionist table.

The man led Lucy out of the building while she tried to walk as fast as she could. Outside, she bottled down a scream and got into her car.

As Lucy drove back to her bakery, she replayed the altercation she'd had with Tabitha and wondered why anyone would want to do something so mean.

4

As Lucy walked through the doors at Sweet Delights, she put a smile on her face to mask the rage she still felt bubbling on the inside. She noticed the bakery was full of customers and joined Hannah in attending to them.

They served the treats they had in stock, and at intervals, Hannah checked on the treats baking in the oven. Lucy's mind still spiraled with thoughts of how she could have handled her interaction with Tabitha. She knew some people would just say it was cupcakes, but it was more than cupcakes to her. She baked each cupcake, hoping it would bring some Christmas cheer to whoever ate them. It was never her intention for them to serve the purposes of a rude and lazy business owner.

"We'll need more supplies if we're going to bake these large amounts for the rest of the holiday," Hannah was saying as she took cash from a customer.

"That's right," Lucy said. She turned to the next lady in the queue. "What would you like to have?"

"A soy-caramel coffee please, and three gluten-free bread, and muffins."

Lucy smiled at her. "Coming right up."

"You know this place has delightful treats and I love coming here, but it's lacking one thing," the lady said as she accepted her order from Lucy.

Lucy leaned in towards the lady. "What's missing?" she asked, her eyes wide. *Did I forget an ingredient in my recipe? Or is there something missing from the dining setting?*

Lucy couldn't figure out what the lady was getting at until she saw a lopsided grin spread across her face.

"Christmas decorations!" she pointed out. "It's the holidays, Lucy. You can add a bit of color and decorations to spice the place up. It'll really make this place more inviting this time of the year," she added and tipped her plastic cup in Lucy's direction before walking away.

Lucy quickly looked around her bakery. The lady's suggestion made sense, and she made a mental note to put up some lights, trees, and fixtures to give the place a festive look for the season. She knew how decorations could alter the atmosphere around the bakery. Plus, putting them up would be fun.

When they finished serving the customers, Lucy let out a deep sigh and leaned over the counter.

"Are you all right?" Hannah asked her as she closed the cash register. "You look flushed, and you have this redness all over your ears. Did something annoy you?"

Lucy opened her mouth to recount the scene with Tabitha, but before she could say anything, Noah Evans stepped into the bakery wearing a full smile.

"Hello, Lucy. How is business today?"

"Great, Noah," she replied.

Hannah patted her shoulder and went into the kitchen while she focused her attention on Noah. "Would you like anything?"

"Yes, some macaroons please, and three coffee-flavored cupcakes. My wife won't stop craving them," he replied with a light chuckle.

"I'm pleased to know she loves them."

Lucy started working on his order, and he continued. "There's an award night event at the church tonight, and I dropped by to invite you. It's a celebration we do to appreciate members of the church and town folk who have contributed over the year."

Lucy handed him the paper bag containing his treats. "I don't know, Noah. Things are quite hectic here today, so I can't promise to attend."

"I understand," he replied, and handed her cash, taking his order. "I would love to have you around anyway, so if you can make it, please do."

"Okay."

"Have a nice day," he said and walked away.

Lucy watched the door swing shut behind him and she rubbed her eyes with both hands. Her cell phone buzzed in her pocket, and she picked it up on the second ring.

"Lucy, honey, will I see you for dinner at Christmas? I'm making plans, dear, and I'd like to have you and Hannah's family around," Aunt Tricia said.

"Christmas dinner sounds like fun, auntie," she replied.

"Great, dear. I'm attending the award night at New Baptist Church today. Are you coming?"

Lucy rubbed her temple. "I told Pastor Evans I'd consider it."

"All right, talk to you soon. Love you."

"Love ya," Lucy replied, and hung up.

Lucy heard Hannah calling her name, so she hurried into the kitchen to help her check on the items baking while Hannah frosted a birthday cake.

"Will you be attending the awards night at New Hope?" Hannah asked as she perfected the design, adding more color to give the cake more beauty.

"Um… not sure. Are you attending?"

"Yeah," Hannah responded. "My sister's presenting the awards alongside Sarah Evans, the pastor's wife."

"Interesting," Lucy said and went to the sink to wash her hands.

"You sure you're all right?" Hannah asked.

"Yeah, I'm fine," she replied, not wanting to bring up the drama she'd had with Tabitha. "I'll be right back," Lucy said and headed up the stairs to her apartment to use the restroom.

*

Later that evening, Lucy drove down to the church to attend the event. She had nothing better to do, and she figured she could pass time there. She went with some brownies and cupcakes to serve the guests and when she made her way into the auditorium, the first face she saw was Becky Anderson's.

"Lucy," the woman greeted and helped Lucy with the packs she held. "It's been a while. How have you been holding up?"

"I've been all right, Becky. How have you been? I haven't seen you around town in a while," Lucy replied as they reached a table in the back row and set her packs down on it.

She had done business with Becky Anderson months ago, and although it had ended on an unpleasant note with a guest getting murdered that same night after eating her cupcakes, Lucy still admired the woman.

"I left town for a while to clear my head, and just got back for the holidays."

"So, you're back permanently? Or will you be leaving again?" Lucy asked, dropping what she was doing to look into Becky's eyes.

"I'm back for good," she replied. "It feels good to have you around," Becky said as she patted the side of Lucy's arm.

"It's good to have you back, Becky. Hopefully, you'll stop by Sweet Delights to indulge in some festive treats. It will be on the house, so you can drop by anytime."

Becky's hand moved to her chest, and Lucy noticed the expensive jewelry she wore on her wrist and finger. "Thank you so much, Lucy. Enjoy the evening."

Becky walked away, and Lucy settled in a chair in the back row. She saw Hannah in front when she whipped her head around, and Lucy grinned, waving at her.

Hannah gave her a thumb's up and turned around to continue

watching the event. Her sister was upfront on the pulpit giving a speech before she called out the first award for the night, and Lucy sucked in a deep breath, and smoothed a hand over the black, patterned dress she wore.

The speech dragged on for a while, and the crowd applauded before Sarah joined Hannah's sister Stacey in the pulpit.

"Now, it's time to give out the awards to those who've merited it for the year. We have a lot of wonderful families amongst us, and we appreciate everyone even though there isn't an award for everyone," Sarah said, and Lucy allowed her gaze to drift around the congregation.

A shiver raced up her spine. She couldn't understand it, but it made every part of her alert, like she was watching out for something, or expecting something to happen.

Whenever she experienced jittery nerves, something always went wrong in the end. Lucy swallowed and diverted her attention to the women on the stage.

"And the first award for tonight goes to the most dedicated member of the charity committee in Ivy Creek," Sarah said, then stepped back for Stacey to announce the winner.

"The award goes to Tabitha Alli."

The crowd gave a muted applause, and Lucy rolled her eyes as she watched Tabitha make her way to the front while enjoying a cupcake she held in one hand.

"Thank you, everyone," Tabitha said, waving. She took the wrapped award and waved again, but this time grinning. "This means a lo—" her words ended in a choke.

Tabitha coughed, and her hand moved to her neck before she slumped to the ground with a loud thud. Murmurs erupted amongst the crowd from different corners, and Sarah dropped to her knees to check on Tabitha on the floor.

"We need a doctor here," she called out with a frantic wave, her voice edgy.

Lucy remained rooted to her chair, unable to move as she watched the scene unfold. The fidgety movements and anxious whispers drowned every other thought, and adrenaline coursed through her.

Three men rushed to the pulpit. One of them said, "I'm a doctor, I'll check her."

Lucy watched the man drop to his knees, and seconds later when he raised his head, he announced in a chill voice that Lucy knew would stay in her head for a long time, "She's... she's dead."

5

The muffled murmurs turned to chaos after the announcement, but Lucy remained rooted to her chair, her heartbeat racing as people scurried to get out of the church auditorium. Mothers dragged their children towards the door, and others hurried out in pairs, not bothering to hide their fear as they screamed and pressed each other to get out.

Stacey still stood on the pulpit, her hands on her lips, and Lucy could see the terror in her eyes as she looked around. Pastor Evans and his wife were by Stacey's side, and the man who checked Tabitha seconds ago stood up from his crouching position.

"She has no pulse, she's dead," he said again.

Panicked voices and murmurs floated past her as the crowd dispersed, and her mind raced.

What just happened? She's dead? How did...

Lucy nearly screamed when a hand touched her. She bolted out of her chair, eyes wide, and lips slightly parted as she turned around to see Richard holding her arm.

"It's me," he said and came to stand beside her.

Lucy looked around the almost empty church, trying to find Hannah or her Aunt Tricia.

"We should get out of here," Richard suggested.

She shook her head. "No... I have to find Hannah and my aunt," she said, willing her head to stop spinning. When she saw Pastor Evans make his way towards where she stood, his eyes drawn together in a frown, she moved and met him halfway.

"I just called the cops," he began. "They're on their way here as I speak."

Lucy's hand moved to cover her mouth, and she asked in a shaky voice. "Is she really dead?" Lucy asked, still trying to wrap her head around what just happened.

Pastor Evans's eyes bored into hers, and she muttered, "Oh God."

Richard's hand came around her shoulder, and he pulled her closer to him. His fingers squeezed into her arm, and she shook her head again.

"Excuse me," Pastor Evans said and headed for the door.

Richard steered Lucy towards the exit. Her legs felt like jelly, and she couldn't stop the dreadful rumbling in the pit of her stomach.

They reached the door at the same time the police arrived. Three officers marched towards the church with quick steps and stopped them from exiting the building completely.

"No one else leaves till we get everyone's statement," one of them announced, spreading his arms to block Richard and Lucy's path.

"Miss, please step back into the building," the officer said to another woman trying to leave the church. The second cop went into the building, and Lucy turned back to Richard.

"Let's go back inside and give our statements," she said in a flat voice. She rubbed her sweaty palms on her sides as they walked towards the entrance. Lucy had a slow flight response; she could have raced out of the hall when Tabitha collapsed, but her body remained glued to the chair.

They walked over to the front, where Stacey and Sarah still knelt beside Tabitha's lifeless body. The pale look on Stacey's face made the knots in Lucy's stomach tighten, and she took a deep breath to keep the rising nausea away.

Richard helped her to a seat, and he held her hand the entire time as they watched the cops talk to Stacey and Sarah at the pulpit. Lucy knew they would come to question her, and she braced herself for the questions.

She knew nothing about this. Just like every other person in the church, she witnessed Tabitha mount the front stage to speak and drop to the ground. The officers finished with Stacey and Sarah in a few minutes, and then they moved to two other women, then Pastor Evans, before they came to where she sat.

Lucy raised her chin a bit and licked her dry lips.

"Miss Hale?" the officer asked, and she responded with a slight nod. "Did you know Mrs. Alli personally?"

"No," Lucy replied. "We met for the first time at the town's Christmas carol."

"I understand you served the treats at the event tonight, and also at the Christmas Carol."

"Yes, I did." Lucy paused for a second. "What has that got to do with this?"

"We are simply covering all grounds, Miss Hale," the officer replied. He took out a notepad, and asked Lucy a few more questions about the treats she served, and if she had run into Tabitha before the start of the event.

"I met Tabitha recently."

"When was this? At the caroling event?"

"No. It was at her hotel."

"What did you think of her? Tabitha Alli, what was your relationship with her like?"

"We didn't have any sort of relationship," she replied quickly and felt Richard squeeze her hand slightly. Lucy tried to control her nerves. She knew where these questions were leading. These cops had a way of implying guilt. She had to be alert not to say anything incriminating.

She had been labeled a person of interest in a previous murder investigation in town simply because of her association with the victims before their death.

"Look, officer, I had nothing to do with this. Just like everyone else here, I'm in shock. I do not know what happened here, and I'd just—" she stopped to catch her breath. "I just want to leave this place."

"I understand that Miss, but we ask these questions as part of our job, and not to accuse you of anything," he replied, then rose to his feet. "We will be in touch if we need anything else."

"Thank you."

Hannah approached where she sat with Richard when the officers left, and she stood up again.

"God, this has been an eventful day," Hannah commented and wiped the hair on her forehead away. "How are you? What happened was shocking, yeah?"

"It was," Lucy agreed. She ran her fingers through her hair and bit her lower lip. "They don't know what happened yet?"

Hannah shook her head. They both glanced back towards the pulpit where Pastor Evans still stood with some officers, his wife, and three other men.

"Did they ask you anything about your treats?" Hannah asked.

"Yes, they did."

"I suspected they would. Someone mentioned they saw Tabitha eating some treats before they called her forward to receive the award. I just can't believe this happened here in church of all the places in town."

Lucy saw Hannah shudder. She had her own anxieties about the inevitable investigation that was already in motion over Tabitha's death and what that might entail. She had experienced it before, and she didn't want to again.

"This seems so surreal. I can't believe this is happening again," Lucy muttered. "Have you seen Aunt Tricia anywhere?"

"I think she left when everyone was rushing to get out."

"We should leave too," Richard chirped in.

Lucy realized her hand was still in his, and he squeezed it gently, looked at her, and gave her a tiny smile.

"Yes, we should."

They left the church. Lucy waved Hannah and Richard goodbye and got into her car to drive back home. On the route back to the bakery, she replayed the tragic scene that had occurred in the church in her head.

337

From what she could tell, Tabitha Alli was not exactly a model citizen of Ivy Creek, so it was possible she had lots of enemies, right?

Why would anyone want Tabitha dead? And who could it be? Or was her death due to natural causes?

Lucy tried not to think about it, but it was all that ran through her mind. She approached her bakery ten minutes later and parked her car in the back of the building. She got out and headed for her apartment upstairs.

Gigi greeted her when she reached her living room and followed her into the bedroom as she took off her clothes. "I'm so tired, Gigi," she murmured, picked up her cat, and settled in her bed.

With a deep sigh, Lucy made herself comfortable and stroked her cat's fur. Once again, someone had died in Ivy Creek, and somehow, she was linked to it.

Why does this always happen to me?

6

Lucy was absent-mindedly mixing a new batch of brownies when the front door opened, and Hannah walked into the kitchen seconds later. The previous night, she had tossed in bed for a while, thinking about Tabitha's sudden death before she finally fell asleep, and Lucy imagined what it would be like for her family right now.

She lost her parents earlier in the year, and it had been a rocky few months since then. Even if Tabitha wasn't an angel, her family still did not deserve to go through the heartache of losing her suddenly.

"Hey," Hannah greeted, and took off the satchel hanging on her shoulder. "Did you get any message of the award you won? The church sent out messages to the other recipients last night.

"You know we might receive an award too. Probably for serving the best treats in town, and making people happy," Hannah continued. She grinned at Lucy when Lucy stole a glance at her and continued. "Winning an award will help our business—expand it and help us gain more publicity."

"You think we would have won an award last night?" Lucy asked.

"Yes… I mean, we obviously deserve one."

Lucy continued sieving flour into a dry bowl for the brownies quietly as Hannah talked. "Well, I didn't get any message," she replied, then raised her head to meet Hannah's gaze. "Tabitha died yesterday, remember? And that ended the event. So, did they still give out awards after that?"

"They sent out messages this morning. My mother received one for the most active member."

"That's nice," Lucy said and reached for her phone in her apron to check. "Maybe I would get one, but so far, I haven't."

"Oh…" Hannah shrugged and joined her at the table and began gathering the items she needed to make cupcakes.

Lucy stopped sieving when Hannah started humming and faced her. "I just can't get Tabitha's face out of my head. What happened was tragic."

"Truly," Hannah replied. "My sister kept talking about it this morning and I couldn't hang around to hear her say more. She said the cops have started their investigation."

Hannah's statement about the investigation made Lucy's throat tighten, and she continued her sieving again. Minutes later, brownies were in the oven, and she had moved on to another task.

They worked together in silence for a while till she heard someone call for her in the front and went out to attend to the customers.

"Good morning. What would you like to get?"

"Three macaroons, please," the young customer replied, her gaze fixed on the display glass. "Make that four, I can't seem to get enough of your pastries."

Lucy attended to a few more customers, and she sold the rest of the cupcakes available, and some bread before she returned to the kitchen to join Hannah again.

"We have a delivery to an office downtown," Lucy said as she bent over the oven to check the brownies. Her recipe always required minimal heat and a little longer baking time because she always tried to avoid burned pans, so she checked to make sure the heat was reduced, and she set the timer.

"They ordered brownies, cupcakes, and coconut bread this morning, and they need their order by evening today."

"Where is the place?"

"Same place I delivered bread to at sixth avenue three days ago. Their office complex is just by Blue River Hotel."

"Right, Blue River Hotel," Hannah replied. "Tabitha owns that place. I wonder if it's open today, you know, after yesterday's tragedy."

"Maybe we can run this delivery together if we finish selling early today, so we drop by Aunt Tricia's place?" Lucy didn't want to drive around that zone alone. If the cops had started their investigation, then they would be around the hotel today.

"That sounds like a great idea. I also want to know what she thinks about what happened last night. It's all the town can talk about."

Lucy shook her head and continued working in the kitchen. Unlike Hannah, she didn't want to think about Tabitha's case at all. She remembered the last personal contact she had with Tabitha, and that she had been offended with her for what she did with the cupcakes she took from her at the Christmas carol. Who else had Tabitha offended? Was the offense so egregious that they wanted her dead?

She pushed Tabitha out of her mind. "Let's just try to finish up work early today," she suggested.

By midday, they closed the bakery to head out to the address where Lucy was to deliver three coconut loaves with three dozen cupcakes with sprinkles.

"That's Tabitha's hotel," Hannah commented as Lucy drove past Blue River Hotel, as she approached her destination and parked her car.

"I will be right back," Hannah said as she got out, and picked the delivery basket from the back seat. Lucy watched her disappear into the building, and she closed her eyes for a second, tapping her fingers on the steering wheel.

When she re-opened her eyes, she glanced toward Blue River Hotel. The hotel was open, and people were walking in and out of the building.

Lucy wanted to remain inside the car, but she couldn't, not after she noticed the hotel was open for business even after what happened to its owner the previous day.

She got out of her car and walked to the front of the building. Standing by an enormous tree in front of the building, she crossed her arms over her chest and pinned her gaze on the sliding doors in front of the building.

Two women stepped out of the hotel holding paper bags, and Lucy shifted her weight from one foot to the other. She knew it was not her business, but she didn't expect that the hotel would be open when the owner just passed away.

She wondered how the staff inside would feel about Tabitha's death. Most of them would have worked with her for some time, and she imagined they would be in a state of shock.

How was Tabitha to her workers? Was she also rude and over-bearing to them?

Lucy imagined what it would be like to work for a woman like Tabitha. She was certain she wouldn't be able to stand her personality or even endure working for her.

She didn't know how long she stood there and wasn't aware that someone had been standing beside her until she heard a voice.

"I can't believe she's gone."

Lucy turned to see a man standing next to her. He was tall and dressed in a black winter jacket with a tartan scarf wrapped around his neck. He offered her a half-baked smile that didn't reach his brown eyes, and Lucy saw his throat bob when he spoke.

"Life is so short. One day you're making plans for the future and the next you're no more. I'm still trying to come to terms with the fact that Tabitha is no more."

"I didn't know her well, but it's sad what happened," Lucy said and turned to the building again.

On both occasions she had met Tabitha, the woman had been rude and inconsiderate, and she wondered if that was how she regularly carried herself. If she was always that way—arrogant and loud, then how did she get along with anyone?

Without thinking, Lucy voiced her inner thoughts about Tabitha. "I wonder what happened, but then again, considering she was rude and greedy, it's no surprise that someone wanted her dead and killed her, right?"

Lucy didn't look at the man by her side as she continued. "A woman as rude as her would have made a lot of enemies, even in a small town like Ivy Creek, don't you think? I met her twice, and she was not pleasant in the interactions I had with her."

She saw the man shake his head from the corner of her eyes and finally glanced at her side to stare at him. His eyes bulged out, and he clenched his jaw hard as he stared at her. She saw his nostrils flare.

"I'm sorry… I don't think we've met before. I'm Lucy Hale," she said and extended a hand to him.

He accepted her gesture, but the hard-line on his lips didn't ease a bit, and his grip on her hand was tight as he said in a gruff voice. "Nice to meet you, too. I'm Justin Alli."

"Alli?" Her jaw went slack, and she croaked as she forced her hand out of his. Her cheeks instantly burned as heat rose there from the back of her neck. She remembered the words she just said about Tabitha and groaned inwardly.

Her stomach rolled over when he swayed his head gently and spoke. "Yes, I'm Tabitha's husband."

7

"Oh God, I'm so sorry," Lucy said as she took a step back. She made a slight hand gesture as she continued, not giving Justin the chance to say anything. "I didn't mean to speak ill of the dead, and I meant nothing I said in a bad way."

Justin's frown eased a little. "It's all right. I'm Tabitha's husband, and I know my wife was a handful," he said in a solemn voice. Justin slipped both hands into his pockets, and Lucy bit her lower lip. "She was difficult to work with, and not so friendly with people. What you said is nothing I haven't heard before."

His flat tone and cracked voice made Lucy's heart stutter. She lowered her head, feeling remorseful. "I'm really sorry," she said again.

Justin lifted his shoulder in a slight shrug.

"I shouldn't have said what I said."

"It's okay, Lucy," he said. "If you don't mind, you can come in with me, and I'll show you around the hotel. I know we've only just met, but somehow I feel like I have to show you the woman Tabitha was beneath the rude exterior she showed others."

Lucy nodded. "Sure, I'd like to see Blue River."

Justin led the way, and Lucy slipped her keys into the pocket of her wool jacket before following Justin into the building. He showed her around the ground floor where they had the reception and took her to a large waiting lounge.

Lucy admired the expensive chandelier in the middle of the foyer that brought the place alive, and she noticed the well-dressed servers carrying trays with glasses on them around the place.

"This is where most of our guests have dinner if they don't want room service," Justin said as she looked around the place.

At the corner of the room, someone sat in front of a huge piano and played a classical tune that the customers seemed to enjoy.

"This place is lovely," she complimented and he pointed to the stairs leading to the rooms. "I never imagined that it would be this big."

"We also have a bar and there's a games room for young families. Would you like me to show you the bar?"

"Yes, please," she replied.

He showed her the bar, and Lucy admired the dimly lit room. The bar was half-empty as most of the customers were still interested in the buffet and silver style service the restaurant offered.

"We got the property from a couple who wanted to move out-of-town years back, and Tabitha's hard work helped build it into what it is today. It might not be as big as what one would find in the city, but it was her life's work.

"We have some smaller rooms we offer at subsidized prices for those who can't afford our standard rooms. It's more like a place for them to rest at night, without having to worry about the high fees."

"I didn't know that," Lucy said.

They left the bar and headed back to the reception area. The elevator door opened as they walked past it, and a couple walked out hand-in-hand, waved at Justin, and walked into the restaurant to take a seat.

"I know you didn't," Justin replied.

Lucy felt another pang of guilt for what she said about Tabitha outside. Her first impression of the woman had led her to say that, but her husband seemed gentle and more jovial with the guests and staff.

She noticed he waved at some servers as they walked around, and a female worker who walked past them smiled at him. "Hello," he whispered to the lady before giving Lucy his attention again.

"Thanks for showing me around. I've only been here once, and I didn't make it past the outer reception where you have the buffet."

"You're welcome, Lucy."

He took her back to the buffet section, and she was about to thank him for the tour when a woman called for him.

"Yes?" Justin responded, and they both turned to see the woman approach them.

"There's someone on the phone for you, sir," she said when she reached where they stood, and Justin gave her a soft nod.

He turned to Lucy and spoke. "Please excuse me for a few minutes. I have to take this call. I'll be right back."

347

"No problem," Lucy replied, and he hurried away with the woman.

She looked around and headed towards the buffet display stand. There was a queue of three people by it, and she wandered close to it. Lucy saw someone dressed as a chef step out from a door to her left, and when the lady went back in, she followed.

Inside the kitchen, the scent of different spices hit her nostrils all at once. She saw the cooks hurry around trying to get everything ready for lunch, and Lucy admired the spacious and simple setting of the kitchen.

She saw one cook bring out a whole chicken from the oven, and another slid in a huge tray of chicken thighs. Chopping sounds filled the room, and the atmosphere was hotter than the rest of the hotel. Lucy had wiped a bead of sweat that was forming on her forehead.

It seems like they make a lot of sales here every day. They're cooking quite a large amount of food.

She stood by the doorway watching the scene till she felt a light tap on her shoulder. "Justin?" she called as she spun around.

Lucy gasped when she saw a woman's frown instead of Justin. She stared back into the stern dark eyes of the woman, and her breath hitched in her throat when the woman's hand formed a grip around her hand.

"What are you doing in here?" the woman asked.

8

Lucy yelped as the woman led her out of the kitchen to the outer corridor. She watched her shut the door behind her, then glare at her again. She took in her fierce dark eyes and the square jut of her chin.

"Who are you, and why are you lurking around here?" she asked.

Lucy searched her mind for words as the woman released her. "I was just... I'm sorry, I didn't mean any harm. I just wandered around and wanted to see what the kitchen was like," Lucy began explaining as the woman's jaw tightened further. She saw the lines on her forehead crease, and she folded her arms over her chest.

"The kitchen area is restricted and as a guest you shouldn't wander that far or else security will show you out."

"I'm really sorry," Lucy said again, wondering how many times she would apologize today. First off, she had almost offended Justin with her comment about Tabitha, and now this lady was glaring at her like she had committed a crime.

Her cheeks burned, and she extended a hand, hoping an introduction would lighten the mood. "I didn't mean any harm," she said to the female staff staring at her with wide, furious eyes. "I just got carried away because the kitchen smelled so nice. I'm Lucy... Lucy Hale. I run a bakery in town. It's called Sweet Delights."

At the mention of Sweet Delights, she saw the frown on the woman's face slowly disappear.

"You're that Lucy Hale?" she asked in an almost breathless voice before accepting Lucy's handshake. "Oh... I'm a huge fan of your bakery, an obsessed fan of your treats. It's nice to meet you. I'm Zara. Zara Stanmore," she continued and raised a hand to her chest. "Forgive me. I didn't know you were the owner of Sweet Delights. I hope I didn't appear rude to you."

"Of course not," Lucy replied, relief flooding through her. She laughed and shook her head. "It's nice to meet you, Zara."

"I'm the chief cook here, and I get worked up when things don't go according to plan," she continued, and Lucy noticed her shoulders slumped a little. "I keep everyone on their toes, so they don't mess up the meal schedule for the day."

"Must be a lot of work," Lucy responded. "It gets quite hectic when I work in the bakery too, and I barely keep it together with the help of just one employee. You seem to handle things here pretty well."

"I try my best, but yes, it does get a tad hectic. I've always wanted to meet you in person. I sometimes order treats from your bakery and also get them whenever I drop in at the grocery store. They always taste amazing, better than anything I've ever had."

"Thank you, Zara," Lucy said, blushing at the compliment. "I work hard to make sure my customers stay happy. It's the only way I can grow the business."

"Oh, tell me about it," Zara commented wryly, twisting her lips to a corner as she spoke. "I've always tried to make a strong point of making sure customers are happy, but it never seems to fly around here."

"What?"

She waved a hand at Lucy. "I mean, you obviously have a good work ethic, and appreciate your customers by making sure you give them the best. This hotel would be the premier hotel in town if we worked that way."

Lucy adjusted the sleeve of her jacket and rubbed the back of her neck. Zara's last statement intrigued her, and she wanted to know what exactly she meant.

Did Blue River have a history of not satisfying its customers?

"What do you mean?"

"Let's just say the customer isn't always right around here," Zara offered and shook her head. "Don't mind me. I should get back to work. I'm glad we met, Lucy," she said, then turned and pushed her way into the kitchen.

The door closed again, and Lucy spun around to see Justin approaching.

"Hey," she said, noticing he was staring right at the door.

"Were you just with Zara?" he asked.

"Yes, I ran into her, and we talked for a while," Lucy replied. "She's a gracious lady."

Justin directed her to the main exit, and when they got outside, she turned to him. "Thanks for the tour, Justin. You have a really nice place here."

"You're welcome, Lucy, and please, drop in anytime. I'll be more than happy to entertain you."

Lucy smiled at him as she turned to make her way towards her car. As she got closer, she noticed Hannah had returned, and she was sitting on the bumper of the car.

"There you are," Hannah said when Lucy got to the car. "I was wondering where you ran off to."

"I went to check out Blue River," Lucy replied. "It's surprising to see the hotel open for business after what happened yesterday."

"Shocking right?" Hannah said and got off the bumper.

Lucy opened the driver's side of the car, and as she got in, she glanced back at the hotel building to see Justin standing out front with Zara. She kicked the engine to a start and put the car in drive.

Before she drove off, she noticed that Justin and Zara were deep in a conversation, and it seemed quite heated when she saw Justin jab a finger at Zara and then at the hotel building.

I wonder what that was about; she thought as she made a turn and drove past the front of the hotel.

As the car bounced down the road, Lucy saw Justin and Zara through the rear-view mirror, still arguing.

9

When they returned to the bakery an hour later, Hannah went into the kitchen to bring out the already baked cupcakes. Lucy helped her display them, and they fell into another rhythmic round of work as customers began trooping into the bakery again.

"What took you so long when you went into Blue River Hotel?" Hannah asked as Lucy arranged a paper bag full of brownies and cupcakes for the customer in line.

"I met Justin Alli, Tabitha's husband. He was a gentleman."

Hannah frowned, and Lucy added. "He showed me around their hotel and offered to host me anytime I dropped by."

"Wow," Hannah replied, but Lucy sensed some cynicism in her tone before she continued. "That's interesting. You know what they say about birds of the same feather flocking together... I assumed he'd be as mean as his wife."

Lucy lifted a shoulder. "Well, he's real nice."

She continued serving the customers in silence, and Hannah did the same. When they finished serving the customers in the queue, Lucy leaned against the standing counter behind her. "The hotel is really beautiful and bigger than I imagined."

"Have you been there before?" Hannah asked.

Lucy nodded. "Yes, once when I made a delivery to that building before the award night at the church. I didn't make it past the reception because Tabitha was rude to me."

Hannah rolled her eyes. "As expected, she has the reputation for being that way."

Lucy sighed and remembered the warmth in Justin's eyes as he took her around the building, and the way he spoke to the guests who greeted him. He seemed genuinely nice, so it made her wonder what caused his argument with Zara.

Could it be about me?

Lucy pushed down the thought the minute it entered her mind. "I also met the head chef there, and you saw their argument, right? It didn't seem like they get along much."

Hannah turned away from her. She began clearing out the plates in the dining area because the bakery had emptied again. "I don't think we should concern ourselves with what goes on there. After the treatment you got from her and the hassle a potential murder investigation into her death might cause, I think we should just keep to ourselves."

"Still, she was someone's wife, maybe mother and relative. I could tell Justin was struggling just from looking at him. It must be so hard on him, and the staff who would still be in shock from what happened yesterday," she said, standing up straight to ease the tension in her back. "I think it's remarkable that Justin is trying to keep it together and run the business," she added.

"Well, your problem is that you care too much," Hannah pointed out before entering the kitchen.

Lucy followed her. "Come on, Hannah, show a little sympathy," she urged. "Think about what it would feel like to lose a loved one, regardless of how horrible the person's personality was. You would still care for them, wouldn't you? It's the same for Tabitha and her family. They'll miss her even though she wasn't the nicest person in the world."

Lucy grabbed a cup to pour herself water, and she wiped her lips with her sleeves when she finished drinking. "You should still show a little compassion."

"You're right," Hannah finally agreed. She pulled out a chair, lowered herself into it, and folded her hands under her chin. "It must be so sad for them."

"Yes."

"But still… I wouldn't feel compassion for Tabitha directly. Her family, I can feel sorry for, but not Tabitha. I know it sounds harsh, but come on, you can't honestly tell me it's shocking someone would want her dead? She must have offended the wrong person, and it led to this."

"That is also true."

"Hello…" someone called from out front, interrupting their discussion.

Both Lucy and Hannah hurried out of the kitchen to attend to the customer.

"What can I get you?" Lucy asked after exchanging pleasantries with the lady.

"Have you got any muffins?"

"Yes, we do."

"Three muffins to go please, and I'd like a slice of coffee cake with that."

"Okay."

Lucy packaged the order and handed it over to her before collecting a cash payment.

"You know, it's time you brighten up this place with some music," the lady commented as she took the receipt Lucy handed her. "It's a festive season. Surely you've got some decorations and music to bring this place to life and give it that holiday vibe?"

"Yes, I do," Lucy replied, and offered her a smile. "In fact, I plan to put some of those up today, so don't worry."

"You do that." The lady grinned at her and bent her head to inhale the pastries in her paper bag before leaving the bakery. Hannah joined Lucy where she stood and crossed her hands over her chest.

"I guess we should go shopping for some Christmas decorations, right?"

"Yeah," Lucy replied. She picked a napkin and began wiping the counter clean as they had finished their sales for the day, while Hannah went to the side of the dining area where they had a speaker, and stepped on a chair to reach it.

"I think it's broken," she said after a few seconds and stepped down from the chair. "We will need a new one because I can't get this one to play."

"I'll get one from the electronic store, but I don't think the store will be open this late," Lucy replied and glanced at the watch on her left wrist. "I'll just have to pick them up tomorrow."

"I think they stay open till much later now because of the holidays. My sister came in late last night with some items she got from there, so we could check to see if it's still open."

"Sounds like a plan. I'll drive by there tonight," Lucy said.

They cleaned up the bakery and made notes of what they would bake the next day before they closed the store for the night. Minutes after Hannah left for the day, Lucy picked up her purse and keys and headed out of the bakery.

She hummed a Christmas carol to herself as she got in the car and drove off. *It is time to put the bakery in a festive mood.*

10

Lucy walked along the aisles in the electronic store and tried to find the right speaker she could get for the bakery. She checked the price pasted on each unit and admired the shiny outlook of most of them.

Most of the speakers were quite fancy and expensive, but she didn't just need fancy or expensive. She needed something durable for the bakery, as it wasn't for her personal use.

What do I choose?

As she surveyed what was on offer, she scratched her head as she tried to figure what to choose. Lucy turned when she heard footsteps behind her, and a salesman grinned at her when he got close enough for her to hear him.

"Hello, can I assist you with anything?" he asked.

Lucy saw his name tag on the pocket of his shirt.

"Yes, I just can't make a choice," she replied, and shifted her gaze from his face to the speakers in front of her. "What do you suggest?"

"Most of the brands on this line are made of IP67 waterproof features, with 15 hours playtime, and integrated with Bluetooth. It has quality dust and waterproof features. It'll set you back about two thousand dollars," he said casually as Lucy tried to hide her shock at the price he had quoted.

"On this other end, we have premium quality speakers at a higher price, but they've all been slashed by about a thousand dollars. These speakers here can serve the purpose of longer play time, and higher bass intensity when you want to get the party started. I can test them out to show you how good they are if you like."

Lucy cleared her throat and offered him a waning smile. "Actually, you don't need to test it out for me. I'm looking for something less expensive and durable too. It's for my store, and I don't think I need something excessively loud."

One of the man's brows shot up, and he continued talking, completely ignoring her last statement about what she wanted. "We have something a little under a thousand dollars if you prefer to spend less. You can be the proud owner of Zealot speakers which are currently nine hundred and ninety-nine dollars and have a one-year warranty on them," he said and she followed him towards the line of speakers he was referring to.

"These are the best prices and products I can offer you, and you have to make a choice on one of these soon."

Lucy pressed her finger to the side of her lip. "Great, thanks for your help. I'll make a choice, and let you know," she replied and turned away from him to check out other products.

He followed, walking behind her as she began searching for a speaker a lot cheaper. His suggestions were perfect if she needed a speaker for a nightclub, and not for a store where people wanted to have intimate conversations with their friends and loved ones while they ate one of her treats.

"I think you should let me show you how great the Zealot speakers are." The man resumed talking behind her, and Lucy had to mentally restrain herself from snapping at him.

"That's unnecessary. Thanks for offering to help me make a choice, but I've got this."

"Miss—"

"Can you please leave, and I'll let you know once I make a choice?" she cut in before he said anything else.

Does he have to badger me to make a choice?

She exhaled when he stormed away from her and continued her search. A few seconds passed, and Lucy turned around when she felt a gentle tap on her shoulder.

"Hi," a gentleman staring down at her said when she raised her head to meet his gaze. "Sorry to bother you, but I kind of overheard your conversation with the salesman and I thought I should make a suggestion."

Lucy rubbed the back of her neck as she tried to avoid eye contact with him.

"Please come with me," he said when Lucy said nothing, and she followed him to the last aisle. "These are the best speakers you can use for your store. I've tried them personally, and they are durable, and not so expensive."

Lucy looked down at the price tag. "Five hundred," she murmured and looked at him again. "Thanks a lot for this suggestion."

"You're welcome, Lucy," he said.

Her eyes widened when he mentioned her name, and her jaw dropped. "How... how do you know my name?"

He gave her a face-splitting grin. "I saw you earlier today when you came into Blue River Hotel with Justin, and I heard your name when you introduced yourself to Zara, the head chef. I'm Reggie Wade."

"Hello, Reggie," Lucy said and matched his smile. "You work at Blue River?"

"Yes, I've worked there for a long time."

"It was a tragedy what happened, and I hope you're not too shocked yourself or devastated."

"It came as a shock to everyone, but we are taking it in stride and holding it together. Your visit caused a stir today after you left."

"What do you mean?" Lucy asked. She fixed her gaze on him, wondering if the stir had to do with the argument between Justin and Zara, which she had witnessed as she drove away.

"What kind of stir? Why, what happened after I left?"

Her questions lay unanswered. She sensed his hesitation when he licked his lips and slipped his hands into his pockets. "I don't think I should say anything."

"Why? You can't leave me hanging," Lucy probed, and she noticed the way his eyes darted around. He took a step away from her like he wanted to retreat, and she reached forward to stop him with her hand.

Slowly, he rubbed his chin, and she repeated the question. "Did it have something to do with me?"

11

eggie stared at her intently, but the frown forming on the corner of his lips made Lucy realize his reluctance to answer her questions. She wasn't going to let that stop her. "Tell me, Reggie. Was it something I did?"

"No, no," he replied with a wave of his hand. "Look, I don't want you thinking it has anything to do with you because it doesn't, but…" he paused, and released a quick sigh. "Most of the staff didn't like Tabitha much."

"Wow! Shocker," Lucy breathed out under her breath. "That's expected. I didn't like Tabitha very much on our first meeting, either. She was plain rude and unwelcoming."

"Yeah, well, she was like that with everyone," he replied. "She bullied the staff at every chance she got. She always undermined our work, and never let us do anything without injecting her ideas, even when it wasn't her area of expertise." He paused and looked left and right before he continued. "She did it to her husband as well, always disrespecting him in front of everyone. It was quite emasculating. I have to mention that some of us are quite relieved she won't be around anymore, even though I know it's a horrible thought."

"Was she this way with customers too?" she asked, wanting to know more about Tabitha. The Blue River staff did not like her from what she learned from Reggie, and even though her husband did not speak ill of her when they met, was it possible that he also harbored some ill feelings towards his wife?

"She was," Reggie replied. "Blue River is a pleasant hotel, with better infrastructure than most of the hotels in town have. That is why most of the staff still work there. Its reputation keeps it going. Besides that, no one would want to work there."

"Zara, the chief cook, had a lot of conflict with Tabitha, mostly. As far as Tabitha was concerned, she always did something wrong."

"It must have been hard working there," she sympathized.

"You don't know the half of it."

Lucy probed again when it seemed like Reggie had relaxed around her a bit. "So why did my visit cause a conflict? I met Zara Stanmore, and she seemed like a wonderful woman. I hope I didn't cause any ruckus or argument?"

She remembered seeing Zara and Justin having a heated conversation as she drove away, and her interest piqued higher.

"I really shouldn't say." Reggie shifted his weight from one foot to the other. His lips parted slowly like he was about to say something else, but his phone rang in his pocket, and he reached for it. "I should go, Lucy. It was nice speaking with you," he said and turned away from her.

She watched him walk away, wondering why he was so cagey with what happened at the hotel. She turned back to the line-up of speakers to make a final choice on what she wanted to purchase.

With no further thoughts, Lucy picked the brand Reggie suggested and noted down the name. She walked around the aisle and headed to the cashier's stand to place her order.

Why was Reggie being so shifty?

As she got to the front, she saw him step outside the swinging doors. A few customers had walked into the store again, and a slow Christmas carol was booming in the background, elevating the mood inside the shop.

Lucy stopped at the counter and leaned forward to speak with the female cashier. "Hi," she said with a wide smile. "So, I came in to get a speaker and I finally made a choice. I would like to pay for it."

"Great! What brand is that? I'll check the price and print out a receipt for you."

"The brand name is Bose, and I believe it's the 251 range."

The cashier keyed in the name while she waited, and when she looked up at Lucy again, she wore a grin. "Right, we've got it for five hundred dollars. Would you like to make payment now?"

"Yes, please."

She reached into her wallet for her card and handed it over to the cashier. Lucy saw the sales representative she spoke with earlier step out of an inner office with another man, and when he spotted her, he hurried towards the counter.

"Have you made a choice, Miss?"

"Yes, I'll go with the Bose 251," she responded without taking her gaze off the cashier processing her payment.

"I suggested three other better brands for you. A little higher in price, but of better durability than what you went for. I think you should go for those," he began.

"I prefer the choice I made," Lucy quickly said before he went on about why she should listen to him.

"But Miss—"

"The young lady is entitled to her choice," the man who stood with him seconds ago cut in as he came towards the counter. He offered Lucy an apologetic smile after shooting a stern gaze at the rep. "Please forgive his approach. I'll come by tomorrow morning to install the speaker of your choice. Just leave your address with the cashier."

"Thanks," Lucy said. She retrieved her card from the cashier and scribbled down her bakery's address on the book provided.

"Have a beautiful night," the cashier said and Lucy waved at her one last time as she headed out of the store.

When Lucy stepped out of the store, she spotted Reggie standing in a corner to the left. He leaned on the wall behind him, with his head lowered, so he didn't notice when she came out.

"I'm sorry it had to end that way, but maybe it's for the best," she heard him say. "Think about it… now we don't have to worry about any of that again."

Lucy thought about going to him for a second, but she shook the idea out of her head and headed to her car parked by the curb. It was already late, and she had to make it back home in time to rest and prepare for work the next day.

As she got in her car and headed back home, she thought of her conversation with Reggie the entire time, and what she overheard him saying as she came out of the store.

What was for the best? What if Tabitha's death wasn't an acci-

*dent, as everyone thought? And if it turned out it was intention-
al, did Reggie have something to do with it?*

Something didn't sit right about the entire situation with Lucy,
but she didn't want to make any wild guesses. She had done
enough guessing when it involved cases like this in Ivy Creek
in the past, and it always ended up with her getting entangled in
something she knew nothing about.

This time, she planned to stay out of it and let the cops do their
job. Whatever happened to Tabitha, it was their duty to find it
out.

12

"Aunt Tricia, I think these should go on the tree," Lucy said, peering into a box of old decorations she found in her apartment upstairs. She remembered her parents had gotten them many years ago and used them every Christmas season. She used to love looking at the tree with elves and socks hanging around. It made the tree come alive, and she was glad she found them.

"They should," Aunt Tricia agreed and took the box from her. She placed it on a table and together they started bringing out the old decorations.

It wasn't fully dawn yet, and Aunt Tricia had stayed over the previous night to help her with the decorations that morning. Lucy also had a lot of baking to do as she had deliveries for the grocery stores and also some out-of-stock pastries she had to replace.

She was humming *12 Days of Christmas* to herself as she wiped the plastic elves clean, and Aunt Tricia joined her to hang them on the tree she just got. When they finished, the only thing they hadn't done was to hang the lights.

Lucy went into the kitchen to check the batter she was mixing with her electric mixer for cupcakes and reduced the speed to give it time to mix properly. When she came out front again, Aunt Tricia was standing on a chair. She was trying to hang the lights on the ceiling board, but even with the chair as an aide, she still couldn't reach the ceiling board.

"I think we will need help for that," Lucy said as she held onto the chair to keep it stable. She stopped humming when Aunt Tricia got down from the chair and put her hands on her hips.

"We've transformed the place, but the lights will make the place look magical, and that is just what we need right now," she said and looked around the bakery.

Lucy had put some lights on the display counter where she kept pastries for sale, and outside the bakery, she had put out some lights on the front door. All that was left were the speakers which she had purchased earlier and putting up the lights, which neither of them could handle.

Still contemplating on how they could do the last bit of their decorations, both ladies spun around when they heard the soft creak of the front door as it swung open.

"Taylor," Aunt Tricia chimed when they saw Taylor, the town's deputy sheriff, walk in. Her aunt went to him before he got to the center of the dining area, and she enveloped him in a hug. "How are you? It's been a while," she continued with an easy laugh.

Taylor wore a smile that reached his eyes as he looked from Aunt Tricia to Lucy. "I have to say, I love what you've done with the place," he complimented, and his smile widened.

Lucy acknowledged him with a soft nod of her head when he

released Aunt Tricia and walked over to where she stood.

"How are you, Lucy?" he asked.

"Great! Just trying to get in the festive spirit, you know," she remarked.

His gaze dropped to the lights she held, and he tipped his head to one side. "Need help with that?" he asked.

"Yes, please." Lucy handed him the lights, and he strode to the chair, and placed one foot on it.

"Thank goodness you dropped by. We were just thinking of how to get that up ourselves," Aunt Tricia said and came to stand beside Lucy.

They both crossed their arms over their chests and watched Taylor drape the festive lights over the board with the adhesive cable hooks.

"I was driving back from the station, and noticed the lights inside were on, so I thought to drop by and say hello," Taylor replied, and cast a glance at Lucy over his shoulder before he focused on his task again.

He finished with one side and dropped from the chair to move it to another part of the room and continue putting the lights around.

Aunt Tricia continued in a cheery tone. "What about your mother? How is she? I haven't seen her in a while. I have to visit more often."

"She is doing well. She always wants to have Lucy's pastries, so she gets a lot from the grocery store every day since it's closer to her."

Aunt Tricia nudged Lucy in her side gently and her smile turned mischievous. "It's good to know she is well," she said.

Lucy cleared her throat and ignored the suggestive look in her aunt's eyes. Taylor's compliments always made her flush, but that was probably because it was hard to get one from him. In the past, they had gotten along fine, but since she returned to Ivy Creek after leaving him years back, he had been distant.

Only recently, he had begun talking to her again, and she was thankful they had at least gotten past the anger he felt towards her.

"Let me check on the batter," Aunt Tricia said and headed for the kitchen while Lucy continued to watch Taylor.

"That should do it," Taylor said and dusted his palms together. He jumped down from the chair and landed steadily on his feet. He turned towards Lucy. "Would you need me to do anything else for you?"

Lucy shook her head. "Thank you so much, Taylor," she said.

"Sure."

"You heading back to the station?" Lucy enquired as Taylor slipped his hands into his pockets.

"Heading home," he corrected and pinned his gaze on hers. "I worked all night."

"On Tabitha Alli's case?" she prompted quickly. Lucy had told herself she didn't want to get involved in the case, but she still wanted information. "Have they found the cause of death yet? Does it really have to do with poison?"

"No, we are yet to get the autopsy results, but it might have to do with health issues, so don't get too worked up over it."

A moment of silence passed between them.

"I have to get back home now," he said and patted her shoulder before brushing past her.

"Thanks again for your help," Lucy said and walked with him to the door. They reached for the knob simultaneously, and his hand brushed over hers lightly before she retreated.

The door gave way before either of them could open it, and Richard stood on the other end holding a box and wearing a grin on his face.

"Happy holidays," he announced. "I love what you've done with the place."

The grin disappeared from his face when he looked at Taylor, and Lucy took the box from him. She set it on the floor by her feet and straightened herself again.

"How are you, Richard?" she asked when he entered the bakery and pulled her in for a hug. The embrace lasted a little longer than it usually did, and when he released her, her cheeks flushed red because Taylor still stood by the doorway watching them.

She couldn't read his blank expression, and he turned away before she could try.

"See you around, Lucy," Taylor said and hurried away.

Richard closed the door after him and turned to Lucy again. He extended a hand to push back some strands of hair falling to the side of her face as he asked. "Did you need help with the decorations?"

"Ah yes," Lucy replied, and offered him a shaky smile. She found a chair to sit and offered him one. "Taylor was driving past the bakery, so he stopped and offered to help. There's no way I could have reached the ceiling boards to put up those lights."

She looked up at the decorated part of the ceiling and smiled a little.

"You know, Lucy, you can always reach out to me for help," he said and placed a hand on hers on the table. "I'm always at your beck and call."

Richard winked, and the full-toothed smile he gave her remind-ed her of his charm. Her insides warmed, and she broke contact to look at the forgotten box on the floor.

"What's in the box?"

"I figured you'd want to do some decorating, so I brought you a box of some stockings and wreath and tinsels I had kept in a box somewhere. And maybe if you're free, you can visit my café to see what I've done with the place."

"I'd like that very much," she replied.

"Me too."

Richard rose to his feet. He leaned in for a peck, taking Lucy by surprise, then he waved at her before heading out of the bakery.

Stunned, Lucy remained seated for some seconds till her aunt came out of the kitchen. "Say nothing," she began before Lucy could muster any words. "I saw everything."

Aunt Tricia's eyes fixed on Lucy's as she added. "I think both of them are into you." Her aunt brought the box to where Lucy sat, put it on the table, and opened it.

Lucy scoffed. "That is crazy," she gasped and covered her cheeks with her hands. Aunt Tricia took out stockings and garlands for their tree.

"Sweet. We didn't have any garlands on the tree," Aunt Tricia said as she emptied the box, then she back-tracked to their for-mer topic again. "Come on, don't tell me you don't see it too, Lucy. Taylor was staring pretty hard when you hugged Richard, and Richard wants you to know you can always ask him for help whenever because Taylor helped you out. I sensed a tiny tinge of jealousy from those words, and with Taylor? Don't even get me started on that look on his face when you hugged Richard. Even a teenager can tell when a guy is into them."

"Taylor and I are a closed chapter, aunty," Lucy said. She ran her hands over her jeans. "And maybe Richard likes me, but it's still early days with him, and I can't really be certain of anything."

Aunt Tricia raised a brow, shooting Lucy a doubting stare.

"I think you're wrong," Lucy continued and stood up to go start her baking for the day. Hannah would be in the bakery soon, and with Aunt Tricia's help, they could get most of the work done before mid-day. She counted what she had to bake in her mind; cupcakes, brownies, and macaroons were on the top of that list.

"If you say so," Aunt Tricia called behind her as they entered the kitchen. "Just be careful not to send mixed signals because I can tell you from experience that that can be very confusing."

Lucy picked up her sieve and walked over to the corner to measure out flour. "Trust me, I won't," she replied as she tied her apron around her neck.

She wasn't interested in Taylor, and with Richard, she had to admit she liked him. Whatever happened, she knew her feelings were as clear as day, so Aunt Tricia had nothing to worry about.

Pushing both men out of her mind, Lucy gathered her thoughts and focused them on the recipes she had in mind for the day.

13

B y mid-day, they had finished the baking for the day, and Aunt Tricia had gone home to freshen up and rest a bit. Lucy and Hannah attended to the customers trooping into the bakery at intervals, and they had almost run out of cupcakes.

She took a break and went into the kitchen to get herself a glass of water, and when she returned to the dining area, Hannah was attending to the last customer in front of the counter.

Lucy beamed when she recognized the lady as the one who had suggested the idea of decorating the bakery the last time she was around.

"I love what you've done," the lady said as she handed Hannah cash for her order. "You see that the decorations really give the place the life and vibe it needs for the season."

"You were right," Lucy agreed and they both laughed.

"Although there is one thing missing," the lady continued and looked around the bakery. "Some—"

"Some music," Lucy said before she could complete her sentence. "I know we need some music to lighten the mood. I'm installing a new sound system today, so when next you're here, you'll be rocking back and forth to some festive tunes. You can count on that."

The lady winked at her, got her package from Hannah, and headed for the door just at the same time it opened, and a sales rep from the electronic store walked in.

"Hi." Lucy quickly went around the counter to greet the man who offered to install her speakers the previous day.

"This shouldn't take me long to install," the man said as he accepted her handshake. Lucy pointed him towards the shelf where she had the previous speaker, and he excused himself to start work.

She returned to the back of the counter and stood there chatting with Hannah about her experience at the electronic store while the man worked on the installation. It took him a few minutes to get the speaker working, then he asked Lucy to connect her phone through Bluetooth to the device and play a song.

Lucy chose *It's Beginning to Look a Lot like Christmas* from her playlist, and as the soft sounds filled the air, she started tapping her fingers. She turned to Hannah and said, "Truly, music makes all the difference."

"I agree," Hannah said.

The sales rep walked over to the counter where they stood and offered Lucy a card. "Here is a company number in case you need anything else. The system comes with a year warranty, so if it develops a fault that isn't due to damage, you can bring it back."

"Oh, I didn't know that," Lucy said, wondering why the nosy sales guy she encountered yesterday didn't think to mention that part. "Thank you…"

"Jay," he offered.

"Thank you, Jay," she repeated. Then, she reached into the counter for the bag of cupcakes she had packed for him while he worked. "Here is a present for you," she said as she extended the pack.

Jay's lips curved into a smile. "You're very kind. Thank you." He peered into the pack and looked back at her. "I've had some of your cupcakes before, and they are extremely tasty, better than anything I've had around here in a long time."

"Really? Do you come by the bakery?"

"No, no. I get bread from the grocery store most times, and I tasted your cupcakes when I had a work meeting at one of Blue River's conference rooms," he replied. "I knew they were yours because I've seen a few colleagues eat them and they always mention your bakery when asked where they got them from."

Lucy's heart jumped at his disclosure of the referrals. Any news about the success of her business made her glad. It was also another force that propelled her to work harder to improve her recipes.

"I love our company meetings at Blue River, although Tabitha always had a way of ruining the atmosphere by belittling one of her team," he added.

"I've heard," Lucy said, suspending her own self-appraisal for a while. "It's a tragedy what happened to her, anyway. It must have been a shock to her workers and family."

Jay shook his head. "Trust me, it wasn't so much of a devastating blow."

"What do you mean?" Lucy said as she leaned on her counter.

"I heard a rumor that the staff was celebrating when they heard of her death. Some of them attended the church's award night and they didn't look so distraught. I don't mean to speak ill of the dead, but honesty, I believe her passing will make Blue River do better."

Lucy pondered on his words as he spoke, and once again the feeling of suspicion she felt yesterday concerning Tabitha's demise returned.

It seems more likely that there is someone who must have gone the extra mile to get Tabitha out of the way.

So far, besides Justin Alli, Lucy hadn't spoken to anyone who was a Tabitha fan. The woman seemed to have stepped on a lot of toes, and Lucy imagined what it would be like for Justin, knowing that a lot of the locals didn't like his wife.

He is such a nice man; she thought. A thorny knot of emotion welled up inside her, and she expressed her pity for Justin out loud.

"Still, her husband must be devastated from the shock. I mean, who would benefit from her death?"

"Who wouldn't?" Jay replied, shaking his head. The sarcasm in his words sent a shiver down her spine, and a knot formed in the pit of her stomach when Jay added. "Every single worker at Blue River will benefit from Tabitha's death. That's the reality of it."

Jay thanked Lucy for the cupcakes again before leaving the bakery, and Lucy chewed on her lower lip as Hannah commented beside her. "Well, Tabitha sure had a lot of enemies."

"It sure seems that way," Lucy responded and went back to attending to her customers when another set trooped in.

14

very single worker at Blue River will benefit from Tabitha's death.

Jay's words rang in Lucy's mind hours after he had left her bakery. She was lost in thought where she sat behind the counter, wondering what he meant by his statement when Hannah suddenly tugged at her arm and dragged her out of her contemplations.

"Look," Hannah said in an excited tone, and Lucy followed the direction of her finger to see an old couple swaying lightly to the song playing.

Santa Claus is Coming to Town played over the speakers, and Lucy realized she had lost track of what was happening in the bakery completely.

"They look beautiful," Hannah complimented as they watched.

Other customers in the bakery also watched the dance the couple performed and when they neared the end, a few others stood up to join them while the rest cheered.

The couple reminded Lucy of her parents, and for a while, she thought of them. Her mother used to dance a lot when she worked in the bakery. There was always a song playing in the background, and it made Lucy enjoy singing and dancing herself.

She remembered during Christmas when she was in high school, they would hang decorations on a tree, and her parents would go shopping for presents, wrap them and place them under the tree at midnight.

Lucy was an only child, so most times she had friends over for Christmas sleepovers. In the mornings, her mother prepared lots of food—roasted potatoes, brussel sprouts, and marinated turkey with stuffing. This had always been her favorite time of the year.

A lump had formed in Lucy's throat as she watched the dancing couple, and her chest tightened with emotion.

I miss you so much, mom and dad…

A tear slipped down her cheeks at the thought, and she laughed it off as she wiped it away with her thumb. She took a deep breath and pressed her fingertips to her eyelids to keep the rest of her tears at bay.

Her heart beat furiously against her chest as she thought of her parents, and she realized for the past several months she had been so wrapped up in work and everything else that she hadn't thought of them in a while.

Her mother always loved this time of the year, and Lucy had grown to love it, too. One reason she had kept the bakery open after their death early this year was because she wanted to keep some part of them alive, and right now, watching her customers dance in the bakery, Lucy felt closer to her mother than she had in months because this was exactly how it was around here when she was alive.

The dance had ended, and everyone returned to their seats again before Hannah spoke. "I want to get off early today to run some errands for the family. I like to finish Christmas shopping early before everyone else, so I don't make a mistake or forget to get anything."

"Sure, you can get off early," Lucy replied. "We've sold almost everything we have prepared and we need to make more for tomorrow."

"Thanks, Lucy," Hannah said and ran a hand over Lucy's back before heading into the kitchen. Lucy gave the adoring couple one last look again before she lowered herself to her seat and picked up a cooking magazine from the table beside her to flip through.

When Hannah finally left for the day, there was only one customer left in the bakery. Lucy thought of closing early to run some errands herself. Watching the couple dance in her dining area had stirred up old memories in her, and she craved a well-grilled turkey with stuffing for Christmas dinner.

She would have to do some shopping for the bakery anyway, and she could use the time to pick out some items for a home-cooked meal. As she pondered on what to do, she returned the magazine she had been reading to a pile she kept in the drawers under the counter.

Lucy heard the doorbell chime, and she said without looking up. "I'll be with you in a second."

She arranged the stack of magazines properly, making sure they stayed stacked on one another. She closed the drawer and straightened to see Zara Stanmore standing on the other side.

"Hi… sorry, I didn't mean to startle you," Zara said when Lucy sucked in a sharp breath."

"That's fine. I wasn't startled," Lucy replied with a smile.

Zara nodded, smiling back at her as she looked around the bakery. "Would you like something?" Lucy asked when Zara's eyes settled on the display counter.

She still had brownies, cupcakes, and coconut bread in stock for the day, and if she could sell some of these before heading out, then that would be perfect.

"I'd like to try some brownies,' Zara said and looked at her again. "And some of those cupcakes with sprinkles."

"Okay," Lucy affirmed and started working on the order. She added an extra brownie for Zara and packed the cupcakes in a fancy paper bag.

"I love how you've decorated the place for Christmas, and the music just adds a wonderful feel to all of it. Good job, Lucy. You've made this place lovelier than it was."

"I'm glad you like it. My aim is to make my customers fall in love with not just my recipes, but also Sweet Delights."

"I understand, trust me. At Blue River, we could hardly decorate this much without consent from Tabitha. She stifled the joy out of Christmas every time."

Zara took her package from Lucy and continued with a wave of her hand. "At least this year we can finally put some decorations up," she said and rolled her eyes.

"I'm sorry to hear that," Lucy offered, and remembered Jay's words again.

Zara stuffed her order into the tote bag hanging on her shoulder. She leaned into the counter, close enough for Lucy to catch a whiff of her strong perfume scent.

"I came around to offer you a business deal," Zara continued, and Lucy's ears perked with interest. "We are hosting a few conferences this month, and a few of them are for businesses from out of town. I thought our guests would need desserts for their meetings, and I cannot think of a better place to get them than Sweet Delights. I'd like to partner with you for this purpose. We sell your pastries at our hotel and serve them to customers who order treats while reserving our conference halls for their events."

"This is the best news I've heard all day," Lucy squealed. Her heart bounced with the excitement, and she enjoyed Zara's short bubble of laughter.

Her eyes danced as she met Zara's, and she could barely stifle the joy rising inside her.

"When do you propose we start? And do you have a specific list of items you'd like for me to deliver?" Lucy questioned. She was already making mental plans for recipes she could add to the usual cupcakes with sprinkles. She could take things to another level by making her fudgy chocolate cake recipe with whipped cream frosting.

This was a new recipe she was considering bringing in for the new year. A lot of her customers already enjoyed her coffee fla-vored cake and carrot cake. It was time for a fresh addition to the menu. She could add berries and tarts to the top of each slice to make it classy and reduce the addition of cream to make it healthy.

"We can start immediately," Zara replied, matching Lucy's en-thusiasm. "I have a list, but of course, add anything else. You're the expert."

Zara handed her a notepad, and she opened it to check the items on the list. "We can make your first delivery next week to give you time to prepare. We have a conference meeting scheduled next week so that works perfectly.

"Yes, it does," Lucy agreed.

"Great. I'll see you around then. I have to run along now." Zara said, turning around to walk away.

Lucy suddenly remembered Jay's words again.

Every single worker at Blue River will benefit from Tabitha's death. She considered asking Zara about what she thought of the murder and stopped Zara from exiting the bakery without weighing her options properly.

"Zara, wait… can I ask you something?"

Zara spun around; her lips slightly parted. "Sure, you can ask me anything," she replied without hesitation and came back to the counter again.

Is this a good idea? What if my questions cause a rift between us? I just got a brilliant business offer from her and I wouldn't want to jeopardize that by stepping on her toes.

Lucy knew she should have considered all this before calling out to Zara, and now she rocked back on her heels, slightly uncomfortable because of the intent gaze Zara threw in her direction.

It's a bad idea… don't ask.

"Actually, never mind," Lucy said, hoping the nonchalant shrug she threw in Zara's direction would make her disregard her initial request.

15

Lucy's cheeks colored when Zara said, "No, I mind. What was on your mind?" and came closer to the counter.

She eyed Lucy, making her more self-conscious, and Lucy wished she had kept her mouth shut. Lucy finally said, "It was nothing."

"Were you going to ask me what my argument with Justin was about?" Zara probed.

Lucy's eyes widened. "I didn't want to pry, so I changed my mind," she said with an apologetic smile and quivering lips. "I was just curious, and I wanted to know if it had something to do with me, or what happened to Tabitha," she added.

"I saw you drive past while we argued, and I know you must have been wondering because it was right after you left the hotel that day." Zara stopped for a second, and Lucy saw her chest heave as she dragged in a shaky breath. "We were arguing about decorations."

"Decorations?" The argument seemed to be about much more than decorations. She remembered seeing lots of fingers jabbing in the air, animated gestures, and eye rolls, and all of that was for decorations? Lucy was interested in hearing the rest of what Zara had to say, but she played down her curiosity by asking in a light tone. "He didn't want to get the place in a festive mood?"

Zara nodded twice. "Justin always had all these great ideas for what the hotel should look like during the festive season, but every time he brought them up, Tabitha shut them down. She never let him have a say in anything, even though he was much more creative than her. Tabitha was blatantly rude to him, and every staffer at Blue River, and if anything went wrong with her ideas, she blamed it on Justin. She always wanted to take the glory for the good stuff and assign the responsibility for failures to him and others. It was very unfair, and Justin just took all of that quietly, to everyone's surprise."

"That's awful," Lucy replied.

"I know," Zara said after a while. "Over time, I watched Justin retreat into a shell, he never contributed to anything anymore, and that day when I brought up the idea of having decorations in the conference halls and the reception, he shut down the idea without even giving it a second thought.

"I had to remind him we had to make changes and look our best for the customers regardless of everything going on or else we would lose our reputation in town."

Lucy shored her frame on the counter as she listened to Zara speak. The woman had the hotel's best interest at heart, she could tell from the passion in her voice.

"He needs to know that his voice is heard now, and the staff at Blue River looks up to him to lead the way."

"I understand," Lucy said in a quiet voice. "I hope you're not offended that I thought to ask about this. I was just curious about it, and I kind of felt like it had to do with me."

"Of course, no it didn't," Zara corrected. "I'm sorry if it came off like I was being rude to Justin on my end, but it was nothing of the sort. Trust me."

Zara put a hand over Lucy's and her lips curled into a smile. "You shouldn't worry about that. We ended up settling for some acceptable ideas for the decorations and we will put them up soon. All you have to focus on is delivering on those treats."

Zara's phone beeped, and she took it out of her pocket. Her brows furrowed a bit as she read the text on the screen before she looked at Lucy again. "I have to go now," she said, backing away from the counter. "Is sometime later this week okay to bring some sample treats over to Blue River?"

"Yes, it is," Lucy replied, and waved at Lucy as she pulled the door open.

Aunt Tricia stood on the other side when the door opened, and Lucy saw her jaw drop when she saw Zara standing there.

"Hey."

"Hi..." Zara replied.

"Wow, you look extremely familiar," Aunt Tricia continued when Zara sidestepped to let her into the bakery. "You don't know me, do you?"

"No, I don't," Zara replied. She glanced at Lucy again, waved, and hurried out of the bakery while Aunt Tricia stared after her.

"Still trying to figure out where you know her from?" Lucy asked.

"Yes... I just can't place the face and I am always good with faces."

"Well, that was Zara Stanmore. She works at Blue River Hotel, and she came here to offer me a contract," Lucy announced, unable to keep her excitement to herself.

"Blue River? Isn't that Tabitha's hotel?"

"Yes. Yes, it is," she responded. Aunt Tricia took a seat and Lucy joined her after she took off the apron and cap she had on.

She sat down and started reading out the items on the list Zara gave her. "Brownies, red velvet cupcakes with frosting and sprinkles, dark-chocolate slices, macaroons, cinnamon rolls, and muffins."

"That's a lot," Aunt Tricia commented and readjusted in her chair. "I think you should be careful with whatever dealings you have with Blue River, Lucy."

"Did something happen?"

"No, not yet. But Blue River staff are still being investigated for Tabitha's sudden death and we want nothing linking you to them," she warned, reminding Lucy of her self-advice to stay out of this case in every way.

16

Lucy entered the conference room the receptionist had directed her to, and she dropped the basket of pastries she came with on the table, adjusted her blue chiffon blouse, and ran her hands over her skirt.

She was never nervous in presentations like this. When she worked in the city, she had interviews from time to time and featured popular restaurants and bakeries in the column she wrote. As a food critic, Lucy had mingled with several high-profile personalities in the culinary world to feel at ease making a presentation.

That life seemed like a long time ago, even though it was only earlier that year that she had returned to her home in Ivy Creek. Alone in the conference room, while waiting for Zara, she wandered to the large window and stood close to it.

The conference room was at the back side of Blue River, and from there, she had a good view of the flat-grass-covered plains.

She saw birds soaring in the sky above a tall tree in the distance, and she admired the clear blue sky. Lucy took off the shawl wrapped around her neck and folded it into her bag. When she left the bakery that morning, the weather was frosty, but now the sun had fully risen. She glanced at the watch on her left wrist and tucked a loose strand of hair behind her ear.

The door swung open then, and Lucy spun around to see Justin step into the room.

"Hi," she breathed out, surprised he was there instead of Zara. "How are you doing?" she asked when he greeted her with a smile. "I'm here to see Zara. We set an appointment for me to deliver some pastries."

"I know," Justin said. "Zara and I talked about it; she couldn't make it in today, so she asked me to do this."

"Oh, great then," Lucy remarked. She clapped her hands together and moved closer to the table to remove the napkin covering the wrapped pastries in the basket. "I brought some of everything she asked for, and you can share some with the other staff once we finish here," she suggested.

"That's very nice of you, Lucy," Justin said.

Lucy took out the cupcakes first for him to try. She watched gingerly as he took a bite and closed his eyes as he chewed.

"Hmmm… amazing," he groaned and took another bite.

Her spirits lifted, and she waited till he dropped the cupcake before trying the muffins next.

The look of satisfaction on his face was the same when he tried the brownies and the macaroons.

Finally, Justin sighed. "I can't seem to make a choice. They all taste amazing to me, and if it were up to me, I'd have you bring us all of them," he said.

Lucy joined in his nervous laugh, and he wiped his lips with the small napkin she handed him.

"But it's not up to me," he added when they became serious again. "I think I should get a chef to come in and taste some of these heavenly treats and make a professional assessment," he said. "If you don't mind, I mean."

"Oh, I don't mind at all," Lucy said confidently. She was a food critic and tasting people's cooking was how she made money for years before she joined the bakery business this year. There was no kind of critical review she hadn't dished out before.

Some of that cynicism from being a critic made her strive to make sure her recipes were perfect.

"Cool, I'll be right back."

Justin left her in the conference room again, and this time she pulled out a chair from the row arranged by the long, boat-shaped table. Justin had left a book on the table when he left, and the picture in front of the notepad caught Lucy's attention.

She took it and looked at the photograph of Justin and Tabitha in front. She guessed it was a pre-wedding photo from how they were dressed, and the back design had a ring by the side of it to confirm that it was.

They looked so young in the picture, and it made her wonder how long they had been married.

Did Justin have to put up with Tabitha, belittling him for a long time? Did they have any kids from their marriage?

Lucy opened the notepad and read the words written on the first page. She realized it was a eulogy for his wife's funeral when she read the first line, and her heart cinched a little towards him.

SILENT NIGHT, UNHOLY BITES

Dear Tabitha,

Many of us gathered here today did not know you well. To some, you were a neighbor, to others a friend, and a boss... a leader and a teacher, an enemy and a friend, but to me, you were my best friend.

The love of my life.

It saddens me greatly that I have to stand here today to speak about you in front of all these people when I always imagined that you would be with me for many years.

It hurts me you're gone, but somehow it also makes my heart rejoice because your going has freed me from the cage I have lived in all these years.

He crossed the last line of the words Lucy had just read. She stopped reading after that line. She quickly closed the book and pushed it back to the spot where it had been.

Why would Justin write such words to read in front of those many people at his late wife's funeral?

Lucy licked her lips and tried to compose herself as her mind raced with unanswered questions. She didn't want it to be obvious she had been snooping when Justin returned, so she had to act normal.

The door opened as she chided herself about what to do, and Justin came into the room. Reggie, the worker she had met in the electronic store, stepped in after him, and Lucy rose to her feet.

"Sorry I took some time. I had to find Reggie, our assistant chef, to come taste what you've brought. Reggie, this is Lucy, by the way. She owns the bakery Sweet Delights, and we are looking to hire her to supply our hotel with some treats."

Reggie simply nodded his head. He stood behind Justin with a blank look on his face, and Lucy smiled at him, expecting him to acknowledge her presence with a smile or warm greeting.

She cleared her throat when he did neither of those things, and Justin waved a hand at the basket and said, "Shall we?"

"Of course," Lucy replied and took out the first pastry to hand over to Reggie. All the time, she couldn't stop thinking. *What if Justin had the most to benefit from his wife's death over anyone else?*

17

L ucy shifted on her feet as an awkward silence settled in the room.

"Your suggestion at the electronic store was really helpful by the way. The speaker is top-notch, and it serves my needs at the bakery perfectly," Lucy said.

"You two have met?" Justin asked, looking from Reggie to Lucy.

"Yes."

"No," Reggie said.

Lucy's brow perked, and she saw a flash of confusion in Justin's eyes as he looked at both again. "We met once at an electronic store nearby," Lucy explained.

Justin turned to Reggie, whose ears had reddened, and Lucy pressed her lips together. She sensed Reggie did not want Justin to know they had met before, and it made her wonder why.

Did it have something to do with what Reggie told her the last time?

"Well, let's get to tasting," Justin broke into the silence. He cleared his throat and pushed back a chair to sit and watched Reggie lift the muffin to take a bite.

After the muffins, Reggie tasted the cupcakes, then the brownies, and everything else. Lucy linked her fingers together in front of her and waited for his remarks while Reggie took his time to wipe his lips clean before he faced her.

"They all taste wonderful," he said. "This is baking at its finest and I think Zara would love them."

"Thanks," Lucy breathed, feeling relieved that she got a compliment from a fellow chef. She was still grinning when Justin rose to his feet again.

"That settles it then," Justin said and adjusted the sleeve of his shirt.

"I will speak with Zara and come by your bakery with some paperwork to complete our business deal together, then you can start working on your first delivery," Reggie said.

"All right—" Lucy started.

"You should get back to what you were doing before I called you," Justin cut in, looking at Reggie with a straight face, before Lucy could complete her sentence.

She was going to say she looked forward to having Reggie come by her bakery, but she kept that to herself.

Reggie hesitated, but he backed away from the table and headed out of the conference room without another word. A second of silence passed between Justin and Lucy before she smoothed a hand over her skirt and said with a laugh. "So, I'll be expecting you then."

"Yes, I might drop by today or tomorrow," Justin replied.

"Cool."

She gathered the pastry wraps together and folded them inside her napkin before pushing the basket to Justin. "Here, for the rest of your workers."

"Thank you, Lucy. I'll see you when I drop by," he said with a pleasant smile, and picked up the basket.

His gaze dropped on his book on the table, and she saw his brows crease when he said. "I had a pen here."

Lucy's breath hitched in her throat, and her eyes darted across the table. She saw the pen at the side of the table where she sat, and she picked it up to hand it over to him.

She shivered as he took the pen from her, but his frown stayed.

"That's weird. Could have sworn I kept it all together," he murmured and pressed the ball of the pen. "See you around, Lucy," he said one last time before he left the conference room.

Lucy stood in the same spot for some seconds, and when she finally exited the room, she prayed silently that Justin did not suspect someone had messed with his things on the table.

She didn't want him to suspect that she knew about his eulogy.

18

Lucy hurried to her car and was glad when she shut the door behind her. She ran her hands through her hair and let out a deep sigh as she remembered the trepidation she had felt as Justin assessed his belongings before he left the room.

She closed her eyes, let out a deep breath, and opened them again to hear her phone ping in her purse. When she entered the hotel, she had forgotten her purse in her car.

Had it been pinging the entire time?

After a brief search, Lucy retrieved her phone from the purse. She saw the text message banner on the screen with the name Richard, and a smile crossed her lips when she opened them and read.

Hey, Lucy, up for a date tonight? If yes, respond with a cute emoji.

Shaking her head, she responded to the text and waited till it double ticked.

Richard replied immediately, and she grinned harder as she read his reply.

Sweet! Pick you up by seven. I can't wait.

Lucy drove back to the bakery after that. Hannah was in charge whenever she was away, and when Lucy returned, the place was swamped with customers. A traditional Christmas carol played from the speakers, and she joined Hannah in serving, putting in additional cupcakes for every customer who ordered.

It seemed like a lot to give to every customer, but Lucy followed her mother's business rules of generosity. Customers loved the attention given to them when they entered a place. No one would return to a place with subpar service, and she had to make sure she stayed on top of her game with the customers here in Ivy Creek. They could be easy to satisfy and difficult to please all at once.

"Have a nice day," Lucy said to the last customer she served. The woman tipped her a five-dollar bill before walking away, and she turned to Hannah.

"So how did it go with Justin Alli?" Hannah asked as she took off the apron tied to her body.

"Went well," Lucy replied. "He will drop by for us to complete some paperwork and I am to deliver my first batch next week."

"This is amazing news, definitely worth celebrating." Hannah strolled into the kitchen and returned with a bottle of grape juice. She waved the bottle at Lucy and continued in a singing voice. "How about a little juice to celebrate your success so far?"

"I'll have to use your offer now because I've got a date at seven," Lucy said.

"Let me guess, Richard?"

Before Lucy could say anything, Hannah raised her hand to signify Lucy didn't have to say anything and went into the kitchen to bring two glasses. Both ladies sat in the empty dining area to enjoy the grape juice with a slice of cake for themselves.

"Yes, he's picking me up."

"That's nice," Hannah commented as she took a sip. "I have a date myself, but over the weekend."

Lucy lifted her glass for a toast. "To a Merry Christmas and an amazing forthcoming new year."

She clinked her glass against Hannah's before they continued drinking.

When they finished their mini celebration, they continued work. It was past six when Lucy and Hannah finally closed the bakery for the day and Lucy raced up the stairs to get ready for her date.

She breezed through the clothes in her closet to find something suitable to wear and ended up settling for a black long-sleeved dress with a V-neck cut and length that stopped over her knees.

Lucy paired it with knee-high boots and wrapped a shawl around her neck for extra comfort and to protect herself from the cold. She finished dressing and stood in front of her mirror, admiring her reflection, when Gigi pranced towards her.

"Hey, Gigi," she called, bent over, and scooped the cat in her arms. "You look pretty. Do I look pretty too?"

Gigi purred, and she stroked its head. Lucy developed second thoughts about the dress as she continued to stare at herself in the mirror.

Do I look too serious? Maybe I should add more lip-gloss, or lipstick to outline my lips.

Her cheeks reddened when she caught herself wondering if Richard preferred a woman with natural looks or a bit of make-up.

Come on, Lucy, get a grip.

She pressed her free hand to her cheek and exhaled before looking at Gigi again. A honk from outside told her Richard had arrived, and she checked the clock on the wall and noticed that he was right on schedule.

Lucy set Gigi carefully on the floor, grabbed her purse, and smoothed a hand over her hair one last time before she headed out of her apartment.

Richard was at the door when she opened it, and he wore a wide smile. His brown eyes danced as his gaze trailed over her. "You look so beautiful," he whispered.

Heat filled her insides again when Richard stepped closer and kissed her cheeks. "Tonight is all about fun," he added, linked their fingers, and led her towards his black sedan.

Seconds later, they were driving down the high street towards the bend that led downtown.

*

They strolled into the restaurant Richard picked for their dinner date, and Lucy matched his steps until they got to their reserved table. She sat with him and picked up the menu to make an order, all the while aware of Richard's stare.

She met his eyes when her attention shifted from the menu, and she smiled at him.

"I'll have the bacon and cheese croquettes," she ordered.

"Same with the lady," Richard said and closed his menu. The waiter returned with their wine first, and two glasses, and they indulged in that while waiting for their starters.

Lucy put down her glass after she had taken another sip and looked around the restaurant. The décor was cozy and had a European feel about it. Everything seemed perfect in a very understated way, which she liked.

"How did you find this place?" she asked, looking around again.

"It's very popular in town," Richard replied. "They have the best steak here, and they are well known for serving the best wine." He tipped his glass in her direction.

Lucy glanced over her shoulder at the area near the entrance. She gasped when her gaze zeroed in on Taylor. He sat opposite a blonde woman, his gaze glued to her face, and from where Lucy sat, she saw his magnificent smile widen before he brushed his hand against hers.

Heat rose to the back of her neck, and she quickly averted her gaze.

"Hey, you with me?" Richard was saying. "Have you heard a thing I said in the past second?"

"Ahh, yes," she lied and covered her shock with a smile. "I was just admiring the scenery. This is a really lovely place."

"What were you looking at exactly?" he probed and scanned the area before looking at her.

She pretended to cough to command his attention, and she was glad when he focused his gaze on her. Lucy placed a hand on his, but before she could think of what to say next, the waiter arrived with a tray.

He set it in front of them, and she picked up a napkin, laid it on her lap, and smiled at Richard again. As she took the first bite of her starter, she cast another glance over her shoulder toward where Taylor sat.

Taylor rose to his feet as she stared, and placed his hand at his partner's waist, leaned into her and whispered something before smiling again.

Lucy rolled her eyes and turned away. She hadn't seen him smile at her like that since she returned to Ivy Creek, and she couldn't believe that he was having a good time here with another woman.

Who was the blonde, anyway? She wondered as she redirected her focus to her meal.

19

The next morning, Hannah arrived early. Lucy couldn't go back to sleep when she was woken up by a noisy truck that went past her building at four am, so she had spent the early hours of the morning in the kitchen baking.

She had cupcakes and brownies ready when Hannah arrived, and she started on the macaroons and muffins for the day. It was a Saturday morning, and the wintry air was a pleasant excuse for Lucy to wear a new sweatshirt to keep the cold away. She stepped away from the center table to wash her hands.

Hannah turned to her. "How did it go with Richard last night?" she asked. Hannah turned on the electric whisker and watched it beat the eggs she already set in the bowl.

"The restaurant we went to was amazing, and their chicken thighs are the best I've ever tasted."

"Really? What's the name?"

"Rossdale," Lucy replied, then she described the lighting and the beautiful scenery inside. "From the outside, it looks like some random restaurant, but inside is beautiful and the service is spectacular. You should try it sometime when you've got the chance, maybe for your date," Lucy said.

"Yeah right."

"You still haven't told me who it is," Lucy continued.

Hannah turned off the whisker. "What did you two do after dinner?" she asked, steering the conversation away from her again.

Lucy shot her a knowing smile but allowed it to slide. She mentioned her drive around town with Richard after, and their stop by an ice cream parlor for some ice cream before he brought her back home.

"I also ran into Taylor with some blonde woman at the restaurant. He didn't see me, and he left not too long after I spotted him."

"Oh," Hannah said and dropped what she was doing.

Lucy shrugged. "He seemed like he was having fun…" she continued, but trailed off and looked at Hannah, who already shot her an amused look.

"You sound like there's a but."

"There's no but," she said, dismissing thoughts of who the woman with Taylor was.

It's not your business, Lucy.

"So why do you sound disappointed that he was having fun with someone else?"

"I do not," she said in a high-pitched tone that made Hannah raise a brow and laugh. "I do not sound disappointed, trust me," she added.

Hannah shrugged. "If you say so."

"I say so."

They returned to work quietly and finished the baking in time to open the bakery for the day. It was almost mid-day when Pastor Evans walked into the bakery, and Lucy welcomed him with a smile. He was dressed in a plain black t-shirt and jeans, and his brown hair was neatly swept away from his face.

She hadn't seen him since the incident at the church, and she suspected he also hadn't dropped by because he was probably swamped with police investigations and dealing with the spooked town members.

"How are you doing, Lucy?" he asked when he reached the counter. "I'm so sorry. I haven't come around here to thank you for the treats you brought to the church the last time. I really appreciate your contribution."

"It's all right," she responded. "How have you been? And how is your wife, Sarah?"

"We are both fine. I would like some macaroons and a loaf of bread, please," he ordered. "Add some brownies to that."

Lucy took care of the order and asked when she handed him the package. "I was wondering, when is the funeral taking place?"

"In a few days," he replied and handed his card over for payment. "We've been waiting for some information from the family and that's now been sorted."

Lucy nodded. "It's a tragedy what happened," she said.

"Indeed."

She remembered Justin's words in his eulogy, and it prompted her next question. "Did they get along? Justin and Tabitha, I mean. Did they get along well as a couple?"

Pastor Evans looked up at the ceiling and rubbed his chin. "They were just like every other couple, you know. Every relationship has its difficulties, and so did theirs. They never had an issue they couldn't work through."

"I understand," Lucy responded in a low tone. "It must be so hard for Justin right now to navigate through his hurt."

"I should head back home, Lucy. Have a nice day," he said and waved at her. She watched him walk out of the bakery, and Zara entered immediately as he left.

"Lucy," she called with enthusiasm and strode to the counter. "I'm sorry you didn't see me the last time you came around. I had a lot on my plate, and I had to attend a business meeting."

"A business meeting?" she asked, walking around the counter to come sit with Zara, who had helped herself to a chair. "I thought you were the head chef at the hotel."

"I was." Zara moved her head from side to side and announced with a bouncing grin. "Justin promoted me to operations director because I have good ideas for Blue River and he made someone else head chef."

"I see," Lucy murmured.

"He made Reggie head chef, and he told me you two met when you came by."

"Yes, we did," Lucy replied. "He tasted the pastries I brought over and liked them. Are you here to deliver the paperwork?"

"No, silly," Zara replied and slapped Lucy's arm playfully. "I am here to say hello, and to get some of those amazing cupcakes of yours."

Lucy went over to the counter and returned with two cupcakes for Zara on a plate.

"They always taste amazing, and I'm going to enjoy having these served at Blue River," she said as she took a bite.

"Me too," Lucy said.

Zara left the bakery when she finished the cupcakes and Hannah joined Lucy in the dining area when they were alone again.

"This is a wonderful offer," Hannah said. "We have a lot to benefit from this deal."

"I know," Lucy said. She didn't doubt that it was, but after her last meeting with Justin, there was this twist in her gut that made her think—what if something went wrong?

"I hope it all goes according to plan," Lucy said and stood up from her chair to get back to work. If it did, then this would only be the beginning of greater things.

20

Since the holidays began, Lucy had barely had time to visit her concession stand at the park. On Saturday morning, she drove there to spend some time and inspect sales while Hannah stayed at the bakery with Aunt Tricia.

The park was full of people; families and kids running around, trying to build and recreate holiday memories.

"How's it going?" Lucy asked Dana, the lady employed to keep the concession stand running. "Lots of sales?"

"Yes… but not as much as it used to be anyway," she replied with a smile as she packed up a muffin for a girl in line. "It's winter. Not so many people hang out here when it snows."

Lucy snuggled into the fluffy coat she wore and adjusted the hoodie on her head. "That's fine. We can change the closing hours till winter's over. Does that sound good?"

Dana replied with a gentle nod and a smile that Lucy acknowledged before she turned around to examine her surroundings. She noticed a man sitting on the street bench not far off from where she stood. He got up and walked away, heading toward the park's exit. Lucy realized he had left a notepad behind on the chair when she went closer to the bench to sit and relax a little.

She picked it up and chased after the man without hesitating. When she got up to him, she tugged on his winter jacket as he turned around.

"You forgot your… Justin," she said when he looked at her. "I didn't realize it was you," she said and swallowed. "You left this behind."

He took the notepad from her. "Thanks Lucy, I didn't even notice I didn't have it with me."

"No problem."

Lucy propped her hands on her hips, and he eyed her a little.

"How are you?"

"I'm great, you?"

"I'm all right. Just thought I could sit here for a while and enjoy the view," he said.

"It actually is a lovely view."

They looked around, and faced each other again, Lucy wondering why Justin was staring at her.

"Are you in a hurry?" he asked. "I'd like to sit with you for a while, if that's all right."

"That's fine," Lucy agreed.

They walked back to the bench, and she adjusted the gloves on her hand. She sat with him on the bench and noticed he still wore his wedding ring when he placed his hands on his lap.

Lucy raised her gaze and met Justin's, and he gave her a smile that didn't reach his eyes. His shoulders sloped, sagging his body down, and he exhaled as if trying to get some load off his chest.

"I saw Zara yesterday," Lucy said, attempting to start a conversation that would ease the awkward silence.

Justin picked up on that and continued. "That's good. I recently promoted her, so she has been really busy running around getting things together. She is an active woman and very business-minded."

"I know," Lucy said. "She mentioned Reggie bringing over some paperwork within the next week before I make the first delivery."

Justin nodded again. "True. I just want to see everything move along smoothly and quickly, and it seems like I am under a lot of pressure from myself to do all of that."

He stopped and ran a hand through his hair. "Tabitha always handled all the business stuff, and since her passing, I've been trying to navigate through it alone. It's been quite difficult."

"I'm so sorry for your loss, Justin," Lucy said. "I heard about the funeral; Pastor Evans mentioned it the last time he was at my bakery."

"You'll be there, right?" Justin asked.

She hesitated. "I don't know."

"I'd like for you to be there, Lucy," he said.

A lump formed in Lucy's throat. She swallowed to push it down, but it stayed when she saw Justin's eyes water.

"Tabitha was a very passionate woman, despite her faults. She loved her business, she loved this town, and I just feel as if...

most of the people here don't know this side of her, so I don't think I will get much sympathy on that day. It's not news to me that my wife lacked fans even within her inner circle."

"I think you'll hang in there just fine, Justin," Lucy said. She touched his hand and squeezed it to show her support, and he sighed again.

"My staff are doing their best to keep the place running, just like it used to when she was with us. They all work very hard, especially Zara. She deserved the promotion. It also seems like some of them have blossomed in her absence. At least I can say business is better than it used to be."

Lucy kept her hand on his and she saw him look down at it. "I would really appreciate it if you showed up for the funeral."

Lucy's throat was too tight for her to speak properly, so she nodded twice before saying, "I'll do my best."

"Thanks for sitting with me, Lucy," he said and pulled away from her. "I need to get back to work."

She waved at him and relaxed on the bench, letting her back rest on it. She turned when someone called her name and saw Taylor standing beside her.

He sat when she straightened up on the bench, and Lucy faced him. "Hey, what's going on? What are you doing around here?" she asked.

"I came to check on someone across the street and I saw you here," he replied. His gaze flickered over her face for a second and rested on her eyes.

"Work related?"

"Yes," he said. "I saw you with Justin, and I came to say hello."

"Oh, that… we were just talking about the funeral and some business arrangement," she replied with a dismissive wave of her hand.

"You're in business with Justin?" he asked.

The ridge of Lucy's back went straight. "You sound like that's a crime," she said when she heard the tinge of suspicion in his voice.

"No, it's not, it's just…" his voice trailed off, and he rubbed his jaw. "We have our eyes on Blue River, and it's best you are careful with your association with them for the time being. At least till everything blows over."

"I know that. Trust me, you don't have to tell me."

"Good."

She saw a smile wrinkle up his lips after a second, and he chuckled.

"What?"

"Nothing. This reminds me of when we were in high school. This park, and winter. We used to come here a lot when it snowed, and we had that spot under that tree," he said and pointed at an oak tree. A couple sat on the bench under its wide branches and the image of them reminded Lucy of the time Taylor spoke about. Back then, she enjoyed coming here with Taylor during summer and every time she had free time on her hands.

They had shared their first kiss at that same spot. Lucy's cheeks flamed when the memory came to her, and she hoped he didn't see her blush.

"It used to be so much fun," she agreed and chuckled. When she quieted down again, she looked at him. "You know, I saw you at that posh restaurant called Rossdale downtown two days ago with some hot blonde."

"Really?" Taylor asked, amused. "I didn't see you. Were you with someone?"

"Yeah," she replied. "Who were you with?"

Lucy found her heart was thudding in her chest as she waited for his reply. *Was she his new girlfriend? A colleague? Or neighbor?*

"She's a new friend," he replied after assessing her for a while. She noticed a mischievous twinkle in his eyes. "What about you? Who were you with it?"

"Richard Lester," Lucy replied and saw his lips turn downward.

Taylor averted his eyes from hers, and shifted on the chair, leaning farther away from her. She saw his jaw muscle firm into a rigid line, and he stood up.

"Make sure you're careful in whatever business you have with anyone affiliated with Blue River," he said and stormed away, leaving Lucy confused.

She didn't understand what made him angry suddenly, and she battled with trying to figure it out the entire ride back to her bakery.

21

The bakery boomed with activity by the time Lucy returned, and she dove right in, serving customers, accepting tips, and sending them off with smiles and well wishes for the holidays.

Hannah came out of the kitchen with a tray of brownies, and she displayed them on the counter, taking her time to make sure they were properly arranged on the tray. Aunt Tricia conversed with some older men who came in together to get their fill of carrot cake, and Lucy smiled when she saw her aunty slip one of them an extra cupcake.

She shook her head and turned to Hannah. "Do you see how Aunt Tricia lights up with those men? It reminds me of when I used to watch my parents talk. They always tried to iron things out between them without an argument."

"That sounds cute." Hannah closed the counter and set down the tray she held. "My parents argue a lot, but it's always worth it in the end because they settle their differences and understand each other better after that."

"My dad hated confrontation," Lucy continued wistfully. Recently, she thought of her parents a lot, and the tug in her heart whenever those thoughts came reminded her of how much she missed them. "My mom knew that, so she tried her best to speak to him without sounding judgy. I didn't know much back then, but I admire what they had."

Hannah put a hand on Lucy's shoulder. "Don't worry, you'll get it," she said and laughed as she walked into the kitchen.

No customer was waiting to be served, so Lucy took a break and followed Hannah into the kitchen to continue their discussion. "Don't read meaning into this... I just miss my parents, that's all. I'm not longing for marriage or babies yet or anything."

"I know," Hannah pointed out in a melodious voice. She tipped the ladle she held in Lucy's direction and continued. "I just think you miss them this much because you're always alone, and you only go out when Richard invites you to. Do something fun alone... I thought that was the idea of this entire blonde thing."

Hannah made a gesture towards Lucy's hair, and Lucy touched a strand.

"My roots are getting darker again. I might need a touch-up soon."

"Yeah, but that's not my point. My point was you should go out more and have some fun. For example, I have an art function tonight with my sister, and it will be fun."

"Your sister is the date you talked about?" Lucy interjected, and Hannah cleared her throat.

"I might have lied about that date," she said with a shrug. "I just didn't want you to think I wasn't having fun myself this holiday season."

"But you're not." Lucy giggled when she saw the exasperated look on her friend's face, and she chuckled. "I'm kidding. If art's fun for you, then you should go."

Her phone pinged in her pocket, and she took it out as she continued talking. "In fact, if I didn't have an event lined up for tonight myself, then I might have come with you."

"You have an event?"

"Yes, Richard and I planned to visit the cinema together last time we were out, and…" her words died in her throat as she read the text she just received from Richard. "And he just texted me to cancel."

"So, you're free tonight, then?" Hannah picked up their conversation again, this time with more enthusiasm. "This will be so interesting if three of us go together."

"I don't know much about art," Lucy said and searched for a more concrete excuse. "And I should just take this time to work on the recipes we will be delivering to Blue River next week."

Aunt Tricia came into the kitchen then, and she took off the cap over her hair. "I'm leaving Lucy. I have a date."

"What?" Hannah exclaimed in a melodious voice.

Her laugh filled the kitchen, and Aunt Tricia joined her.

"You're the only one who isn't doing anything fun tonight. Don't you think you should join me?" Hannah urged again.

Lucy rubbed the back of her neck and tried to decide, but in the end, she shook her head. "I should stay back and work on the recipes, but you should have fun."

She faced her aunt. "Enjoy yourself, Aunt Tricia."

"I sure will, honey," Aunt Tricia replied.

She was waving as she left the kitchen with her bag, and Hannah came over to where Lucy stood. She began taking off her apron and cap, then combed her fingers through her hair to free her blonde tresses.

"I'll see you tomorrow, Lucy."

She hugged Hannah briefly and left. Thirty minutes into working on her recipes and Lucy wished she had gone out with Hannah.

It was so silent inside the bakery that she sat outside on the front porch for a while. At least that way, she could enjoy watching the sunset while working on the recipes.

She finished early, locked her front doors, and turned on the speakers to listen to some Christmas songs while she fixed a quick dinner for herself and Gigi. Lucy usually made sure Gigi stayed upstairs, to avoid her coming into the bakery when she had customers, but tonight, she opened the middle door, and allowed Gigi to come stay with her in the kitchen.

Lucy danced alone while the water for her pasta sizzled, and went around the kitchen, gathering items to prepare some sauce. When she finished preparing her meal, she fixed Gigi a quick one and sat down to eat in silence.

Time dragged slowly, and Lucy read through the modifications she intended to make to her recipes one last time before she cleaned up to retire for the night.

She heard a loud bang on her front door as she locked the kitchen to head upstairs, and she froze in her tracks.

Who could it be?

She wasn't expecting anyone, and so far, she had gotten no calls or texts. Lucy hesitated, not wanting to let anyone in at this time of the night.

The knock came again, followed by a familiar voice calling her name. Lucy let Gigi down from her arms and crossed over to the side window of the bakery.

She saw Zara standing outside from where she stood, and she relaxed a bit before going to open the door.

"Hey, Zara," Lucy said when she opened up.

"Good evening, Lucy," she greeted and adjusted the bag on her shoulder. "Should have come sooner, but I got caught up at work, and I couldn't make it earlier. Can you let me in? Let's go over the deal. I have the paperwork here."

"Right now?"

"We should finalize it before Monday, and I won't have time after now. So yes, right now," she replied, her words ending in a plea.

Lucy sighed and stepped away from the door to let Zara in. She closed the door and latched the lock again. "All right, so what are we looking at?"

22

L ucy invited her into the kitchen, offered her a glass of water and a seat, then poured herself a glass of water before she sat.

"Here are the documents for you to sign, and these are special recipes I would like for you to add. We sometimes have special guests who have special diets because of health issues and we have to meet the needs of these VIP guests."

"I understand," Lucy responded as she flipped the pages of the bonded document.

"Your payment and every other detail are written there, so take your time and go through it."

Zara sipped from her glass, and Lucy adjusted herself on her chair as she read the pages. She felt Zara's gaze on her the entire time, and it almost made her squirm.

Zara Stanmore had intense dark eyes. It made Lucy wonder if anyone had ever told her how disconcerting they made people feel when she looked at them. Or was she just being overly sensitive?

She finally got to the last page after minutes of reading the document and looked at Zara. "I will have to get a pen."

She went to the counter where she kept her notepad to get a pen and when she looked back, Zara had left her chair. Zara stood by the counter where Lucy kept some dry ingredients for her baking, and she pointed. "Wild cats?" she asked.

Zara pointed at the sticker on the counter and asked again. "You attended University of Arizona?"

"Yeah, my mother went there," Lucy replied. "She talked about the school a lot. Did you go there too?"

Zara nodded. "I grew up in Arizona with my parents... My mom, actually, because my father left when I was six. He moved far away, so I never got to see him much, at least not till I lost my mother."

"I'm so sorry to hear that," Lucy said. She sat down again and signed the document and closed the file.

Zara shrugged. "Thanks. When she died, I moved away and finally settled here. Seeing this sticker just reminded me of what my life was like those many years ago in Arizona, you know. Your childhood is one time of your life you can never forget if you know what I mean."

"Oh, I know what you mean," Lucy replied sincerely. Her decision to stay back in Ivy Creek after her parents' funeral earlier that year made her realize how much she had missed home, and Lucy had learned to be grateful for support from family and friends since she returned.

"Ivy Creek helped me discover my passion for hospitality and cooking, and also helped me grow my career, so I don't regret moving here at all," Zara said. "Working at Blue River helped me grow my skill too."

"But it must have been so hard working for Justin and Tabitha, right? Considering how Tabitha treated her staff and how Justin could never stand up to her."

The smile on Zara's face faded in the blink of an eye. "That has nothing to do with Justin," she snapped. "Don't you dare talk about him that way."

"I'm sorry, I didn't mean to upset you, I just—"

"Stop talking!" Zara raised a hand to hush her, and she took a step towards Lucy. "Justin has done nothing wrong. He is a victim of everything that happened."

Lucy's stomach churned when Zara's face paled, and she averted her gaze.

"My God, what's wrong with me?" Zara said in a broken voice and tendered Lucy an apologetic smile as if she hadn't just snapped moments ago. "I'm so sorry. I didn't mean to snap like that. I guess I'm just tired from a long day at work, and my nerves are a bit on edge."

Lucy took in a long, shallow breath. "Its fine," she said with a nervous laugh to ease the tension that hung in the air moments earlier.

"When you work with people for a long time, they become family to you, and it's only natural that I would defend my family like that," Zara said as she started to pace the kitchen. She raked her hand through her hair and stopped again when Lucy straightened up.

"I mean, if anyone talked about my father in a certain way, or my mother, then I would also react the way you did. It's normal to defend the people you care about," Lucy said.

Zara froze in her steps and shot Lucy an unflinching look. Her pupils dilated, and she dropped her hands to her side. The cold look in her eyes sent a chill down Lucy's spine, and a wave of nausea reached her as it suddenly dawned on her.

Was it possible? What were the chances that Justin was Zara's father?

Lucy's entire system pumped with adrenaline as she asked in a shaky voice.

"Is Justin your father?" Lucy blurted.

She gasped when Zara nodded in affirmation, and her knees nearly gave way. "I came out here because of him. After my mother passed away, I had no one else, and I thought I should find him, but he... he had forgotten all about his daughter, and he couldn't even recognize me. I don't blame him. He left because my mom wanted him to, but a part of me was still hurt that he didn't even look for me. I wondered for a long time if he loved me at all, and when I met him again after all these years, I realized he did. He just couldn't show it because he wasn't free."

Lucy's stomach churned harder the more Zara talked. "Who else knows about this?" Lucy probed further.

"Tabitha recently found out," Zara replied. She took a step closer to where Lucy sat, and Lucy gripped the edge of the table in front of her so tight, her knuckles turned white. She fought against the cold, paralyzing terror tearing at her insides when Zara's lips curved into a cynical smile.

"She wasn't supposed to find out, but she did. It was my secret to keep, and she couldn't keep out of my business, so I had to do something."

Lucy's head swooned. Her right hand moved to her pocket for her phone, and when she didn't touch anything, she gasped.

"Looking for this?" Zara asked and pointed at the phone on the side counter of the sink.

Oh, sugar… I left it there when I got her a glass of water.

Lucy licked her dry lips and rose to her feet slowly.

"So, you killed her? Because she knew your secret?"

"I didn't want to," Zara said and continued pacing again.

Lucy had moved from where she stood. If she could distract Zara long enough to make it to the door, then she could run upstairs and use the landline in her living room to place a call to the cops. She just had to make sure Zara kept talking.

"I hated the way she treated him. He's my father, and he deserves more than some woman who wouldn't respect him, even in front of strangers. I had to set him free. You get that right?"

Lucy suspected Zara wanted sympathy from her, but how could she look her in the eye and lie? She didn't get it—her heinous act could never be justified. No matter what Tabitha did, Lucy believed Zara had no right to kill her.

She didn't voice out any of these thoughts, instead, she kept her eyes glued to Zara's.

"It must have been hard watching your father every day and knowing he didn't recognize you must have made it worse, but…"

"Are you going to stand there and justify Tabitha?" Zara cut in.

"I'm not doing that; I just don't think that…"

"She deserved what she got," Zara interrupted again. She took three menacing steps towards Lucy who backed away, and Lucy's heart began to pound against her ribcage.

Try to hold still, Lucy… deep breaths. There's always a way out.

The distance between her and Zara was short, and she tried to calculate her options. If she made a run for the door, Zara would get to her before she touched the doorknob. She also couldn't risk staying here with her.

It was nearly ten pm, and no one was coming this way. How could she get out of this situation?

"I could not watch her disrespect him anymore. With her out of the way, he now sees me," she said as she kept coming closer, and Lucy backed towards the wall.

"With her dead, I can finally be happy with my father, and not have to worry about what insults he would get if she ever found us speaking. Everything that went wrong in my family was her fault."

"Zara," Lucy murmured when she got so close. At this point, Lucy could barely breathe without the tightness in her chest closing in on her.

"Now, you know the truth, and you have to go too."

Lucy lunged for the doorknob then and pushed the door open, but she wasn't fast enough. Zara dragged her back, shut the door with a loud bang, and hurled her against it.

She whimpered when her back crashed on the door, pain radiating through her. Zara's hands encircled her neck, shutting her air supply with one squeeze.

"I'm sorry, Lucy, but you have to die."

Lucy fought her off with every bit of her strength. Her nails dug into her wrists and she tried to dislodge Zara's grip, but she failed.

Slowly, her fight faded, and her gaze became blurry. Air stopped getting to her lungs, and she felt her eyes bulge out of their sockets.

Someone help me! She tried to scream but couldn't form any words, not when Zara's tight grip was crushing her windpipe.

Her eyes fluttered, and she gave up, slipping away into the terrifying darkness consuming her. Lucy opened her eyes one last time and stared into Zara's dark eyes. The dreadful smile on her pale face etched into Lucy's memory and she didn't think she could ever get it out.

If this was her last moment on Earth, then she didn't want to go down alone. With the rest of her strength, she jerked her knee forward, bringing it in contact with Zara's pelvic region.

Zara yelped and staggered away from her, giving Lucy time to inhale a large chunk of air. She grabbed the door and dashed into the stairway, shutting the door, and locking it behind her before she hurried to her living room.

She fell on her knees when she got to the living room, her hands shaking as she struggled to get on her feet again and get to the phone. Downstairs, she could hear Zara hitting the door.

It was a wooden door, weakened from years of use, and Lucy knew with the right amount of force it would cave. She got to the phone in time and dialed 911.

"I need help," she said and screamed when Zara's hands closed in on her again.

They wrestled to the ground, Zara staying on top of her. Her hands snaked around Lucy's neck one last time, and she pressed hard.

"It's a shame, Lucy, I liked you," was the last thing Lucy heard before she blacked out.

23

L ucy opened her eyes with a loud gasp, and she struggled to free herself. She fought against the tightness in her throat, wanting to breathe, and she felt warm hands come around her arms.

"It's all right… Lucy, it's me, Tricia, you're safe."

The sure words cut through the terror clouding her brain, and Lucy's fight slowly disseminated. She broke into tears, and the sobs wracked through her body as her aunt's arms came around her body.

"You're safe," Aunt Tricia murmured and consoled her, patting her back and running a hand down her back. "I'm with you.

Her shoulders sagged, and she sank into her aunt's arms, wanting the warmth of her embrace to offer safety.

"I thought I was going to die," she murmured, her voice a bare croak when she could finally speak.

Her throat burned, and she lifted a hand to her neck to feel the soreness.

"I came right on time. Zara had her hands around your neck, strangling you when I arrived, and I stopped her with a bat I found in a corner."

"How did you know to come?" she asked.

"I finished my date and decided to spend the night at your apartment because you were alone. When I came, the doors were locked, but the lights inside were on. I tried calling but couldn't reach you, then I heard the loud crash from upstairs and knew I had to get in," Aunt Tricia explained.

"I was right on time," she repeated. "I remembered you always kept a spare key under the flowerpot on the porch and I used that to let myself in. When I got upstairs, I found you struggling for your life."

"What about Zara?" Lucy asked. She continued forcing herself to take deep, relaxing breaths, and she wanted to ease the wild race her nerves still hadn't recovered from.

"I knocked her out hard, and by the time she regained consciousness, the cops had arrived. They took her away immediately, and just in time, because they were going to search for her at her house."

"They found out she's the killer?"

Aunt Tricia's head bobbed twice. "The autopsy report came back. Turns out she poisoned Tabitha with a strong substance."

"The cops found out?"

"They knew she died from poison, but wanted to investigate where it came from quietly, so they held back the details of the case from everyone. It was a smart move because Zara would have skipped town if she suspected they were onto her."

Lucy remembered Taylor warning her about associating with any staff from Blue River. She sank into the bed, sighed, and closed her eyes.

Her body still ached, and she was feeling dizzy again. "I'm just glad you're safe, Lucy," her aunt said and this time picked her hand up from the bed. "Today is Tabitha's funeral, and I promised Justin I would come on your behalf. He was here to check in on you hours ago."

"Oh," she murmured, already slipping away. Her eyes closed for a second and when she opened them again, a doctor had come into the room.

"I'll be back, honey," Aunt Tricia said when the doctor asked her to leave. "Don't worry about a thing and rest. This Christmas will be filled with many beautiful things, just like you love it."

Aunt Tricia kissed Lucy on the cheek and left the room. The doctor checked the IV connected to her arm and administered an injection that instantly made her drowsy.

"How long will you keep me here" she slurred as the drug took effect.

"Not for long, miss. Don't worry. As soon as we're certain you've passed some tests, you'll be free to go home."

"Good," she whispered and licked her dry lips. "I would hate to spend Christmas here." A smile crept on her lips as she dozed off and for a second, she thought the doctor smiled back at her.

Lucy fell asleep and dreamed of making snow angels in her backyard with her parents. At some point, she heard a deep voice speak to her softly, and her eyes twitched open. She thought she saw Taylor through her hazy vision, but she couldn't be sure.

She went back to sleep for the second time and dreamed of a happy Christmas, full of music and laughter, just like the ones she had in her childhood.

Lucy wanted a Christmas full of laughter and joy, and she hoped she'd get it once she could get this grogginess out of her system.

24

T hree days later was Christmas eve, and Lucy was very much in the Christmas spirit the entire day. The bakery emptied early, and all she did since she got up was sing carols and festive songs as she worked.

Now, with Hannah, Aunt Tricia, and Richard, she danced to another tune playing in the background. Richard pulled her close, and they moved slowly to the song while Aunt Tricia went into the kitchen to bring some mulled wine.

They made a toast to the coming year and all the good things they wished would happen in their lives. Lucy was especially thrilled with how things had turned out in her life after her parents' death.

The bakery was doing better than she expected, and she had escaped several brushes with death. She was grateful for all of that.

"To Christmas," Aunt Tricia said after refilling everyone's glass.

They clinked and cheered as they bobbed their head to a popular Christmas song playing over the speakers. She threw her head back and laughed when Richard winked at her, and she danced with him some more.

"We should all attend the carol at the church together tonight," Richard suggested. "I am sure it'll be fun."

"I think so too," Lucy agreed.

The bell above the door rang as the door slid open and they stopped dancing when Justin came into the bakery.

"Bad time?" he asked.

"No, no, come in please," Lucy ushered him in. "How are you?"

Justin slipped his hands into his pocket and rocked back on his heels. "Compliments of the season, Lucy, and I am doing great. How are you? I should have come by sooner, but I have been swamped with work at the hotel and trying to get everything in order since the funeral and the investigation."

Hannah had turned down the music, and Aunt Tricia offered him a seat.

"I'm so sorry about what happened to Zara," Lucy consoled. "It must be hard for you to lose a daughter and wife in a short period," she said.

Justin sighed. "Zara wasn't mine," he said after a minute of silence, and she saw his eyes sink into their sockets in sadness. "She was too little to know what happened back then with her mother, but when I found out she wasn't mine and confronted her mother, she kicked me out. I left Arizona because there was nothing for me there, and when I met Tabitha, she helped me build a life. I loved her, and I knew she loved me too, even though she was rude and inconsiderate. There's no way I would have abandoned my own child, ever."

"You've been through a lot, Justin," Aunt Tricia said. She disappeared into the kitchen and returned with a glass for him. "You should join us to toast to a great year ahead."

"Both women loved me, but in the wrong way," he muttered as Aunt Tricia poured him a glass of wine.

Justin toasted with them, and they drank again. Another song came on, and Lucy sang along at the top of her voice.

On the first day of Christmas, my true love sent to me: a partridge in a pear tree...

They sang the song to the end and clapped when it ended.

"Did the cops finalize the investigation?" Richard asked.

Justin nodded. "They found the substance used to kill Tabitha in Zara's apartment and confiscated it. "It's so sad that she had to go to such lengths, poisoning Tabitha the morning before the award. It took time for the poison to work its way through her system, and she used that substance so no one would suspect it was something she ate earlier in the day. The poison killed her slowly and according to the autopsy, there was no way she would have survived the amount of poison found in her system."

Lucy shuddered, as Justin gave them details of the entire case, and Richard must have noticed this because he put his arms around her to pull her into his side for a hug.

"It's all over now, thank God," Hannah whispered.

"Yes. Both women loved me in their own way, and I just wish things turned out differently between Zara and me. Maybe if she talked to me, she would have found out the truth before she did something so diabolical."

"True," Aunt Tricia agreed. "Tabitha was not a saint, but she still did not deserve what happened to her. No one should die like that… I'm just relieved justice was served in the end, and Zara will be punished for her crimes. There are a lot of charges against her, and she will be away for a long time, maybe for life."

"Me too," Justin said. "And I'm so sorry for all that happened, Lucy. I hope we can put it all behind us and work together as agreed."

"Water under the bridge," Lucy replied with a wave of her hand. "I already signed the papers Zara came with that night, and I made a list of what I will be delivering."

"Well, it's time to put it all behind us and celebrate," Aunt Tricia said and everyone agreed. They turned on the music again and Justin thanked Lucy for welcoming him, even after everything that had transpired over the last few weeks.

"To a new start," Aunt Tricia toasted, and everyone joined her.

"We will move forward with the business as planned and will be expecting your deliveries this coming week," Justin continued, after sipping his wine.

"I can't wait to get started," Lucy replied with a smile.

That night, they attended the town's carol at the church together. Lucy sat with Richard in church and as they sang along to the carols, she hoped the new year would bring more than everything she hoped for.

The End

WAFFLES AND SCUFFLES

AN IVY CREEK COZY MYSTERY

ABOUT WAFFLES AND SCUFFLES

Released: April 2022
Series: Book 5 – Ivy Creek Cozy Mystery Series
Standalone: Yes
Cliff-hanger: No

Lucy's excited about the new year and all the dreams she hopes will be fulfilled over the coming months. She's glad when her customers make the right noises when they taste her latest treat.

She's happy to offer this treat as her main item when she's invited to serve her pastries at the local theatre.

She knows her treats are delicious and to die for but when a fight breaks out over them, she's left wondering if she's witnessing fact or fiction. Things take a turn for the worse when a prominent personality in town drops dead in the middle of a rehearsal at the theater.

The death of this prominent person attracts the attention of local and national media who descend upon the small town of Ivy Creek. Lucy is left feeling despondent and lonely when all her customers desert her bakery after a popular reporter twists her words, which paint Lucy, her bakery and her town in a very bad light.

Lucy has also come to a crossroad in her relationship with one of the most eligible bachelors in town. Have things turned sour beyond repair or is her relationship about to soar?

Will she set aside past hurts, and her pursuit of happiness to find a killer who seems to hold all the aces in a murder investigation that appears unsolvable?

1

Lucy unwound the lights from the celling board
frames and dropped them into the box her Aunt
Tricia held. When she stepped down from the
chair, she dusted her palms together and sighed.

"That's all of it," she said, and looked around the store.

They had just finished taking down the Christmas decorations,
and now the bakery's dining area was back to its regular look.

Lucy smiled as she looked around, hands propped on her hips.
"Seems like the place is back to its old self, and we might need
something new to spark things up for the new year."

"Maybe a new addition to the menu? Like the waffles you made for your delivery today," Aunt Tricia said as she was closing the box.

"That sounds like a brilliant idea," Lucy responded as she walked over to the counter. It was still the first week of the new year, and she had just re-opened the bakery. There was a lot she had on her list for the new year, and one of them had been expanding Sweet Delights.

"Maybe waffles and another kind of cupcake? I'm thinking cheesecake," Aunt Tricia was saying as she carried the box into the adjoining office and came back out.

Lucy had pulled out her notepad and was now scribbling down the idea her aunt suggested.

"It's a new year, so we should start out with something new to excite the customers. I love the waffles idea..." Lucy closed the notepad and looked at her aunt. "Personally, I also have some new goals for the new year."

"Really? Like what?" Aunt Tricia asked as she pulled a chair towards herself. The bakery had opened for the day, and they were yet to get their first customer. Lucy took the chance to sit with her aunt in the dining area. She was still expecting her friend and assistant, Hannah, and she was sure she would arrive at any moment.

"I don't know... I just think I want to find true love this year," she said, and rested her chin on both hands with her elbows balanced on the table in front of her. "The kind my parents had," she added with a wistful sigh.

The holidays had filled Lucy's mind with memories of her childhood. Her parents spent every moment together. Lucy remembered they went on brief trips during the holidays, and in those times, she had envisioned her life with her future husband being just as splendid as her parents. Her parents had died the previous year and Lucy couldn't help reminiscing about the good times she had with them.

"I always admired your mother's relationship with Tom," Aunt Tricia said, referring to Lucy's father, Tom Hale. "At first, I thought it would wear out... the way he adored her from the start, but it never did."

"I crave what they had," Lucy said as she sighed again. "Maybe I'll have what they had someday?"

"Of course, honey," Aunt Tricia replied. "I mean... what about Richard? That young man cares for you."

Lucy had been dating Richard Lester, the owner of a cafeteria, for some months now, and although she liked him; his kind personality and attentiveness... she still didn't want to rush things.

"We're still taking it slow, getting to know each other," she told her aunt.

"He seems like a real nice young man, and I think both of you should think about taking things to the next level? It's been some months now."

Lucy flushed at her aunt's statement and waved her hand dismissively. "I do like Richard. That's why we're taking it slow."

Her aunt shrugged, raising her hand in the air. "Well then, I think you don't need to worry too much about true love for now. It will come in its own good time."

Lucy was about to change the subject to something more work related when the new doorbell she had installed rang once, and the door swung open.

Hannah walked into the store alongside a customer. Lucy had made her way to the back of the counter to attend to the customer while Aunt Tricia relaxed further in her chair.

"Hey, hey," Hannah greeted as she came to where Lucy stood and hugged her briefly before greeting Aunt Tricia. "Happy new year," Hannah continued.

Lucy was smiling as she quickly attended to the customer, then went around to join Hannah and her aunt. "I haven't seen you since the start of the new year," she said as she sat down.

"I went on a holiday with my sister, and just got back. How did your holiday go?" Hannah asked.

"It went well. Oh my God, I love your new haircut," Lucy said as her eyes settled on Hannah's platinum blonde hair. She admired the pixie cut style.

Hannah smiled at her and touched some strands of it. "It's a new year, so I decided to go with a new look."

"I love it," Lucy complimented again. "It frames your face, and it makes your smile stand out."

Lucy watched Hannah look around the bakery. Her eyes settled on a basket of cupcakes and cookies she arranged on the left end of the counter.

"Are those for delivery?" Hannah asked, one brow quirking up.

"The town council is having their first meeting for the year, and I was asked to deliver some treats. I'm taking them there soon," Lucy said and glanced at the watch on her wrist.

Hannah went into the office to hang her coat and returned to the counter.

"Will you come with me to deliver the treats for the council meeting?" Lucy asked.

"Yes, sure… are you ready to go?" Hannah asked.

Aunt Tricia rose to her feet. "I'll stay here till you both get back," she said.

Lucy walked over to the table and picked up the baskets. Minutes later, she was driving down the street with Hannah, and listening to some pop song on the radio.

They passed the police station as they headed for the town hall, and Lucy saw some cops standing out front. They seemed knee-deep in their discussion, and she stared for a long time, trying to see if she would spot Taylor, the town's deputy sheriff, amongst them.

During the holidays, Lucy had spent some time with the deputy, who was her ex, before she left Ivy Creek years ago. He had frequented the store during the holiday to buy her treats almost every day.

Her relationship with Taylor had been frosty when she first arrived back in town and she didn't think it could ever get better, but recently, they were communicating better whenever they ran into each other; most of the tension that had hung in the air whenever they had bumped into each other had eased away.

"It's my first time coming here during the meeting," Hannah said when they arrived at the hall, and Lucy stepped out of the car with her. They headed towards the entrance, both holding baskets, and Lucy greeted the first woman she saw at the reception when they entered.

"Hi, I'm Lucy Hale… I'm here to deliver treats for the town's local council meeting today."

The red-haired woman behind the reception desk gave them a warm, welcoming smile. "It's a pleasure to meet you, Lucy. I'm Judy… Judy Cousins, a member of the board," she said. "The meeting has already begun. Would you like to join us?"

Judy took the basket Lucy handed her.

"I should be on my way," she said and was about turning around when Judy stopped her with a light touch to her shoulder.

"I was hoping you would join us for the meeting," she said. "It's a good opportunity for me to introduce you to the council members."

"Uh… I didn't plan to," Lucy replied.

"Come on… like I said, it's a good opportunity. You shouldn't let it pass," Judy urged. "The meeting won't last that long."

Lucy shot Hannah a glance to know what she thought, and Hannah responded with a slight shrug.

"Alright," she agreed.

Judy led them into the main hall where other council members had already gathered, and they found a seat at the back.

Lucy and Hannah watched Judy walk away, her three-inch heels clicking against the floor as she headed to the front of the hall where some members were seated. She took a seat amongst them, crossed her fingers, and kept her hands on the desk in front of her before she began speaking.

The council members talked about the town's welfare, and near the end, Judy and some other lady shared the treats before Judy announced. "The last item on our agenda is to discuss the open auditions at the theater."

"I hope we don't have to attend?" one man asked, raising his hand from the crowd.

A few others murmured, and Judy lifted her hand to gain their attention again. "It's being organized by Pete Jenson," she announced. "He'd expect us to be there."

The mention of the name made the crowd fall into a hushed silence, and Lucy scanned the crowd. She noticed most of the council members wore concerned looks on their faces, their brows furrowed as they listened to Judy.

She turned back to Hannah and asked in a low tone as people began filing out of the hall. "Who's Pete Jenson?"

2

"Pete Jenson is Ivy Creek's famous director. Haven't you heard of him?" Hannah asked. Lucy turned to Hannah as she tucked some loose strands of hair behind her ear. "He used to run the local theater and direct plays there before he became a global star when a play he wrote and directed became a hit on Broadway. Now he has his own production company, and he's a major player in the theater industry."

Lucy shook her head. She had never heard of Pete Jenson, but she was curious to know more about him after she heard all his achievements.

"How is it I've never heard of him?" Lucy asked as she drove back to the bakery after they left the town hall.

"Let's just say he's not everyone's cup of tea. People still remember how he cut corners and left some businesses in a pickle. You probably don't know him because he changed his name. He used to go by Pete Gruden."

Lucy replayed the words in her head and wondered how many toes Pete had stepped on in his pursuit of success. She could recall the name Gruden, even though she couldn't remember the face. Her parents had to have mentioned him when they were alive.

"Judy probably mentioned that people should be wary of him because he has a reputation of going back on his word," Hannah said as they passed the traffic lights on the road next to the bakery.

"It'd be nice to meet him," she said, as she parked her car.

"I don't think it would be a good idea to," Hannah replied as she got out of the car.

They entered the bakery, and Lucy heard laughter from the doorway even before she stepped in. Taylor and her aunt sat at a table having what seemed like a friendly chat. Taylor rose to his feet when he saw her.

"Hey," she said as she got close. Her hands moved into the pocket of the coat she wore, and she stopped in front of him.

"Taylor dropped by shortly after you left and we've just been catching up."

"You dropped by for some carrot bread?" she asked.

Taylor smiled and nodded. "How did you know?"

Her eyes latched onto his for a second before she walked past him and headed to the counter.

"I know you… It's your favorite and your mother's too," she replied.

Hannah made her way into the kitchen while Lucy began packaging some carrot bread. She wrapped up a bag and handed it to Taylor over the table.

"Say hello to your mom for me," she said when he took the pack.

"I will. See you around, Lucy."

When he left the bakery, Lucy caught the mischievous gleam in her aunt's eyes that made her flush.

"He came to see you," Aunt Tricia said as she pulled on an apron and wrapped her hair into a bun. "I had to delay him a little till you got back."

Lucy shook her head. "He came for the bread, aunt. Let's not get any ideas."

Lucy kept smiling as she entered the kitchen to join Hannah. They started baking and had made three batches of cupcakes and brownies.

Aunt Tricia sat in the dining area when they entered, and Lucy joined her after getting a glass of water from the kitchen. Minutes after they arrived, Richard walked in.

Lucy dropped the napkin she wiped her hands on, went around the counter, and flung her arms around his neck.

"Happy new year," he said, bringing his hands out from behind him to hand over the flowers he held.

Richard had been away on a skiing trip with some of his friends, so they hadn't seen each other since the start of the new year.

"How are you?" he said.

"I've never been better," Lucy replied, grinning as she accepted the gift, and out of the corner of her eyes, she saw Aunt Tricia give her another knowing grin. "Give me a moment while I find a place for this."

When she returned to the dining area, she found Richard and Aunt Tricia talking. He laughed to some joke she had made, and she put her hand on his arm.

"Walk with me," Richard said when she joined them. "I've missed you, and I'd like to spend some time with you."

"Uhm… I have to stay in the bakery," she started, rubbing the back of her neck.

"Come on, Lucy… it's the first week of January. There's no customer here anyway as everyone's trying to reduce the number of sweet treats they have this time of the year," Aunt Tricia said.

Lucy's rubbed the back of her neck because of her aunt's obvious matchmaking, and she bit her lower lip.

"Just go with the gentleman already," Aunt Tricia said, chuckling this time. "I will handle things with Hannah, okay?"

There was a grin on Richard's face when she looked at him, and she gave in.

"Alright… let's walk."

Minutes later, they were strolling down the street hand in hand. A chilly wind blew in their direction, but they kept their pace, passing the first curve out of their street.

They were heading towards the town's local church when Lucy angled her head towards him. "How was your trip?"

Richard looked at her and tightened his grip on her hand.

"It went well… not so much fun because I missed you. I enjoy skiing anyway and wished you had come with me."

Lucy rubbed her hand over his and lifted it to her cheek. "I enjoyed Christmas here in Ivy Creek as well. It reminded me of so many happy memories and helped me decide what I want for the new year."

"Care to share?"

"I'm thinking of expanding," she launched right in. "Business is booming, and even the concession stand has loads of customers during the week. I'm thinking of making the bakery into something bigger. That way, we can make more and host a lot more customers."

Richard was quiet as she spoke, and when she looked at him, his lips were pressed into a thin line that made her pause. "Why do you have that look? Do you not like my idea?" she asked.

"That's not it," he replied. Richard dragged in a deep breath, closed his eyes, and lifted their joined hands so he could kiss her knuckles. His lips lingered for a bit before he continued. "I've tried expanding my business before, and I have to tell you, it's hard. The financial burden becomes a lot at some point, and it will weigh you down. I don't want any of that to happen to you. I like the pace at which you run the bakery right now."

Lucy took in his words and toyed with them in her mind. Expanding the bakery seemed like a brilliant idea to her from the minute she thought about it, but she also hadn't weighed the other aspects Richard just brought up.

She turned to face him again, but she suddenly noticed a queue on the other side of the road. "What's going on there?" she asked, as she observed a few people crossing the road to join the queue.

"Wanna find out?"

Richard was already pulling her across the road with him before she could reply, and they stopped when they made their way past the side of the queue and managed to get into the foyer of the building.

"This place used to be the local theater till it got moved to a new location, and all these people here are…" Richard's voice trailed off when someone walked behind them.

"Are you here for the audition?"

Lucy and Richard both turned to the lady asking.

"Pete Jenson's open auditions for the new play," she continued. "Is that why you're here?"

"There's a new play?" Richard asked the lady.

"Yes," she replied with a smile. "Pete's putting one together, and he intends to take this one around the world. It will be a huge one, judging by the looks of things." She clapped her hands together when she finished, and Lucy noticed the elated look on her face. "So will you be auditioning?"

"No... we're here to watch," Lucy replied, easing her hand away from Richard's so she could tuck her hair behind her ear. "We can watch, right?" she remembered Judy mentioned he was hosting the open auditions, and frankly, Lucy wanted to see for herself what Pete looked like.

She was in luck because the woman standing with them suddenly gasped and looked past them. "That's Pete," she announced, and hurried away before Lucy or Richard could say anything else.

The crowd outside cheered, and Lucy saw Pete wave at some people as he came out from another adjoining door into the foyer. He wore a wide smile as he waved, and she took in his physical looks.

He had a tall, lean figure, and the blue shirt he wore complimented the golden-brown shade of his hair. Pete stopped to listen to what the woman was saying, and as they spoke, she paused and pointed in Lucy's direction.

Lucy's jaw dropped momentarily. Her hand moved to her chest, and she shot Richard a curious look. "I wonder what that's about," she said.

Pete said something to the woman, patting her shoulder as he spoke before he walked away from her with long strides towards Lucy and Richard.

"Pete Jenson," he said when he got to them.

"Lucy Hale," she replied, accepting his hand before Richard mentioned his name.

"Owner of Sweet Delights? That Lucy Hale?" Pete asked, one brow rising with the question.

"Yes, that's me," she answered.

He exhaled and slipped his hands into his pockets. "I've heard so much about you, and your treats, too. I've always wanted to try them as the reviews say you're doing a brilliant job with your recipes. It's good to see young minds creating outstanding products in town."

"Thank you," Lucy replied, flattered that he had a lot to say about her bakery when she had only just met him.

He seems like a nice man, she thought as she assessed him. His eyes were a deep shade of blue and his cheekbones were prominent when he smiled. Lucy could see how he earned a reputation in the entertainment industry. The man had good looks, and there was an easy aura around him.

Two ladies walked past them, and he waved at them, before turning to her and Richard.

"I understand you asked about watching the open auditions. We're yet to start for the day, but there's always room for spectators."

"I'd love to watch, but I have to get back to my bakery," Lucy said, looking at Richard, who nodded in agreement.

"That's sad. You would have enjoyed it. I hope you'll find time to come watch tomorrow. The auditions will last for a week," he said. "By the way, I'd like to contract you to deliver some pastries for the auditions starting from tomorrow. I'd like the production team and main cast to have something to feast on during the rehearsals."

Lucy's insides bounced with excitement at the mention of the offer. Her eyes darted from Pete to Richard before she asked. "That's an amazing offer, and I'd like to take it on. Do you have a list of pastries you'd like to be served? And how about the payment?"

"My secretary will get back to you on both counts as I have to go attend to some business before the auditions start for the day. Don't worry, she'll contact you soon," he said.

Pete gave her one last smile and waved at them before he continued down the hall, entered a room, and closed the door behind him.

"I got an offer," Lucy said, almost letting out an excited squeal as she turned to Richard again. He didn't share in her excitement, and the look on his face dampened her celebratory glow.

"We should go," he said, took her hand and led her out of the foyer again.

Outside, the crowd had reduced because most of the people had entered the theater. Lucy stopped Richard from walking any further and turned to him. She got the sense that he wasn't too excited about her new job offer because it came from Pete.

"This is good news for me, but you don't seem so happy."

Richard faced her. He took out one hand and stroked her chin with it before the lines on his forehead creased. "I am happy for you, Lucy…. The thing is just… you need to be careful when doing business with a man like Pete. Everyone in town knows he's a cunning businessman, and he likes to rip people off. I wouldn't want to see that happen to you."

Her heart swelled with warmth when she saw the look of genuine concern etched onto his face and she sighed.

"I know you worry about me, Richard," she began softly. "But I have a good feeling about this, and I think it will turn out fine," she said. "Trust me on this one."

He shrugged his shoulders. "Just be careful, okay?"

"I promise."

Richard adjusted the lapel of the coat she wore with both hands and pulled her to his side. They continued their walk back down the track they came from. On the way back, Lucy focused her mind on the new job offer, and she tried to think of the possible treats Pete and his secretary might want.

It was the start of the new year, and things were already looking up. With the crowd she saw at the old theater a few minutes ago, Lucy was certain a lot of people would be tasting her treats.

That meant a large order, and good money. She had finally met Pete for herself, and he didn't look like some sleazy man ready to swindle her. If anything, Pete looked professional and she could tell he was adored by many.

What could possibly go wrong with this deal?

She wondered as they arrived at the bakery again.

Nothing.

Lucy answered the dilemma in her head herself as she waved Richard goodbye for the afternoon and entered the bakery to share the good news with her aunt and Hannah. Her new year was truly getting off to a great start.

3

Early the next morning, Lucy hummed to herself as she wrapped the last cupcake and put it in the basket. She glanced at Aunt Tricia, who had just finished making a cup of coffee, and smiled. "Is it ready?"

Aunt Tricia looked up at her from the coffeemaker. "Yes, I just need to add some sugar," she replied. "Are you done packing the treats?"

"Yes, that's all of it for today. Once I get there, I will set up a stand and start selling immediately."

"And how about your payment?" Aunt Tricia asked as she filled a cup. She handed it to Lucy, then filled another for herself. Lucy added cream to hers and tasted it before she sat down to have a sip.

"His secretary contacted me, saying my first payment will come today."

Aunt Tricia paused, and the frown on her face made Lucy smile. "Don't worry about it, Aunt Tricia. I told you I have a good feeling about this," she said.

"Are you sure? I've heard some things about Pete in town myself. People have a lot to say since he started these open auditions, and I don't want him treating you like some of his team."

"Nothing of the sort will happen,' Lucy reassured her aunt before sipping from her cup again.

The door to the bakery swung open and Hannah walked in like a ballet dancer about to put on a performance.

She greeted Aunt Tricia with a hug and rushed to hang her jacket before taking a seat at the table. "The pastries for the sales are ready?"

"Yes," Lucy replied. "I was waiting for you to get here. I'm heading out by ten and before that, I thought we could make a list of the items we need."

"Sure."

Hannah went into the office and returned with a notebook. Lucy started making a list, and she noted down the items until she ran out of what to add.

"I will get them on my way back from the old theater."

"Has Pete paid you for this job yet?" Hannah asked.

Lucy looked from Hannah to Aunt Tricia whose ears had perked up.

"No," she replied, as she noticed a displeased look cross Hannah's face.

"That man does the same thing to everyone. You've got to be careful, Lucy... he might try to rip you off, and not pay for your services."

"Come on... guys," Lucy said, rising to her feet. She kept the optimism in her voice as she continued. "Pete's play is going international, and from the crowd I saw at the theater the other day, there will be a lot of people around for the audition. This is Sweet Delight's chance to go international, too. Try to look on the bright side."

Her positivity didn't rub off on her aunt and Hannah. Both women blinked and stared at her, so she tucked the excessive smile away and dropped her shoulders with a defeated sigh. "All right, I will be wary of Pete Jenson, as you both have advised."

"Good," Aunt Tricia said then and focused on her coffee again. The bakery opened minutes later, and Lucy attended to a few customers before it was time for her to leave.

She ran up to her apartment floor to change her clothes and stood in front of the mirror with her Persian cat, Gigi, sitting at her feet.

"This is a chance for us to get famous, Gigi," Lucy whispered as she played a glamorous scene of her at an international baking talk show being interviewed by some celebrity chef in her head.

Sweet Delights will go international if this goes right... I think this is a good sign.

She smiled again when she bent over to pick Gigi up for a belly rub, then set her on her feet again before picking a brush to ease the strands of her hair.

When she finished applying some makeup, she headed downstairs dressed in a white shirt and black jeans.

A quick drive from her bakery took her to the old theater, and Lucy watched the crowd from her car for a minute. A smile crept up to her face at the thought of everyone complimenting her treats. She had added a new item—waffles, to the list Pete's secretary, Joselyn had asked for, and she knew it would be a hit with anyone who bought it.

Lucy made her way into the theater, and she found Joselyn in the foyer, addressing some men.

"Joselyn," she called with a brilliant smile.

"Lucy… so nice to have you here with your treats. I'm sure everyone will love them already," Joselyn said as she left the people she stood with to meet Lucy. Joselyn was the first woman Lucy met when she first came here with Richard days ago.

"Come with me. There's a stand for you inside the theater, but at the back of the theater," Joselyn said and led Lucy away.

When Lucy arrived at the stand she spoke about, she set her basket on the table and began setting up for the day ahead.

*

Thirty minutes later, Lucy had nearly sold out the waffles she came with. She sat on the chair behind her to rest her legs for a moment but was back on her feet when another man approached the stand.

"One cupcake, please," he said, his head lowered as he placed the order. She handed one to him, and he paid for it before taking a bite. When he raised his head, Lucy saw the dejected look on his face. His eyes were sunk deep into its sockets, and his forehead creased into many frown lines. She didn't ask before he began. "I can't believe I paid a lot of money to get here only to be embarrassed by the famous Pete Jenson."

"What?" Lucy asked. The man raised his head and looked at her.

"I came for the auditions," he continued. "And it was horrible in there. Pete was mannerless, and while I acted out the part he gave to me, he asked me to do some things I found disrespectful. I've been in so much awe of him my entire career, I can't believe he's such a jerk in person. Can you believe he doesn't give anyone a second chance? And he's mean when he tells you off... it's a complete horror show in there."

"I'm so sorry to hear that," Lucy sympathized with him as he finished the cupcake. She saw him scan the other items she had displayed on the table, and he pointed at a doughnut.

"Can I have one of those to-go?"

She nodded her reply and began wrapping the doughnut. Lucy handed it to him and waited for payment. The man stuck his hands into his pockets, but the wallet he pulled out was empty, and it also seemed like he had nothing else left on him when he searched the other pocket and groaned.

Lucy watched him adjust the cuff of his shirt before he looked at her again.

"You can have that one for free," she said, trying to save the man more embarrassment. He already looked mortified, and she didn't want the feeling to increase.

"Thank you," he said. "You're very kind... I wish I hadn't come here; I should have saved myself the embarrassment."

Lucy watched him walk away, then she sighed and ran a hand over her hair. Over the next few minutes, she saw more people walk to the theater. They all wore grim expressions, and it made her wonder how horrible was Pete to these actors?

Lucy remembered her aunt's warning as she lowered herself to her chair again. Was this a terrible idea? She thought, letting self-doubt creep in. Maybe I shouldn't have taken this gig from the start.

4

B y mid-day, the queue in front of Lucy's stand had lengthened considerably. Lucy was down to her last waffle, and the other treats were nearly exhausted, too. She served the man in front of her the last waffle and closed the basket.

"We have cupcakes and doughnuts left," she said when the next man in line asked for a waffle. Lucy saw his lips form a tight line before he turned and pulled the last customer before him back.

"You bought the last of the waffles, and you weren't even the next in line," the man said.

"Excuse me?"

Both men faced each other, and the tense expressions they wore made it obvious that the scene would soon turn heated.

"You skipped the line, and now I can't get any waffles because it's gone. It's rude to do that when there are others waiting in line for the same treats you just had."

The man who cut the line poked the other in the chest. "What are you going to do about it?"

He raised his chin and puffed his chest out when the other man shoved him back.

Lucy hurried away from her stand and moved to the scene when hushed murmurs erupted from the rest of the people on the line. She stepped in between both men and raised her arms like a referee warning two opposing players.

"There's no need to argue over the waffles," she began when they pinned their glares on her face. "I'll call my assistant and have her send over more waffles… enough to go round."

Seconds passed before both men parted, walking away in opposite directions, and Lucy exhaled as she took out her phone to place a call to Hannah.

She was excited that people enjoyed her waffles, but she didn't expect that they would fight over it.

"Hannah, good thing you picked up on the first ring. I need you to send more waffles through a dispatch driver to the old theater," she said, looking around to check on the queue of other customers waiting for her to return.

"Sold out the first batch?" Hannah asked from the other end.

"Yes, some men were even fighting over not getting any of the waffles. I confess, I didn't expect to sell out this fast compared to the other pastries I've been selling."

Hannah's breezy laugh tickled her ears.

"I'll send a driver soon, or will you be free to come pick it up?"

Lucy turned to the queue and realized they had already dispersed, some of them walking out of the theater while the others headed towards the rehearsal wing.

"Actually, I'll drop by to get them," she replied quickly before hanging up.

"Everyone, gather around. We're about to start." Joselyn's voice boomed as she came out of the rehearsal wing. She clapped her hands together to gain their attention. "Let's get back on stage, people."

Lucy picked her purse from the table and headed out of the theater. In a few minutes, she had arrived at the bakery. She noticed Hannah was closing the basket she had prepared on the counter.

"How's it going at the auditions?" Hannah asked as Lucy got to the counter. "Is it all glamorous?"

"Not in the least. I had two men fighting over the pastries because one of them cut the line, and it seemed like things would have gotten heated if I didn't step in. Everyone there just wants a shot at being featured in the latest Pete Jenson production, and I get it... they all want a chance to be famous."

"Well, an actor has to suffer for his art," Hannah replied with a shrug.

"Yeah," Lucy murmured before she snatched the basket from the counter and waved at Hannah. "I should get back to the theater."

She was out the door, and in her car again in seconds.

When Lucy arrived at the theater, her stand was empty, so she dropped the basket and headed towards the rehearsal wing.

I can watch the auditions for a bit since I have some time, she thought as she entered.

Inside the auditorium, a lot of the actors were gathered at the front of the stage. She saw Pete address them from where he stood, making dramatic hand gestures as he explained his point.

Lucy stepped closer to the front so she could hear what Pete was saying to everyone.

"When the classical musical comes on, that will be the cue for money to begin to fall from up in the rafters. I need everyone to scramble to get their share of it. Am I clear? I need you all to make this scene believable."

The actors replied in unison, and Pete clapped his hand. When he turned around, her gaze landed on his, and he waved at her, smiling gently before he faced the stage again. He didn't seem too pleased by the way he spoke to the woman beside him. Lucy suspected she was one of his assistants because she nodded and crossed over to the stage to address the actors.

Lucy crossed her hands over her chest as she watched the scene. Pete sat down, and the music came on. The actors in front immediately rushed towards the stage when the cash started raining from above, and their exclamations filled the room.

Although Lucy thought the scene played out perfectly, and the actors looked natural, it didn't seem like it was good enough for Pete because he rose to his feet and stomped towards the stage, waving his hands in the air as he shouted, "Cut!"

The noises continued from the stage. The actors crowded over one another, each of them struggling to get a dollar note from the stacks flying around the stage.

"Cut," Pete shouted.

He dashed towards the scene and tried to get them to stop.

"This is nonsense," he said as the crowd parted for him. "I need you to make it real," he yelled. His voice subdued the clamors coming from the actors.

Lucy crossed her arms over her chest as she watched Pete shove his fingers through his hair and continue. "Let's do it again."

The actors replayed the scene, this time a bit more frantic in their actions, scrambling over each other as they tried to get some of the cash pouring down to the stage.

"Cut," Pete yelled again.

This time, he rushed to the stage. "This is how you do it."

More dollar bills rained down on the stage as Pete joined the actors on the stage. More screams erupted as Pete showed them how, and for a second, Lucy lost track of him in the crowd.

The uproar grew intense this time with people struggling to get some notes dropping to the ground. She saw more people hurry to the stage from the spectators' seats and join in the rabble.

Suddenly a loud piercing scream tore out of the crowd, and slowly everyone dispersed, making room in the center of the stage.

"He's dead," a woman yelled, her tone of voice a hollow sound that sent a chill down Lucy's spine.

Color drained from her face, and she blinked, rooted to one spot as hushed silence filled the auditorium. She spotted Pete Jenson's lifeless body on the floor.

5

D id someone just murder Pete Jenson?

Lucy blinked as she took the left turn leading to her bakery and pressed her foot on the accelerator pedal harder. Her mind still reeled from the shock of what happened at the theater. One minute Pete Jenson was on the stage, directing and voicing his displeasure at the actors' performance, and the next he was lying on the floor, lifeless.

A chill raced through Lucy, and she shuddered from it.

How did this happen?

She tried not to think about it as she continued her drive. If Pete is dead, then the cops will find out about it soon, she told herself. Her mind drifted to the terrified screams of the people on the stage. When the uproar broke, Lucy had hurried out of the auditorium without looking back. The last thing she needed was

465

to get caught up with whatever had happened back there.

Minutes later, Lucy was at her bakery. She slammed the door of her car and dashed into her bakery, holding her purse in one hand, and the full basket of her second batch of treats in the other. Aunt Tricia and Hannah were talking when she entered, and they both turned in her direction.

"How did it go?" Hannah asked, standing to her feet while Aunt Tricia put down the glass of juice she held in her right hand.

"You're back early. I didn't think you'd be back till evening, and why do you still have those?"

Hannah was at Lucy's side as she asked. She took the basket from Lucy, opened it, and peered inside. When Lucy met her gaze again, she saw the question in them.

"Did something happen?" Aunt Tricia asked.

"I… I think Pete Jenson's dead," Lucy announced.

She heard her own heartbeat speed up as she said the words out loud. Hannah's jaw dropped, and out of the corner of her eye, she saw Aunt Tricia push back in her seat and walk to them. The bakery's dining area was empty, so both Hannah and Aunt Tricia steered Lucy towards a chair.

"How? What happened?"

"Pete was trying to get the actors to perform a scene some certain way," Lucy began explaining. "I just got back, and there was no one in the queue at my stand, so I joined the spectators for a bit. Half-way into the scene, and Pete's obviously on edge, complaining that they weren't doing it right. He goes up onto the stage, and shows them how, then there's this loud scream and suddenly people are shuffling away. I only glimpsed Pete lying on the floor. I didn't stay long enough to find out if he was really dead."

Silence filled the dining area when Lucy finished. Her eyes dropped to her hands on her lap, and she licked her dry lips. She replayed the shrill voice that screamed, He's dead in her head, and shut her eyes for a second to get it out of her mind.

"I don't think he's dead," Hannah said suddenly. "Pete's a show-man, and he's made his fame from his brilliant productions. It's probably just a stunt to drum up media coverage for his new show."

"You think so, too, Aunt Tricia? Is it possible what happened was just for show?" Lucy asked her aunt, who was still quiet.

"I can't tell. We might have to wait till word gets around."

"I'm not just being skeptical," Hannah continued. "I once watched one of Pete's short plays he performed at some event in Rome on YouTube. In it, he was locked in a cage with lions, and he had to get out alive. A lot of the audience had this stunned expression you have on, but when I watched the making of the video, I realized it was special effects and there were obviously no real lions in that cage.

"Pete's a talented director and actor. You probably witnessed one of his many stunts."

Lucy saw Hannah relax in her chair when she finished speaking, and she moved to join her.

A customer came into the bakery then, and Lucy rose to her feet. She carried the basket of treats into the kitchen, leaving Hannah to attend to the lady and three other customers that walked in.

Inside the kitchen, she unpacked the cupcakes and waffles in the basket, set them on a tray, and returned the basket to the top shelf before letting out a sigh.

Was it possible that scene was a part of some special effects for the production, like Hannah said?

Lucy didn't know what to think. She washed her hands in the sink before carrying the tray of pastries out to the dining area. Hannah and Aunt Tricia worked hand in hand to attend to the customers in the bakery when she returned, and she joined them to assist.

The lady right in front of the counter whispered to the woman by her side as she waited for Hannah to pack her order. "I hear Pete's doing something elaborate for this show he's producing; it has to do with a lot of special effects. I don't know the full story, but a friend of mine is auditioning for the lead role."

"Really?" the second woman replied as their conversation continued.

Lucy shot Hannah a glance as she closed the counter door and took a paper bag from the pile they had to attend to another customer in line.

"I told you it was probably a stunt," Hannah whispered, leaning closer to Lucy as she picked one paper bag for herself.

The women on the line had turned to walk away from the counter, and Hannah moved onto the next customer. "What would you like?" she asked.

They continued to work in rhythmical silence, Lucy pondering on the scene she witnessed, and trying to convince herself that it was just like Hannah had said.

If it's a stunt, then it's a good one because they had me fooled.

They had soon run out of waffles, and Lucy adjusted the apron she wore. "I will go start another mixture for more waffles," she said to Hannah and Aunt Tricia before returning to the kitchen.

Lucy took out a bowl and scooped out some flour. She finished adding the other dry ingredients. She mixed it up while wondering about Pete and his stunts. Could he go to such extreme lengths to add more flare to his production? Maybe that's why he's so famous, she thought.

Lucy knew the ability to go the extra mile could help anyone's career. It certainly helped her when she was in culinary school.

After mixing up the waffles, she set the waffle maker into the oven to pre-heat and set the timer before heading back to the dining area to join Hannah and Aunt Tricia.

She joined them serving, packing up cupcakes and brownies for a man with his wife while Hannah worked on serving some cinnamon rolls and donuts.

Lucy had thought about expanding the area to accommodate more customers, and created more room behind her counter for work, but she had started re-considering the thought after her discussion with Richard.

Lucy wiped her hands on a towel as Hannah turned to her and murmured, a concerned look on her face. "You still worried about what happened at the theater?"

"Yes, it looked like more than a stunt,' she replied. "I mean, you had to hear the terror in the actors' screams as they rushed away from the scene."

"It could be part of the scene," Aunt Tricia commented. "Hannah might be right... you might be worried for no reason. You also said you didn't stick around to see how things developed. So..."

As they conversed, the door opened, and they all turned to see Taylor walk into the bakery. He was dressed in his full uniform, one hand on his waist as he approached the counter. His blonde hair swept away from his face and his jaw was set in a tight line as he stepped over the threshold.

Lucy walked around to greet him first.

"Hi," she began, pasting a smile on her face.

She shook off her anxiety about Pete as she stopped in front of him and pushed her hands deep into the pocket of her jeans. "How are you doing? Are you here for more cupcakes? Or bread?"

Taylor shook his head. She noticed the grim expression on his face as he scanned her bakery before replying. "I'm not here for some treats, Lucy. I'm here on an official assignment."

He faced her squarely, the heat from his blue eyes boring into her face. An inkling that this had to do with Pete filled Lucy's mind even before he said anything else.

"What business?" she asked, her eyes searching his as she tried to maintain her cool, even though her mind was spinning in different directions.

"I'm here to question you about the murder of Pete Jenson."

6

"What?" Lucy asked with a tilt of her head, her voice visibly loud enough to cause heads to stir in the dining area. She drew in a stuttered breath and pressed a hand to her chest, trying to regain composure. Murmurs filled the bakery, and out of the corner of her eye, she saw two customers whisper to each other before glancing in her direction again.

I suspected it, so this shouldn't be that shocking. Still, she struggled with allowing Taylor's words to sink in. Pete was so full of life this morning at the theater, and now he was dead?

"Is everything alright?" one older woman sitting at the far-right end of the bakery asked from where she sat. "Did something happen?"

"Not at all. Lucy just got some good news," Hannah responded before Lucy could speak. Hannah walked around the counter to where the older woman sat and continued speaking to her while Lucy looked at Taylor again.

"Come with me to my office. We can talk privately in there."

She led him into her office, her knees knocking against each other, and shut the door behind them before facing him again. "Pete's dead?" She repeated in a low voice, barely hearing herself, and he simply nodded.

Taylor took off his cap and held it with both hands.

"His body was found on the front stage; he was stabbed, and the paramedics confirmed he was dead when they got to the scene. I understand you were there when it happened, so I came here to get your statement."

Lucy's hand stayed stiff at her sides, and she cleared her throat. "I was there to sell some treats and decided to watch the auditions for a bit. I went into the auditorium, and stood at the back to watch, and Pete was trying to explain a scene to the actors on the stage when suddenly there was a scream. I saw his body on the floor, but I joined the crowd and hurried out before finding out anything else," Lucy said and paused to catch her breath.

"My God, I can't even begin to imagine how this happened," she whispered, looking away from Taylor for a second. When she looked back at him, she saw he was watching her, a furrow between his brows, like he was deep in thought.

"So, what happens next? Am I under investigation because I was at the scene? I was just there to sell my treats as Pete asked me to, and I have no link to any of this," she said, the urge to clear the air filling her even when Taylor hadn't said anything about investigating her.

"Relax, Lucy. I'm just here to get your statement. Nothing else for now."

"For now?" she asked, her brows quirking up.

"Yes, for now. I will be in touch if I need anything else from you because even though we know the cause of death, we know nothing else about the case. You just need to remain watchful till the department figures out what's going on and why Pete was murdered," he advised. "A full investigation will begin, and because of Pete's fame, the town will get a lot of national media descending on the town. This may turn out to be a long investigation for everyone in town."

"Seems like things are about to get interesting around here," she muttered, rubbing a hand on her forehead.

"Yeah... things are about to get very interesting," he repeated. His eyes drifted over her face for a second before he added. "Just do your best to stay out of the spotlight, and don't stir any trouble."

"I won't," Lucy replied almost immediately. She didn't intend to get involved in anything pertaining to Pete's murder.

It's a new year... I've had enough drama in Ivy Creek to last me a lifetime, she thought, remembering the murder investigations she had somehow become entangled in throughout the course of the previous year.

"Good. Take care, Lucy," Taylor said, turning away from her to walk out of the office. She escorted him out to see that the bakery had emptied and waved him goodbye as he walked out the door.

Hannah and Aunt Tricia looked at her with curious stares when they were alone again.

"What did Taylor say?" Aunt Tricia asked, as Lucy lowered herself to a chair and placed her hands on the table in front of her.

"He just confirmed that Pete's dead. I told you it felt like more than a stunt," she said, shifting her attention to Hannah. "He was stabbed right there on the stage."

"Oh my," Hannah muttered. "I heard when he said he came to investigate Pete's death, but I didn't want to believe it was true."

Lucy saw Hannah pale visibly, and her aunt's shoulders sagged.

"I told him I was at the scene, but I got out as soon as the commotion started," Lucy continued. "He said he will be in touch if he needs anything else, and that the investigation would most definitely shake the town."

"That figures," Aunt Tricia muttered. "Pete gained a lot of international attention over the past few years. Many people believed his work was exceptional and a lot of upcoming actors here in town wanted a chance to work with him. It's probably why he came to produce a play here with local actors, years after he gained fame from this same town."

Lucy sighed. Pete's dead. What happens to his show now?

She remembered the pleasant smile he gave her when they had met the first time, and the way he complimented her on her treats. Pete seemed to her like a gentleman, even though she didn't know him much.

So, who would have wanted him dead, and gone through with the plan to murder him?

Lucy couldn't shake the question out of her mind for the rest of the day, no matter how hard she tried.

*

By the end of the day, Lucy closed the store with Hannah and strolled down the street with her to get some personal items she needed. They crossed the street, and Hannah walked with her into a convenience store.

"It's such a tragedy," Hannah said as they walked down the first aisle. They stopped and Hannah picked up some shower gels. "I was looking forward to what Pete would come up with for this production. I even considered sending in an audition tape."

Lucy looked at her as she picked up a bottle. "Audition? You can act? I thought you didn't think much of Pete Jenson?" she asked.

Hannah shrugged. "I wanted to give it a shot. You never know when lightning will strike. It's such a pity I won't get to find out now."

After tossing a shower gel into her cart, she looked at Hannah again. "Don't worry, I'm sure another opportunity will present itself," she said with a light smile. "As far as I can tell, I think Pete's production has come to a grinding halt. I can't imagine the show going on without him... he had such a captivating aura."

"Yeah, I know," Hannah agreed.

Together, they walked to the front of the store, and as Lucy dropped her items on the counter, the news playing on the TV caught her attention. A female journalist was reporting from somewhere that seemed familiar.

"The murder has left the citizens of Ivy Creek in shock, as Pete Jenson was a pivotal member of their community."

A picture of Pete was displayed on the screen as the reporter continued. It was an image of Pete smiling, his hands raised in a wave.

Who could have done this? She wondered for the hundredth time that day.

"That will be ten dollars and ninety-nine cents please," the attendant said to Lucy, gaining her attention again. She paid with her card and headed out onto the cold streets with Hannah again.

"It's all over the local news, and I'm sure the national one as well," Hannah commented.

"Yes," Lucy replied. She snuggled into the coat she wore and pushed Pete out of her mind. "Good night, Hannah, I will see you in the morning."

"Goodnight."

Lucy watched Hannah cross the street, flag down a cab, and get in before she started down the opposite direction towards her bakery. Once inside, she shut the door and went into her apartment upstairs.

Her cat, Gigi, welcomed her with a purr. Gigi's tail was in an upright position as she waded across the living room with Lucy till she fell onto her couch. Lucy switched on her television and the channel on was the international news station. A huge question mark was displayed on the screen after a short clip of Pete at an award show.

Lucy read the words on the bottom of the screen.

Breaking News - Famous Movie director and actor—Pete Jenson was murdered at a local theater in his hometown.

7

Lucy tied her hair into a bun and swiped her hand down her side.

"Let's say Pete didn't come back to town. Would someone still have murdered him? Or could his killer be someone who's been holding a grudge for years?" she asked, looking at Gigi who sat beside her foot.

She spent the early hours of the morning thinking about Pete's murder and replaying the scene that led to his death in her mind.

His killer must be one of the people on that stage.

Lucy headed into her kitchen to fix Gigi a quick meal before she wrapped a shawl around her neck and headed down the stairs to the bakery. Hannah had sent in a text a few minutes earlier to tell her she wouldn't be around today, so Lucy was looking forward to having Aunt Tricia around to help.

She started the baking early because she was unable to sleep well during the night, and by seven, she turned the door sign to 'open'.

Lucy welcomed her first customer minutes later.

"Good morning, what would you like?" she asked as the man inspected all she had displayed on her counter.

"Three apple pies and a loaf of bread, please," he replied.

"Would you like a coffee to go with that? It's on the house."

The man nodded his head as a smile spread across his face and Lucy proceeded to prepare his order. After him, other customers came in groups, and the next time Lucy got a chance to check her time, it was nearly eleven am.

She took a break since the bakery was empty and took out her cell phone to call Aunt Tricia.

She was supposed to be here hours ago.

Aunt Tricia picked up on the first ring.

"Hey, Lucy, I'm so sorry I couldn't make it there this morning."

"Did something happen?" she asked when she heard the breathlessness in her aunt's voice.

In the background, someone asked, "Can you try to stand on your own, ma'am?"

"It's nothing serious, dear. On my way to the bakery, I tripped on the sidewalk, and I think I hurt my back a little, but I'm all good… you don't have to worry about it. The nice doctor here will patch me up and send me on my way soon."

Lucy frowned. "Oh my God, you should have called me earlier. I'm coming to you now," she said, rising to her feet in a hurry. "Are you badly hurt? You don't have to downplay it, Aunt Tricia. Which hospital are you at? I'm heading there now."

Lucy was already heading for the door when Aunt Tricia protested.

"I'm fine, Lucy. I didn't call because I didn't want you to worry… you're good at that," she said with a tiny laugh.

Lucy didn't believe her aunt was fine, and she would only relax when she saw for herself, so she stepped out of the bakery, turned the sign to 'closed', and locked the door. "Just tell me where you are, Aunt Tricia," she countered, turning her car engine on.

She pulled out onto the road, did a quick reverse, and headed down the road as Aunt Tricia replied. "New Mercy Hospital."

"Great, I'll be with you soon."

She dropped her phone and focused on the road ahead. The sky was clear today even though it snowed the previous day, and Lucy was mulling over her aunt's dilemma. It wasn't uncommon for a woman her age to miss a step, but she worried her aunt took things too lightly.

Lucy remembered once during the holidays; Aunt Tricia nearly slipped in the kitchen. She had blamed it on the shoes she wore, but she was starting to think maybe her aunt wasn't paying attention to the signs her body was telling her she was getting older.

As Lucy drew closer to her destination, she drove past a floristry. The display of flowerpots and the bright yellow color of daffodils displayed in pots caught her attention, reminding her that Aunt Tricia loved the spring flower so much because it reminded her a lot of her childhood in Ivy Creek.

Lucy parked by the store, got out, and walked in to get some flowers for her aunt. She looked around the store when she entered, admiring the botanically designed interior of the shop, and the lush ornamental flowers set aside on the front desk.

"Hi, Lucy," a voice hollered, and Lucy turned to see Judy walk into the store. "I went behind to get some tools, and I noticed the car parked out front. How are you? Are you here to get flowers?"

"Hey, Judy," Lucy greeted. "I didn't know you were a florist," she commented as she smiled at Judy.

Lucy looked at the tiny shovel Judy held, and the gloves in her other hand. Judy wore a brown leather apron over her clothes, her hands were dirty, her cheeks had a smudge, and overall, she looked sweaty, like she had been knee-deep in some work.

"I am," Judy replied. "The shop belonged to my mother, and I love the life flowers give, so I kept it when the chance came. It's just like you did with your mother's bakery. I love what you've done with Sweet Delights."

"Thanks, Judy," Lucy said, admiring Judy's charm and kind words. "I would like a bouquet, please," Lucy said, getting to the business of why she had stopped by. For a second, she wondered if Judy would bring up something about Pete's death.

Everyone in town was talking about it. She wondered if Judy knew Pete well or if their relationship had strictly been work based.

She ought to wonder what happened too.

Judy had walked over to the counter where her pots were displayed, and she waved a hand at them as she pinned her eyes on Lucy's. "All right, what kind do you intend getting? Have anything specific in mind?"

Lucy paused and looked around the collection on the table in front of her. She touched one petal of a lily, and looked at Judy again, meeting the woman's blue eyes. "Something that depicts healing."

"I think a bouquet of lavender is what you're looking for," Judy replied, pointing at an already prepared bouquet. "As you know, the scent is therapeutic, and the color is just so lovely."

Lucy agreed with her. "I'll take it."

She watched Judy gather her a bouquet, and she looked around the store one more time. The setting was like something Lucy envisioned for an upgrade to her bakery. A larger setting, with space for more tables, and larger, rectangular windows to let in more light."

"Thank you," Lucy said as she took the bouquet from Judy and reached into her coat's pocket for her wallet. "I really love your shop, Judy. Pleasant setting, and very spacious," she commented, but stopped mid-way when she realized she didn't have her wallet.

I must have left it in my apartment in a rush to get to Aunt Tricia, she thought, chiding herself internally at her forgetfulness.

"I know… I started out small with very few customers, but with a commitment to excellence and improving, I now have a steady flow of customers, even from the big cities, who trust my judgment, and always patronize me."

"That's so lovely." Lucy smiled again and rubbed her eyebrow. "Judy… I kind of left my wallet at home in my rush to get out," she said, stretching her hands out to return the flowers. "I don't think I'll be able to get these."

"Oh, no, no, don't worry about that, Lucy. You can drop by to pay me later," she said, pushing Lucy's hands back. "I insist."

"Thanks for this, Judy," she replied. "And for the contract to deliver treats to the town's council meeting."

Judy waved her hand and let out a short laugh. "That was nothing… you're doing a good job of keeping up your parents' legacy and I like that. You just need to always think of growing because if you're not, then you're dying. Business wise, of course," she added after a second of silence and chuckled again.

"Thanks, Judy. I'll drop by to pay for these later today," Lucy thanked her again as she waved goodbye.

She got to the door and pushed it open when Judy said in a light tone behind her. "Have a nice day, and I wish whoever gets the flowers a quick recovery."

As Lucy came out to the front porch, she had to quickly side-step to let a woman enter the flower shop. Lucy's head snapped to the side as the woman passed her. She caught the familiar scent of a perfume.

Where have I seen that face?

Lucy contemplated for a second before continuing to her car. Through the large windows, she saw Judy smile at the woman inside the store and laugh at something they said to each other.

She looks familiar, she thought again as she set the flowers on the passenger seat and continued her journey.

8

Lucy found her aunt at the out-patient unit after inquiring at the nurse's station. Aunt Tricia sat upright on the hospital bed, her hands in front of her, as she listened to what the doctor standing by her bedside was saying.

Her body sagged with relief when she saw a smile on Aunt Tricia's face, and most of her worry ebbed away. Even in a hospital gown, Aunt Tricia seemed at ease, her hands crossed on her lap as she wriggled her ankles on the bed.

Thank goodness, she's actually alright.

"Hi," Lucy breathed out as she got to the bed and hugged her aunt briefly before handing over the flowers she held. "How is she?" she asked the doctor as Aunt Tricia took the flowers from her and inhaled them deeply.

"Lavender… I love them, thanks Lulu, they're really lovely…"

she said with a tiny smile that Lucy returned as she watched her inhale the scent of the flowers again.

Lucy placed her hand on her aunt's shoulder, waiting for the doctor's reply.

"Everything looks fine, and she's lucky she didn't break anything from her fall," the doctor replied. "We will keep her for a few days for more observation, and you can come for her on Friday," he added.

"Friday?" Aunt Tricia protested. "That's three days away... can't I go sooner?"

"No madam," the doctor replied, then left them after giving Lucy a brief nod.

Alone with her aunt, Lucy dragged in a deep breath, and turned to her. "You need to be more careful, aunt," she cautioned. "That fall could have gone badly in many ways, and I don't think I can stand you getting hurt."

"I'm fine, Lucy," Aunt Tricia replied, and took her hand. "Now don't ruin your lovely face with that ugly frown, dear. I put on some weight during the holidays and it's affecting my balance. It's nothing too serious, so you shouldn't worry."

Lucy sat on the chair near the bed and put her hands in front of her. "You should be more careful," she said before putting her hands into the pocket of her coat.

"I will, I promise," Aunt Tricia replied. "Did you lock up the bakery to come see me?"

She answered with a nod and relaxed into the chair. "I rushed out, just turned the sign to closed because I had to make sure you're fine."

"Thanks, dear, but you really should get back to the bakery. It's lunch hour at this time, and you'll miss a lot of customers if you stay."

Aunt Tricia had a point, and even though Lucy was reluctant to leave because she just got there, she still rose to her feet.

"I'll come check on you in the evening," she said, and kissed her aunt on the cheek. "Try not to fall off the bed this time."

Aunt Tricia chuckled. "All right, dear."

On the drive back home, Lucy noticed an older woman strolling down the sidewalk with the help of a younger lady. The picture of them both together brought back her anxiety about Aunt Tricia.

Her aunt wasn't getting younger, and it was growing obvious that she needed more help and assistance in getting around.

Living alone probably isn't ideal, she thought as she took the bend leading to the bakery. While Aunt Tricia lived on her side of town, she was still not close enough for Lucy to check up on her as much as she'd like.

Would having her move in with me be a good idea?

The second the thought entered her mind, she deliberated on it. Having Aunt Tricia closer to her was a better option for both. That way, Lucy could keep an eye on her while still going about her business.

The only issue was her apartment above the bakery would be cramped to accommodate them both. She drove past the town's local church and continued down the road, speeding past the turn leading to the high street without even realizing it.

She drove past her intended turn, and when she realized, she stopped and did a U-turn to get back on track. Lucy was familiar with this street as it was where she grew up. Her parents' house stood by the left side towards the end of the road, and when she got to it, she parked by the curb and got out.

With quick strides, she got to the front of the picket fence separating their house from the main road and propped her hands on her waist.

It feels like I haven't been here in years when it was only just last year that they passed away.

As she stood there in front of the house, a memory flashed in her head, one of her riding her bicycle around the yard, and her mother shouting for her to be careful from the porch where her father worked on a broken stair.

"I'll be careful, mommy," Lucy remembered her reply like it happened just yesterday. A short laugh escaped her lips as tears filled her eyes. Seconds after she promised to be careful, she fell from the bike, and her mother had dashed to her side immediately.

More fond memories rushed through her, creating a swirl of emotions Lucy hadn't felt in a while. Her lung clenched for a second, and when she released the breath she held, it came out in a whoosh. There was a cold bite to the air that stung her ears. Even though the day started out warmer, the weather was gradually changing.

Settling her shaky insides, Lucy walked past the lawn to the front porch. She reached under the flowerpot at the far end of the wooden, narrow porch and grabbed the keys she kept hidden there.

She entered the house, taking her time to walk around the living room. The place looked the same, except it was covered in dust, and cobwebs swamped the corners of the celling boards.

This place is big enough to house Aunt Tricia and me.

Lucy hadn't once thought of selling her parents' house even though she also hadn't considered moving in. It was the first time since she had arrived back in town that she had considered moving in.

Her phone rang in her pocket, pulling her out of her thoughts. "Hey, Hannah," she said when she picked up on the second ring.

"Hi, Lucy… I stopped by the bakery on my way back from my outing with my sister, and you aren't here. What's happening? We just drove off now, but I had to call to check in."

"I'm on my way back," she replied. "Had to check in on Aunt Tricia. She had a nasty fall earlier this morning, and she's in the hospital."

"Oh, my God! Is she all right?"

"Yes, yes, she's fine—she insists I shouldn't worry, but you know how I get. I just had to make sure she was all right. I'm driving back to the bakery now; I'll be there in a few minutes."

When she dropped the call, Lucy's eyes swept around the kitchen where she stood. She walked out, locked the door behind her, and this time, slipped the key into her pocket.

I'm moving back in, she told herself as she got into her car and turned on the engine. It was time to act on the urge she had to do something different this year. Expanding the bakery had been her first option, and she planned on moving on with it.

As Lucy drove away, she stared at her reflection in the center mirror of her car. Judy's words played in her mind. If you're not growing, you're dying.

"I can do this," she said to herself. The expansion of the bakery would take a while, and she would move back to her parents' house before starting.

That way, she could be with Aunt Tricia, monitoring her while the work went on. It was a brilliant idea, and Lucy knew the first thing she had to start with was changing the narrative of how she thought of the house.

From now on, it was her house… not just her parents'. Lucy stepped on the accelerator pedal to speed up so she could get to the bakery faster. It was lunch hour, like Aunt Tricia said, and she had to get back to work.

9

L ucy and Hannah finished cleaning the next morning after baking. It was quite early, and the first stream of customers for the day just left the dining area when Lucy faced Hannah. "I've decided to expand the bakery. It took me a while to be convinced about it, but yesterday, after the incident with Aunt Tricia, I finally decided."

"It's an excellent decision, Lucy," Hannah said.

"Thanks," Lucy replied as she opened the display glass to pick a cupcake. She nodded as she bit into it. "Yes, it will give this place a fresh look for the year, and also allow the customers more space to enjoy their treats."

Hannah was wiping the counter with a napkin as she turned to Lucy again.

"It also gives us more preparation room. If we can make the kitchen bigger, the table and shelves can be expanded as well. Speaking of shelves, that reminds me, we've run out of syrup and whipped cream."

"I'll get them today," Lucy replied.

They continued their conversation for a while, Lucy going over the plans she had already formed in her head concerning the expansion.

"If the counter comes forward a bit, then we can even make a stairway leading up to another dining area. It will be cozier up there, and customers who sit there will have a good view of the high street and the mountains in the distance."

"So that means you'll be moving out?" Hannah asked.

Lucy cast a glance over at her as she counted the cupcakes left. She saw Hannah's hands come over her chest as she leaned against the counter.

"Yes, I'll move back to my parents' house," she replied, then remembered her new narrative. "I'll move back to my house," she corrected with a smile. "With Aunt Tricia, I'm thinking of keeping a keen eye on her, really for my peace of mind."

"That's a good idea," Hannah agreed. "I think you moving in there will be great. Besides, it shows you're actually planting roots here."

The door opened, and a customer walked in wearing a cheery smile. "Hello… Happy new year," she greeted as she got to the counter. "I'd like some waffles, please. I had them yesterday, and I can't stop remembering how wonderful they tasted, especially the ones with the sliced berries."

"Coming right up," Lucy replied.

She immediately started packing the order while whistling to herself, and when she was done, she handed the paper bag to the lady. "Here you go. That will be three dollars."

The lady reached into the pocket of her coat. Her eyes widened suddenly as her hands flew to her mouth. "Oh shoot, I think I left my wallet at home. Oh God, I was in such a hurry to get to work, I didn't even realize—I'm so sorry," she babbled.

Lucy blinked. She smacked a hand on her forehead, her mind jumping to the previous day when she promised to return to Judy's store. "Oh no," she exclaimed.

"Please don't be mad. I truly didn't know," the lady whispered again.

"It's fine, really. I'm not mad," Lucy answered. "You actually just did me a favor, reminding me of something I have to do real quick. I have to go now, but you can have the waffles for free," she continued, giving her a sidewards glance as she rounded the counter, dashed for her coat hanging in the office, checked it for her wallet and keys before heading out of the bakery.

When Lucy arrived at Judy's store a few minutes later, Judy was standing on the patio. Judy welcomed her with a wide smile.

"I'm really sorry, Judy. I promised to come back yesterday, but I skipped on that. It genuinely escaped my mind, and it just came to me, so I had to rush here."

"It's nothing, Lucy. I trust you… I knew you would come eventually," she said.

"Thank you," Lucy replied. She reached into her coat for her wallet. "How much did the flowers cost?"

"Thirty dollars," Judy replied. "Come in, I should write you a receipt for that."

491

Lucy rubbed a hand on her chest as she inhaled the crisp air deeply, filling her lungs with it. Inside the store, she looked around again, admiring the wooden stands where Judy displayed her flowers.

"Here you go," Judy said when she returned from the table, where she wrote a receipt. "Thanks for coming back."

"I should be thanking you," Lucy replied as Judy took the cash. "My aunt really loved the flowers."

"You can come back anytime if you want more. Maybe something to brighten up your bakery or house. Flowers are nice aesthetics, and they brighten up the mood."

"You're right, maybe I should look around," Lucy agreed.

She followed Judy around, checking the vases of lilies and pansies. When she reached the last stand, she noticed a newspaper lying on it.

Lucy's heart somersaulted when she saw the picture of Pete Jenson. She scanned the headline on the front page before facing Judy again.

"It's a tragedy what happened to Pete," Judy said, starting the conversation about Pete. "Even though he had many flaws, he didn't deserve to go down like that."

"Flaws?" Lucy repeated. She slipped her hands into her coat pocket and gauged Judy's expression as she talked.

Judy's brittle smile showed again when she answered. "Yes, flaws. Whenever he was in town, he threw his weight around, stepping on toes and leaving a cloud of strife and anger. But it all goes away once he leaves town. All he does is talk bad about the town when he's away."

"I see," Lucy murmured the words, as she chewed on her thoughts. "But who would have killed him?"

"Probably someone he must have offended," Judy replied with a shrug. "Someone who can't get over what he did to them."

Lucy was about to comment when the door opened, and a lady walked into the store. Lucy recognized her from the last time she was there. The woman had striking looks. Long blonde hair that fell to her waist in straight strands, and delicate facial features.

Lucy noticed the poise of her body as she walked into the store, and her gaze lingered as the lady took off her coat, looked in their direction for a second, but made her way into the back of the shop without saying anything to them.

Lucy cocked her head to one side and rubbed a finger over her lower lip.

I'm sure I've seen her somewhere, Lucy contemplated, trying to figure out the face. "I have seen her before," she mumbled.

"Seen who?" Judy asked.

Lucy looked up at Judy and sighed. "It's just... the lady who walked in looks really familiar. I'm certain I've seen her before," she replied.

"Oh... that was Thelma," Judy replied, her lips curving. "She's my daughter."

"Oh..."

"You probably know her because she starred in a toothpaste commercial when she was younger. Thelma gained a lot of attention after that commercial."

Judy struck a pose then and went ahead to act out the commercial.

"Want a brilliant smile?" she said at the end, propped both hands on her hips, and widened her grin just like it was acted in the commercial.

Lucy chuckled, recalling the commercial as she watched Judy act it out. "I remember when that commercial first aired. I loved it so much and always admired the girl's lovely smile," she teased, laughing as Judy straightened.

"You're good at acting yourself. The way you just played that out, it was like I was watching the commercial all over again," Lucy said with a hearty chortle. "I just wondered because it also seems like I've seen her recently."

"You probably have," Judy replied as Lucy started walking towards the door. "She's an actress, and she was in Pete's production."

10

Lucy stopped by the grocery store on her way back to the bakery. She checked her watch after pulling into a parking spot and hurried into the store to grab the items Hannah mentioned earlier.

"Syrup, and whipped cream," she muttered to herself as she got to the baking aisle and searched for the products she enjoyed using. She picked them up, and walked towards the counter, but stopped when her eyes caught the papers hanging on a rack.

Lucy looked and shoved her fingers through her hair. She wondered when his death would be old news.

Two men stood in front of it, their hands inside their pockets. She moved closer to see Pete's picture on every front page. Lucy shook her head.

"I think he deserves what he got if you ask me," one man said to the other as they stood in front of the newspaper rack.

"Don't say that… it's bad enough that Pete came back to town when no one really wanted him around. Now, his face is plastered on every newspaper, and there will be a lot of useless publicity this town doesn't need," the other replied. "I didn't like Pete either, but I feel he should have died elsewhere."

Lucy stood beside them quietly, reading the headlines on the newspapers as she held her cart.

"What do you think about it?" the taller man asked, turning to face her. "Don't you also think that his death has caused a nuisance in town?"

Lucy shook her head. "I don't think it's my business," she replied, meeting their gaze. The shocked look on the men's faces satisfied her as she walked over to the counter to pay for her items.

Some people need to gossip less, she thought to herself as she got to her car and drove off.

Lucy walked into her bakery to find Hannah serving customers at the counter. Some women seated at a table were also talking about Pete's death in hushed tones.

"How were things while I was gone?" Lucy asked as she fell into rhythm with Hannah behind the counter. She handed prepared orders to the customers while Hannah took more orders.

"I don't want to be insensitive, but I'd like to turn off the news for a bit," she commented when they served the last one in the short queue and had some time to themselves.

"Pete's death is all anyone's talking about."

Both Lucy and Hannah stole a look at the table where the women talked in audible tones about what happened at the theater. She remembered the scene vividly but tried not to relive it.

"I was right there when it happened, and I think it must be one of the actors… it had to be one of them," a lady at the table said.

"It's best we don't get involved," Hannah replied, drumming her fingers on the countertop. "We have a good thing going on here and getting involved in this murder case might ruin it."

Lucy didn't need to be reminded what could happen when she meddled with anything that didn't concern her. When she moved back to Ivy Creek, a murder was committed on her property, and it affected her business in every way. She couldn't let that happen again.

"You're right," she said, and exhaled. Lucy looked around the bakery to see it had emptied, so she reached for the remote under the counter and turned off the TV.

"Today, I met the young girl from the famous Crest 3D white commercial," Lucy began. She put her hands on her waist, struck a pose, and mimicked the commercial. "Want a brilliant smile?"

Hannah chuckled, covering her mouth with her right hand as she laughed out loud. "I remember that advert, and also the girl… what was her name again?"

"Thelma," Lucy replied.

"Yes, Thelma. She was in my year in high school, and we finished together. She was always so full of herself because of the popularity of that ad."

"Well, I met her today. More like glimpsed her actually… she's Judy Cousins' daughter, the woman we met at the town's council meeting the other day."

"Really? I didn't know that."

Lucy and Hannah moved to the front porch to relax a little with a glass of water.

Hannah voiced her opinions on the expansion plans, and Lucy went over it with her, vividly imagining what the new bakery would look like, and trying to figure out how they could work on this project without affecting sales at the bakery.

Lucy waved her hand to the end of the narrow porch where they sat. "We can make the porch wider a bit since we're adjusting things. It will give more room for the dining area downstairs, and the stair that will be constructed."

"I think it's a good idea to re-paint the wood and give the place a total make-over… more vibrant colors."

Lucy experimented with that idea in her head. "What of pastel shades?" she asked.

"Sounds terrific," Hannah beamed, clapping her hands together.

Lucy's insides rumbled with her building excitement. The building would look better overall if she went along with this plan, and she could almost see how the improved look would attract more customers and improve her bank balance.

Relaxing in her chair, she looked at the lawn out front, and back at Hannah. "I will need to work with a professional, someone with more in-depth knowledge on renovations and interior designs because I want to give this my best."

Her heart swelled at the thought of starting something new.

This is the kind of energy I need this new year… more things to get me pumped up for the months ahead.

"I have an uncle who's in that field," Hannah responded immediately. "His name is Keith, and he runs an interior design firm here in Ivy Creek. He's the finest interior designer in town as far as I'm concerned." Hannah paused, took out her phone from her pocket and began showing her some pictures. "Here, let me show you some of his work," Hannah continued.

"He worked on our house recently, totally transforming our fireplace and the kitchen. My mom fell in love with the wall designs immediately."

"I also love them," Lucy agreed. "I think you should ring him up," she said.

She waited, watchful of Hannah's facial expressions as she dialed the number. Lucy saw her eyes suddenly light up.

"Hey, Uncle Keith, how are you? I'm great, too. Are you in town? I have a friend here who needs an interior designer, and she's looking to book an appointment."

Lucy kept her focus on Hannah as the conversation played out.

"Right, thanks so much. I'll let her know."

When Hannah dropped the call, she said, "He says he's around, and we can come check on him today or tomorrow if we'd like. I can go with you, or give you directions, whichever you'd prefer."

"There's no rush at the bakery today," Lucy said as she looked around. "We can go now... I'd like to go now."

She couldn't hide her excitement, and most of all, her instincts told her this was the right time to push forward. "I'm too excited to wait, actually," she added as she rose to her feet.

Hannah followed her inside, and they headed back out together after checking around the kitchen to make sure they hadn't forgotten to turn off anything.

Lucy turned on the radio as they drove down the road, and she changed the station when the first thing she heard was a report on Pete's death.

I don't want anything spoiling my mood right now; she thought as she tuned in to a music station. Hannah knew the lyrics to the R n B song playing, so they sang along as she followed Hannah's directions to their destination.

"I so loved this song growing up," she commented, grinning as she tapped the steering wheel while keeping her attention on the curvy road ahead of them.

Lucy had a good feeling about the plans she had set in motion.

Everything will turn out all right. I just can't wait to see what designs Hannah's uncle will have to suggest to me.

11

"Keith Meyer," the man said when Lucy walked into the office with Hannah. "Nice to meet you."

"Lucy Hale. Likewise," she replied, and took the seat he offered. "Hannah said a lot about your designs, and I couldn't wait to see them."

"I've also heard a lot about your bakery, and I've tasted a few of your pastries. They are absolutely the best. I knew your parents, God bless their souls, and I think you're doing a good job keeping the family business alive."

"Thank you, Mr. Meyer."

"Please, it's Keith."

She saw him smile at Hannah.

"How are you, Hannah? It's been a while since I dropped by at the house. How are your parents?" he said.

"Everyone's great," Hannah replied.

Keith took a seat at his side of the table, and Lucy joined him after taking off her apron.

"You should have a look at my catalogue," he said, reaching into the drawer by his side.

Lucy took the catalogue from him as he said, "I have these designs for businesses like yours, and I think one of these should work well with the structure of your bakery," he continued, pointing at the picture on the catalogue she was viewing.

Lucy met his gaze, and he added. "I've been inside the bakery once. I think I remember what it looks like in the dining area, but I will need to take another look."

"What do you think about these floor patterns?" Lucy asked Hannah. They went over the designs and the size of the expansion they were looking at. Lucy wasn't sure what she wanted yet, but she knew something subtle and yet different would suffice.

"Would you mind if I took a few days to mull over this? Everything I see here is great, and I'd like to decide."

Keith grinned. "Sure, you can do that. I will email you a brochure, so you can ponder on the designs there until you make a choice."

"I appreciate that."

She scribbled her email on a piece of paper he offered, and he gave her his business card in exchange.

When Lucy and Hannah stepped out of the firm, they stood by the car for a second. "His designs looked really lovely... I think I liked the ones with the white tabletop joined to the display glass by the side, and the lights dropping from the ceiling."

"Me too… that one really gives off a cozy vibe with the spaciousness. There are shelves on the wall too and you can display bread and some other pastries there. The seats in front of the counter also give the customers a chance to seat while waiting for their order."

"I might decide on that one," Lucy said. "I'll just give it some time."

She glanced at her watch and looked across the road. Richard's café was just a few blocks away from there, and she considered giving him a surprise visit.

"Do you mind going back to the bakery alone?" she asked Hannah. "I'd like to check on Richard."

A flicker of a mischievous smile crossed Hannah's lips. "You should have packed him a tiny basket," she suggested. "It's always fun to have surprise visits with a present at hand."

Hannah winked at her and shook her head as she walked to the side of the road. "It's all right. I'll head back to the bakery."

Lucy waited till Hannah got in a cab before she drove and parked at Richard's café. When she entered, Richard was scribbling a name over a plastic cup, and the wide grin on his face immediately made Lucy smile.

He paused for a second when he saw her but recovered from his surprise as she got to the counter. The ladies he served hurried away, giggling amongst themselves as they exited the cafeteria.

"Caramel latte for me with soy milk, please," she said in a light tone.

Richard winked at her. He put his hand over hers on the count-

503

er briefly before he replied. "Coming right up. Soy milk is nice and if you don't mind, I'd like to sit with you and have some."

"Are you always this charming with the customers?" she asked, laughing as he handed her a cup, then walked around the counter to meet her.

Lucy took a seat, sipped from the cup, and waited till Richard took off his apron and joined her.

"It seems to drive the customers in," he said. "It's a strategy. People feel comfortable in places where they are treated with care, and I try my best to do that."

He stopped for a second, his hand drawing circles on hers on the table. "Are you in the neighborhood for something? Or was this just a surprise visit? If it's the latter, then I'm really loving that you came. We can spend some time together this evening if you aren't busy."

"This is a surprise visit, but I was around here to see someone."

When he quirked a brow, she continued. "Keith Meyer, the owner of the interior designs firm. I'm thinking of moving through with the expansion of the bakery and moving back into my home."

"Your family house?" he asked.

She nodded. "It's mine, and there's no reason to run from it. I think this is a good thing, the expansion... moving back into my house... it's a sign that I'm growing."

Lucy expected a different reaction from Richard. Maybe his usual charming smile and witty words, or some enthusiasm, but he stared at her blankly for a second before withdrawing his hand.

"You moved forward with the expansion anyway," he said, and pushed back on his chair to rise to his feet.

Lucy stood up after him. Her cup of latte lay forgotten as she followed him, closing the distance between them.

She put a hand on his arm and stopped him from walking any further. "Why do I sense that you're not in the least bit excited for me?"

When Richard simply shrugged, picked up a napkin, and began wiping a table, she scoffed. "I can't believe this... you should be happy for me. What is the problem?"

"It's not like I'm not happy for you, Lucy. I am, but..." his voice trailed off, and he shoved his fingers through his hair. "Why do you have to expand? It's a hassle, and you'd spend a lot. Why not keep running things smoothly as you are now? Even though it's small?"

His words echoed through her, sucking wind out of her lungs like she was punched in the face. She licked her lips once and rubbed her forehead.

Richard looked at her again. "I'm sorry, it's just I don't get why you need to grow bigger."

"I get it," she answered, and pushed the strands of hair falling to the side of her face away.

Richard's eyes drifted over her again before the door opened and some students walked right past her to the counter.

He was instantly his usual charming self again as he attended to them, and Lucy turned to get back to her seat. She lifted her cup to her lips again, but the latte had gone cold, and she had lost the urge to enjoy it.

Why isn't he supportive of my decision? He should be happy for me... this is a good decision. I don't get him.

She stole a glance at him again and exhaled deeply. There's definitely a reason why he is being this way.

With a sigh, she dropped the cup and got up to walk out of the cafeteria. Just then, the door opened, and a man walked in. He looked over his shoulder as he closed the door behind him, wiping the sweat beading on his forehead with the sleeve of his coat. His hands shook visibly as he dropped them to his side and adjusted his coat.

Lucy recognized him as one of the men fighting at her stand at the theater the day Pete was murdered. Her pulse skipped a beat as he drew closer, but walked right past her like he hadn't seen her.

I don't think he recognizes me.

"Hello, what would you like to have?" she heard Richard ask when he got to the counter. Lucy put her hands deep into her pocket and contemplated confronting him for a second.

Richard was smiling when she looked back, and she saw the man take the plastic cup Richard offered, exchanging it for some cash.

Lucy sucked in a deep breath, and without re-thinking her choice, she stepped forward to have a chat with him.

Who knows, he might know something useful about the ongoing investigation.

12

L ucy tapped the man on his shoulder once, and he spun around. His eyes widened when they landed on hers, and his coffee spilled a little from the plastic cup he held.

"Holy moly, you scared me!" he exclaimed, eyeing her.

"I'm sorry, I didn't mean to," Lucy apologized. "Do you mind having a little chat? There are some things I'd like to ask you."

The man looked over his shoulder at the counter where Richard was now attending to a customer, and Lucy adjusted her coat as she waited for his reply. He pretended to cough, then followed her to a corner of the café where they sat facing each other.

Lucy took a second to take in the man's physical looks. He had straw-blond hair and looked like he had just gotten a tan. His lips parted as he took a sip from his cup, and Lucy noticed his wiry fingers.

"I'm Lucy Hale," she said. "We met at the theater on the day of…" she stopped as she was about to say Pete's murder. "On the day of the open auditions," she said instead.

The man nodded. "Freddie Burrow. I remember you from the theater. You're the lady who sold the treats that day," he replied, proving to Lucy that he remembered her, too. "And it's all right to say Pete's murder. I admit it bothers me when I think about it, but I'm trying to be more comfortable accepting what happened."

He dragged in a deep breath when he finished talking and took a sip from his cup.

"Why does it bother you?" Lucy asked, gauging his expression.

"Pete was a tough boss. I performed in some of his productions when he lived in Ivy Creek, and when he came back, I was one of the first people he reached out to. He was a perfectionist, I knew him well, but… what happened that day shocked every-one. The cops have questioned me a few times about it, and I still can't get comfortable enough with the way everyone looks at me when I'm in public."

As he talked, Lucy noticed a few people glance in their direc-tion.

"What did the cops ask you about?" she questioned, focusing on him again. "Do you know if they've found out anything about the murder?"

Freddie shook his head. "They asked a few questions about what happened before the murder. Where Pete had been, and who he'd been with. I told them all I knew. The scene we were rehearsing was already perfect, but it's in Pete's nature to make it exceptional, so he pushed harder. He wanted it to be more frantic because he believed that would make it better. I told the police this, and that I had nothing to do with his death. They asked me not to leave town till the end of the investigation."

"I see." Lucy twisted a button on her jacket as she watched him.

Freddie adjusted himself on his chair and emptied his cup before standing up. "I need to go… I'm sorry for the commotion I caused at your stand that day. I wasn't my best self that day."

"It's alright, it happens to the best of us," she replied.

Freddie gave her one last look before he turned and walked out of the café.

Sitting alone, Lucy looked at Richard again. She realized she was waiting for him to come over so they could continue their conversation, but Richard hadn't looked in her direction the entire time she sat there with Freddie.

She rubbed her forehead and rose to her feet to get out of the store. Lucy checked her watch as she drove off from the store and dropped by the hospital to check on Aunt Tricia. When she walked into the ward, her aunt was being her usual charming self with the nurses, and she was rolling around the corridor in a wheelchair.

"How are you feeling?" Lucy asked when she got to her. She put a hand on her aunt's shoulder and massaged it gently.

"I'm great, Lucy. I can even stand and walk properly on my own."

They began making their way to her aunt's ward. When she got to the ward, she helped her up from the wheelchair.

"What's happening at the store?" she asked. "I feel like I've missed out on a lot."

"You've not missed out on much," Lucy said and sat beside her on the bed. "I'm thinking of expanding the bakery, and that means I will move back into the house on Easton Street. I want you to come with me. That way, I can monitor you and make sure you don't have another incident."

"You worry too much," Aunt Tricia said with a laugh.

They spent some time together; Lucy went over the details of the idea she got from Keith Meyer, and she showed her the brochure Keith emailed to her.

"I love this one," Aunt Tricia said, pointing at a picture.

"Me too… It was one of my favorites." She returned her phone to her coat pocket and sighed.

"But you don't look so happy though," Aunt Tricia continued.

"It's just…" Lucy rubbed the back of her neck to ease some of the tension there, but it still ebbed through her veins slowly. "I told Richard about the expansion, and even though I was so excited, he didn't feel the same way. He practically told me to continue being small, that he likes me that way."

"Nonsense, dear," Aunt Tricia responded immediately. "He obviously didn't mean that."

Lucy replayed the conversation she had with Richard, and the way he dismissed her after that, acting like she wasn't still in his café as he attended to his customers. "No… I think he really wasn't pleased to hear I'm expanding. He also didn't hesitate to show his disapproval." She fell silent for a second, then added with a shrug. "Not that his approval will make me change my mind. I just thought he would at least be happy for me and show some support."

"You will get all the support you need from Hannah and me, all right?"

Lucy chuckled when Aunt Tricia reached out to stroke her hair. Her aunt was the confidence boost she had needed, and hearing her words of encouragement was enough to push Lucy on.

"I should get back to the bakery and help Hannah out," she said, rising to her feet again. "You'll be out of here soon, and hopefully the house will be ready by then."

"Take care," Aunt Tricia said.

Lucy waved at her one last time before she exited the ward. As she walked to her car in the parking lot, she noticed a flier stuck to her windscreen.

Lucy looked around to see if anyone sharing fliers was hovering around. When she found no one, she picked up the flier and read it.

Audition for a role in the latest Pete Jenson production.

Lucy stared at it for a long time. She wondered what would happen at the theater in Pete's absence. She had expected the production would stop, or maybe pause until the investigation was over.

Who would distribute these leaflets even though Pete's dead?

A wild thought flew in her head just then as she rumpled the paper in her hand. What if the secret to Pete's murder lies at the theater?

She scratched an itch on her nose and got in her car. Lucy drove by the theater to see what was going on there for herself.

I might find a clue if I look closely, I'm almost certain of it.

13

It was nearly three pm as she headed for the theater. The road seemed unusually busy as Lucy drove past a few diners and stores before taking the turn leading past the station.

She noticed a crowd of reporters gathered in front of the station, taking pictures, and clamoring for a chance to ask their questions.

She focused ahead again when she passed the station, and minutes later, she was pulling up in front of the local theater. Lucy got down from her car, walked towards the entrance, and paused as a frown spread across her face. She expected to see a crowd gathered around her for the ongoing auditions, or maybe more people inside, but the place looked deserted.

With careful steps, she neared the door, pushed it open, and entered. Inside, the theater was empty too, no sign of a soul hovering around.

Maybe the flier I saw was an old one?

There was slow music coming from inside the rehearsal wing, and as Lucy stood there, she considered checking if anyone was in there. The music played slowly, the instrumental tone filling the air. Its sound reminded her of the ominous scene Pete had been trying to pull off on the day of his death.

Stilling the sudden rumble growling in her stomach, Lucy took the first step towards the rehearsal wing. Her head whipped around fast when a voice called from behind her.

"Who are you?" the low timbre voice called, sending a shiver through Lucy.

She froze from the shock, but it lasted only a second before she spun around on her feet to see a tall man across the hall, walking towards her.

"Who are you? And what do you want here?" he asked again when he got to her. His lips were pulled back as his eyes narrowed on hers, and deep lines marred his smooth forehead.

Lucy hadn't seen the man before, but the frown on his face eased off when she mentioned her name. "Lucy Hale," she said, sticking a handout. "I sold treats here at the theater a few days back during the auditions."

"I remember you," he replied, but ignored her hand, so she withdrew it, and stuck it into the pocket of her coat. "Why are you here? There're no auditions and you don't have treats on you to sell, do you?"

Lucy forced on a smile even though she didn't appreciate the hint of sarcasm laced in his question. "I thought the auditions were still ongoing, so I dropped by."

He looked at her again, and Lucy also took in his features. He was several inches taller than her, so she had to angle her head a bit to get a good look at his face. His square-shaped jaw slacked a bit when his frown faded, and she noticed he had a jagged scar on the left side of his cheek.

"You want to audition?" he retorted, accessing her with his probing brown eyes. "You don't strike me like an actress, Miss Hale."

Lucy shook her head. "I'm not here to audition." She looked around where they stood. "I saw a flier showing dates for special auditions."

"It's an old one… The company in charge of distributing them might have continued without realizing Pete died."

His icy tone compelled Lucy to ask more questions. She noticed he shifted his weight from one foot to the other before speaking again.

"I'm Tim Humphrey, by the way, and I have to compliment you, Miss Hale. The treats you serve are the best. I enjoyed them, but I'm afraid coming here was a mistake… you shouldn't even have considered that the auditions would continue after what happened to Pete. If you ask me, I think it's good riddance."

Lucy lifted a brow. "Good riddance?"

"Pete was a terrible boss," Tim continued. "Many didn't like him, and I can tell you, he had it coming. If it didn't happen that day, someone else would have done it."

"Are you saying you think someone here killed him? One of the actors? Or someone else close to him?"

A muscle ticked in the side of Tim's jaw as it hardened. Lucy saw something flash in his eyes. Anger… she couldn't explain the expression he wore, but from the set line of his jaw, and the way his eyes darted away from hers then back, she could tell Tim had a lot on his mind about the murder.

Her breath hitched in her throat when she thought, *Oh Lord, could he be the killer?*

The thought swam in her head for a millisecond as she stared at Tim.

He looked into her eyes, keeping his hard look. "I have nothing to say… the cops will find out what happened, so I think you should leave."

Lucy backed away from him, walked out of the theater to her car, and drove away. His sudden change in mood made it look like he had something to hide, but she didn't want to make any assumptions.

But what if he's the killer? What motive would Tim Humphrey have to kill Pete?

From her conversation with Tim, it was obvious he disliked Pete, and Lucy even sensed that he was pleased with what happened. His words made his dislike clear. But was Tim the kind of man with the guts to kill?

She couldn't tell because she didn't know him at all. But… Tim Humphrey looked guilty to her… his shiftiness and dismissiveness made it look like he had something to hide, and if Lucy was a cop, she would investigate him.

But I'm not a cop, she reminded herself. Best to let the professionals handle the case.

She arrived at the bakery a few minutes later, and Hannah was wiping the tables when she walked in.

"Hey," Lucy said as she got out of her coat and hung it. "Sorry for taking time. I dropped by the hospital to see Aunt Tricia and stopped by the local theater. Hope it wasn't too hectic here at the bakery?"

"Not at all," Hannah replied. "It's not been frantic today, but we had a few customers drop in, and we've sold out all the waffles and brownies, so we need more for tomorrow. How is Aunt Tricia, by the way? I plan to visit her this evening on my way home."

"She's better," Lucy answered. "I planned to bake some cookies. I've been craving some. We will add brownies and waffles to the list," Lucy replied.

Hannah walked to the counter to drop the napkin she held and added as she rounded it. "Also, there's someone here to see you. She came in a few minutes ago, and it's a good thing you didn't take long to show up as she insisted on waiting for you," Hannah pointed at a woman at the extreme right end of the bakery with her back to them. Lucy looked and saw the woman sitting with her back straight and hands on the table.

"Who is it?" Lucy whispered as she walked towards the woman with Hannah by her side.

14

"It's Thelma Cousins," Hannah replied as Lucy got to the table where the woman sat. Thelma immediately rose to her feet when Lucy got to her and extended her hand.

"Hi, I'm Thelma," she said in a steady voice.

Lucy thought she oozed the charm and confidence of a Hollywood celebrity, and she remembered something about Judy saying her daughter was still an actress.

"I'm here to see the owner of the bakery," Thelma said when Lucy sat with her. "Do you have any idea when she'll be back?"

"I'm the owner," Lucy replied, crossing her fingers in front of her. "I'm Lucy Hale."

"Oh, thank goodness you're back in time. I was hoping I wouldn't wait here too long." Thelma grinned this time before she adjusted herself in her seat and ran a hand over the sleeve of her blouse. "I'm Judy Cousins' daughter, and I saw you at my mother's shop a few days ago," she began, not taking a break before she launched right into the reason she was there to see Lucy. "I was wondering if I could work for you. It will only be for two weeks, and from what I've heard about your bakery and what I can see, it will be really nice to work here."

Lucy leaned further on her chair as she accessed Thelma. Her bright countenance was probably one of her best qualities, and the charming smile she wore might get her a lot of roles, but Lucy thought it couldn't land her this job.

"I'm not in need of an extra hand now," Lucy replied, slowly getting her words out as Thelma's smile dropped. "It's still early in the year, and there's no major event going on for now. Also, I don't think you have the particular set of skills for this kind of job."

Thelma lit up again at the mention of skills. "Actually… it's more like an internship for me. I'm playing the role of small-town baker in a Denver production, and hands on experience of what it's like to work in a bakery would be helpful. I like to get into my role and play it like it's my life. I don't know if this makes sense to you."

"It does," Lucy replied, reconsidering. "So, you're looking for experience as a baker… to help with your role?"

"Exactly," Thelma replied. "It will only be for two weeks, and I don't even need to get paid. I think it'll be fun working with you, Lucy," Thelma said, then leaned closer to add. "Besides, I have connections with cool people, and celebrities, and if I put in a word about your bakery, you'll be getting lots of attention. Pretty soon, you might even look at opening multiple branch-es."

Lucy rolled the idea over in her head for a short time. "It sounds like a good idea," she replied. I'm not so hyped about her celebrity connections, and I'm the one who'll be doing her the favor if she works here.

Thelma clapped her hands together in excitement and chuckled as she tossed some part of her hair over her shoulder in a glamorous style.

"This will look good on my Instagram timeline," she said. "A few snapshots of the bakery and the wonderful service you offer is more than enough to drag customers here, but of course, that will only be after I'm done with the internship," she said.

Lucy smiled at her. "I will offer you a stipend for interning here," she said. "It's not right to let you work for free."

"Ahh, you're very kind."

Lucy saw her glance around the bakery again. When her gaze landed back on Lucy's, she was rising to her feet and thanking her.

When Thelma left the bakery, Hannah came to where Lucy sat and joined her. "I think this is a bad idea," she said, looking directly at Lucy. "Thelma is more of a socialite… she pulls a crowd but I sincerely doubt she'll be of any help here even as an intern… she might just be extra weight."

"Well, you were right when you said she pulls a crowd, and I think the bakery needs some media attention. Besides… she might know something about Pete's murder."

Hannah sighed, and to ease her mind a little, Lucy suggested. "Let's bake some brownies and cookies."

She led Hannah into the kitchen, and they threw themselves into work. By evening, when she closed the bakery, she was exhausted. She went to her apartment upstairs and threw herself on the couch with a loud sigh.

Gigi was immediately by her side, purring and clamoring for attention, so Lucy stroked her fur a bit.

"I'm so tired, Gigi," she muttered, closing her eyes. She was still dressed in her work outfit, and even kicking off her shoes seemed like too much work. Lucy took off the boots, and the shawl wrapped around her neck.

She turned on the television, went into her bathroom for a quick hot shower, and when she returned to the living room, the 9pm news had begun.

Lucy sat with a glass of fruit juice and crossed her legs on the center table close to the couch, where she relaxed. Gigi climbed onto the couch to stay close to her, and she brought her pet close, patting her as they listened to the news.

The report talked about Pete's murder, and a few minutes into the report, there was a sudden cut to a female reporter in front of an old building. The woman who came on the screen spoke with a slight shrill in her voice, immediately capturing Lucy's attention.

The fatigue she felt earlier was being replaced by an interest in the news report, and she massaged the back of her neck as she listened, her eyes glued to the television screen.

"We're live at the local police station in Ivy Creek, and the cops here are reluctant to release any information," the reporter was saying. "Everyone wants to know what happened to Pete Jenson, the Broadway producer, and the authorities are being highly secretive about the investigation. The lack of transparency in this investigation is worrying. We hope genuine efforts are being made to find the killer."

Lucy had never seen the reporter on the channel before, and she read the words below the clip - Stephanie Appleby, Hollywood Investigative Journalist and Reporter.

The dark-haired woman continued speaking, and Lucy paid

attention.

"Ivy Creek might look serene, but looks obviously can be deceiving," she continued. "Regardless of the excellent reports we've heard about this remote Colorado town, the public now knows that the town is harboring secrets and a murderer."

A footage of the scene at the police station came up next, and as the rowdy voices of the reporters' asking questions played on the television, Lucy turned to her cat. "This is bad, Gigi," she mumbled. "Really… Pete's death is creating a ruckus. This case is dragging the town's name in the mud," she murmured.

Gigi kept looking at Lucy, her ears perked up like she understood what Lucy was saying.

"We need to do something before things get worse. Our town's good name will be tainted if the killer isn't found soon."

Gigi purred, and Lucy closed her eyes. She zoned her mind out of what the news report was saying, and as she dozed off to sleep, she replayed all she had found out so far in her mind. She planned to check on Taylor and see if she could find anything out from his end.

We need to find the killer before things become worse, and Ivy Creek becomes the most unpopular town in the country. That won't be good for anyone.

15

The next morning, Lucy and Hannah had finished baking new batches of waffles and cupcakes for the day. Lucy sat on a stool in the kitchen, her back to the door as she enjoyed the lemon tea Hannah had made. "This is amazing," she said as she sipped again. "I want to have it every day."

Hannah was bent over in front of the oven, checking the cupcakes. When she straightened, she took off the gloves she wore, dropped them on the table and placed her palm flat on it. "It's almost opening time, and your new intern isn't here. I told you this was a bad idea," she said.

"Come on, Hannah. Quit being so grumpy," Lucy said as she rose to her feet and set her mug on the table. She walked over to where Hannah was and put her hand on her shoulder. "She'll come... she'll be here."

They heard the front bell ding then, and Lucy rushed out to the dining area with Hannah to see Thelma strolling into the bakery, a wide smile on her face, and phone in one hand.

"All right, I'll talk to you later… Bye."

Thelma ended her call and slipped her phone into the pocket of the fur coat she wore. "Hi, Lucy," she said in a cheery tone, adjusting the sleeve of her coat. "How's it going?"

Thelma blinked as she spoke, still grinning, and Lucy glanced over her head to see the look on Hannah's face. She sighed, rolled her eyes, and faced Thelma again. "You're late on your first day, not a good impression."

Lucy crossed her hands over her chest and Thelma began taking off her coat. "I'm sorry, but I'm here now," she said in a sing-song voice as she walked over to the stand to hang her coat. "We can start."

"You're late, and I won't tolerate lateness, Thelma. We keep to time here."

"I'm sorry," Thelma replied, lowering her head a bit. "It won't happen again, I promise."

Hannah had gone back into the kitchen, so Lucy took Thelma around to show her the basic setting of the bakery. She showed her the price list and pointed out the packages she usually added as a side-order or a freebie when she had a customer who bought a lot from her.

"We sometimes get online orders through calls on this phone, so if you ever pick up, all you need to do is scribble down the order and get it to me or Hannah."

Thelma nodded. "Hannah's your…" She dragged out the sentence for a second.

Lucy answered, interrupting her. "Hannah's my assistant. She handles things when I'm not around, and she's here if you don't understand anything."

Thelma put on a sly smile, then leaned closer to Lucy. "I don't think she likes me very much," she whispered, a mischievous look in her eye. Lucy ignored her and turned around to walk into the kitchen and continue their tour.

The first customer for the day came in when they finished going around the kitchen. Lucy went behind the counter to attend to the man while Thelma leaned over the wall and took out her phone to text again.

She noticed Hannah staring at Thelma as she served cupcakes, and Lucy shook her head. Lucy moved closer to Hannah and poked her in the side gently. "It's only for two weeks," she said.

Hannah exhaled and went into the kitchen. The morning was busy, and by the time Lucy finally had time to rest, it was nearly mid-day. She turned on the speaker to listen to some music for a bit while she relaxed.

Thelma immediately put her phone in her pocket and came to the counter. "These are your famous waffles," she began. "I'm not so into baking, but I'd definitely like to learn how to make these."

"During interning, aren't you supposed to be actually learning?" Hannah asked in a low tone. Thelma rubbed her palms together as she stared at the waffles, and Lucy noticed Hannah's frown deepened.

"Hannah, we should check on the bread dough," she said, trying to lure Hannah into the kitchen.

Lucy walked into the kitchen first, and Hannah followed, closing the door behind her.

"All right, I sense something else is going on here, between you and Thelma," she said. "Care to share?"

Hannah dragged her fingers through her hair and rubbed her lips. "When we were in high school, Thelma and I were in the same year, and we used to be friends at some point. At least I thought we were, but turned out she was just using me to make herself more famous. She didn't really like me as a friend, and all I did was follow her around like a fool till I realized I was just her puppet."

"I'm so sorry to hear this, Hannah," Lucy said in a solemn voice. She put a hand over Hannah's shoulder and pulled her in for a hug.

"Yeah, I got over it a long time ago, but I can tell you, Thelma isn't the person you want to work with."

Lucy heard a clang from outside and rushed out of the door to check on what was happening. Thelma was standing outside, a pale look on her face as Lucy dashed past her.

"Did you break something?" she asked.

Thelma shook her head in response and pointed at the paper bag on the counter. "I was trying to pack an order for a customer."

Lucy sighed and finished packing the items for the customer. When she collected the payment from the customer and turned to find Thelma, she saw her standing by the light stand in a corner and taking a selfie.

The phone suddenly rang, distracting Lucy before she could say anything. She picked it up before it rang again.

"Yes, I have waffles and brownies available for delivery. All right, I will get down to your address and you will have them in a few minutes."

Lucy scribbled down the address, thanked the caller, and went into the kitchen to prepare it.

"Hannah, help me with the delivery basket, please," Lucy said as she counted the packed waffles to make sure it was complete. When Hannah brought the basket, she arranged them inside, and hurried out to pick some freebies.

When she got to the dining area, Thelma was standing by the door again, her hands twisting in front of the other.

"Why don't you help Hannah in the kitchen, Thelma?" Lucy said. "You shouldn't be out here staring at nothing."

"I wasn't staring, I just…" Thelma turned and pointed at a woman standing with her back to the counter. "A customer came in," she said. "She's famous."

The woman turned around at that moment, and Lucy's eyes widened when she recognized her as the reporter on the news the previous night.

"Oh my God, that's Stephanie Appleby."

"Yes," Thelma said, looking starstruck.

"She looks smaller in person, though," Lucy commented as she looked at the woman again.

"Well, there's a saying that TV puts weight on you or something along those lines," Thelma replied.

"I'll go talk to her." Lucy went to the woman and tapped her lightly on the shoulder. "Hi, would you like something to eat?"

"Yes, please, but as soon as I finish this call," Stephanie replied with a pleasant smile before returning her attention to her phone.

Lucy left her and returned to the kitchen to pick up the basket she had put together. Hannah was washing her hands at the sink when she entered.

"Guess who we have as a customer today," Lucy announced when she got to her. "Celebrity reporter Stephanie Appleby."

Lucy wondered what had brought a Hollywood celebrity to her bakery.

Did she get referred here by someone? Is she here on official business or to buy some of my treats?

"You're kidding," Hannah replied, turning to her.

"You should go see for yourself then."

"Holy…" Hannah exclaimed. "What do we do? We should do something, right? Is everything set? We have enough pastries for sale?"

Hannah was rambling, and Lucy put her hands on Hannah's shoulders to calm her.

Lucy said, "Relax… Everything is set, and we're always ready to welcome any customer."

Hannah sucked in a deep breath and nodded. "All right," she murmured.

"I will go deliver these, so you will be here to take her order when she's ready to make one. I don't think we should leave Thelma out there with the customers alone because—"

A crashing thud from the dining area interrupted Lucy's sentence. She moved spontaneously, dashing out of the kitchen with Hannah behind her to see what was happening.

16

What in heaven's name happened? Lucy wondered as she dashed into the dining area with Hannah behind her. "What was that?" she asked, her heart in her throat as she rounded the corner and stopped in her tracks when she saw Stephanie standing with both hands over her mouth.

Thelma stood frozen to a spot in front of the broken vase, a horrified look on her face, and Lucy repeated her question to get her attention.

"Oh my God," Stephanie exclaimed before Thelma could reply. Stephanie dropped her hands and angled her body to face Thelma.

Stephanie's brows knotted into a frown, and she jabbed a finger at Thelma as she continued. "You almost killed me."

Lucy looked from Thelma to Stephanie, trying to understand what had happened with the broken vase on the floor.

"I'm so sorry," Thelma blurted just before Stephanie huffed, adjusted her shoulder bag, and hurried out of the bakery. When the door closed behind her, Lucy folded her arms over her chest, arched a brow and faced Thelma.

Thelma shuddered and squeezed her eyes shut for a second. "I didn't try to kill her, I swear it," she said when she re-opened them.

Hannah stood at the kitchen's entrance, her hand folded over her chest, and Lucy saw her shrug and walk back into the kitchen before she faced Thelma again.

"What happened?" she asked, contemplating dashing out of the bakery after Stephanie. "How did you break the vase?"

"I'm sorry… I noticed it was out of place, and I was trying to fix it, but it just dropped, and I couldn't stop the fall. Please, trust me."

Lucy sighed. She pushed her fingers through her hair and rubbed her forehead for a second. "Stephanie's a famous reporter from the city, and whatever she tells the world about Sweet Delights is definitely going to stick. Your clumsiness might ruin my business," she scolded.

Thelma lowered her head, and Lucy released another sigh before she walked past Thelma and headed out of the bakery to find Stephanie. She didn't think Stephanie would have gone far, so she doubled her steps, hoping to find her.

As a one-time food critic, Lucy was mindful of her customer service because she knew what a critical review could do for a business. Especially one from someone as influential as Stephanie Appleby.

Lucy walked down the first three blocks she passed, scanning her surroundings to see if Stephanie had entered one of the local shops around. She passed a diner and noticed a crowd of locals in front of a bookstore across the street from her.

When she crossed over to the other side, Lucy noticed they were staring at Stephanie inside the bookstore through the windows. Stephanie seemed engrossed in a conversation with a lady, probably the store's manager. She was holding a book in one hand, making hand gestures with the other as she spoke, and it reminded Lucy of the news report she watched the previous night.

Lucy lifted a hand to rub the back of her neck as she made her way into the store. It's best I apologize to her. I don't need the bakery getting the wrong review from a reporter.

Inside the store, she approached Stephane immediately as the lady walked away from her.

"Hi," Lucy said when she drew closer. She slipped her hands into the pocket of the jeans she wore and continued. "I'm so sorry about what happened at my bakery earlier. Thelma, the lady you met, is an actress, interning there to learn some skills for her next role as a baker, so she really does not know about baking or customer service."

Lucy noticed Stephanie took a step back at first before speaking. "Really?" she asked.

"Yes, really… it was an accident, so I came here to apologize."

"Alright then, water under the bridge."

Relief flooded Lucy, and she released an audible sigh. "Great. I'm Lucy, by the way… Lucy Hale. I'm Sweet Delights owner."

"Nice to meet you, Lucy," Stephanie responded. "I'm Steph."

Lucy gave a soft nod before her gaze dropped to the book

Stephanie held in her right hand. She read the title quickly and looked Stephanie in the eye. "That's an enjoyable book you're holding there."

"It is?"

Lucy responded with a nod. "I've read the first two parts. It's a trilogy, and it has one of the best plots if you ask me. You won't regret getting or reading it."

"Thank goodness. I was having second thoughts about getting it because it's an author I don't know but getting a review from someone who's read it has definitely cemented my decision."

Lucy noticed it was quite easy to get into a conversation with her.

"I read it in an entire day when I first got it, didn't want to put it down for a second. If you get it, I'm sure you'll feel the same way about the story."

"It's a good way to pass time," Stephanie said, continuing their conversation. "Especially in an uneventful town like this. I mean, how slow can time pass? I've been out and about since dawn broke and it's not even twelve noon yet," she said with a laugh as she glanced at her watch.

"Ivy Creek isn't so bad… this is actually a peaceful place to be in," Lucy replied.

"You sound like you've lived here a long time," Stephanie said as she picked up two more books and accessed them.

"I was born here. Ivy Creek is my home."

"So, you probably know or have met Pete Jenson?"

The question reminded Lucy that the lady was a reporter when she threw the bold question. "Yes, I met Pete Jenson a few times before the incident," she admitted.

"What did you think of him? And the incident?" Stephanie probed.

"Well, I didn't know him so well, but I know a few things. Most people here believed he always put the town down when he had time to speak about us, and that made him disliked by many. Also, I got to find out that he never appreciated talent from town, and always tried to cheat the people he worked with. Either way, I think what happened is a genuine tragedy. No one deserves to die like that."

"Right," Stephanie said. "It was nice speaking to you, Lucy," she added. "I'll drop by your bakery before I leave Ivy Creek. Hopefully, that won't be long from now."

"Thank you," Lucy replied as she shook hands with her. "It's a pleasure talking to you."

"Same."

She watched Stephanie walk to the counter to pay for her books and faced the shelf to scout for a contemporary novel that could keep her busy during her leisure time on Sundays. After a quick search, Lucy settled for a crime thriller. She paid for the book in cash, then headed out of the store and back to the bakery.

When she entered, she noticed Hannah was alone at the counter, attending to customers, and Thelma was nowhere in sight.

"How did it go with Stephanie?" Hannah asked as Lucy joined her after putting the novel she bought in her office.

"Turns out she's really nice. I apologized, we chatted a little, and she even said she would drop by sometime."

"Thank goodness it went well," Hannah replied as she accepted cash from a customer. "Would have been a real disaster if you didn't get to her in time, and if the bakery got a bad review from a famous reporter, that would have been Thelma's fault."

Lucy understood why Hannah was always harsh with Thelma, and she also thought Thelma needed to take her internship seriously.

"I don't think she can commit to this position, and she might actually ruin things for me," Lucy admitted to Hannah. "I guess maybe you were right about her."

Hannah went into the kitchen to check on the muffins in the oven while Lucy continued attending to the customers in line.

The rest of the day, Lucy attended to the customers in line and made one delivery to the town's hospital before she closed the bakery for the day.

On the news that night, the town's deputy sheriff, Taylor, was on the news with a local reporter.

"The investigation is still ongoing, and the department asks for all citizens of Ivy Creek to remain calm and patient. We will find the perpetrators of this heinous crime and justice will be served."

Lucy hoped there would be a quick resolution to the murder investigation as the good name of Ivy Creek was hanging in the balance.

17

The next morning, Lucy hummed a song to herself as she strolled around the counters in the grocery store. She had picked a basketful of cooking ingredients for her kitchen, and now she needed to get some baking soda for the bakery.

When she finished picking the items on her list, she rolled her cart towards the front.

She had woken up that morning with the urge to do something brand new, and a lemon meringue pie seemed like a good way to start the day.

I will put some on sale to see how much the customers like it, she thought as she rolled her cart forward when it got to her turn.

"Hi," Lucy greeted the cashier.

The woman grinned as she looked up from her computer screen, but her grin slowly faded when she looked at Lucy, and her lips formed a tight line. Lucy wondered if she caused the cashier's change in demeanor.

Behind Lucy, two women argued between themselves. Lucy heard her name and glanced over her shoulder to look at them.

"It's her, Lucy Hale, the owner of the bakery," one of them murmured, eyeing Lucy with a nasty look.

"That will be fifty dollars, please," the cashier said, dragging Lucy's attention back to her.

Lucy tapped her fingers on the counter before she reached into the pocket of her coat for her wallet. She noticed to her side an elderly man glare at her. His eyes fixed on hers for a second when she looked at him, and he only turned away when a younger boy steered him away from where he stood.

Is something wrong with my dress? Lucy wondered, feeling self-conscious. She gave the cashier a shaky smile, took out cash to pay for her items, and waited for her change.

"Thank you," Lucy said when the cashier handed her the shopping bags.

"I thought you loved Ivy Creek," the cashier said, shaking her head.

Lucy looked behind her to see if the cashier was talking to someone else.

"Hello, let me check that for you," the cashier continued, turning her attention to the next person on the line, and forcing Lucy to step away.

Gathering her bags, she walked away from the counter, still analyzing what the cashier meant by her statement. When Lucy walked out of the store, she went to the first car she saw parked. She checked her face in the side mirror to see if anything was amiss.

"Why is everyone staring at me?" she wondered out loud. Straightening again, she scanned the surrounding area where she stood, noticing that some people who walked into the store stopped to stare at her and murmur to themselves.

Rubbing her forehead, Lucy started her walk back to the bakery. It was only a short distance away, and she had planned to get back in time to work on the lemon pie before noon.

When she crossed the road and took the street leading to her bakery, she glanced at her watch to make sure she was still on time. A few minutes' walk down the street, and Lucy saw Richard jogging down the road.

She stopped walking when he drew closer to her, slowing down his pace but not stopping entirely.

"Hey," Lucy said. She hadn't seen him in days since her last visit to his cafeteria, and Richard hadn't bothered to call either. "I haven't seen or heard from you in a while… How are you?"

"Great… you seem good too," he replied, jogging on a spot as he talked.

Lucy watched him wipe a hand over the sweat on his forehead.

"The entire town's talking about you. At least now you're certain your bakery is going to get a lot of media attention."

Lucy arched a brow in confusion. "What are you talking about?"

"I can't slow down. Maybe we'll talk later?" Richard responded and resumed his jog. He waved at her briefly, and her gaze followed him as he continued down the street.

Lucy was still frowning when she continued her walk back to the bakery.

What a weird day, she thought. Inside the bakery, Lucy set the bags down in the kitchen and took out her mixer to prepare her pie when her phone pinged in the back pocket of her jeans.

She got two texts from Hannah and Aunt Tricia. She opened the latter first.

Thanks for the flowers and for showing up the other day. Will you come around this evening? It'll be fun to have someone around for the last round of tests before I get discharged.

Shaking her head, Lucy quickly replied to her aunt.

Yes, sure! I'll try to round up at the bakery in time to be there with you.

She read Hannah's text next.

Hey Lucy, could you please text me the recipe for the coffee cake? I want to make some at home today.

The text reminded Lucy that it was Hannah's free day. She sighed as she looked around the kitchen, remembering that she would have to handle things on her own all day. The chances of Thelma also coming in for work were slim. Since she took off yesterday, Lucy hadn't seen or heard from her.

Lucy texted Hannah the recipe, then began preparing her lemon pie.

She was glad when her first customer of the day walked through her doors.

"Good morning," Lucy said with enthusiasm as she placed both hands flat on the counter. "What would you like?"

The woman looked around the bakery, and when her gaze landed on Lucy's again, Lucy sensed there was a bit of hesitation in the way she looked at the display glass of pastries.

"Seems like you're having a slow day," the woman commented as she looked at Lucy again, shaking her head.

Lucy kept her smile, trying not to appear too worried about the lack of activity in her bakery. It was nearly past eleven am, and she just got her first customer for the day.

Something seems off today. It all started at the grocery store she had visited earlier that day. With everyone staring at her, the cashier's weird comment, and the run-in with Richard on the street, Lucy could only conclude that she was having a very peculiar day. She just hoped things would return to normal… fast.

"Perhaps people need a brief break from treats, but they'll be back," she replied with optimism. "In the meantime, what can I get you? You should try our lemon meringue pie… I'm sure you'll like it."

"Sure, let me have that," the woman replied, tapping her fingers against the counter as Lucy began packing her order. She paid in cash and walked out of the store.

Lucy dropped to a stool behind her and exhaled deeply. What's happening today? She was still wondering why she had no customers when the door opened again.

This time, it was Taylor who walked in, and Lucy was on her feet before he got to the counter.

"Hey," he said. "Busy day?"

"Not in the least. Would you believe I haven't had more than a customer all day? It's really a slow day. People have been funny to me all day, too."

"Funny?" Taylor asked.

She looked at him, noticing his interest in what she was saying, as he fixed his eyes on her face.

"Yes," she answered. "I had people stare at me all day in the grocery store, and on the street. It made me feel green... like an alien who just landed from outer space." Lucy shuddered as she spoke and wrapped her arms around her chest.

"Maybe you caused it," Taylor said with a shrug. Lines pulled at the corner of his mouth. "I mean, why else would every-one be so interested in staring at you if you haven't done or said something? You know how people love to gossip around here... but there's no smoke without fire."

Lucy chuckled at his turn of phrase, and he laughed with her for a second before clearing his throat.

"I'm serious, Lucy," he added. His voice remained soft as he spoke.

What could I have done?

"What do you mean? I don't think there's anything interesting I've done recently."

Taylor shook his head. He reached into his pocket and took out his phone. "It's best if I show you," he explained in a low voice, his eyes soft on hers.

Lucy's heart pounded in her chest as she waited, watching him scroll through his phone for whatever he was about to show her.

18

Taylor moved closer to the counter for Lucy to get a closer look. Her eyes widened as she read the headlines linked to the video.

"This is trending?" she asked Taylor, dismayed at the news she was watching.

"The owner of the local second-rate bakery, Sweet Delights, told me personally that many people in this town didn't have many good things to say about the deceased. It makes me wonder if this murder was planned and supported by some locals," Stephanie was saying in a news report. "This local baker, Lucy Hale, boldly mentioned that Pete Jenson wasn't exactly loved by the members of this town."

Stephanie quoted Lucy's statement about Pete belittling the town and watching this made Lucy's jaw drop.

"Everyone has probably seen this clip," Lucy muttered as

Stephanie's words faded in her ears.

"Yes, this broke out on the local news channel late last night, and it's been trending around town since morning. I'm surprised you didn't know or see this on the news."

"I haven't watched the news all day," Lucy replied and fixed her attention on the video again.

She listened to Stephanie spout more untruths about Ivy Creek.

"I don't think Ivy Creek is peaceful at all. If anything, I think they are a bunch of hypocrites."

Lucy turned away from Taylor and shoved her hands through her hair, sighing in frustration. Taylor paused the video when she faced him again, shaking her head.

"I would never say a thing like that about this town. That woman is completely taking what I told her out of context."

Taylor was quiet, and Lucy replayed what had happened at the grocery store earlier that morning. It made sense now why she was getting all those icy stares and whispers from people around, and Richard's comment about her business strategy.

"This will ruin my reputation and business in town," she continued as she started to pace. "I can't believe this. I've gotten myself involved in another investigation again. This time around, the backlash might be hostile."

"Hey… hey," Taylor said.

She turned to him as he slipped his phone into his pocket and met her gaze. His eyes were soft on hers as he spoke.

"Nothing like that is going to happen. This is just a rumor, and the view of one investigative journalist who is not even a member of our community. I know you would never speak ill of our town, and I'm sure there are others who know this, too."

His words had a relaxing effect on her, and Lucy's shoulders dropped as the worse of her worries faded. Still, she had to find a way to make sure Stephanie corrected her public statement about her.

"I won't sit back and let her ruin my reputation. There must be a way to make sure she says the truth and tell everyone that I never said any of those things or insinuated that Pete was murdered by someone here in Ivy Creek. Besides, I would never give a customer any bad experience here at Sweet Delights."

It was Taylor's turn to sigh. "You shouldn't worry so much, Lu… this will blow over soon," Taylor consoled.

He smiled at her, the corners of his eyes crinkling up as he did. "The storm will be over soon, and you'll be able to get back to business as usual. So far, you've done great, and this little issue won't change all the hard work. Trust me."

Lucy returned his smile, her heart warming up at his confidence. Hearing encouraging words from him relieved some of the tension already growing on her shoulders.

To her surprise, Taylor reached over the counter and put a hand over hers on the counter. The contact lasted briefly, and her skin tingled as he pulled away.

"Once the investigation ends, everyone will return to their lives and all of this will be history."

"Thanks for your kind words, Taylor," she said after a second of silence passed between them again. "It means a lot."

"It's nothing…" he answered. "I know how hard you've worked since you returned, and I admire your dedication. You should keep the hard work going, and soon this place will be bigger than you imagined."

"Would you like some lemon pie?" Lucy asked. "I made some this morning. I think you should try it and take some home to your mom."

Lucy was already packing him three slices of pie as she spoke, and he thanked her when she handed it over to him.

"I'll see you around," she called after him as he waved at her, then made his way out of the bakery.

Alone again, Lucy sat on the stool behind her and closed her eyes for a second. What a disaster, she thought, mortified at how things had turned out with Stephanie. After their conversation, and with Stephanie promising to drop by the bakery sometime later, Lucy had thought things were off to a smooth start with the reporter.

She can ruin everything I've worked so hard to build here with her words.

Lucy was lost in her thoughts for the next hour, and the alarm she set on her phone to remind her of her visit to the hospital dragged her out of it.

No one had walked into the store or called to place any order all day, and frankly, she was exhausted from the waiting.

Lucy got on her feet, cleaned the counter, and packed up for the day. She closed the bakery after a quick drop into her apartment upstairs to feed Gigi, and drove out, heading for the hospital.

Lucy drove onto the main street, her attention on the road and the incidents of the past twenty-four hours.

How much will this affect me? She thought as she turned into Easton Street and stepped on the brakes when the traffic light turned red.

To clear her head, she turned on the radio, hoping to listen to some music, but Stephanie's clear tone hit her ears the minute she tuned in.

"The owner of the local second-rate bakery, Lucy Hale, specifically told me that the town members didn't exactly like or worship Pete Jenson…"

Lucy rolled her eyes. Is she saying this on every channel?

She changed the station to one playing music and spent the rest of the drive singing along to the pop songs. Lucy dropped by Judy's store to get her aunt flowers and for her apartment.

Something colorful and fresh will brighten my mood. Aunt Tricia had loved the last flowers she had gotten, so she would get the same ones for her.

Lucy parked by the side of the road across from Judy's store and got out.

She slipped her hands into the pocket of her coat as she crossed and strode towards the entrance. Through the windows, she spotted Judy bent over a pot of flowers, inhaling their scent.

Judy straightened and turned in her direction as she stepped over the threshold, and Lucy quickly put on a smile.

"Hey, Judy," she said in a light tone, tucking the loose strands of hair falling to the side of her face behind her right ear. "How're you doing?"

"You again?" Judy said in a stern voice.

Lucy froze at the unwelcome response. Judy's frown deepened, marring her facial features, and Lucy's heart pounded in her chest as Judy folded her arms over her chest and spat in a gruff tone. "What do you want?"

Woah! Seems like I've become public enemy number one, Lucy thought, blinking and reeling in shock at the hostile welcome from Judy Cousins.

19

"What do you want?" Judy asked again, her blazing eyes fixed on Lucy for a second. Lucy paused in her stride as she reeled from the unexpected cold welcome from Judy.

Without a word, she spun around to walk out of the store, but gasped when she saw Tim Humphrey standing behind her, a grim expression on his face.

"I was talking to Tim," Judy said again, making Lucy turn back to face her.

"You can stay Lucy, I was asking Tim to leave, not you."

Tim Humphrey took another step forward into the store, despite Judy's instruction. He clenched his hands at his side, and Lucy didn't miss the obvious tension in the air between them.

"You're kicking me out now?" Tim retorted. "You promised to settle everything the next time I came here, and now you're pretending you don't know what I want?"

Judy's eyes widened and darted across the room to Lucy's. "I don't know what you're talking about," she denied, dropping the flower she held carelessly on the table.

Lucy remained on the same spot, watching Judy close the distance between her and Tim. Judy raised her chin defiantly as she spoke to him. "I want you to leave my store right now. Let's not cause a scene, please."

A long minute of silence festered in the store, then Tim raised both hands in a gesture of surrender.

"Right," he spat as he backed away. "Don't come running to me for help when next you need it."

Tim cast one sideways glance at Lucy before he walked out of the store. Judy faced her then, released a shuddering breath and pushed back the strands of hair falling to the side of her face.

"Sorry, you shouldn't have seen that," she said, angling her body towards Lucy. "He's come here three times in the last week, and I don't know what he wants. I don't want to have anything to do with Tim Humphrey, especially now that the cops are investigating him for Pete's murder."

The cops are investigating Tim. Lucy pondered on this fresh development as she listened to Judy complain.

"Sorry if it came off like I was kicking you out of my store. I wouldn't do that…"

Lucy adjusted her bag on her shoulder. She followed Judy to the counter when she walked away.

"Maybe he needs something from you," Lucy said. "Have you tried figuring out what that is?"

Judy shook her head in response. "He did some gardening for me a few weeks ago, and I paid him for it, but he's demanding more money. I'm all for helping people, but my generosity will not be used to blackmail me."

Lucy nodded, noting Judy's judgement of Tim. She could understand where Judy was coming from regarding not letting one's kindness be abused by other people. For a second, she contemplated asking Judy about what Tim meant, but changed her mind when she remembered her decision not to involve herself in this investigation.

Judy was already gathering the flowers she dropped earlier into a vase. When she faced Lucy again, she was dusting her palms together.

"I came in for some lavender flowers," Lucy said. "My aunt loved the previous ones I got."

"I knew she would." Judy brought another bouquet and handed it to Lucy. "This should do the trick once more."

"Thanks, Judy." She collected the flowers and inhaled its scent before looking at Judy again.

"I heard about what happened with the reporter. I'm so sorry, Lucy. Thelma isn't always that clumsy. I wonder what got into her that day," Judy said.

Judy looked genuinely concerned as she spoke, worry lines forming on her forehead, and Lucy sighed.

"It's alright," Lucy replied. "What happened was an accident. It wasn't Thelma's fault entirely."

"I'm glad you think so," Judy said almost immediately as her hand flew to her cheeks. "I was so worried this would affect your working relationships," she continued. "I didn't want that to happen. It's good to know I have nothing to worry about."

Lucy cleared her throat, feeling uncomfortable with the way Judy was staring at her. She shifted her weight from one foot to the other and reached into her pocket for her wallet. "I'll take a bouquet of lilies for myself," she said as she took out some cash.

"Thanks for dropping by, Lucy," Judy said after she paid for the flowers.

"You're welcome."

Lucy was about to leave the store when the door opened, and Thelma stepped in. Thelma gasped when Lucy saw her. The bags she held dropped to the ground, and at the spur of the moment, she spun back around on her heels and ran out of the store.

"Thelma," Judy called after, but she didn't look back. Lucy saw Judy's apologetic smile when she glanced over her shoulder one last time at her. She acknowledged the smile with a nod and walked out of the store.

While heading to her car, Lucy looked around to see if she would spot Thelma. She drove off when she didn't and arrived at the hospital a few minutes later to see Aunt Tricia sitting on her bed, both hands clasped to the side of the mattress before she rose to her feet and tried to find her balance.

Lucy rushed forward to support her after dropping her bags.

"You made it," Aunt Tricia said softly.

"Yeah."

The doctor checked Aunt Tricia's ankle one last time after asking her to walk around, then he scribbled a prescription on a piece of paper and handed it to Lucy. "For her arthritis," he said. "She can go home in the morning."

"Thank you."

Lucy frowned at her aunt when they were alone. "I didn't know you had arthritis," she said, waving the paper at Aunt Tricia.

"It's not important," Aunt Tricia dismissed with a sort of laugh. "I'm just happy I finally get to go home."

Lucy sat on the bed with her and handed over the flowers she bought. "You're moving in with me, so I will keep a closer eye on you now," she said, satisfied with her decision to look after Aunt Tricia.

"How are things at the bakery?" Aunt Tricia asked. "What have I missed?"

Lucy spent the next hour telling her aunt all about the experience with Thelma and Stephanie, and what she noticed at Judy's store earlier.

It was evening when she returned to the bakery. Lucy parked her car behind the bakery and by the time she got to the front again, she saw Stephanie waiting at the door.

Stephanie seemed engrossed in her phone until Lucy drew closer to her. Her head snapped up when Lucy climbed onto the patio and stopped in front of her.

"I didn't think you'd be stopping by here," Lucy commented, allowing her eyes to drift over the woman's face. She wished she could wipe the smug smile off Stephanie's face, but that was not an option.

"Why wouldn't I be back? The locals say this place sells the best pastries in town."

Stephanie looked around and put one hand on her waist, striking a pose. "It doesn't look like there's much going on around here, anyway."

Lucy's hands formed fists at her side, and she replied through gritted teeth. "You lied in your report about what I told you. I

549

don't remember insinuating that someone here murdered Pete."

Stephanie shrugged. "It changes nothing. We both know some-one here did anyway, so what's the difference?"

"I would never speak ill about this town. You need to make this right and tell the truth."

Lucy held Stephanie's gaze for a moment. It didn't seem like Stephanie would back down. Her eyes danced with mischief as Lucy stared, and she scoffed, angled her head to one side and parted her lips in a sigh.

"I decide what I report," Stephanie began, spiking Lucy's irri-tation. She took a step towards Stephanie, and the blare of cop sirens behind them interrupted Lucy's attempt to tell the report-er her mind.

"Miss Appleby?" A cop called from behind them.

Lucy stepped away and turned to see three cops come out of the police car.

"What's happening?" Stephanie asked.

"We would like a word with you, please," the cop said again.

"I'll think about changing my statement," Stephanie said as she breezed past Lucy and sashayed towards the cop's vehicle.

Lucy gave her one last look as she fiddled in her bag for her keys.

She opened her bakery, got in, but moved to the window to watch Stephanie and the cops from there. Stephanie spoke to them for a while, making many hand gestures as she did before she got into the car and drove off with them.

Is she part of the investigation? Lucy wondered as she saw the car disappear into the distance.

20

Two days later, Lucy handed Aunt Tricia a cup of coffee when she joined her in the kitchen. They spent the night in her apartment upstairs, but she planned to speed things up and move back into her house before the end of the week.

"This tastes amazing," Aunt Tricia commented as she took a sip. "Soy milk?"

"Yes. A new recipe I tried out for myself. It tastes heavenly, and I think I'll be having this every morning now." She chuckled as she emptied her mug and set it on the table before moving in to have a slice of toast on the table.

"It will not be a busy day today, so I'm reaching out to Hannah's uncle, Keith, with my choice for the interior designs."

"What did you settle on?"

Lucy took out her phone, opened the brochure she spent the past few days deliberating on, and showed Aunt Tricia her top choice. "This," she said, handing the phone over to her. "This one is lovely; I think it will blend well with the colors on the wall."

"I think so too," Aunt Tricia replied.

"I already set up an appointment with Keith to come around this morning. I should call to find out if he's on his way."

Aunt Tricia went through the brochure briefly, then handed her back the phone so she could call Keith. The call lasted for a few minutes and when it was over; she emailed the cleaning agency she had contacted the previous night.

Lucy started the baking for the day when she finished the call, and Hannah joined her as soon as she arrived. They talked about the decrease in activities at the bakery for the next few weeks during the renovation, and Hannah's idea was to set up a pop-up shop in front of the bakery's building so they could serve the citizens of Ivy Creek.

Keith and his team arrived before any other customer, and Lucy quickly showed them around the bakery. The expansion would create room for a bigger kitchen, and once the apartment upstairs was gone, they could create a sales station up there for other treats she was thinking of adding to their menu for spring.

She turned to Keith when they came into the kitchen again.

"That's all I need for now. I will get back to you with a quotation and list of items needed," he said.

"Sounds like a plan," Lucy agreed with a smile.

She escorted Keith outside, handed him a free pack of cupcakes Hannah had prepared, and bade him farewell before heading back inside to meet Hannah and Aunt Tricia.

"This is finally happening," Hannah said with an excited squeal, and Lucy matched her excitement with a laugh. She heard the doorbell ding and hurried out to receive the customer.

"Hey," she greeted when she saw Taylor walk in.

He wore a casual t-shirt and shorts with a base-ball cap, and he took the cap off as he got to the counter.

"Free day?" Lucy asked.

"Yes," he replied. "I came to get some of those lovely lemon pies you made the other day, and also check on how you're doing." He looked around the dining area before his gaze settled on hers again. "How are you holding up?"

"Things are slow but great," she replied, tapping her fingers on the counter. "I'm moving forward with the expansion, and I've had someone come in to view the place and take measurements. I want it done before spring, and I'm so excited."

"I can tell you're excited," he replied. "You're doing that thing you do with your fingers when you can't keep the joy down and need to share it with someone else."

Lucy grinned. "You know me too well."

She nodded. "Let me get your order."

She packed the lemon pie and an extra cupcake for him, handed it over, and thanked him for the order. "Bye… Have a nice day."

Taylor waved at her before leaving the bakery and she returned inside to join in Hannah and Aunt Tricia's discussion about the report Stephanie made about Lucy's comment.

"It's outrageous that she could take what I said and twist it into something else," Lucy complained as they moved their discussion onto the patio. The day rolled by quickly, with only two customers besides Taylor coming in for the day.

Later that evening, Richard dropped by at the bakery. Lucy greeted him outside while Aunt Tricia and Hannah excused themselves and went inside.

"It's been a while," she said as she relaxed in her chair. "I haven't seen or heard from you since our run in on the street that morning."

Richard nodded. He sighed as he lowered himself to the chair Hannah had occupied moments earlier. "I'm sorry. I should have called or responded to your texts, but I got caught up in work."

Lucy assessed him as he apologized, and shrugged, determined to let their lack of communication slide. She hadn't thought about Richard much in the past days either. Her mind had been too pre-occupied with everything happening around her, and then there was the conversation they had at his café the last time she was there.

"I see you're moving on with the expansion as planned." He paused for a second and looked around before continuing. "You're doing just fine as you are now, and I don't understand why you need to make this bigger than it already is and risk losing what you already have."

"You're being insensitive, Richard," she pointed out in a flat voice. "The news Stephanie reported chased customers away."

I don't know if I'm more annoyed or disappointed; she thought as she looked at him.

"You know, I thought at least you would be one of the few who would believe that I'd say nothing bad about this town. You know how much this bakery means to me, and how much work I've put into it. How can you belittle my efforts?"

"Belittle? I merely stated that it was a good move, which it was. I mean Lucy, look around you. No one here cares about how big your bakery is but you."

"How can you say that? You're trying to say that I shouldn't grow?"

"It's too much pressure on you. A kind of pressure you don't need. And what if something goes wrong? You'll suffer losses. Is that what you want?'

"Oh, I get it now. It's not that you don't want me to expand… It's that you don't believe I can do it," she said and rose from her chair.

"Lucy—"

"You've said enough," she interrupted, raising a hand to stop him from proceeding. "You know what saddens me, it's that you don't think I can pull this off. I get that you're not a big fan of the expansion and everything else, but at least you could try to pretend you're happy for me and support me regardless of anything else. It's what I would have done for you."

Without another word to him, she walked away and re-entered the bakery. Aunt Tricia and Hannah probably over-heard their conversation because she noticed the look of concern on their faces as she entered and hurried past them to get to her apartment upstairs.

Lucy lay in bed, focusing her mind on the business at hand and trying to ignore the obvious ache in her heart. She realized the relationship with Richard was on its last legs.

I can't be with a man who doesn't support me.

When Lucy went down to the bakery later, Hannah had closed for the day, and Aunt Tricia was sitting on the front porch enjoying a glass of cool lemonade.

"You're alright?" Aunt Tricia asked when she joined her and took a sip from the glass on the table.

"Yeah, I'll be fine," she replied. It wasn't the first time Lucy had to end a relationship with someone she really cared about, so she was certain she would recover from this one, too.

"Good, because you have a lot going on for you, Lucy, and you can't afford to get distracted. You're doing great and that matters more than anything else."

"Thanks aunt," she replied gently. "You're my rock every time I need one. I love you."

"Love you too, Lucy. Now cheer up… a smile suits you better every time," she said.

Lucy laughed then and picked up the glass again. "It sure does."

They recalled memories of Lucy's childhood in town, and the times Aunt Tricia came to visit.

It was nearly past nine pm when they retired for the night, and Lucy made sure Aunt Tricia was comfortable on the bed first before she took her spot on the couch in the living room.

She woke up to a text from Hannah the next morning, and yawned as she sat on the couch, took the phone, and read through it with sleepy eyes.

Hey, Lucy… I can't make it to the bakery this morning because I had to go to the hospital a few minutes ago. I'll talk to you when you see this.

Lucy immediately sat up on her bed, alarm bells ringing in her head as she re-read the text.

What could have happened to Hannah?

21

L ucy hurried past the nurse's station thirty minutes later. She followed the direction a nurse
gave and entered the emergency ward unit. She
didn't make it far before she spotted Hannah
standing by a bedside.

"Hannah," she called, putting her hands on Hannah's shoulders
to examine her. "You're alright? What happened?"

"I'm good," Hannah replied with a sigh. "It's Thelma who's
hurt," she added.

Lucy's eyes fell on the bed then, and a pale Thelma gave her a
weak smile.

"Hi Lucy," Thelma greeted. "It's me who got hurt, and Hannah
was on the scene, so she volunteered to come to the hospital
with me."

Lucy dropped her bag on a chair and moved to the side of the bed so she could stand beside Thelma. "Oh honey, what happened? Did you get badly hurt?'

Thelma shook her head. Lucy put a hand on the bandage on her forehead and stroked it gently. She looked at Hannah, waiting for someone to tell her how Thelma had gotten injured.

"A drunk driver hit her car from behind," Hannah said. "She hit her head on the steering wheel, and probably sustained a concussion, but besides that, the doctors say she's fine."

"Thank goodness," Lucy exclaimed. She pulled a chair close to the bed and sat. She rubbed Thelma's hand as she listened to Thelma explain what happened on the road.

"The cops arrested the culprit on the scene," Hannah added.

"I'm relieved you're all right, Thelma," Lucy said again as she looked at Thelma. "When I got the text, I thought something bad had happened."

Lucy saw Hannah glance at her watch, then at her. "Is Aunt Tricia alone at the bakery? She will need help because Uncle Keith and his team are starting work today."

"Yes, we should get back to the bakery in time before their arrival," Lucy agreed.

She gave Thelma a soft smile as she rose to her feet. "I'll come check on you in the evening."

"Lucy," Thelma called when Lucy turned to walk away with Hannah. Lucy turned back to face her. "I'm sorry about the incident with Stephanie," she apologized, hanging her head low. "I feel like it's my fault she made that report about your bakery. I should have been more careful and should have taken responsibility instead of walking away and not showing up for work."

Lucy remained quiet as Thelma apologized. Thelma's actions

played a role in damaging her bakery's reputation in Ivy Creek, and she was still working on getting things back to normal. It would take a while for things to return to normal for her, yes, and she could hold that against Thelma. But that was never Lucy's approach to life.

She preferred to hope for the best and believe the best in people.

"I hope you can forgive me," Thelma repeated, this time meeting Lucy's gaze.

With a sigh, Lucy crossed over to the bed and touched Thelma's hand again, squeezing gently to show her affection. "I understand, and I forgive you. Don't worry about anything for now and focus on getting better."

"Thank you so much," Thelma said.

Lucy laughed. "Sure... I have to get back to the bakery now, but I'll come check on you later, okay?"

"Alright."

On her way out of the hospital, she spotted Taylor with some other cops questioning a doctor and waved at him briefly before exiting the building.

"I see you're getting friendlier with Taylor," Hannah commented as they drove back towards the bakery. "He drops by often and even smiles whenever he sees you."

Lucy caught Hannah's mischievous look when she stole a glance at her. She understood what it implied, and shook her head, laughing it off with a wave of her hand. "There's nothing to it. We're just getting back on good terms. When I first moved back to town, it seemed like he resented me a bit for our breakup, but I think we're past that now, and we might even be friendly neighbors now."

"That sounds good," Hannah replied with a chuckle.

Few minutes after they arrived at the bakery, she saw Keith's quote in an email.

She texted him to say that she'd get back to him shortly and then headed into the kitchen to start work for the day.

Once the expansion work started, she would have to minimize the amount of baking she did in a day because she would bake from her house, but she planned to keep the concession store and the pop-up stand running. That way, she could still make sales while expanding.

Later that evening, after the long, busy hours, she drove Aunt Tricia to her house on Easton Street and helped her settle in. She then drove to the grocery store to get some items. As she strolled around picking what she needed, she spotted Richard on the other end of a row where she stood. He looked at her for a moment before walking in her direction.

Lucy cleared her throat and kept her head high when he got to her.

"Hey," he said. His face lacked any obvious expression, so she couldn't tell what he was thinking as she looked at him. "How are you?"

"I'm good," she replied. "You? How is business going?" It was an awkward question, and Lucy felt herself cringe inside when she asked.

Richard simply nodded, then they fell into another moment of awkward silence before he tipped his head to the side. "I should get these to the counter," he said, pointing behind her.

"Yeah, you should." She side-stepped him so he could roll his cart past her, but he stopped in his tracks.

"For what it's worth, I didn't mean to be a jerk to you. I guess we just don't have the same take on this situation."

Lucy nibbled on her lower lip. An ache spread through her heart at his words, and even though she had concluded earlier in her mind that her relationship with Richard was over, it still didn't make it any easier.

"I know," she answered. "I respect your take… But this is something I must do, regardless of your opinion."

"I believe you will do great, Lucy. You should know that… for what it's worth," he said, repeating the phrase.

"Sure… See you around."

She turned to watch him walk away with his cart and exhaled. That was the most awkward conversation she had ever had, and she was glad it didn't last long.

Lucy hoped they could one day relate with ease again, but right now, she didn't need anyone discouraging her about her choices.

She rounded up her shopping, paid for her items, and headed to the hospital to check on Thelma, as she had promised.

She greeted the doctor who treated Aunt Tricia at the ward's entrance, and another familiar nurse as she passed the nurse's station, drawing closer to Thelma's unit.

Lucy stopped in her tracks when she saw Judy standing by Thelma's bed, knee-deep in the conversation they were having. She wasn't far off from the bed so she could hear Judy clearly when she said. "I did it for you, Thelma. You should know by now that I would let no one walk all over you like that. No one can do that to my precious daughter and get away with it. I told you not to take that deal, but you didn't listen. Now look what it caused."

"It wasn't your choice to make, mom," Thelma countered

fiercely, the tone of her voice attracting the attention of a few others around them. "That deal was a once in a lifetime opportunity. I had to take it... you don't know what it's like to be in my shoes, so you don't get to tell me what to do," Thelma argued. "You always ruin everything, just like you did with dad. If you hadn't told him about me, then maybe he'd still be here today."

"Watch it, young lady," Judy countered, forming a fist with her right hand at her side.

Lucy's first instinct as she watched the scene was to continue towards them.

This is probably a family issue, she thought, observing the tense stance Judy assumed when Thelma mentioned her father.

It's best I don't interrupt. She spun around and walked away before either of them noticed her.

22

The next morning, Lucy was still replaying the scene between Thelma and her mother in her head. She was slicing some carrots for the salad she wanted to make, and the kettle on the stove sizzled, reminding her she had put water there to boil.

She turned off the stove, then returned to the table to continue her slicing. Her aunt was still asleep as it was not yet dawn, but Lucy had a lot to prepare. She had moved the basic baking ingredients to her parents' home with Aunt Tricia's help the previous evening, and now all she had to do was bake.

Lucy finished preparing the items for the salad, and she was mixing it all up with cream when Aunt Tricia finally came down the stairs.

"Good morning," Lucy greeted her with a smile as she entered the kitchen. "Did you sleep well?"

"Of course, I did. It's been years since I was last in this house. I've forgotten how cozy it can get, and if not for my alarm, I would have slept the morning away."

Lucy chuckled at that. She offered Aunt Tricia a bowl of salad and set a glass of water in front of her before settling to eat hers. She had whipped up a coffee cake batter first thing when she woke up, and the heady aroma of the ground coffee beans filled the atmosphere.

"Yesterday, I dropped by the hospital to check on Thelma's recovery, and I witnessed something unusual," Lucy began when she finished her salad. "She's better, but I overhead her having an argument with Judy, and there was a lot of tension between them."

"What was it about?" Aunt Tricia asked, wiping her lips with her thumb.

"Something about a deal Judy didn't want Thelma to take, and then Thelma mentioned her father. That got Judy worked up, and defensive. Do you have any idea what happened to Judy's husband?"

Aunt Tricia shook her head. "I think he died of a heart attack. I didn't live in town back then, but I heard from your mother. Judy's just looking out for Thelma. Considering how her acting career has panned out, it's only normal for her mother to be concerned about the kinds of deals she makes with agencies."

"What happened to Thelma's career? Isn't she like really famous or something?" Lucy asked, in the dark to what her aunty was saying.

Aunt Tricia shook her head. "Thelma had bad reviews on her last performance that would have buried any aspiring actor's career, and she found it hard to get another role after that."

"Woah… you're kidding," Lucy exclaimed. Her brows knitted together as she listened to her aunt continue about the movie

Thelma failed to act properly, and how horrible her scenes were.

"I thought she was a natural," Lucy said. "I didn't know."

"Guess she didn't take her mother's talent. When I was in college, Judy was famous in town for her acting. She starred in many high school plays and local productions in her time. Everyone naturally expected her daughter to follow suit but turns out Thelma wasn't that gifted."

"So that last role almost ruined her acting career?" Lucy asked.

"I guess she's been auditioning for new roles," Aunt Tricia replied. "I don't think her acting skills compare to her mom's."

She recalled Thelma's argument the previous day. That deal was a once in a lifetime opportunity... I had to take it.

"You think maybe Judy didn't want her to take the baker role?" Aunt Tricia asked.

"I don't know."

They both fell silent for a minute, then Aunt Tricia spoke again. "Her first role was in a Pete Jenson production. I remember he used to brag about his latest prodigy in his interviews, but things turned sour when the play started running, and it didn't do well. Pete didn't hesitate to dump her and move on to the next star he could find."

"Seems like Pete was a real jerk when he was alive," Lucy commented.

"He was," Aunt Tricia agreed. "The agency that signed her dropped her after that. I remember running into her at a grocery store once when I came to visit your mother. She wore this black hoodie and shades to make sure no one recognized her, and I just thought that it was so sad."

"I think Thelma aims to improve her acting skill," Lucy said.

"She's putting in some effort into her new role by interning at my bakery."

"Is she serious about the internship?"

Lucy exhaled. The answer to her aunt's question was a big no because since Thelma started her internship, which was to last a few weeks, she hadn't been of use to Lucy or Hannah. She only came in once so far, and that day nearly ended in disaster.

"She's not been of any help, though," Lucy stated. "I just want to give her some credit and the benefit of the doubt that she will make something out of the internship."

Lucy rose to her feet to clear out the table and wash the dishes as she spoke. When she finished, she hurried to her bedroom, showered, and dressed for the day before feeding Gigi.

She stood in front of the mirror, brushing her hair, while Gigi feasted on the kibbles in her pan. "Today's going to be a long day, Gigi," Lucy whispered as she tied her hair into a bun on top of her head and brushed away the strands in front to each side of her face.

Aunt Tricia had dressed, and she was ready to join her when she got back downstairs, and they headed out together. Lucy's first stop was the bakery to check on the progress of the work Keith and his team had already begun.

*

Two days later, Lucy and Hannah were chatting by their stand as the day drew to a close. Lucy adjusted the sleeves of her shirt as Hannah packed the rest of the treats they had left for the day.

Keith came out of the bakery wearing his work overall, and he smiled at Lucy when he got to her small stand near the curb.

"My workers loved the pie you shared," he said.

"Thank you, Keith. I'm glad they enjoyed it," she replied, smiling. "How much more work needs to be done? Can I come in and look?"

"Sure."

Lucy followed him into the bakery, with Hannah behind them. Her jaw dropped in astonishment when she saw the new ceiling boards and the lovely eccentric chandelier light already installed in the middle of the dining area.

They had piled the chairs up in one corner, and the stairs that would lead to the upper level were already in construction.

"This is lovely," Hannah said.

"Yes, it is. Now I can't wait to re-open in this new bakery setting," Lucy agreed.

"It won't be long now," Keith answered. "Let's give it a week or two and we should be finished."

"Alright."

Lucy went on a brief tour around with Hannah and they were discussing the new look when they went outside to join Aunt Tricia.

"Today we had more sales than I had in the entire week. I'm glad things are getting back to normal again," she said.

"Yeah, me too," Hannah said.

They stopped talking when a car pulled to a halt by the curb.

Lucy watched and saw Thelma get down. She got to them with quick strides and took the free seat at the table.

"How are you?" Lucy asked. "When were you discharged?"

Thelma beamed at her, and Lucy wondered if Thelma or Judy had seen her at the hospital yesterday before she left.

"I'm alright… thanks for looking out for me, Lucy," Thelma replied. "They discharged me yesterday after all the check-ups."

"Thank goodness, you're alright," Lucy said. She saw Thelma's eyes drift towards Hannah, who had been quiet since Thelma arrived.

"Thanks, Hannah, for going to the hospital with me," Thelma whispered. "If you hadn't been on the scene, then I would have probably been alone the entire time."

Lucy saw Hannah's tentative smile before she replied. "I would have done the same for anyone else," Hannah replied.

For the first time, Hannah didn't frown when Thelma spoke to her, and to Lucy that was a good sign they could one day reconcile their differences.

When Thelma left, Lucy turned to Aunt Tricia and spoke. "I don't think she knows I overheard the argument with her mother yesterday. It's better that way, but something tells me there's more to the argument I witnessed."

"Just be careful, Lucy," Aunt Tricia advised.

"I will. You have nothing to worry about, trust me."

23

On a Sunday morning, Lucy went for a jog to start the day. She stopped after a mile, put her hands on her knees to exhale and relax a bit. The morning breezed wafted through her nose and tickled the skin at the back of her neck. She marveled at it, thankful that spring was drawing ever near.

Her usual route was down Easton Street towards the gas station that led to a bend where she could connect with the high road. When she lived in the apartment above her bakery, she usually jogged in the opposite direction of the route she jogged that morning. That way, she ended her exercise at the end of Easton Street, then walked back to the bakery.

Lucy stretched her legs, straightened her spine and resumed her jog. She made it a few blocks away from her resting point before she saw Tim Humphrey coming out of an adjoining street.

He spotted her too, and paused in his stride, jogging on a spot till she got to him.

"Good morning, Tim," Lucy said. "You jog down this route often?" she asked, wiping her forehead dry as he rotated his arm.

"Yes," he replied. "I live not too far from here, and it is the perfect route for me. What about you? You live around here?"

"On Easton Street, yes," she replied.

"Oh, great."

Lucy looked around them for a second and brought her gaze back to Tim.

"It's a good thing I ran into you. I planned to drop by your bakery to apologize for the last time we saw each other at Judy's shop. I wasn't my best self that day, and I realized I've been grumpy on the two occasions we met. It has nothing to do with my usual personality and everything to do with how life has been for me. It seems being out of work really affects me," Tim said. He shoved his fingers through his dark hair as he spoke, and his eyes landed on Lucy's again. "My apologies, Lucy."

"No problem," she replied, gesticulating with her right hand. "I understand… not being able to work in the theater these past weeks must have been frustrating for you."

"It really is," Tim continued. "I used to enjoy having to handle the preparations for rehearsals or productions, and watching the show was a source of entertainment. I can't do any of that now that the production has been shut down."

"You were a part of the productions?" Lucy asked, not bothering to hide her surprise.

"Yes, yes… I'm not just the janitor," he replied. "Pete and I used to organize rehearsals and produce the plays in town before he had his big break on Broadway. We were a team, and our productions always attracted large audiences. Some of our plays were turned into TV shows and films. But I was never compensated."

"Why is that?"

He shrugged, and his voice dropped a notch as he answered. "Pete never mentioned he had a partner. He's done stuff like that before to a few locals. You help him with something, and he takes all the glory to himself."

Lucy fell silent as she listened to Tim speak. She didn't miss the hint of jealousy in his tone as he continued about how Pete continued using most ideas from their work together to enhance his career, completely forgetting all about Tim and their history together.

"It must hurt for you to watch Pete excel on his own," she sympathized. Putting a hand on her forehead, Lucy stroked her brows and pondered on her next question for a second before asking. "During the open rehearsals Pete organized before he died, did you see Judy's daughter Thelma Cousins there to audition? Do you know if she was at the theater the day Pete died?"

"I'm not sure," he replied, his brows knitting together. "Why do you ask? I'm not shocked though. Pete had a thing for casting many characters in his play. It's one thing we never agreed on... he would cast every Tom, Dick or Sally that popped out of every corner and find a role for them, even when he was certain they had no acting talent."

"Perhaps he just wanted to give them a chance," Lucy suggested.

"Nonsense," Tim cut in, his eyes flaring with anger.

A sudden shiver raced up her spine, and she met his blazing eyes as he added. "He thought he was always right, but he wasn't. Sometimes scenes with a lot of characters are difficult to handle and organize. I tried to tell him this even during these open rehearsals, but he completely shut me up and asked me to do my job, which was being the janitor."

Lucy nodded as she took in the deep frown marring Tim's face and the dissatisfaction that was etched in the lines on his forehead. She licked her dry lips. "Is that why you killed him?" she blurted, unable to stop the question from slipping out of her lips.

"What?" Tim growled.

"Did you kill Pete Jenson?"

He scoffed and took a menacing step towards her. "Watch your back, Lucy," he said in a dangerously low voice. "Don't go around asking stupid questions or digging into matters that don't concern you. It's how you'll get yourself killed."

His threat rang deep in her, and she remained rooted to a spot as he turned away and continued his jog down the road. Lucy blinked, ushering herself back to reality after being stunned at his swift change of character.

She turned to continue into the adjoining street opposite where she stood, still dazed, and the loud blaring honk of a car's horn jarred her out of her thoughts.

Lucy screamed and her hand flew to her chest. She stumbled to the ground by the car that nearly hit her as the door opened and a young man dressed in a prim, black fitted suit stepped out.

"I'm so sorry," he said as he walked over to her and extended his hand. "Are you alright? You seem pretty out of it, and I had to honk that loud to get your attention."

Lucy exhaled. She swallowed, trying to steady her heartbeat by taking slow breaths. The scene reminded her of when a car nearly hit her the previous year.

"I'm alright… I'm fine, I'm not hurt."

"Sorry about this," the man said again. "I'm Joseph Hiller," he added. He reached into his suit pocket; he handed her a card. "I'm going to be the resident producer at the local theater."

"Lucy Hale," she replied. "I own Sweet Delights, a bakery here in Ivy Creek. Nice to meet you."

Joseph Hiller gave her a full smile. He adjusted the lapel of his suit and looked around them. "Care for a ride? I could take you to your destination before continuing to the theater. I don't mind, and it will be a way to apologize for almost knocking you down."

Lucy looked at him, and his smile widened. His green eyes danced as he looked at her.

"Please, don't say no," he said.

Lucy agreed to the offer with a soft nod of her head, and he led her around to the front passenger's seat and held the door open for her to get in before he returned to the driver's seat.

She directed him to take the turn leading into the main street and sat in silence as he drove.

"What production will you be working on?" she asked.

"We hope to bring Pete's production back to life. Because of the ongoing investigation, we'll have to bide our time."

"Sounds like you really believe in Pete's production."

"Pete was like a mentor. He laid the groundwork, and my team and I will finish it in his memory. He was a very talented man, and he deserves to be recognized for his contribution."

Joseph slowed down when they reached the bakery and said, "I'm guessing this is your bakery," he said, pointing at the sign.

"Yes, it is. Thanks for driving me, Mr. Hiller. Really appreciate it."

"It's Joseph and you're welcome. You're one pretty lady, Miss Hale and you should be careful when on the road next time."

Lucy thanked him again and got out of the car. She watched Joseph drive away before she turned and headed for the bakery. It was Sunday, and she was only there because she needed to pick up some baking soda and foil wraps for her round of baking tomorrow morning.

After grabbing the items she needed, Lucy started her walk back to her house. She hummed a popular classical song to herself as she walked, moving her head to the rhythm as she sang. She was enjoying the melody when the blares of oncoming sirens filled the air.

Two cop patrol cars dashed past her, leaving gusts of fumes in their wake.

She stared after the next van that passed, her curiosity spiking when she saw the cops lined up in the open back of the truck.

Something must have happened, she thought. The sirens became distant as they drove farther away from her, leaving Lucy wondering who they were out to arrest.

Have they found who killed Pete Jenson?

24

On Monday morning, Lucy and Aunt Tricia brought out the pastries for sale, arranged them on the display counter by her makeshift stand, and sat under the shade they had created for themselves. She got the first text from Hannah thirty minutes after they settled down to wait for customers for the morning.

I won't make it to the bakery today. Something came up at home, and I must take my sister for an appointment. I'll tell you all about it when I get back.

"Hannah's not coming in today," she said to Aunt Tricia when she raised her head again.

"Is she alright?" Aunt Tricia asked with concern.

"Yes, she's fine… she says something came up with her sister," Lucy replied. She sighed and slipped her phone into the pocket of the apron she wore over her dress. "That leaves us both to handle everything for the day. It's a good thing we have little to do. Keith and his team will be here soon and once they are done for the day, we can close up early and go back home."

Aunt Tricia agreed with her. They spent the next few minutes talking, and Lucy mentioned seeing the cops drive downtown the previous day on her way back from the bakery.

"That was after my run in with the new producer at the theater, Joseph Hiller," she said.

"Do you feel they caught someone? If they did, then news will be all over the local stations already."

"I do," Lucy responded. She rubbed her jaw as she considered any other possibility for the cops to descend on the town in their numbers on a Sunday morning.

Maybe it's an unrelated case?

She was still contemplating the workable options when Aunt Tricia tapped her hand on the table, drawing her attention. "It's Taylor," Aunt Tricia said when Lucy met her gaze.

Lucy looked up to see Taylor approach where they sat with a smile. Lucy rose to her feet to greet him, and he took off the cap on his head.

Taylor ran his fingers through his hair as he spoke. "Hey Lucy, how's it going?"

"Great," she beamed. "How are you, Taylor?"

"Good, good." Taylor greeted Aunt Tricia with a wave of his hand and answered a few questions about his mother before Lucy led him to her stand near the curb.

"I see the workers are making progress," he commented when he stood in front of her and slipped his hands into his back pocket.

Lucy glanced at the bakery's building. "Yes, the workers are yet to get here for the day, but they should be here any minute now."

When she looked back at him again, she noticed he was looking at her. His eyes searched hers for a second before he spoke again. "So, when it's all done, you'll have a bigger dining area, and what else?"

Lucy took time to give him a description of what the bakery would look like on completion.

"That sounds great, Lucy. When it's all done, you should celebrate with a launch party. You deserve it."

"Thanks, Taylor." A thought suddenly flashed across her mind, which she knew Taylor might help with. "I noticed some cops drove down the street yesterday. It looked like they were in a hurry to get somewhere. Did something happen in town?"

"We have a few suspects in Pete's murder case," Taylor replied.

She gasped in surprise.

"It's nothing concrete yet. Yesterday was just a search after getting a warrant."

She was about to ask if the suspect was Tim Humphrey, but he wagged a finger at her. "I can't mention any names, but you have to be careful with whom you are in contact. We've been investigating those who worked at the theater, and the actors who auditioned that day. Some fingerprints besides Pete's were found on the shirt Pete wore that day, and soon we'll match it with some fingerprints we have on our database."

"Hmmm," she whispered, a shiver racing through her at the

thought of the killer possibly being found soon. "I hope it's all wrapped up soon," she continued. "Nearly everyone has been on edge since Pete's death and catching the killer will normalize things."

"You're right," Taylor said.

They both fell silent for a second, and she heard him take in a deep breath before pointing at the cupcakes she had on the counter. "I will have some of that, and three brownies too."

"Sure."

Lucy handed him the paper bag as her phone buzzed in her pocket. "Oh, excuse me."

The text was from Thelma, and she shook her head as she read through it.

Hey Lucy, how're things going? I won't be coming in today. I thought I should let you know.

Lucy typed her reply quickly, tired of allowing Thelma the space to make up excuses and not take her internship seriously. She had given her the weekend off after her accident, and the morning was already far spent before she came up with this excuse.

Take all the time you need. You also shouldn't bother resuming tomorrow.

When she looked up at Taylor again, he was watching her closely.

"That was my intern, Thelma Cousins," she said as she tucked the phone away. "She keeps making excuses not to come to work, and I just can't handle her anymore, so it's best she doesn't work here at all."

Taylor put a hand on her shoulder, surprising her. "Take it easy," he said, his eyes warm on hers. "I should get back home now."

"See you later," she said.

She joined Aunt Tricia again, and minutes later, Keith and his team arrived for the day's work. Lucy and Aunt Tricia attended to the customers that trooped by throughout the day. The day went by without incident and Lucy was glad when she noticed it was almost time to close for the day.

Lucy had taken in her stand and was closing the windows when she saw Judy approach the bakery. Judy walked with quick strides, glancing over her shoulder briefly.

"Good evening, Judy," Lucy greeted as she stepped out to greet Judy at the entrance.

"Lucy," she said in an icy tone as she adjusted the shoulder bag hanging loosely on her left hand. "Were you locking up?'

"Ah, yes… I was just leaving for the day," Lucy replied. "Do you want to buy some treats? I still have some left."

Judy shook her head. "No, no, I'm not here for some treats, Lucy. I'm here to see you, and it's quite urgent, so may I come in?"

Judy pushed past her and entered the bakery as she asked, and Lucy followed.

She wondered what Judy's visit was for as she closed the door behind her and walked past Judy to where her previous display counter stood. "What did you need?" Lucy asked, crossing her

579

hands over her chest as she met Judy's gaze.

The corner of Judy's lips lifted into a crooked smirk as she answered, "I saw you at the hospital that day… I know you were there."

25

L ucy froze where she stood as Judy continued. "I saw you right before you turned and hurried out."

"I…" Lucy's words died in her throat when Aunt Tricia appeared on the stairway, beaming as usual.

"Judy," Aunt Tricia called in a singing voice, her eyes opened wide as she descended the stairs and hugged Judy. "It's been ages since I last saw you. Oh, my goodness," she exclaimed, laughing as Judy hugged her back. "How have you been? Look at you, you're… Different."

"I'm alright, Tricia," Judy responded, giggling as she hugged Aunt Tricia again.

Lucy swallowed. The ice she had heard in Judy's tone a moment earlier had completely disappeared, and she wondered if she had imagined it. Her palms had turned sweaty, and she closed her eyes, told herself Judy wasn't here to attack her before opening them again.

"I was telling Lucy the other day about how you used to be Meryl Streep back in school. You would have made a fantastic actress. How come you never pursued that?" Aunt Tricia asked. She still held Judy's hand in hers as she talked, and Lucy backed away from them into the kitchen to make sure the back doors were locked.

"Life happened," Judy replied as Lucy walked away. "I met my husband, got married, had Thelma and the rest, as they say, is history. I have no regrets, though. I have a wonderful flower shop that serves Ivy Creek and beyond. My daughter's doing well with her acting career. I get to help our town as a member of the town council. I love my life."

"Amazing... Lucy gave me a bouquet she bought from your store, and they were really therapeutic. I loved them so much."

"I'm glad you did, Tricia," Judy replied.

Inside the kitchen, Lucy switched off the lights after admiring the progress of the work for a while. When she got back to the dining area, Aunt Tricia and Judy were still catching up, and she waited, her hands behind her back.

"It was nice seeing you again after all these years," Judy said as Aunt Tricia pulled away from her.

"Same here, Judy... I need to run along now. I have an appointment. See you around soon."

Lucy caught Aunt Tricia's gaze as she backed away, and Judy faced her again.

Aunt Tricia walked out of the bakery, and Lucy sucked in a deep breath as she looked at Judy.

"Your aunt was a good friend of mine when we were in college. I haven't seen her in years and it feels good to re-unite with an old friend."

Judy's tone held a wistfulness that was charming, but she was more concerned with the reason for Judy's visit.

"I saw you at the hospital with Thelma, and I didn't want to interfere, so I left," she said, causing Judy to arch a brow as she looked at her.

"Fine, but that's not why I'm here, Lucy."

"Then why?"

Judy took off her bag and set it on the ground gently. "I've had a very busy day, but I had to stop what I was doing when Thelma called and mentioned you fired her."

Lucy blinked. "I can't have Thelma working here," she replied after a moment. "She's not dedicated to learning, and honestly, she's just not cut out for this kind of work. It's best she tries to do something else she will be good at."

Judy put her hands together in front of her. She then massaged her temples and looked at Lucy again. "I beg you, Lucy," she said, coming closer. Her blue eyes searched Lucy's desperately, and she lurched forward to grab Lucy's hands. "She needs this… I need this. The role Thelma got is a once in a lifetime opportunity and I did a lot to get her that spot in the production. It'll be a stepping stone to bigger and better things," she said. "She needs to do this," she added in a hoarse voice, spacing her words to sound convincing. "Please…"

Lucy dragged her hands from Judy's. "I can't do that, Judy," she said. "Thelma's clumsy… the incident with Stephanie affected sales and damaged my reputation. I'm yet to recover from that and I can't afford a worker who isn't of help."

"Thelma can be of help," she rushed to add.

"But she's not. She's not helping, and she's certainly not learning. I thought I could put up with her attitude, but I really can't, and I don't want any trouble, Judy. It's best she finds someplace else to intern."

Lucy turned away from Judy but stopped when Judy clamped a hand on her arm and spun her back around.

Judy's lower lip quivered as she stared at Lucy. Her eyes turned watery, and for a second Lucy thought she was about to cry.

"I gave so much to get her to where she is, but she's never able to keep up. I've spent so much on acting classes, dance glasses... I even hired a teacher to teach her Spanish in case a role came up in the Spanish-speaking world. Everyone remembers her as the kid in the toothpaste commercial, but she has so much more to offer. This role she's got is her ticket out of this town. I know Thelma can be a spoiled brat, but I know if she applies herself, she can be good... maybe great. I suggested she come and intern with you as nothing beats living and breathing a role."

Lucy rubbed the back of her neck and sighed. "I can't do what you want, Judy. I'm so sorry, but this is my business on the line, too. Thelma almost ruined it, and I can't give her another chance."

Judy sneered. She turned away from Lucy and began pacing, one hand on her hip and the other on her forehead. "This is all his fault and now, even after his death, we still can't recover from the havoc he caused."

"Judy..." Lucy began.

Judy's head snapped up, and she took menacing steps towards Lucy, who staggered backwards and collided with a table behind her.

"I begged Pete to give her a chance, just like I'm begging you, Lucy. He was just too stuck up to see that she's talented... just like you."

"Judy…" Lucy began. Her eyes widened as Judy stopped in front of her.

"You, Lucy of all people, should know that everyone needs a second chance. Look at how much progress you've made with your business. I'm sure you came this far because you had support from others and all I'm asking is that you give Thelma that same support. She really needs to excel in this role. It's her dream."

Judy's tone had regained the same chill it had earlier when she entered. Her face had paled and now she was giving Lucy a crazed look that made Lucy's mouth dry up. Her chest rose and fell with the force of her breathing as she asked. "Thelma's dreams? Or yours?"

The question made Judy back away from Lucy for a while, and suddenly she burst into a full cackle that filled the room.

Lucy saw sweat beads on Judy's forehead. Her eyes were red as she sneered at Lucy.

"She's my daughter," she started through gritted teeth. "Her dreams are mine… and… My dreams are hers. I would do any-thing to see her shine like she's supposed to." Judy scratched her forehead and added. "Even if it means getting stumbling blocks like yourself out of the way."

The threatening words set alarm bells in Lucy's head off. She dashed for the door, intending to breeze past Judy's side and get to it, but Judy was faster. Judy's firm hands grabbed Lucy's ponytail, and she yanked hard, dragging Lucy back to her.

"It took little to end Pete, and I'd do it all over again if I got the chance," Judy was saying as she tightened her grip. "And it won't take much to end you, too."

Judy's hands came around Lucy's neck, squeezing until Lucy

felt like she was going to pass out.

Her skin flushed, her chest deflated, and she struggled, holding onto the last chunk of air she had inside her. Lucy held on to Judy's crazed gaze as she fought to hold on to her consciousness. An eerie feeling of déjà vu crept over her as, once again, she was in a battle to stay alive.

26

The blares of sirens filled the air as Lucy fought to free herself from Judy's firm grasp.

Her eyelids fluttered closed as she looked at Judy one last time. Lucy's hands clamped over Judy's wrists, and she tried to break free again at the same time Judy let go of her and rushed for the door.

Lucy scrambled away from Judy. Her hands moved to her neck, and she swallowed against the burning sensation rising in her chest. The door swung open just as Judy was about to run out, and cops came barging into the bakery. Lucy saw her stagger backwards and make a run for the kitchen, but she was too late.

The cops surrounded Judy. One of them grabbed her hands and cuffed her wrists behind her before she could run. Aunt Tricia entered the bakery and ran towards Lucy to hold her.

"Are you alright, honey?" Aunt Tricia asked. "Did she hurt you badly?"

Lucy managed a nod. She didn't think the lump in her throat would let her speak, and frankly, her dazed brain couldn't form any words.

Grateful for support when Aunt Tricia put a hand around her waist, Lucy leaned into her body; her breaths kept coming out in strained puffs as she watched them drag Judy away.

"I'll make you pay for this, Lucy. I swear I'll make you pay," Judy cursed, and tried to free herself from the cop's grip. "I will make sure you pay… I'll kill you, Lucy, just like I killed Pete," she continued, laughing hysterically.

"She's completely unhinged," Aunt Tricia murmured at Lucy's side, shaking her head.

"She's crazy," Lucy murmured as she slumped to the ground. Her backside contacted the floor with a loud thud, and her shoulders slumped as she exhaled. Taylor appeared at the doorway, and she met his gaze as he hurried towards her.

"Are you alright?" He asked, his hands coming around her. He pulled her in, one hand patting her hair and the other rubbing her back. "You're safe now. I'm here and you're safe," he said.

Lucy shuddered and allowed herself the liberty to enjoy the warmth of his comfort. She closed her eyes as he brushed tendrils of hair away from the side of her head and helped her to her feet.

"Oh, Lucy," Aunt Tricia called as she returned to the bakery. "I just gave my statement to the cops," she said, coming closer to take Lucy out of Taylor's embrace. "It's a good thing I hung around and called the cops immediately."

"Yes," Taylor replied. "Judy did not know you were still around. That's how Lucy got lucky."

Taylor looked at her as he spoke. He rubbed his chin for a second before adding. "Once the paramedics get here, they'll assess you and determine if you need to go to the hospital."

"That'll be unnecessary," Lucy said, finally finding her voice again. Her throat still hurt, the skin there burned, and she had to keep her hands against the section that hurt. "I'm fine. I don't need to go to the hospital."

"You're not fine," Taylor and Aunt Tricia chorused.

"Your neck and cheeks are all blotched, and you need to get checked," Taylor said.

His hands were on his waist as he spoke, and he looked around the bakery. The door opened and two paramedics entered. Aunt Tricia brought Lucy a chair to sit on and Lucy snuggled into the blanket the paramedics wrapped around her shoulders before a cop came to question her.

She told him everything that had happened. Judy's consistent begging to give Thelma her job back and the dramatic change in her behavior when Lucy had refused. By the time she finished, and the cops excused themselves, Lucy turned to see Taylor standing near the entrance to the bakery. He stood with his back to her, his attention completely engrossed in the conversation he was having with the cop next to him.

With a sigh, she tried to get on her feet, but gasped when she swooned and nearly fell to the ground. Taylor hurried to her side and steadied her with both hands.

"You should come with me to the hospital," he said, this time hooking her arm in his and turning her towards the door.

"I'm fine," Lucy insisted. "I have Aunt Tricia here, and she will be with me at the house tonight, Taylor."

"It's not enough," he argued just as Aunt Tricia entered the bakery again.

"The paramedics are waiting," Aunt Tricia said, letting them through the door. Lucy didn't put up any more fight as Taylor helped her into the van with her aunt's help. She lay on the stretcher there, sighing as her body relaxed against it.

Her head still spun from what just happened, and even though she wasn't physically hurt, Lucy knew she needed time to wrap her mind around her near death experience. Taylor had saved her again, and she was thankful for that.

Lucy's eyes closed as the ambulance door closed. Her aunt sat by her side, so she could relax. The next time she opened her eyes, her heart was trembling inside her chest. She sat up with the rush of adrenaline that filled her. Her eyes took in her surroundings, and the surge subsided when she remembered she was at the hospital.

Hannah came into the room then, a soft smile on her face as she opened the door.

"Hey," she whispered, coming close to Lucy's bed to hug her. "Aunt Tricia already filled me in... Who would have suspected that Judy was one crazy lady?"

"I can't still believe it myself," Lucy replied, allowing herself to get squashed into Hannah's tight embrace. "Turns out she's controlling and manipulative."

"Taylor was here earlier, and he told me everything," Aunt Tricia said. "Judy became hysterical once they got to the station. She confessed to killing Pete because he refused to give Thelma a lead role in his new play. She hadn't meant to kill him when she disguised as one of the actors in the stampede scene, but she considered it sweet revenge when she found out he had died."

"The news already has reports on this, and Judy's picture is pasted across every media outlet. There's no way she'll get out of this without a maximum sentence," Hannah added. "The police matched a stain of Pete's blood to a hoodie found in the basement of Judy's house after a thorough search."

Lucy and Hannah continued talking about Judy for a few more minutes till Aunt Tricia came into the room with Taylor right beside her.

"Ah, you're awake," she exclaimed, beaming as she walked over to Lucy and enveloped her in a hug.

Taylor grinned as he stood at the door with his arms crossed over his chest. "The doctors confirmed that you're fine, but we insisted you stay the night on bed rest. It was unanimous," she said, pointing at Taylor and Hannah. "So, you're not getting out of it."

"Okay," Lucy replied, grinning. She was thankful for life and didn't want to argue with anyone for now. She had people to support her, so she was fine.

Hannah and Aunt Tricia left her in the room with Taylor, and he crossed over to the bed and sat on its side. "It's all over now. Judy will get the justice she deserves, and now you can go back to business and baking," he said, his eyes not leaving hers.

"It's finally over," she repeated, her words ending on a sigh.

A minute of silence passed between them, and Taylor rose to his feet, patted her hair away from her face tenderly, and turned to walk away.

"Thank you," Lucy said.

He stopped and faced her again, his lips curving into a smile that reached his eyes. "For saving my life every time," she said, her voice rich with emotion.

"You're welcome," he replied. "Stay safe, Lucy."

Lucy watched him walk away, and her heart filled with a slow flutter as the image of his smile registered in her head. When she angled her head to one side, she saw Aunt Tricia and Hannah standing by the room's shutter windows, giggling as they watched her.

27

hree weeks later

Lucy clinked her glass with Hannah's, and then Aunt Tricia's, before sipping her sparkling grape juice.

"Cheers," the three women chorused and drank again, then Lucy turned on the music playing on the speaker, flung her head back and danced to the rhythm of the song playing.

"Tell us, how did it go with the health inspector?" Aunt Tricia asked when they sat down after the first song had ended.

Lucy picked up her fork to cut into her steak, and Hannah filled her plate with some mushroom sauce.

She had prepared that Sunday lunch to celebrate their new success. The renovations were complete, and the overall look was brilliant. Lucy especially loved the patterned floorboards compared to the regular brown ones her parents had installed when they first bought the building.

The walls were now a blend of pastel colors; there was a spacious aisle between every table set-up to avoid congestion, and her kitchen felt wider because it had more space considering they had removed the wooden walls demarcating it from the dining area and expanded it.

"I passed the check and I'm looking forward to a more fruitful spring," she replied, beaming at her aunt as she took the first bite of her steak.

Their discussion continued over lunch. Lucy had given Hannah the weekend off after they had arranged the bakery, and tomorrow was the start of a new business era for her. She was yet to take pictures of the overall outlook, but that was something she could do sometime later.

Aunt Tricia and Hannah were going over the new flower vase on the front porch when the bell rang and Thelma entered the bakery. Everyone around the table fell silent as she approached, and Lucy stood up first to greet her.

"Hi, Lucy," Thelma said in a shaky voice. Her eyes were wide, and beneath them, Lucy noticed large dark circles. "You look good."

Lucy offered her a seat, noticing how she clung to the shoulder bag she carried. Thelma twisted the hem of the blazer she wore as she looked around the bakery. Hannah cleared her throat and lifted her glass to her lips. Lucy met Hannah's questioning gaze before she turned her attention to Thelma again.

"I thought I should drop by to congratulate you," Thelma began, nibbling on her lower lip when Lucy didn't break eye contact. "I heard about the renovation… everyone in town is wondering what the new look is like, and I think it's lovely."

"Thank you, Thelma. How have you been?"

Thelma lifted a shoulder in a shrug. "I've been holding up, trying to keep my head up amidst everything else."

She didn't need to get into explicit details for Lucy to know what she was referring to. Judy's court hearing ended in a week because all evidence had pointed to her. Coupled with her threatening Lucy's life, and her confession as the cops dragged her away, it was already over before it began.

Seeing Thelma now made Lucy feel sorry for her. It must have been hard trying to live with a mother like Judy who controlled everything about her life, she thought.

"I'm really sorry, Lucy. For what my mother did, and for…" Thelma's voice trailed off before she finished the sentence, and a heavy log of pity for her formed in Lucy's chest.

"You shouldn't apologize," she spoke and reached out a hand to take Thelma's. "I know you're sorry, and it's all over now. Everyone's moving on, and you should do so, too."

"I'm trying to," Thelma said, releasing an unexpected laugh. "But it's hard to do that when everyone in town keeps murmuring whenever I pass. I'm leaving for a while. There's a photography internship in Denver I got into, and I plan to be serious with this one."

"Is photography what you want? Is it your dream?"

"Yes, it always has been. When I mentioned to my mother that I took the internship, she didn't want me to go. I told her it was a once in a lifetime opportunity, but she thought it was mediocre and nothing compared to what I could be if I was an actress. There's nothing stopping me from taking that path now."

"There isn't," Lucy agreed, smiling at her. "I want you to do what your heart wants because that's the only way you will be happy."

Thelma nodded. She spoke to Hannah and Aunt Tricia for a while and by the time Lucy walked her to the door; they hugged goodbye before she walked away. Lucy didn't re-enter the bakery immediately because she spotted Taylor's car parked across the street from her building.

He got out, crossed the road, and walked to her, holding a bouquet of daisies in one hand.

"You look amazing," he said when he got to where Lucy stood and handed her the flowers. "I also remembered how much you love daisies."

"Thank you," she replied, grinning at him.

She had invited him for the celebratory lunch, and although he was a bit late, she was still glad he made it, anyway.

"Thanks for coming," she said, stepping aside to let him into the bakery.

"I wouldn't miss celebrating with you for anything in the world."

He entered the bakery and moved to Aunt Tricia, hugging her lightly before greeting Hannah and taking a free seat at the table.

Lucy took the flowers into her office, set them in a vase, then joined them at the dining area again to make another toast. The afternoon spanned into an evening full of laughter and joy after their lunch, and Lucy stole glances at Taylor as he conversed with Hannah and her aunt.

When the year started, she had been so full of hope, and she felt a renewed surge of that energy fill her again as the peaceful sounds of their laughter tickled her ears. Lucy was looking forward to what Ivy Creek's spring offered.

The End

COOKIE
DOUGH
AND
BRUISED
EGOS

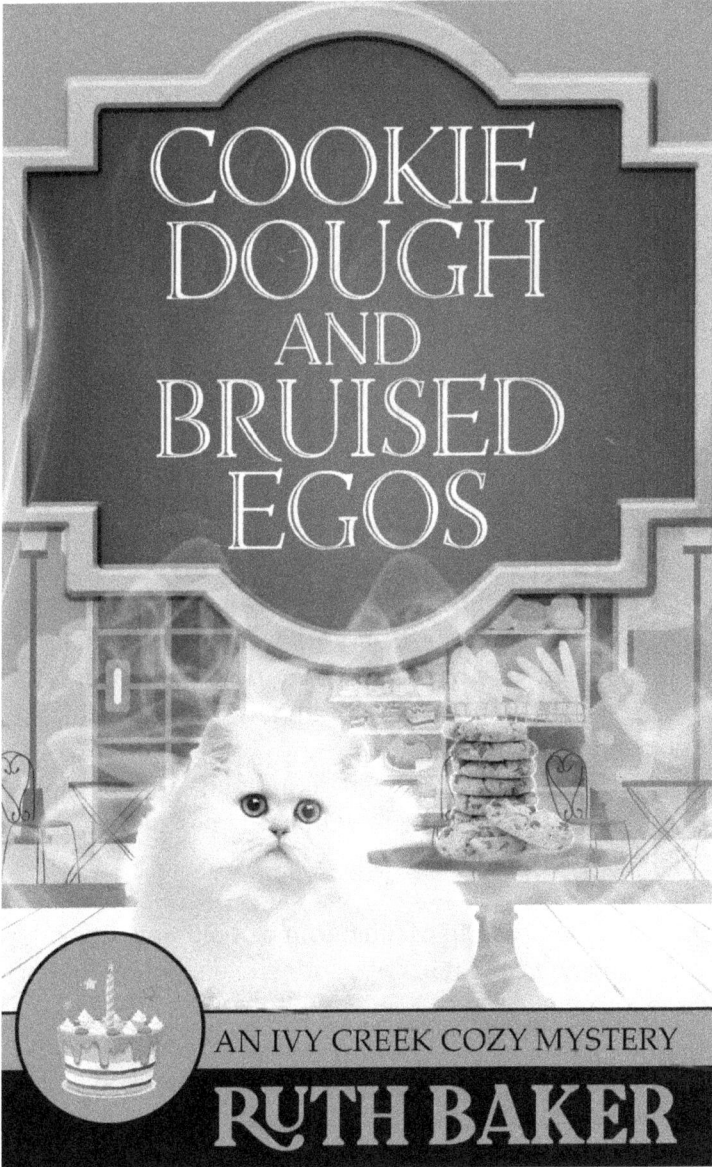

AN IVY CREEK COZY MYSTERY

RUTH BAKER

COOKIE DOUGH AND BRUISED EGOS

CHAPTER 1 SNEAK PEEK

"Is it straight?"

Lucy spared a quick glance over her shoulder at her Aunt Tricia, while concentrating on maintaining her balance. She was perched on a stepladder in front of her bakery, Sweet Delights, clutching one end of a banner with her right hand. Her left hand curled around the porch overhang in a death grip. Heights had never been her favorite thing.

"Hannah... drop your end by about an inch," Tricia suggested, standing on the front walkway with her hands on her hips, eyeing the homemade banner critically.

Lucy turned her gaze to Hannah, on a matching stepladder to her right. Hannah caught her eye and winked, before inching her side down...again.

They had been at this for a solid fifteen minutes and Tricia had still not deemed the banner straight enough. Lucy was beginning to wonder if the sidewalk her aunt was standing on was crooked.

"Perfect!" Tricia finally crowed, clapping her hands, and Lucy gratefully descended from the ladder, her knees a bit wobbly.

She joined Hannah and Aunt Tricia on the walkway, and the three of them admired their handiwork together.

SWEET DELIGHTS GRAND RE-OPENING PARTY
JOIN US AS WE CELEBRATE OUR NEW LOOK
FOOD, FUN & FRIENDS GALORE

Lucy sighed happily. "It looks great! Hannah, you did a fabulous job with the colors." Her friend and assistant never failed to amaze her with her many talents.

Hannah smiled, pleased by the compliment, and the three of them walked inside.

The bakery had undergone a massive transformation in the last month. New countertops, a fancy patterned tile flooring, and bold colors on the walls gave the interior a fresh vibe. Hidden speakers in ceiling corners piped soft music, and recessed lighting added a warm glow. The seating had doubled, with more tables downstairs, as well as an upstairs veranda where customers could enjoy their treats in the open air. Lucy had moved the office and stockrooms upstairs, into the former apartment space, and that had allowed her to expand her square footage substantially.

"I can't wait to see everyone's reactions." Aunt Tricia settled comfortably into a chair at their favorite table, next to a window overlooking the quiet street.

Lucy set a pitcher of lemonade down and poured them each a glass, while Hannah brought over a plate of cookies.
"I would say champagne is called for," Lucy said, raising a glass. "But we'll save that for the launch party. Here's to a job well done, ladies."

They clinked glasses, and Hannah snagged a cookie. Their newest recipe was called Peanut Butter Cup Crunch, and Hannah couldn't get enough of them. She nibbled and sighed blissfully.

Lucy watched her with amusement.

"How is it you can eat cookies all day long and never gain an ounce?" She shook her head, marveling at her friend.

Aunt Tricia chuckled, reaching for a cookie herself. "Oh, to have a young person's metabolism again…"

The phone rang and Hannah swallowed, announcing, "I'll get it. Mrs. Fox said she would call about her daughter's graduation cake today." She pushed her chair back and dashed across the bakery.

Aunt Tricia looked around the bakery's colorful interior with appreciation. "Well, you did it. It looks fabulous, honey." She laid a hand on top of Lucy's and gave it a squeeze. "Your parents would be so proud."

Lucy smiled nostalgically, her thoughts turning to her late parents. Sweet Delights had been their life's work, and Lucy had grown up helping at the bakery. She'd moved away after high school, living in the city and working as a professional food blogger. Upon the tragic death of her parents almost two years ago, she'd decided to try running the bakery herself. Ivy Creek was her home once again, and now she couldn't imagine ever living anywhere else.

It's funny how things come full circle, she mused.

"Lucy!" Hannah called her name and Lucy turned her head. Hannah was holding the telephone, with the mouthpiece covered. Her eyes were wide as she announced in a stage whisper, "It's Richard."

Lucy froze for a minute, then stood slowly. She and Richard had dated for a few months, and though they'd never officially broken up, they had stopped seeking each other's company.

In her heart, she knew their relationship was over, and she took stock of her feelings now, walking to the phone. She really didn't feel any sadness. She'd only invited Richard to the bakery's launch party to be polite, leaving a message on his café's answering machine. She was positive he would decline, since one of the reasons they'd drifted apart was his lack of enthusiasm for her plans for expansion.

Lucy held the phone to her ear, saying cheerfully, "Good morning, Richard."
There was a beat of silence, and then she heard his familiar voice. "Hi, Lucy. How've you been?" He sounded a bit uncomfortable.

"Super! Everything turned out even better than I'd hoped. The bakery looks fabulous. I'm really excited to re-open." Lucy babbled, then made a conscious effort to stop talking.

"Yeah…" Richard sighed out a breath. "About the party. I appreciate your invitation, Lucy, but…"

Lucy waited silently, knowing what his response would be.

"I think it would be awkward," Richard blurted out. "I… really do wish you the best, you know. But I won't be coming."

Lucy nodded her head, wondering why she'd bothered to invite him. As two business owners in the small town of Ivy Creek, she thought they should support each other… celebrate each other's successes. But apparently, Richard was not on the same page.

"OK." Lucy kept her voice emotionless. "Thanks for letting me know."
They said their goodbyes and hung up, and Lucy crossed the room to slump into her chair. She wasn't sad; she told herself. Just disappointed.
Aunt Tricia looked at her sympathetically. "He's not coming?"
Lucy shook her head and reached for a cookie. "It doesn't matter," she proclaimed. "I guess I just expected more of him." She bit into the cookie, savoring the delicious combination of flavors.

Hannah frowned, forever loyal. "He was never good enough for you. You deserve someone who will always stand by you, celebrating your victories with you... helping you get through the tough times. A real man. A partner." She took a sip of her lemonade and crunched on an ice cube.

Aunt Tricia nodded. "I agree. Like the kind of relationship your parents had. Together, through thick and thin."

Lucy shook her head ruefully, with a weak laugh. "Yes, sounds great. Does anyone know where I can find a fellow like that, here in Ivy Creek?"

As soon as the words left her lips, the bell on the bakery door jangled as it opened.

A familiar, deep voice sounded. "What does a man have to do to get a decent piece of pie in this town?"

Discover how things unfold in this murder mystery. Get your copy of Cookie Dough and Bruised Egos

ALSO BY RUTH BAKER

The Ivy Creek Cozy Mystery Series

Which Pie Goes with Murder? (Book 1) – OUT NOW

Twinkle, Twinkle, Deadly Sprinkles (Book 2) – OUT NOW

Eat Once, Die Twice (Book 3) – OUT NOW

Silent Night, Unholy Bites (Book 4) – OUT NOW

Waffles and Scuffles (Book 5) – OUT NOW

Cookie Dough and Bruised Egos (Book 6) – OUT NOW

A Sticky Toffee Catastrophe (Book 7) – COMING SOON

Newsletter Signup

WANT **FREE** COPIES OF FUTURE **CLEANTALES** BOOKS, FIRST NOTIFICATION OF NEW RELEASES, CONTESTS AND GIVEAWAYS?

GO TO THE LINK BELOW TO SIGN UP TO THE NEWSLETTER!

https://cleantales.com/newsletter/